...nda Windsor's talent for creating a faraway land and time is flawless."

"A captivating fictional chronicle of Christianity's dawn in Ireland. Remarkable for its appeal as both a historical saga and inspirational novel *Maire* achieves success that few other books can boast."

SUITE101.COM

"This enthralling tale reveals God's miraculous power at work and how His love conquers all. The thrilling finale will bring chills—as well as the assurance of God's incredible omnipresence. A definite page-turner."

INSPIRATIONAL ROMANCE REVIEWS

"*Maire* is an exciting work of historical fiction that brings to life the Celtic heritage mindful of the great Beowulf. The current story line is exciting and fast-paced, while centering on the conflict between Christianity and Druidism. Readers will want to read this tale even as they impatiently await the sixth-century (*Riona*) and seventh-century (*Deirdre*) novels."

MIDWEST REVIEWER'S CHOICE

"Ms. Windsor's writing is creative and informative to say the least. She captures the reader with her characters' wit and charm, keeping them enthralled until the very last word."

ROMANCE REVIEWS TODAY

"An exciting fictional tale of love, faith, and war.... The plot is smooth from start to finish and holds the reader enraptured, unable to put the book down."

BOOKBROWSER

—◦◦◦—

NOVELS BY LINDA WINDSOR

Love on the Lam (Fall 2002)
It Had to Be You
Not Exactly Eden
Hi Honey, I'm Home
THE FIRES OF GLEANNMARA SERIES
Maire
Riona
Deirdre

DEIRDRE

BOOK THREE OF THE FIRES OF
GLEANNMARA SERIES

LINDA WINDSOR

Multnomah®Publishers *Sisters, Oregon*

DEIRDRE
published by Multnomah Publishers, Inc.
published in association with the literary agency of Ethan Ellenberg Agency.
© 2002 by Linda Windsor
International Standard Book Number: 1-57673-891-4

Cover illustration by Douglas Klauba
Cover design by Kirk DouPonce/UDG DesignWorks

Scripture quotations are from *The Holy Bible,* King James Version.

Multnomah is a trademark of Multnomah Publishers, Inc.,
and is registered in the U.S. Patent and Trademark Office.
The colophon is a trademark of Multnomah Publishers, Inc.

Printed in the United States of America

For information:
MULTNOMAH PUBLISHERS, INC.
Post Office Box 1720, Sisters, Oregon 97759

Library of Congress Cataloging-in-Publication Data
Windsor, Linda.
    Deirdre / Linda Windsor
        p. cm. — (Fires of Gleannmara series; bk. 3)
    ISBN 1-57673-891-4 (pbk.)
        1. Pirates—Fiction. 2. Princesses—Fiction 3. Castaways—
    Fiction. 4. Ireland—Fiction. I. Title.
    PS3573.I519 D45 2002
    813'.54—dc21

                                                            2001007012

02 03 04 05 06 07 08 09—10 9 8 7 6 5 4 3 2 1 0

Dedication

To my friends and *anmcharas*: Connie Rinehart, my stalwart critic who would accept nothing but my best writing, no matter how much I complained; Sue Coleburn, my champion and a true queen of hearts; my editors Karen Ball and Julee Schwarzburg, as well as the entire Multnomah staff, all who worked as a team to make *Deirdre* shine on the shelves for God's glory. May He keep you ever in the palm of His hand as I keep you in my heart.

—◦◦◦—

Dear readers,

In an effort to maintain historical accuracy, I've used several terms or mentioned historical figures that may be unfamiliar to you. You will find these explained in the glossary at the end of the story.

Speaking of the glossary, the earthy speech with which I have Erin present the foreword, the glossary, and the bibliography is not reflective of the educated Irish, either by past standards or those of today. It is intended to effect the earthy speech of an old storyteller, or *seanchus*, and is reminiscent of that which filtered down through my grandmother from her grandmother, an uneducated mother of eleven. This lady supported her children as a laundress, surviving three husbands. I am proud to claim her as an ancestor. Like those who fled to Ireland in the dark ages of Western Europe, she was a brave, devout, and honest soul who came to America with a dream: building a better life for her children.

Linda Windsor

A FOREWORD FROM ME HEART TO YOURS...

Dear *anmcharas,* 'tis a sheer delight to chew the proverbial fat with ye again as I look back at yet another time dear to me heart in the annals o' my children: the seventh century o' me Golden Age. Ah, what days those were. Me saints looked eastward, where their British kin held fast to the cross against the flood tide o' Anglo-Saxon heathens. Driven into the hills o' north and west Albion (the Scotland and Wales o' today's Great Britain), the Christian Romano-Britons bitterly struggled to muster and reclaim their lost land for Christ by the sword...

But no sword, no matter how worthy its cause, could unify them like the Word o' God.

And so it is in this tale that, armed with this holy sword, Gleannmara's Irish and Scottish Dalraidi cousins sally forth to Albion to clear the way for the salvation of Albion's barbarian conquerers. They take with them a message that, instead o' takin' the edge off their weapons, softens the hearts behind them until there is no desire for the use o' steel or spillin' o' blood. Faith, the likes o' magic and miracle bring back stirrin' memories o' me own fifth century, when Christ first entered the hearts o' me dear offspring. In a wink o' the good Lord's eye, the Britons—most of whom were educated upon Erin or Scotia Minor's (Scotland's) shores—are caught up in the fight for souls.

The biggest threat, dear hearts, came from within. Me Celtic children, separated a century and a half from Rome and the church growin' elsewhere in the world, enjoyed a spontaneous faith unencumbered by ritual and organization. 'Twas inevitable that the Celtic church and the Roman one would clash. Mind ye, I'm not takin' a stand for one or the other, for both have withstood the test o' time. Sure, one man's meal is but a morsel to another. But Rome, ascribing to their interpretation of Peter and Paul's vision, had built cathedrals and set into place rituals and decorum appropriate to the royal promise of

Christ's heritage, while me children lived in earthly example o' the Savior Himself and Saint John.

Fittingly enough, the clash was settled in a prayerful and peaceful debate among these saints in the Synod of Whitby. Oddly enough, 'twas decided by a Northumbrian king, who, at least in the service of his tongue, was a Christian. Let's just say, Oswald didn't want to offend God, just in case He was more powerful than the pagan gods Oswald hadn't quite dismissed. Besides, he was gettin' on in years and startin' to fret about what lay beyond death.

Oswald ruled for the Roman Church after hearing one of Jesus' metaphors—the one where Christ intimates that Peter, upon whom the church of Rome was founded, had the keys to heaven. Now, friends, this was a time when images or metaphors carried more weight in winning pagan souls than talk o' the Spirit. Even Christ Himself used stories to reach the common multitudes. And so Oswald decided if he wanted into heaven after his death, this Peter was the man at heaven's gate with the keys, not Saint John.

Thus began a controversy that centuries later divided the Christian church—the conclusion o' which I leave to the good Lord to lay upon yer hearts, for men far more faithful and learned than meself have never satisfied all, much to the sufferin' o' many innocent souls.

But I say all this to paint a picture o' the world at the time o' me story, and of the Irish Celtic and Roman saints who united despite their differences to save Albion's lost souls and abolish the sellin' of captives into slavery. This is the century o' me darlin' Deirdre, the strong-willed yet faithful princess of Gleannmara, and her captor, Alric, a pagan pirate prince who knows she's the key to an earthly kingdom denied him by his illegitimate birth. But what he knows not is she is the means to an eternal kingdom as well. And the key, dear hearts? Why, 'tis love.

May it bless ye, each and every one.

(Oh, and don't be forgettin' the glossary/reference in the back for help with names and terms strange to yer tongue, as well as tidbits of interest to them with a Celtic heart.)

PROLOGUE

Northumbrian kingdom of Galstead in the year of our Lord 657

Alric of Galstead drove his noble steed toward the gates of the fortress where his mother lay upon her deathbed. The horse snorted, tossing its head and sending foam splattering back. It was lathered and weary. Much as he'd like to, Alric could offer no reprieve from the hard ride that had begun the moment his ship had put into port and he'd found the dread news awaiting him.

He had to get there. He had to speak to his mother one last time, to let her know how much she meant to him before…

Alric shuddered, reluctant to even think of the world, much less his life, without Orlaith. His mother was like the sun, nourishing to the body, heart, and soul—a peaceful refuge from the darkness of a daily existence riddled by treachery and war. Only with her did Alric feel truly at ease. It was unfair that she be taken so soon.

Unfair! Unfair! Each pound of his heart screamed in protest. Surely it would shatter before he reached his destination.

Nightfall edged out the sun on the horizon behind him as Alric cleared the city gates at a full gallop. The sentries hailed their young prince, but he paid them no heed, racing by the cluster of A-framed dwellings toward the one that loomed over their roofs ahead: his father's royal hall. Yet it was not to this hall that Alric headed after handing his panting, sweat-soaked horse to a servant, but a small cottage near it.

The cottage was no guest house, as were the others nearby. It had been built for its beloved occupant many years ago, after the birth of the king's son. Even though Orlaith was King Lambert's slave, she was no ordinary servant. She'd been a princess of the Dalraidi Scots to the north, captured by their Northumbrian enemies and purchased by

Lambert the moment the Saxon king laid eyes upon her. His love for Orlaith was no secret—not to his queen Ethlinda, nor to the people. Some thought the king's eyes shone a little brighter for Alric, the Christian slave's son, than for his elder half brother, Ricbert, the legitimate heir to Galstead.

Bracing himself with a deep breath, Alric approached his failing mother's side. The fever that ravaged Orlaith's body bled her face of color even as it bled her body of strength. She was as white as the fine linens on which she lay. Her eyelids fluttered and opened, as if she sensed his presence.

"Alric." His mother tried to raise her hand to him, but weakness would not allow it.

Her golden hair was only beginning to silver. *Surely this can't be happening.* Alric gathered the slender hand in his own. "Mother, I came as soon as we put in."

Orlaith drew in a shallow breath through her nostrils. "You smell of the sea. I believe it has bewitched you."

"It has. But you should rest. Save your strength."

"God will give the strength I need to say what I must." She turned to Abina, who'd been her handmaid at the time of their capture. Lambert bought Abina for his lovely royal captive, but the two were more like soul mates than mistress and servant. "Leave us, dear friend."

Tears bright in her eyes, Abina gave her mistress a kiss on the forehead and rose to leave. "She's held on for you, Son," the stooped servant mouthed to Alric, her words less than a whisper.

He nodded. The woman still acted like his nursemaid, though he was man now in his twenties.

"Abina has a slight limp," he said as he watched her leave.

The surprise in his voice caused Orlaith's lips to twitch. "None of us are as we were."

And he was away so much, he'd not noticed. His mother didn't say it, but Alric knew the truth hovered at the edge of her mind...and his.

"Seeking my fortune has blinded me to the changes," he admitted. "But I don't want a share of Ricbert's birthright."

Lambert had told Alric to establish an estate on the seacoast, which he knew Alric loved. But that was a part of the kingdom the elder legitimate son would inherit and so, while it was a generous offer, Alric graciously refused. He determined to seek his own fortune, than either win or purchase the land. *His* son would have a legitimate birthright. No child of his would know the ridicule and contempt Alric had suffered.

The very thought of it tasted of bile in his mouth.

"Your birthright lies beyond the sea, my son. God has shown it to me."

Alric held back his response, not wishing to upset her. Her Christian God had allowed her to be taken from the royal womb of her home in the north. Pampered and loved as she'd been, she was still Lambert's property.

"It is not here in Galstead," she went on, then shook her head wearily, the limp strands of her perspiration-darkened hair falling away from her ashen face.

Alric needed no holy vision to know that. By law, his birthright would not be among his father's people any more than it was among his mother's Dalraidi kin. No, the only way he'd have a Celtic kingdom was to take it by force.

Once King Oswald, *bretwalda* of Northumbria, chose the Christian faith for himself and all his subkingdoms, the newly baptized Lambert finally succumbed to Orlaith's pleas that she and her son would visit her family and see that Alric was properly educated according to his noble bloodlines. It was not unheard of for Saxon princes to seek a universally esteemed Irish education. While Lambert's belief in Oswald's new Christian God was not that strong, his faith in Orlaith's promise to return to him was.

Orlaith's family had received the returned princess and her son as Celtic hospitality demanded, but Alric and his mother were treated worse there than among the Saxon heathens. Alric's sword arm grew stronger defending his mother's honor than it had in practice. Soon his Celtic cousins dared not challenge him. He'd worked just as hard to surpass them in academic study, until his wit was as keen as his blade—

"You are a prince, my son, and your true kingdom will be won by faith, not by the sword."

"Ah, the kingdom of heaven." Alric tried to suppress the bitterness with which he usually responded to his mother's sermons. For her sake, he hoped she would inherit that kingdom when her last breath was spent…unless her God rejected her the same way her family had. She deserved a place of honor for all she'd suffered. Although, even the cold grave was a relief from the broken heart he believed had sapped away his mother's health and given this fever its lethal teeth.

And it was her own people—Christians, no less—who'd broken her heart.

"But God also revealed to me your earthly kingdom."

His mother's hold on Alric's hand slackened, but the light that shone in her eyes would have shamed the sun. Or was it fever? Still, the mention of an earthly kingdom reached through his drowning ocean of anger and grief and pricked his curiosity.

"Oh?"

"Its colors are the royal blue of a sky lighted by the moon and its full consort of stars." She licked her dry, cracked lips to no avail. Death was drawing breath and water from her body by the moment. "And the gold of your hair." She'd always marveled at his warrior's mane with motherly pride.

With a pang of guilt, he leaned closer that she might touch his hair once more as she had so oft in his life. He could give her that, even if words of comfort eluded him. Anguish had cut them from his tongue, holding him hostage. His mother was the only truly good thing he knew in this life. Her only ambition was to love.

"And the symbol on the cloak I made for you. You will know it by that."

"Enough of kingdoms, Mother. Save your strength."

What did kingdoms or birthrights matter without her? Alric held her hand so that she could finger one of the natural curls that gave her such pleasure. She straightened it and let it go, smiling as it sprang back into shape.

"My *muirnait,*" she sighed.

Beloved. She hadn't called him that since he was a weanling.

"Always," he assured her softly. It felt as if stones enough to build a wall round his father's kingdom had been laid upon his chest. There was so much he wanted to thank her for, so much love he needed to declare, but never had he known the right words to do so. The one thing he believed in could not be measured. But nothing could hurt so much and not be real.

"And your earthly kingdom, Son, will be won by love."

Not this love. It was reserved only for his mother. Then there was the poet's game to be played upon the fairer sex, or the mutual respect he and his father held for each other...but the love his mother spoke of—

"I've seen her."

Alric's furtive musings stumbled. This was something different from Orlaith's Scripture-based prophecy, which was vague now and certain only after death.

"Her namesake is sorrow, yet she will bring you great joy. Her chatter will be like birdsong to your heart."

He cleared his throat. "Have you a name?" Why he asked, he didn't know. Certainly he didn't believe these feverish mumblings.

Whether she did or didn't, Orlaith closed her eyes and took a deep, shaky breath. In a whisper, it escaped her lips. "God be with you, muirnait, until we meet again." Her chest dropped, ever so slowly, as if death's unseen hands pushed the last remnant of air from her body. The hand in Alric's grew limp.

His mother was gone and with her, the only real love he'd ever known.

Desperate to hold on to her warmth until death took that away from him as well, Alric pressed his mother's hand to his cheek. The blades of anguish and anger that held his tears at bay, shredded the words he spoke into it: "This I vow to your memory, *Maîthar,* that I will not repeat the crime my father committed against you. She who bears my son will be my lawful wife."

ONE

Seventh century, beyond the coastal waters of Erin

L ess than a day from Wicklow's shore, the Irish merchant ship *Mell* shuddered beneath Deirdre's feet. The wind caught the leather riggings and clapped overhead, like gulls' wings at the lofty promise of freedom. Excitement infected the young princess of Gleannmara with a wild longing to shed the trappings of her disciplined albeit privileged station. *Oh, to fly before the wind—at least in spirit!* Yet all that expressed that abandon were the flaxen tendrils of her hair, waving bannerlike away from the regal set of her oval face and squared shoulders.

The fine woven material of her dress billowed about her as she let go of its folds and gripped the ship's rail, lest fantasy become reality. She could not allow that to happen. She was the princess of Gleannmara, and she was on a mission on behalf of her ill father—a grievous task that pricked at her pride and faith. The thought of it struck like a rain cloud, dousing the whimsy in her heart with the dark flood of memories...

Deirdre had been at academically reknowned Clonnard, devouring her studies in her private quest to someday become a teacher, when a grim messenger rode through the gates demanding an audience with her. She feared her stepmother had found yet another suitor in her quest to marry Deirdre off. Though she had made it plain to both her father, King Fergal of Gleannmara, and to his second wife, Dealla, that she'd choose her own life mate in her own time, her stepmother was resolute.

Bracing against a shudder of anxiety, Deirdre thinned her lips—lips that her last admirer had likened to the color of a rose. Would that another prospective husband *had* been the news the man brought to them.

"Would you like me to fetch your cloak, milady?"

Deirdre turned to Orna, her attendant, and shook her head. "Nay, leave it in the chest." She took a deep breath. "This sea air is blood stirring."

"More like bone chilling, to my notion."

Three years Deirdre's junior and clearly not of the same mind, Orna drew her own cloak closer, shivering enough for the two of them.

"Then take cover amidship." Deirdre nodded to where a makeshift tent had been constructed for their passage.

Orna shrugged. "No, I'll stand for a while. I get queasy if I remain inside over long. 'Tis what I deserve for agreeing to sail on a ship named for lightning." She broke into a smile, the freckles she tried futilely to rid herself of fading of their own accord.

"It was also the name of the mother of seven saints," Deirdre reminded her gently, considering it aptly named for both excitement and piety. "To think, it was from the sea that God brought forth the first living creatures. Did you ever wonder why He chose the sea first rather than the land?"

"Far be it from me to question our creator, milady. The motives of men are confounding enough." Orna gave a sniff of pure disdain.

The girl had received her education at Dromin, which was enough to serve her well, given her sole purpose in life was to marry well and breed children. Her latest prospect, Dromin's heir, had failed to show at their early morning departure, and the maid was miffed.

"I suppose." Subjects of this meat were best shared with scholars of the church, though they were no less exasperated at Deirdre's curious inquiries. It wasn't as if she were challenging God's choice—the usual assumption when they had no answer. She merely wondered about the why of it.

"Perhaps it's better to ask the good Lord why the heathen Saxons invaded our shores and took your brother among their hostages," Orna added.

Deirdre was forced to agree. "Aye, and don't think I haven't."

With a pang of guilt for trying to escape the weight of her duty for a few moments, Deirdre focused on the events of the last few days as due penance.

She'd ridden with the messenger straight for Gleannmara, a good two-day journey even on horseback. The shock of the new Northumbrian king's invasion, the details of the carnage and pillaging he invoked in the name of God against not just the kingdoms on the coast but the sacred monasteries, still curdled her stomach. Surely God would not let the atrocities committed against the nuns and priests go unavenged.

Her brother, Cairell, and other young nobles from the nearby university had rallied to stop the onslaught, but the aspiring young warriors were no match for the seasoned attackers hurled against them by this demon-possessed Ecfrith, who claimed to be championing the church. Now the pride of fine Irish families were captives, bound for slave markets in Rome. Because Cairell was a prince, the heathen dogs, under the guise of civility, had offered his salvation through ransom from a prosperous *tuath*. The other prisoners, hailing from lesser kingdoms or poorer clans, were not so fortunate.

Deirdre's father had only one moon cycle to deliver the money.

"Would that King Fergal was well enough to take the gold and a host of warriors to pour it, molten and hot, down the devils' throats." Orna relaxed her folded arms for a moment on the rail, clearly savoring the idea with the same indignation Deirdre felt.

As the ambassador of Gleannmara, she had to keep a level head. So her father insisted when she'd given in to a fearsome rant as she placed one of the tuath's most cherished treasures—the sword of her ancestor, King Kieran of Gleannmara—in to the ransom chest. A century ago, Kieran had surrendered his weapon and his life to Christ and laid the jeweled sword upon the church altar with a prayer that it never be used against God's will. There it remained, only removed to fight for Gleannmara and the One God who blessed it...until now.

"Cairell is a good man, raised and educated to be both a king and a servant of God. 'Tis the man himself, not the sword, that will carry on God's glory," Deirdre murmured, as if to convince herself. She'd cut her teeth on the tales of Gleannmara's glorious past, and her country's indomitable spirit lived in her. Would that her ancestor's sword be used against the villains rather than handed over to them.

Perhaps if Gleannmara's warriors had not been summoned into the high king's service, Fergal might have responded differently, but the time needed to summon them back home was not on their side. And while Deirdre was no novice at swordplay, she was no warrior queen like the legendary Maire.

Here was a situation where the spiritual strength of the ancient queen's husband, Rowan, was needed. He would truly believe, as Gleannmara's priest suggested, that the attack on the innocent clergy and the kidnappings might be turned into a blessing by God. Unlike Rowan, Deirdre had dwelt more on the pursuit of practical knowledge than of spiritual. Sadly, it was the latter she needed now.

"He'll make a fine husband, as well," Orna added wistfully beside her.

Aye, a man like Rowan would suit her just— "Who?" Deirdre cut her eyes sharply at the maid.

"Why your brother, milady. Were we not just speaking of him?"

Deirdre mentally backtracked. It was yet another fault of her eager mind, running ahead of conversation on some tangent and leaving her clueless when it came her turn to speak.

"Yes, he will…when he meets the right woman." Faith, how many men did the woman want on her string? "Like as not, he'll seek a princess…or at least a marriage that will ally a great clan to Gleannmara."

"And one no more than seventeen or eighteen in years," Orna added pointedly, stung by the reminder that she was not among that select group. Her people belonged to one of Gleannmara's subsepts.

The maid's pluck was well matched with ambition. Deirdre laughed, and her gaze traveled to where the newly ordained Father Scanlan, another of Gleannmara's sons, spoke with the ship's captain. Although they traveled on the same ship, their objectives were different. The priest was intent on saving the very souls who demanded the ransom from Gleannmara, while Deirdre, God forgive her, leaned toward condemning them.

"You mean unlike me?" Deirdre knew full well that was exactly what Orna meant.

Deirdre had just attained her twentieth year, still engaged in academic studies rather than wedded to some nobleman who would want her only to make his life comfortable and provide an heir. Admittedly, it was unusual for a woman not pledged to the church to reach such an age without marriage, but it was certainly no crime.

"Oh no, milady," Orna recounted hastily.

"You would not be the first to bring this to my attention, nor the last, I'd wager...but I want to be more than a peace weaver, or the instrument of a political alliance, or a vessel for producing heirs, or a Saint Brigid, dedicated to saving souls."

What exactly she *did* want, Deirdre wasn't certain, but she knew true love—the kind glorified in legend and in Scripture—was central to it. She yearned for adventure and travel, but not the sort in which she was engaged now.

"To be a scholar is a high aspiration, milady," Orna offered without conviction.

Deirdre struggled not to laugh at her attendant's confoundment as to why a princess with so many more prospects than she found academic study and discussion preferable to marriage. "Aye, it is," she reflected, straight-faced. "And far easier than having to live with a man one simply doesn't understand."

Relieved for the common ground Deirdre offered, Orna nodded eagerly. "Aye, that it is. I cannot for the life of me explain why Corc of Dromin did not come to see us away as he promised most fervently last eve. I vow, the only *heart* he has lies in his name."

"Moonlight passion cools in the warmth of the sun, or so I've heard."

"His kiss did warm me like the sun never has," Orna admitted. "And I am considerably cooled this day and see him in a much clearer light."

"Ah, I see." At least in theory, Deirdre mused. Moonlight passion is hotter than the sun and addles clear thought...like too much sun.

Her thoughts shifted instantly to her ailing father. He'd not been well since he married his younger brother's widow, a woman scarcely a decade Deirdre's senior. Dealla had boldly flirted with him before his grown children and all Gleannmara, though their sainted mother was scarcely cold in the tomb. Enough gossip circulated about the winter-summer affair as it was, echoing the sentiments that filled the air when their uncle Eber had taken Dealla as his wife years before. At the time, all Deirdre knew was that it was difficult to call a woman so few years her senior *aunt,* and impossible to call her *mother.* At his brother's funeral, even Fergal confided that Eber's marriage to a woman half his age was enough to kill the aging warrior. So why had her father up and done the very same thing?

Now he was so weak that the news of Cairell's abduction sent him to bed. Proof positive that passion addled the brain and the physical constitution, at least for some. Deirdre frowned. Why was her father so affected?

Biting back the question teetering on her lips, she glanced at her attendant. There was no point in asking Orna if too much, or perhaps ill-matched, passion could really drain a body of health. The maid was no more keen than she of such things. Well, perhaps a mite more, Deirdre conceded. Orna had at least been warmed by a kiss, where Deirdre had found kisses a curious physical attempt by her suitors to win her favor.

"You ladies appear to be enjoying this glorious day that the Lord has made," Father Scanlan commented as he joined them, folding his coarse gray-frocked arms on the rail.

"Aye, and I've enjoyed all I can stand, save taking a fatal chill," Orna answered with a shiver. "Lady Deirdre, will you have your cloak now?"

Deirdre shook her head, dismissing the attendant in silence. Piece by piece, she was getting to the core of what troubled her most about this mission, that burr which was hidden by the obvious.

"Something weighs heavily on your mind, milady. Perhaps you'd care to share it with me?" Scanlan's look was enshrouded in compassion. His perception was uncanny but slightly off the mark, just as her own had been. He believed, as had she until this moment, that her mission alone furrowed her young brow in the midday sun, when, in truth, it merely deepened it. Faith, she had been loathe to leave her father, seeing how frail he'd become.

In particular, she'd not wanted to leave him with Dealla.

"Do you think Father has been drugged by my stepmother?" As the compassionate fix of his dark Irish features gave way to wide-eyed shock, she explained quickly, "His health has faded since their marriage."

"Your father is aging, milady. From what I've seen, your stepmother has helped him regain a portion of his youth. Remember, your mother's death left him old beyond his years." His words were slowed by a concerted effort at tact. "Besides, what possible gain is there for her in his demise, when Cairell is the undisputed heir?"

Cairell is gone, she wanted to say. And yet…her father's health began to deteriorate long before all this came to pass.

"Suppose this drugging was inadvertent," she hypothesized. "The result of…" The age difference. That was it. "Mismatched passion!"

"I b-beg your pardon?" Scanlan's eyes looked ready to pop from his head.

With analytical tenacity, Deirdre switched from the obvious to the scriptural. "We are wonderfully made, the Word says so, does it not?"

Scanlan's nod was slow, hesitant.

"So when we disrupt that order, intentionally or unintentionally, we are corrupted."

"That all depends on—"

"And passion outside of wedlock is corrupt," Deirdre went on, hot on the philosophical trail. "It makes people do sinful things that they ordinarily wouldn't think of…like David's pursuit of Bathsheba. His brain, even his soul, was addled by his passion." Faith, he first saw her at night, bathing no less. Moon addling *was* more intense than sun addling.

Scanlan dug in with saintly resolve. "I would hardly compare Fergal's marriage to David and Bathsheba's story. Your father married Dealla. It is a blessed union."

"But physically, they are mismatched by age and hence in…um…vigor." In truth, she could feel her cheeks gaining warmth on the sun, but she felt close to a marvelous theory backed by Scripture itself.

The young priest retreated. "This has nothing to do with drugs or physical ailments. Nor is it a matter for man to discern, but for God."

"But it does! When a body ingests food that is overly rich, yet not tainted, does the stomach not turn sour? Bilious juices are manifested within the body itself, like a poisonous drug, making it ill." She had to keep herself from clapping her hands with the thrill of this intellectual hunt. "And just as unwed passion can impair one's sensibilities, cannot a union, mismatched in vigor—the bland with the rich—render similar health-impairing effects?"

"Well I…I don't know what to say."

"That science and Scripture concur!" Deirdre reined in the triumph she felt, lest it sound as though she delighted in what had happened, not only to her father, but to her uncle as well. "Passion must be restricted to wedlock and matched according to the order of time or, in the case of mankind, age."

"Yes, I do know what to say," Scanlan announced even as blood infused his face. "This is not a fit subject for a princess but best left to physicians and scholars. How *do* your tutors deal with this unbridled curiosity and tongue of yours?"

Soundly put in her place, Deirdre took a stubborn stand, jaw jutted for emphasis. "I *am* a scholar, or I will be when my studies are complete." She'd hoped for more from a man as well-read as Scanlan, but he was as shortsighted as her suitors when it came to conversation beyond subjects of their interest or experience. Or comfort.

Father, somewhere out there, there has to be someone like me, a dreamer, a thinker, someone unafraid to explore the unknown…a young, strapping, and, not quite so saintly, Saint Brendan, if You will.

A precocious smile tugged at her lips, but she mastered it out of reverence. If God truly loved her like a father, then He would smile behind a stern countenance when she slipped into harmless mischief. His love was first and foremost, and she was certain He liked to laugh as well, what with all the truly serious matters He dealt with day in and day out. A feeling of comfort swept over her, as if she sat on her Father's knee, as beloved as she had been as a child on Fergal's.

Without notice, a shout of "Sail ho!" from above drew her attention to the sea. An approaching vessel that hadn't been there only a few moments ago was practically upon them, as if conjured from the belly of the sea itself. Its single sail strained toward them, full of the wind their own vessel seemingly lost with the collective gasp of surprise echoing round the deck.

Deirdre stood riveted by the sight, one word too loathsome to utter coming to mind…

Saxons!

TWO

The sides of the vessel were barren of the shields of a war ship, yet it was too lightly fitted, in Deirdre's admittedly limited estimation, to be a merchant vessel. It rode much higher in the water than the one beneath her feet, which was laden with goods bound for Albion's western coast. Unlike the leather-wrapped Irish *curraghs,* this vessel was enclosed with narrow strakes, gracefully tapered down from the carved wolf's head of its sharp prow and up to its equally high and narrow stern stem. Painted a dark shade of blue-green, it blended well with the sea that had hidden it to the last. Now, as though the good Lord's wind was not sufficient to speed it along, a long row of oars worked in concert from each side, like the spindly legs of a giant insect, propelling it closer at a startling rate.

"Is it unfriendly?" Deirdre whispered to Father Scanlan. It was a question she'd not have posed before the Saxon invasion. Incursions against Erin were scarcely heard of, isolated as it was from the continent.

"I'm not likin' the looks o' them oars poking out both sides of 'er, Cap'n," a seaman called down from his lofty perch above, preempting the priest.

"There's no markings on the sail," Scanlan observed to no one in particular.

"Stand ready, lads. Friend or foe, we'll not outrun 'em with our cargo aboard!" At the captain's roar, the helmsman shifted the wheel hard to the leeward, struggling to remove their vulnerable side as a potential ramming target.

The *Mell* shuddered in resistance, groaning sails lashing at the lines in protest as the bow dipped into a trough. Holding to the rail for balance, Deirdre stood fast as the gaping mouth of the sea opened before her very eyes. Her heartbeat outpaced the seeming eternity the ship took to level off again. Much to her astonishment, weapons of all manner, hitherto concealed, appeared in the hands of the more nimble-footed seamen. In the rigging above was a veritable hornet's nest of men waiting with ready sting.

"You'd best get below, milady," Father Scanlan said, prying Deirdre from the rail. He ushered her toward the open hatch leading below. "And take Orna with you."

As one of the only two women aboard, it made sense, but Deirdre stopped abruptly. "I can fight if I must." She'd been indulged in training by the men of her clan.

Scanlan smiled. "I remember. But these may be pirates, not a doting uncle or your father's men."

"They'd as soon cut us in half as look at us," Orna said. "Think of those poor nuns." She crossed herself hurriedly for their sisters, who had not just been robbed and violated but viciously mutilated on the grounds of heresy against the Roman-established order of worship.

Deirdre shuddered that the Saxon King Ecfrith used the excuse of faith to feed his hatred of his mother's people. She wanted to fillet this vermin with Kieran's sword of righteousness, but that was not her place. Hers was a conciliatory mission to save her brother, not nearly as blood stirring as it was pride bending. Besides, a female on deck might distract the captain and his men.

"Come, then." She stepped back so that Orna might descend the ladder first.

As Deirdre descended into the hold, she saw Scanlan kneel by the grate cover. After offering a short prayer, he closed them up in the hold. It took a moment for Deirdre to adjust to the eerie darkness broken only by checkered shafts of sun leaking through the latticed grate. Neither the air allowed in by the grate nor the leathery presence of the cattle skins or wooden casks filled with salted meats and wine could override the fetid breath of mold.

Inhaling only because she must, Deirdre settled on Gleannmara's gold- and jewel-embossed ransom chest. Next to her Orna prayed, lips moving with the fervor of a backslid saint at hell's gate.

Rather than waste more time pondering the identity of these people, Deirdre switched her thoughts to what she might do if they were the enemy. Pray, yes, by all means. *Father above us, deliver us from evil...* Ever so gently, Deirdre moved Orna to the crate next to the ransom chest. "Keep praying, friend."

But should You allow them privy to us, Deirdre continued with her own spiritual plea, *then show us what we must do to meet the foe. Give us the strength and grace to*—She removed a key from the embroidered bag slung at her side and slipped it into the trunk lock—*do Thy will.* As she sprang the lock, the *Mell* jarred with such force that she fully expected to see the prow of the other vessel rip through the side.

Orna screamed as she was flung to the wattle floor separating them from the slime of the bilge. Deirdre scrambled for her dropped key. Simultaneously, an ungodly roar echoed above them, met with the shouts of the merchantman's crew, conjuring the image of a pack of wolves seizing upon weaker prey.

Father, save us! Deirdre helped Orna to her feet. *They mustn't take the ransom. It's my brother's only hope.* She slipped the key back into the safety of her purse.

Her first thought was to hide the gold between the ship's ribs, under the wattled flooring they supported, but, God forbid, should the *Mell* go down, the treasure would be lost anyway.

Father, show me what to do! She winced as something heavy fell on the deck above them. A body? It was likely, given the screams and growls, the clash of metal and wood, the scramble for footing on unsteady ground that chorused in bloody horror above them.

Orna's ear-piercing shriek filled the close confines of the hold, assaulting Deirdre's senses with the sharpness of a butcher's knife. Looking up, she saw the source—a hand separated from its body lay on the grate, fingers still trying to clutch the hilt of a long knife. Deirdre jerked away and bumped against a lashed stack of barrels, wine from the monastery on the Liffey. An idea struck her with a glimmer of hope. She could hide the contents of the treasure in one of the wine barrels! The top barrel had already been tapped for the use of the crew. Hurriedly, she wrung at the tap. While the rich red wine poured into the bilge, she unsheathed her dining dagger to cut the barrel free from the secured stack of kegs.

"Orna, open the chest. We're going to transfer the gold to this barrel."

"B-but where can we hide it?"

"Behind these bundles of hide," Deirdre told her. "The brigands will never know they have it…not at first, leastways." Making it difficult for the enemy was the least she could do, pitiful as it was.

"For all the good it'll do our rotting dismembered flesh." Orna sniffed.

"More like they'll take us as slaves," Deirdre retorted with impatience.

At this, Orna became inconsolable as well as useless.

With no time to rally the maid to her senses or acknowledge her pang of guilt, Deirdre set about the task herself, shutting out the blood-letting fury above. God willing, if this ploy worked, she might somehow get the ransom back.

Her diligent ministrations had a sobering effect on Orna. "Milady, have you lost your wits?" The maid hiccoughed, struggling to her feet beside Deirdre as the latter packed the container tight with her royal cloak, her jewels, and every other item of clothing that might give away her identity.

"There's no need to let the devils know they've a royal captive for whom they can further rob my father." Faith, it would kill him. "Now, hold this tight." Deirdre stripped off her rich overdress and packed it in as well. "All they'll find is two Irish lasses bound for God's humble service."

"And what of the sword?" Orna glanced at the bottom of the chest, where Kieran's legacy to Gleannmara lay in its sheath.

It was too long to fit in the cask and too precious to risk losing if they scuttled the ship. "I'll hide it under my priest's robe, *Sister* Orna. Now help me lift this, and then we'll get two robes from Scanlan's trunk."

Her companion's expression left nothing to be said regarding her doubt. Together they pushed the cask behind the stack of barrels. After looting the priest's trunk of two robes bound for his brethren, Deirdre donned one, while Orna simply stood agape at her madness.

Thank God, she was tall for a woman, Deirdre thought. Wth a

darting look at the hatch, she tied the king's sword to her thigh with one of the woven belts from the trunk. Now the only sound above them, beyond the moans of the wounded, was the barking of orders and their acknowledgment in a harsh tongue. It slashed at the senses like a whip, unlike the poetic song of Irish tongue or the romantic staccato of the Roman.

At footsteps echoing directly over their heads, Deirdre hastily let the robe and her shift drop to the floor, concealing the weapon. The coarse, ill-fitting garment pooled at her feet as the hatch cover was jerked up.

Orna gasped, dropping the robe she was supposed to have donned. Deirdre took a slower, deeper breath to fortify her resolve against the regret being squeezed from her thudding heart. There was no time now.

A hideous face, painted and squinting at the darkness, appeared where the cover had been. Grease-laden, crudely shorn hair fell around it as the creature grinned. What teeth were not black-edged with rot or missing altogether had a brownish-yellow cast to them. Turning away, he barked something in his oafish tongue.

Deirdre refused to cower against the stack of hides as Orna did but stared boldly up at the warrior who took the other's place. In no rush, he removed his helmet, a princely piece embossed with silver and brass inlay. As he cradled it in one arm and swept a long, liberated mane away from his face, she saw the glittering ornament of a wolf as the armor's crest. Blood still dripping from the long, single-edged knife hanging at his lean girded waist, he eased down to one knee and peered into the hold.

Deirdre's breath seized at the lock of their gazes—blue fire within a steel gray as hard as the hidden blade pressed against her flesh. No doubt his heart, if he had one at all, was just as cold. The corner of his mouth pulled with a grunt of indifference, probably the most intellectual thing he'd given voice to today. Though wordless, it still managed insult. She lifted her chin at the condescension.

"Will you stand there gaping like a village idiot or will you help us out of this stink hole?"

Was that her voice upbraiding this giant of muscle and blood in flawless Latin? The universal tongue of world trade, surely even pirates would have some knowledge of it.

The other corner of his mouth pulled back, transforming his lips into a smile. Undaunted, he offered her his hand. "By all means, milady, do come up where my men and I might have a look at you and yon friend there."

His smooth reply took her aback almost as much as the size and strength of the hand that enveloped hers. He spoke like a scholar, not a brigand. As he assisted Deirdre's unsteady climb up the ladder, he called over her shoulder to Orna, who still cowered against the cargo of skins. "There's no need to fear us, sweetling. Come along after your..." He locked gazes with Deirdre once again, his own softened by curiosity. "*Sister,*" he finished without certainty.

The hidden sword hampered Deirdre's progress, but that was the least of her concerns at the moment. She felt as if the stranger looked not just into her eyes but into her very soul. The eyes were, after all, the soul's window. She lowered her gaze hastily before he could name the number of jewels on Kieran's hidden scabbard. She could not, however, resist challenging his reassurance.

"Is that what you said before you slaughtered our sisters in God's own house?"

His cordial demeanor darkened, and he growled like thunder's own god. "Neither I, Alric of Galstead, nor my men make war upon women *anywhere.*"

As Deirdre searched her memory for either the name or the place, he tilted her face so she could not avoid his penetrating look. The scowl that had been etched in her mind from his guttural declaration mellowed along with his voice.

"Women are for making love, not war." He ventured a lazy smile that seemed far more dangerous than his fury. Her eyes widened with the rush of heat singeing her neck on its way to her face. Was he flirting? How dare he! She was a princess, her bloodline traceable to the Milesian kings who conquered Erin for the Celts. He was nothing but a bloodthirsty swine.

Deirdre raised her hand to slap Alric, but he seized her wrist just short of contact with his gold-stubbled jaw. Over his shoulder, he made some remark in his native tongue, evoking laughter from his men. She refused to dignify it by asking what he'd said, but he shared with her anyway, taking infuriating pleasure in it.

"I told my men that your study in Christian humility has been a waste of time. Besides, to waste such fiery spirit in a marriage to your church would be a pity."

"No more wasteful than praying for your black soul."

The Saxon's eyebrow shot up, arching higher than its mate in surprise. Father Scanlan rushed to Deirdre's defense before the mockery in her captor's gaze found voice.

"My colleague is new to the order. She only wears the mean garb of our church community because—"

"I clumsily dropped my belongings overboard," Deirdre finished, sparing Scanlan further involvement in her charade. God would forgive them, surely, but Scanlan might not forgive himself. Sometimes, she dared to think, he and his kind walked a fine line between faith and foolishness.

Splattered with innocent blood, the pirate leaned over to help Orna out of the hold. "I *had* noticed," he answered over his shoulder—he could surely carry Deirdre on that one and her handmaiden on the other—"that grace is sorely lacking among your more obvious charms. You took to yon ladder like a fool on stilts."

"If you—" Deirdre choked off her reply just in time. *If you had a sword strapped to your leg, you'd walk like a fool as well.* "Better an affliction of the limb than of the mind."

The pirate captain turned back to her. Far from stung by her sarcasm, he seemed to be enjoying it. Stepping back, he boldly assessed her, the silver gray of his eyes seeming to dance in mercurial speculation—slow, yet quick; warm, then cool; amused, then something that made her shiver.

The heat she felt vanished when she heard two heathen words she understood. "Did you say *slave market?*" Deirdre's challenge clearly took him, as well as his men, aback. She allowed a smile of smug satisfaction. "There are some words in your distasteful language well known in my country. Your reputation precedes you."

"It's a shame none here took it seriously," he answered with unsettling gravity. He waved his arm in a circle about him. "A surrender to our obvious fighting strength would have spared all this."

Deirdre looked around her for the first time and caught back a gasp.

Of all the men aboard the merchantman, only Father Scanlan had been spared. The rest lay lifeless, hacked by a single-edged Saxon *scramasax* or impaled by their deadly spears. The bloody sight would have made a lesser woman retch, exactly as Orna, who'd run to the rail, was doing that very moment. The bile that rose to the back of Deirdre's throat resisted swallowing, but she would not yield to it either. Not here. Not in front of *him*. With as much dignity as her bound leg would afford, she walked over to where Orna held on to the rail to keep from buckling to its deck.

"They wouldn't stop fighting until they'd spent their last breath," Alric told her.

"Wouldn't you prefer death's freedom to slavery in life?"

"Life offers the chance to escape from slavery. There is no escape from the grave."

Deirdre spat out her contempt. "There's none for your heathen likes anywhere."

The golden giant threw back his head and laughed, and then said something to his crew, which sent them into a chorus of amusement as he translated for Deirdre.

"Indeed, if I hope to fetch any price for you, I shall have to parade you with your tongue bound securely. No man in his right mind would expose himself to its sharpness unless he cut it out.... Now *there's* an idea." He scratched his chin thoughtfully and, for one terrifying moment, his other hand moved toward the hilt of the blade at his waist. Only the faintest twitch at the corner of his mouth gave her a whit of reassurance—that, and the way the sunlight cavorted in his gaze.

Deirdre let out a short breath of relief—for with the likes of Alric of Galstead, she was certain relief would be nothing if not short-lived.

THREE

Alric stood, arms folded, feet planted squarely on the rolling deck of the merchant ship. A quick inspection showed the vessel had suffered little damage during the battle. He allowed a small smile. Sale of both the *Mell* and its cargo would fatten his purse. Indeed, the tribute due the Northumbrian subkingdom of his father, denied forever to Alric by birth, would someday pale in comparison to what he took from the sea.

He'd show his family that the illegitimate son of his father's captive Scottish princess neither wanted nor needed Galstead—not even that which his father offered out of earnest affection. The offer had only worsened the tension at court, making his stepmother, Queen Ethlinda and half brother, Ricbert, green as their greed. How could his father expect Alric to someday pay homage to his elder half brother as Galstead's king when no love had ever been lost between them? Not in this world, at least, and there wasn't likely a next.

"I reckon this will put us ahead some," Gunnar, his second in command said. "Did you find the treasure chest yet?"

They were much like brothers, both noble second sons who would have to make their own fortunes, although Gunnar was not the bastard of a slave.

"Yes, it's fine as any you've ever laid eyes upon but empty as a witch's heart." The loose lips of a drunken merchant in Dublin had tipped the two pirates that a royal treasure chest was included in the hold that carried his future fortune. At least he'd been half right.

His dark-haired mate looked stricken at first and then returned to his usual good humor. "Ach, to hear you speak of our beloved queen so."

Lack of love for Ethlinda and Ricbert was yet another commonality they shared. Gunnar beat his fist against the hard leather plate of his armor, his only body protection save his helmet. His mail shirt, like

Alric's, had been left ashore. One false step and that particular protection could prove death in the water.

It was a less bloody demise, that was for certain, Alric mused, watching as the last of the dead were tossed over the side. Water was as good as earth for a grave. Either way, creatures waited to devour a man's flesh and bone.

"Do you suppose our drunken friend meant a treasure *chest* and not a royal treasure?"

"Or mayhap he was spinning tales from his imagination." Alric glanced over to where the curious sister of the church and her companions tended the wounded. It was a shame such beauty had a lame leg, for she'd be a delight to chase about a plump bed, given the right frame of mind. Alric had never forced a woman to placate his needs, but he had managed to charm a few into forgetting their initial refusals.

"Imagine her in silk instead of sackcloth," Gunnar reflected beside him. "By Frig's sweet breath, she's as long-shanked as a warrior and twice as comely.... Although I favor the more compact, brown-haired lass she's escorting."

"Well, don't dwell overlong on either, for they are worth more to our Frisian partners untouched...at least the little one is. The other claims to be a sister of the church."

The force in Alric's voice was as much to convince himself as his friend. That he had to do so astonished him. There was something about the wench, something that reached beyond her beauty. It was her fire that swirled beyond the blue glass of her gaze, stirred by spirit. It was a shame if she was really intended for the church—and not just because Alric's respect for his mother would not permit him to sell clergy into slavery.

"Have the young priest and the women brought aboard the *Wulfshead*. Then fit this ship with a crew to sail for Albion."

"No point in transferring the cargo when our destination is the same," Gunnar agreed.

It wasn't the first time they'd taken a ship intact and done the exact same thing, but Gunnar was drunk with easy triumph and more than likely had already calculated his share of their prize, just by the position of its waterline. It was exasperating that his longtime friend was always within his own blood worth of being correct, whether the cargo be wool or gold.

Alric preferred the sure way of doing the sums himself. Nothing was certain until he knew it was his and his alone. Estimation was as unreliable as the wind—like an empty gilded and jeweled treasure chest.

Or a prophecy.

Frig's mercy, it had been five years, and Alric could still see his mother and hear the strain it took to draw breath enough to tell him what she'd clung to life for. Out of respect for her, he'd taken no part in King Ecfrith's travesty on the Celtic church. There was plunder aplenty in the Irish ships bound for Argyll, heavy with supplies to aid the Scots and the Picts in their border war with Northumbria. The seamen, at least, were armed, and if they were not…well, Alric had no mercy for fools.

Gunner's startled voice struck through Alric's unwitting lapse into the past. "Ho, what's this slipping out from beneath your robe?"

The note of alarm sent Alric's hand to the hilt of his scramasax as he turned to see his first mate back away from the flaxen-haired female in sackcloth, his mouth agape, an empty scabbard in his hands. And what a scabbard it was, inlaid with jewels and precious metals—worthy of a bretwalda or high king. The wench wielded its sword with no lack of skill. Nearly as many riches sparkled on its hilt as did on the scabbard. Both she and Gunnar struggled to maintain their footing on the swaying plank that connected the two ships.

"Hand over the weapon, milady…I mean, Sister…" Gunnar swore in exasperation. "Whatever the blazes you are!"

"Never! This sword is a sacred relic of the church. I'd rather die than hand it over."

So *that* was the source of her affliction. Almost smiling, Alric inched his way toward the plank, trying not to catch the fiery vixen's eye.

"Milady, have you taken leave of your senses?" the other woman cried from the deck of the *Wulfshead*.

"Orna's right, Deirdre. Give up the weapon. It's not worth your life," the priest said.

This was no nun, of that Alric was now certain. The way the priest and the other female addressed her seemed to confirm it.

"Hold, Galstead, or I'll skewer your comrade where he stands," the woman called as he came within good lunging distance.

She had a warrior's stance and eye. His certainty regarding the female's station with the church faltered. He had read of both priests and nuns who were accomplished with swords of righteousness. The famous Columba of Iona was one such anomaly. And there were rumors that the small abbey near the coast was run by a woman of God, who, on her first mission into heathen territory, cut down a horde of armed unbelievers bent on murdering her small party. Lightning had followed her blade, killing any and all—some without so much as a scratch—who stood in her way.

Alric looked beyond this enigma to Gunnar. "Let her be." Most likely it was more Christian nonsense, but he saw no reason to challenge it. The day was his.

Gunnar wasn't as easily dissuaded. "But look at it!"

"Use your head, mate. Where is she going to go with it?" Alric jerked his head toward the *Wulfshead*. "Just leave her be. She'll have to yield to one ship or the other eventually."

Scowling, Gunnar leaped to the deck.

With a victorious smirk, the female turned slightly so that both decks were within the periphery of her vision. Had a man struck the same lofty tilt of the jaw, the pirate would have taken great pleasure in breaking it with his fist. With the lady, he resorted to a verbal jab. "With luck she'll fall overboard and save us all a great deal of aggravation."

Her eyes widened, spitting defiance in reply. Suddenly, she dropped to the plank between the two vessels in a huff and puff of sackcloth, her garment taking moments more to settle than she did.

"*Now* what?" Gunnar called to him, *I told you so* ringing in his cryptic tone.

"Put another plank over till our business is done. Sister Deirdre can keep watch on *our* sword."

Deirdre clamped her mouth shut, most likely swelling with the indignation building within, and laid her prized possession over crossed knees. She had pluck. Much as it annoyed him, Alric had to admire it.

The rise and fall of the sea beneath the two vessels made Deirdre's perch no more precarious than a pleasant horseback ride. Nonetheless, she kept a keen eye on the ends of the board to be certain they didn't work their way clear under the constant movement. Now that the heat of her defiance had waned with the indifference afforded her by her adversaries, she felt foolish. But when the strip holding Kieran's sword to her thigh had given way as she climbed up on the plank, her gasp of dismay was involuntary. She caught the precious weapon before it fell overboard, but not without drawing the attention of the dark-haired man in front of her.

Gunnar had pounced upon it like a hungry cat upon a fat mouse, but his greedy hands claimed only the scabbard. Before he knew what had happened, Deirdre drew the magnificent weapon. Only Providence kept her from stumbling over the hem of her robe as she swung around into a ready stance, but ready she was for whatever the dogs had in mind—except being ignored altogether. Her pride had crumbled around her like her robe as she sank to the plank out of sheer spite.

Oh, heavenly Father, how short is the fall from holy warrior to earthly fool! Father, I bleed with remorse…and confusion. What am I to do now? Must we lose the sword pledged to You to that heathen swine?

Much as she listened and stared into the sea's blue-green depths, Deirdre heard only the creak of wood against wood as the current see-sawed the two vessels. *Stu-pid, stu-pid,* it seemed to say. As if that weren't harsh enough, even the to and fro swish of the brushes on deck joined the chorus. The stream of blood-stained water pouring out the drain and spilling into the untarnished sea drew her attention from her personal contrition. It was as if the vessel shed tears for the dead. Surely God did.

Deirdre hung her head lower, stricken by the thought. Aye, she'd tended the wounded, aching for them, but keeping a lifeless length of jeweled steel had preoccupied her mind rather than the prayers Father Scanlan said with both friend and foe. The sword was not worth anyone's life. Besides, how could she be of any use to her brother, or her friends, if she risked death for something so paltry in comparison?

She ran her fingers along the taper of the blade, memories of its history—Gleannmara's history—stirring afresh in her mind. What joy she'd taken in the bards' accounts of Kieran and his lady, Riona—he a wild man of the sword and her example of faith—the weapon that tamed him.

"Well, fair warrior of the church, your time to decide what you will do has expired. We all await milady's wish."

The comforting cloak of nostalgia in which Deirdre wrapped herself vanished, torn away by her captor's derision. *Father, forgive me, but this is one enemy I cannot love. I hate the man.*

With a look as hard and sharp as the steel in her hand, Deirdre handed him the weapon—point first. "It will never serve the likes of you, you know," she told him, drawing what little satisfaction she could from the moment.

A single golden eyebrow arched in challenge. "Oh?"

"It won't spill innocent blood."

He smirked. "Neither do I."

Deirdre swallowed a dubious and unladylike reply. To voice it would only prolong the game he was enjoying entirely too much. She was tired. He held Kieran's sword *and* the day. Tomorrow remained to be seen.

"Well?"

Deirdre gathered up the folds of her robe, balancing carefully on the swaying plank as she steadied herself on her knees, no different than she did when preparing to stand on the cantering horse her father gave her. When confident, she stood as straight and proud as her situation allowed, unprepared for the sharp jerk of her clothing on one squared shoulder. Grace and dignity abandoned her as she scrambled for a foothold and grasped at thin air for support.

The gasp of alarm that filled her lungs one second was knocked from her chest as she struck the icy water below. Her shriek of bubbles rose toward the surface as she sank into the depths.

Deirdre struggled toward the bright water over her head, but the gangly robe strangled her efforts. Her lungs ached, devoid of life-sustaining air, choking her from within.

I won't give up!

With all her strength, she kicked her feet in the course tangle and used her arms to propel her body upward, but her garment seemed to partner with the monstrous sea to draw her deeper into the suffocating shadows of the vessels.

Surrounded on all sides, Deirdre fiercely battled the oppressive foe toward the water's surface. Against her will, liquid death seeped into her lungs.

Father...

Unmercifully, panic snuffed out her prayer with its impenetrable fingers.

FOUR

The impact of Alric's dive threatened to force the air from his lungs, and the cold water assaulted the pores of his flesh with a million pinpricks of ice. The algae-rich water made it hard to see more than an arm's length away. Making wide sweeps with his arms, he searched blindly for the wench in the silent but deadly pull of the current.

Suddenly something brushed his foot. Spinning around, he grabbed blindly and snagged a coarse fold of the clerical robe. Reeling it toward him, he soon encountered the woman struggling within its confines, but instead of accepting his assistance, she began to kick and claw at him as though he intended her harm.

The impact of her foot—for surely no female had the strength in her fists to strike so hard—knocked the remainder of air from his lungs. If he shot to the surface for air and came back down, he might not find her. With no choice save letting her drown, Alric lunged toward the flailing figure and gathered robes, arms, legs into his embrace. Lungs constricting, he propelled himself and his struggling baggage toward the blinding, brilliant surface.

Just as he breached it, gasping for air, he felt a searing pain on his forearm. Frig's teeth, she'd twisted in his grip and bitten him! But at least he now knew where her head was. As he tried to strip the cumbersome garment from her, her struggles began to diminish. Slinging the robe aside, Alric hooked his arm under her chin, lifting her nose and mouth above the water, and tackled the distance the tide had put between them and the two ships, where a line had been cast toward him.

Alric held on to the limp form of his captive with one arm and grabbed the rope and nodded for them to haul away. Heave by heave, the men pulled him from the water, the dead weight of his burden seeming to grow twice her size. When his men finally relieved him of the woman, he rested a moment, gathering breath, and then pulled himself over the rail.

The other female captive began screaming. "She's dead! God save us, she's dead!"

"She's just got a belly full of water." His protest was more against the brittle blade of alarm penetrating his chest than the woman's outburst. The vixen didn't dare die on him, not after he'd risked his neck to save her!

Shoving aside the priest, who knelt beside the still form crossing himself and mumbling, Alric seized Deirdre by the waist and hauled her up, her back against him. Crossing his arms beneath her rib cage, he shook her and constricted the locked bands of muscle in one sharp movement. Twice there was nothing but the listless fling of her arms and snap of her head. Her long, wet hair dragged like a mop through the pools of water on the deck.

Curse the little fool, where was that indomitable spirit of hers? She'd not been underwater that long. With a growl starting deep within his belly, Alric jerked her again with such force that he feared he might have cracked one of the woman's ribs. But better a rib lost than a life.

The muscles of Deirdre's abdomen rebelled against his arms in a spasm, and then another and another. Seawater shot from her lungs, hardly enough to properly wet a man's boot yet deadly when taken in lieu of air. Her arms no longer flailed but wrapped weakly over his. Around him, his men cheered.

"Yes, that's it, *feisty!*" Encouraged, Alric gave her another hearty squeeze.

"No!" At her moaned protest, her frantic fingers dug into the bloody bite she'd inflicted on him.

With a yelp, he let her go, dropping her into a heap at his feet. "Frig's teeth, woman, 'tis a harsh thanks you hand out."

Life flowed back into her long limbs, their graceful shape exposed by the wet folds of her sleeveless shift. She pushed herself up with arms that were slender and gently golden from the kiss of the sun. And no nun he'd seen while in Argyll with his mother wore artfully worked armbands of pure gold, such as glistened before him now.

"Just who on Frig's green earth are you?"

Deirdre's shoulders squared in a prideful pose. Slowly, her soaked and tangled tresses all but obscuring her face, she raised her head.

"Well, milady?"

"I...am not...your lady." Her voice gained strength with each clipped word.

All fire and spit, she was. Alric crossed his arms, suddenly aware of the soreness of his wound. If he'd wondered before, he need not do so now. The vixen had all her teeth, and he bore the evidence.

"Very well, then. Whose lady are you?" No matter whom she belonged to, she was a handful. He'd seen grown men reduced to tearful babble by what she'd just been through, and yet she stood there, prideful and straitbacked.

In less time than it took for the corner of his mouth to twitch in appreciation, Deirdre lurched forward and promptly heaved the remains in her belly onto Alric's feet. Too late, he jumped back, then forward again as she swayed unsteadily. He reached down and caught her just before she struck the deck face first. As he turned her on her back, her eyes rolled toward an equally blue sky overhead.

While consciousness played tag with its counterpart, her bloodless lips moved with one last parry. "I belong to God in heaven, and no one else."

Fickle women and their God would be his death! Alric motioned the priest over with a jerk of his head. "Here, Father, *you* take her. You're as close to her God as any on this ship. Truth, I don't envy *either* of you."

"But where shall I put her?" the priest called after him as he gave the nod for the lines connecting the two vessels to be released, with Gunnar in charge of the *Mell*.

Alric swung around, but his anger found no voice. *Where indeed?* he wondered, scowling. This was a pirate ship, not a passenger transport. The only sheltered area left in place was midship, a canvas cover over his own pallet. Others were erected as needed during inclement weather.

He motioned to his second mate. "Wimmer, show the man to my quarters. The women can use it for the duration of the voyage."

"I can…walk." To Alric's surprise, the resilient creature found footing on the deck. "But bless you, Father Scanlan." She leaned heavily on the priest's arm, raised her head, and ran Alric through with her gaze. "You will not get away with this, Captain. God won't let you."

God *again*. Alric leaned forward with a mocking bow. "Your gratitude for my pulling your hide from the water takes my breath away."

"Were that the case, I should fall prostrate anon before heaven and all witnesses for such a blessing."

Alric bit his tongue. The only thing predictable about women was that they'd have the last word, even if it spent the last breath they'd ever take. A good warrior knew when to dig in and fight and when to retreat. In this case, he'd do as well trying to hack the crests off every ripple on the high seas.

The remainder of the day closed with the sun gathering a mantle of clouds about it, as if reminding all eyes of the blood red sky that gave it birth. Better than halfway to the island of the sea god, Mona, Alric ordered the men to batten down what they could and prepare for the sky's prophecy to be manifest.

The crew met the storm fortified by a cold meal of dried beef and hard bread, for the fire in the small stove had been banked to prevent fire during the rough ride. It was not the first they'd weathered, nor, the gods willing, would it be the last. They'd learned to take the sea as it came, much as Alric's father accepted his neighbors—as friend or foe.

Pelted by stinging rain and dodging lightning, the seasoned sea warriors spent the night in a game struggle with oar, sail, and bucket to keep the vessel steady toward the east.

At last the day broke before them in yet another scarlet-glazed sky, but the signs of another storm paled compared to the lookout's cry of "Land ho, to the stern!" Instead of Mona's marbled shore of sand and moss-patched rock nestled in the sea before them, the landfall was *behind* them and green as spring itself, rising gently toward cloud-comforted hills.

Erin.

"Are you certain?" Alric stared in disbelief. Never had a storm turned him completely around.

"Yes, sir! There it be."

"Now how the bloomin' bones—" Wimmer started beside him.

"Any sign of Gunnar's ship?" Alric searched waters placated by the fiery red fingers of the sun, looking for sail, but aside from a few Irish curraghs out for a catch off their coast, he saw nothing.

"I've never seen the like," he heard one of the men at the oars remark. Indeed, unsettled whispers rippled up and down the oar benches.

His men were spent, and their provisions were diminished, yet they'd made no progress toward home. None at all. The wind must have shifted unnoticed in the turbulence.

"I warned you that God would not allow you to get away with your evil."

Vexed, Alric turned to see Deirdre sitting on a keg of salt beef near his lodging, working her fingers through the tangle of her hair. She'd fashioned one of his blankets into a cloak, fastening it with a cumbersome knot. Color had returned to her face—along with the biting edge to her tongue.

He snorted. "Nonsense."

"I prayed all night long that He'd see us delivered safely home…and He *did.*"

The smug quirk of her lips pricked at Alric's sleep-deprived humor. "'Tis the work of Thunor's foul mood, nothing more!" He was not given to superstition, nor to believing that gods controlled the elements for that matter, though they made excellent scapegoats. He could not say the same for the beliefs of his men.

"Storms are a part of life, as normal as breathing." He made sure he spoke loud enough for all ears that would hear. "And winds change like a woman's mind."

She smiled, clearly undaunted. Under other circumstances, Alric might have admired the pearly show of her teeth and the ripeness of the lips that framed them. Instead, he was wary as a dog heeling its master's steed.

"Then, if this Thunor of yours is real, you must have displeased him as well."

The way the sun took to her shining tresses, she could be mistaken for some heavenly creature—one of his mother's angels perhaps—in a mantle of spun gold.

"Although anyone with the wit of a salmon's egg knows it's God, not some thunder being, who controls the sky, wind, and sea. He created it. He of all should be privy to its temperament."

Still, the only angels Alric could recall from Orlaith's teachings had male names, and now he knew why. Imagine having to listen an eternity to a female's chatter. "Woman, you alone could talk down a flood tide. Would that you'd put that tongue to use last night and saved us all great effort."

The scattered chuckles among his men gave Alric scant comfort. The vixen had cast her seeds of doubt upon fertile minds.

Later in the day, as the three Christians knelt on the deck in prayer, Alric noticed the keen attention they drew from the men. Although his crew was not well versed in Latin, they knew enough to allow the fair magpie's chatter to undermine common sense. Contrarily, the stiff wind that picked up at midday boosted morale as it carried them eastward without further exertion on their part. With luck, they would make the shelter of Mona by nightfall.

The fire was banked at the sight of the first clouds hurtling over the spines of sea behind them. They hurried the darkening of the day and riled the water from its previous calm. The remains of the fish the men netted and baked on the coals in the firebed that afternoon were tossed over the side. The wind that had aided them earlier calmed, as if the wall of clouds to the stern blocked it. Robbed of breath, a lifeless sail hung from the rigging. Accustomed to stretches of calm, the men took the matter into their own hands on the oars, but their unease was thick as the air itself.

In the dim light of the lantern hanging by Alric's quarters, his captives knelt again for evening prayer, sparking mumbles of speculation up and down both sides of the ship.

"Father," Alric interrupted when he could tolerate it no more, "kindly reserve your show to my quarters. You distract the crew and hence put the ship in peril."

"'Tis *they* who put us in peril by following your orders against God's will," Deirdre volunteered. "You've stolen from the Lord thy God."

"If He created everything, then let Him create more that there is enough for us all." Alric seized the moment she took to formulate a reply and put it to use. "Now under the canopy with you—*all of you*— and stay low until the blow has passed."

"He sees to our needs, not our wants—"

"He created enough for all, milady," Father Scanlan cut in, ending the discussion. "Let us move inside as the captain said. God will hear us there as well as here."

With a scathing glance at Alric, Deirdre ducked under the canopy, following the other female, who, by her greenish color, had not yet adjusted to the roll of the sea. A curious trio of personalities, if ever there was one—a puzzle for a man who considered himself a fair judge of character. If either of the women was a nun, it was the smaller of the two. The taller lass rebuked humility with every word. Clearly, she was accustomed to having her own way.

Alric gave himself a mental shake to banish the plaguing fascination with his captive and turned to focus on the threatening sky. The sooner he was rid of the woman, the better. He froze in midstep at the sound of a strangled sob.

"Milady, I don't think I can b-bear another storm. There's nothing left to wring from my body but life itself."

"Orna, we have no choice."

Alric's ears pricked, but the feisty one's tone was soft with compassion rather than the cutting edge she reserved for him.

"Perhaps milady might consider her own advice while dealing with the captain," Father Scanlan put in. "He did risk his life to save yours. Indeed, he has been more than gracious, given our circumstances."

Indeed he had, Alric agreed, straining to listen above the murmur of the vessel and its crew. Predictably, the priest's words fell like fat on a fire.

"Father, Galstead is a scoundrel. A dog might lick your hand and share his bedding, but it is still a dog with teeth and fleas."

Scanlan clearly knew not what manner of beast he dealt with, but he plied on. "Nothing happens that cannot be used to God's glory, child. You must remember this."

"I am not your child, Scanlan. You're scarcely ten years my senior." Alric could picture the petulant purse of the fair one's lips.

"*God's* child, Deirdre…and He'll not take to you bandying His name for your own satisfaction."

Frig's breath, she's worried the holy out of the priest! Alric grinned, not feeling nearly so burdened now that he had company in his frustration. He waited to see what the prodigal would say next. He could well imagine the storm clouds gathering in her cerulean gaze, yet when she answered, it was with nothing less than a whimper of contrition.

"Father, forgive me. I—"

Her voice broke and with it, something snapped in Alric. Surely not pity. Perhaps disappointment.

"My mission means so much to me. Pride is the bane of my existence."

Alric had seen his mother's inherent strong will tempered by her regard for her mission or God's will. It was a confounding combination of stubbornness and humility that led him to wonder if it was a strength or a weakness.

"Pride is a demon that's undone the strongest of us," came Scanlan's placating reply.

"Aye, well I know it."

Her agreement seemed crushed out of her by the burden of her guilt. Foolish as this God nonsense was, it was as real to her as it had been to his mother. Alric shook himself again. Another moment, and he'd want to gather her in his arms and offer her comfort. Like a scolded kitten, she'd be soft and yielding, not defiant and irritating as a wet cat—

"But pride isn't the only demon to overcome," she stipulated, backbone returning as she glared in Alric's direction. "The oaf."

Or a burr in the stride. Alric's fists tightened at his side.

"Then *he* is the weakness you must overcome to remain in God's favor. Humility prevails where indignation cannot. More flies are trapped with honey than vinegar."

"Faith, spare me talk of food," the woman Orna moaned. "The very thought makes my insides twist."

There was some hasty movement inside the enclosure and the scrape of wood across the floor. Alric would have heard more, but at the sound of Orna's retching, he retreated aft to where the helmsman watched the growing menace approaching them. The thought of the tall, lithesome captive humbling herself before him was entertaining at the least. Perhaps this faith of hers might prove to his advantage.

"Smells like a wild ride, sir," the man at the tiller remarked.

Homing in on the matter at hand, Alric dismissed the twinge of guilt that tainted his whimsy. He'd send Scanlan and his prickly charge to the closest monastery. Between the Irish and the Scots, the coast and islands were peppered with them.

Turning to where the wind was picking up, Alric stiffened at the sight of a dark, ominous column rising to their stern. It was at least equal to the one that had sent them back toward Erin. Alric's pulse thrummed at the prospect and a slow smile spread upon his lips. The *Wulfshead* would dance with the sea sprites tonight.

Like a great monster, the storm gained upon them, its teeth the waves gnashing at the stern of the ship, flooding the deck and washing all that was not tied down into its watery throat. By nightfall, the *Wulfshead* tossed like a toy boat in a torrent, dodging bolts of lightning that spawned sprites of blue fire dancing on the water.

"Father, Yours is the hand that calms the sea. Yours is the breath that feeds the wind. Yours is the thunder that pierces our ears and the lightning that blinds our eyes," Scanlan prayed.

The first storm was surely to punish their Saxon captors, but why this one? Guilt niggled at Deirdre until she could no longer bear Orna's suffering and Scanlan's pleas. Though he'd said no more, the sting of her clansman's admonition festered within her. They were all going to die, and it was her fault. She'd flaunted God's power in the face of the captain, not for God's triumph but her own. Her pride and rebellious nature were her downfall, but it needn't be everyone's.

Leaving the cover of the enclosure, Deirdre stepped out into the wet fury. The wind and spray lashed her face, but she refused to back down—not from the storm or from God's wrath. She shouted into the monster's breath, her penitent tears mixing with its briny spittle.

"If Your anger is at me, then, I beg You, Father, spare the innocent among us, that our mission to free Cairell might be accomplished. All I ask for myself is Thy forgiveness."

Before her, a curling claw with frothy nails rose and poised, as though awaiting a command from a higher authority to carry out her sentence. Standing as tall as the thrashing ship would allow, Deirdre refused to stand down.

"Yea, though I walk through the valley of death, I fear no evil—"

The water struck her like a hammer, slamming her downward and swamping the deck around her. The rib of the ship's rail bit into her side, knocking out what little breath she'd clung to. Brine seeped in to replace it, burning her throat and lungs. She wasn't going to drown in the sea, but right here on the deck.

The thought no more than registered in Deirdre's staggered mind when the water subsided. Yet its sinew tightened even more about her, with no relief of its weight nor wane of its roar.

"By all the gods, woman, have you lost what wit you have?"

It was the Saxon, who twice now had plucked her from the sea's watery grasp. As he rolled away from her, she coughed up the salt wash from her lungs. Was this God's answer to her prayer? That she not be punished by death? She buried her head weakly in the curl of her arm. But she'd been ready for death…not life at the mercy of—

A terrible crack resounded overhead, and beneath her the deck shuddered to its skeletal frame. Suddenly, Deirdre was jerked up by her waist like a rag doll, but when Alric hesitated, as though uncertain which way to toss her, she looked up and saw what held him fast. The mast swayed at them, a deep crack making its way toward the deck. Alric broke, scrambling from where it would surely fall, when the ship shifted in the other direction, offering a temporary reprieve.

Before she knew what he was about, he shoved her under the tarp enclosure, barking hoarsely, "By thunder, you stay there or I'll toss you over the side myself!"

With a reluctant admiration, she watched as Alric and his crew pulled together without panic, as if the mast split upon every voyage. He climbed the mast, lashing it section by section with ropes, riding the tossing pole like an unbroken horse with little more than his powerful thighs to hold on with. Where she'd been willing to accept her fate, he fought his with muscle and sheer will, even laughing like a madman at the lightning bolts striking about them.

Yes, that was it. He was worse than a pagan. He was insane.

FIVE

The following morning, Deirdre awakened from an exhausted sleep to the bark of Alric's orders and the scurry of the crew. Once the mast was secured, the storm began to abate enough that Deirdre and Scanlan could leave Orna to help the weather-beaten sea warriors bail out the swamped bilge. Although she bore the burn of the captain's glare at first, he said nothing to her until the ship's free-board was restored to a seaworthy level.

"I'd best see to those hands before you go to sleep, milady."

A quick trip to the forward compartment produced a tin of balm. It had some sort of glorious numbing ingredient for her bloodied, rope-burned palms, yet it did nothing to dull the effects of the Saxon's min-istrations upon her senses.

"You make a decent sailor when you follow orders," he said in a soft timbre that smacked more of contentment than his customary hostility. Did wolves purr?

It was hard to believe the same hands that had wrestled a ship from certain death with a few ropes and a lot of determination could tender such gentleness. And when he produced a blanket, miraculously dry, from his seachest and wrapped it around her shoulders, she'd grown warm and giddy as a fool.

Of course, it was fatigue and nothing else. Once she and Orna had shed their soaked clothing, she promptly gave her servant, who was violently shivering in a delirium, the dry blanket in lieu of the damp bedclothing they unrolled. Deirdre was too tired to fret over why the bone-melting warmth and giddiness didn't leave with the blanket. Sleep was her priority—after thanking God for their deliverance.

"Perhaps milady might find some warmth in my cloak."

Alric tossed something else inside the canvas flap just as she uttered a teeth-clattering "Amen."

His cloak. The fur on it—most likely wolf—tickled her nose. The garment, like the man, was large and warm. As she fell asleep, she couldn't shake the fancy that it was he who wrapped around her, snuggling out the cold and sealing in the coziness.

Now, having abandoned the warmth of their pallets and shaking as if to shed their skin, Deirdre and Orna hastily dressed. It was hard for Deirdre to discern if her companion was feverish or simply as chilled as she, for the garments still smacked of dampness against their bed-warmed bodies. Deirdre donned the blanket and fur-trimmed cloak over all, then they emerged from the enclosure to face the new day.

Listless, Orna made her way to one of the rowing benches, while Deirdre inspected the skillfully woven cloak in bright sunlight. It was a beautiful midnight blue and adorned with nothing so mean as wolf or fox but a breathtaking ermine that glistened silver or white, depending on how the light struck it. Before she could examine the garment further, she was distracted by the movement of the crew.

The *Wulfshead* was no longer at sea but approaching under manpower a river beachhead just short of a small, port-side village. Sand and volcanic rock gave way to a rise behind the smattering of buildings, as though the small cove had been hacked out of the higher ground with divine thought to sea access. A few other ships, with foreign flags waving from the mast tops, were moored offshore in the quay, floating light in the water. At the village dock was the *Mell*, in all her seaworthy splendor and unharmed by the namesake that had plagued the *Wulfshead*.

Alric's second in command stood at its prow, shouting across the distance. "What took you so long, friend? I'd begun to think you were lost in the storm, and I'd not get my drink."

Alric cupped his hands round his mouth, answering, "I always make my bets good, gamecock. Join me at the Boar's Head after we've put in."

He pointed at the buildings that sprouted on the sandy rise of the bank. On the bank's crest was an ancient fortress built of the same stone that had been used to shore up the dock. It told of times when the sea approach had been guarded by a people more advanced in skills than its present inhabitants. Undoubtedly, trade had flourished for generations of Romans, Britons, and now Saxon and Frisian spawn, perhaps with coal from Northumbria's spine of mountains.

The wafting land breeze carried the scent of freshly baked goods mingling with the salty pungency of fishing boats and nets strewn along the shoreline. For the first time since their capture, Deirdre thought of food with longing. Not as disciplined as her mind to such things, her stomach growled, drawing the captain's attention.

Alric smiled, looking entirely too refreshed and winsome to her liking. When had he time to shave that angular jaw and tame his golden mane so that it fell away from his face with rakish disregard, brushed by the wind? And surely he'd had no more sleep than she, yet his eyes sparkled like the sun-silvered ripples of the water.

"Good morning, *Sister.*" He gave Deirdre a sweeping bow, his ebullience sticking like a thorn in one side of her humor, while his mockery jabbed at the other. "I daresay, we have arrived and are none the worse for wear, despite the tempest."

"Speak for yourself, sir. I fear Orna has taken a fever in her weakened state. She's not eaten since we were seized." The guilt she slung at him ran off his broad shoulders like rain off one of the heathered granite slopes in the far distance.

"As soon as we are secure, I'll have Wimmer see you are brought a fresh, hot meal. Then you and Father Scanlan are free to leave. Perhaps you'll find a fisherman willing to take you along the coast to one of the monasteries. Our people exchange goods regularly."

"I would ask that you leave Orna in our care, at least until she's well enough to be sold like a piece of cargo." She should have made some show of gratitude, but she could not. Slavery was detestable. Gleannmara's people had been free for generations, even if all the tuaths of Erin did not follow the practice.

"You'd stay aboard the ship then?"

"Ready, ho!" one of the crew shouted before she could reply.

The *Wulfshead* struck the beach, grinding into it with the force of its momentum. Deirdre steadied herself on the rail, eyes widening. Who'd have thought a ship this large had such a shallow draft?

Members of the crew leaped over the side into the wading-depth water and put their shoulders to the work of shoving the *Wulfshead* further onto the narrow beach. Lines were tied to stakes that looked to have been driven deep into the sand for a good while. Evidently this was the ship's usual berth.

A group of men approached from the village, burly sorts with broad backs and weathered faces. One of the younger among them hailed Alric.

"Good morning to you, Captain." He waved heartily. "Will you be needing to unload the ship?"

Alric shook his head, pointing to his prize at the dock. "No, Kaspar, we left all the cargo aboard and kept the ship as well."

"Aye, Gunnar said to wait for your order to see her unloaded." He looked at Deirdre. "We worried you'd run into the Dalraidi navy when Gunnar came in so far ahead."

"We saw none of the Scots-armed ships this time," Alric went on. "I thank you for your concern. Are you a father yet?"

The familiarity with a man so far beneath him in station surprised Deirdre. Alric seemed genuinely interested in the man's family.

The man grinned widely with what looked to be a full count of teeth. "No, and I swear, Hilda is fit to burst at the beam."

"After I see to my passengers, then meet us at the Boar's Head later and hear all about it before fatherhood puts its noose about your neck." Alric turned suddenly, catching Deirdre in her bold observation. That smug twitch of his lips made it clear he misunderstood her attention for admiration rather than disdain. "You were saying that you'd stay aboard the ship?"

Deirdre resisted setting his overblown ego aright as Scanlan approached them from the ship's cold hearth. There was little point in antagonizing Alric just as she asked a favor of him.

"I was just saying that Orna isn't well, Father, and that the captain should consider leaving her in our care until such time as she is fit for whatever fate he has in store for her."

"Milady speaks as though I alone instigated the practice of slavery just to spite her."

The devil take her transparent humor.

Scanlan sucked in his cheeks, choosing his words carefully before he spoke. "Milady has a large heart, which she wears upon her sleeve, sir. Like myself, she is distressed to see her friend destined for such a fate."

"It pains me deeply," Deirdre admitted, affecting humility as best she could. She'd rather have stomped the captain firmly on his polished instep. "But the captain has graciously offered us quarter on his ship until Orna is well. For that, I'm thankful." Perhaps God already prepared the way for their escape, although His purpose in their capture and the death of the *Mell's* crew still eluded her.

"It's safer than going into town," Alric informed them, his earlier humor fading. "With all manner of man and nations sailing in and out, the ship is always under guard."

"You mean even thieves have to be on the watch for thieves?" And the beast might as well take her runaway tongue as well. *Oh, Father, help me, for I cannot help myself.*

Alric ignored Deirdre's peeve. "If you wish, sir, I can have someone ask around to see if any of the vessels are headed farther up or down the coast."

"That won't be necessary," Scanlan assured him. "The Lord God has led us here for a purpose. My calling is to carry the Light to the unlit wick of humanity."

With a spontaneous laugh, Alric clapped the man on the back. "Then, Father, you have come to the right place, although the breath of decadence may well extinguish your earnest fire before you can fan it. Just look, man." He pointed to the parapet crowning the ancient stone. "Beyond that tower, lies every temptation flaunted before man. Here thieves parade as merchants, and merchants as thieves, depending on which end of the transaction they are on. The finest and most tawdry of the world passes through those gates. Linger long inside and it can cost you, not just your purse, but your life and your soul."

He mocked and threatened Scanlan with his eloquent tongue, but the priest was not the least daunted. If anything, the prospect excited him like a meaty bone tossed to a starving hound. "Then I have my road cast before me."

"The lady will not last." Alric's mercurial gaze shifted to Deirdre.

"They will lap her up like wolves with fresh blood. Only the strong survive here, for whatever such survival is worth."

A thief with contempt for others? What a hypocrite he was. "Then why do you fancy yourself up for such a place, if you find it so depraved?"

Indeed, the man had decked himself in finery. His tunic of brightly bordered linen cost no mean sum. Nor did the girdle, fastened with a silver wolf's head buckle, its eyes inlaid with garnet. Where his trim, dark trousers left off, *hemmings* skimmed the balance of his long frame. Made from the hind leg skin of a deer, the noble footwear was bound by lacings that were surely as long as Deirdre was tall.

"Because, *my derling lady*—" again came that low, threatening mockery—"I am the proverbial wolf in sheep's clothing, intent on finding a tasty lamb for my beastly edification."

Deirdre actually jumped, moving backward with a startled "Oh!" Her dismayed gaze grew wider still as her foot took the too-long cloak up short, jerking her by the neck. Alric caught her by the waist and rolled her into the curve of his arms as if they'd practiced the maneuver for hours.

Off balance, she found no escape from the ravenous lips that consumed her protest. The kiss threatened to draw the life from her body and leave it pleading for its return. Senses foundering in a sea of sensation well over her head, Deirdre closed her eyes, groping blindly at the front of his shirt to keep from sinking beyond retrieval. Somewhere above the whirling dervish of blood racing round her brain, she heard Father Scanlan's protest, but it was drowned by the wolflike pant that mingled with the panicked shortness of her own breathing.

When the beast returned to its human form, Deirdre lay in the trap of its arms like ravaged prey. With her breath returned enough for her to pull away, she staggered against Scanlan, wiping her lips with the back of her arm as if to erase what had just befallen her.

"That was hardly necessary, sir!" the priest stammered in indignation. "And unbefitting a gentleman of your station."

Ignoring the priest, Alric moved back, staring at her with something akin to wariness. What on earth had *he* to be wary of? "And *that,*

milady—" he swallowed as if purchasing time for further thought—
"that is why *you* will not be safe outside the walls of a holy cluster."
With obvious effort, he forced the raggedness from his breath and
turned away. "Wimmer!"

"Aye, sir!" The mate hurried toward them with an embarrassed
glance at Deirdre.

"See that food and drink are brought to our guests. They've chosen
to remain aboard until their companion is well. Since our Frisian
friends aren't in port, there's no rush regarding the other woman."

"Aye, sir. And will you be riding to your father's court at Galstead?"

"Frig's breath, Wimmer, you're as worrisome as a wife." The captain
swore, leaping to the rail light as a cat.

Deirdre flinched inwardly. Faith, but he was a dangerous creature—a shape-shifter to be sure, part human, part animal. Perhaps he
was a wizard as well.

"Sorry, sir. I meant no harm."

Alric capped the volatile rise of his aggravation with the contrite
second mate. "Only our guests and the watch are to remain on board
until further orders," he instructed with forced patience.

"Consider it done, sir. I'll see to the guests personally."

With a curt nod, Alric started down the planking that had been
raised against the side of the ship. Once on the beach, he spoke with
the two of his crew who had not already left the shore and then headed
up the narrow strip of sand toward the town and who knew what
depredation.

Deirdre unfastened the soft, woolen cloak and, with a shudder,
wadded it in a ball. "Here, Wimmer. I don't need this now."

She handed the dark blue garment over to the mate and wiped her
sore hands against her hips, as if to rid herself of the devastation its
owner had wreaked upon her sensibilities. He had pushed her beyond
annoyance to something that made her feel…what? Tarnished? No
man had ever handled her so roughly, nor exercised such dangerous
work upon her defenses. While steady on the outside, she trembled
inwardly, vulnerable in a way that defied words.

"I'll be putting it back in the captain's trunk then. Just ask if you need it." Wimmer shook out the garment. "I reckon I've never seen the captain wear this before."

Sooner than dignify her curiosity as to where Alric headed upon reaching the shore, Deirdre decided to help Wimmer. As she smoothed out the other end of the cloak, a strangely familiar embroidery caught her eye. In disbelief, she stared at the image of the Gleannmara brooch, embroidered in golden thread and studded with sapphire buttons where the real gems lay. Where on earth could Galstead have come across this?

"But it's such a fine piece." She rubbed her fingers over the expert stitches in perplexity. "You say your captain has never worn it?" She recalled how it had been wrapped in a package when he'd retrieved it from the trunk.

"He doesn't dress so fine on the *Wulfshead,* like he does at his father's court." Wimmer shook his head and then grinned widely, exposing his haphazard display of remaining teeth. "But for you women aboard, he would not wear a shirt unless he expects a fight."

Saints preserve us! She focused on the mention of the court, unable to recall if Alric had mentioned his father's name. "His father being…?"

"King Lambert, of course." The man looked astonished that she didn't know. "He is lord of all the land you see and more."

"So the captain is really a prince?"

"More of a prince than Ricbert, I can tell you that." Wimmer's emphatic nod tolerated no doubt. "It's to Galstead's misfortune that the captain's mother was a slave and Ricbert's the queen. When her mother named her after a serpent, 'twas an omen."

"Praise God!" Scanlan's chest swelled, most likely with a holy sense of purpose at the challenge that lay before him.

Deirdre shivered, wondering if her fellow countryman had lost his mind. Only a few chosen were equipped to deal with a supernatural enemy. Was Scanlan one?

Regardless, it explained Alric's almost mystical nature. And if this Ricbert were any more dangerous than his illegitimate brother, heaven help them all.

In the name of Christ, protect us from demons.

Retreating before she babbled like Orna, Deirdre returned to the mystery of the cloak. More than likely it was stolen. But from whom? Deirdre watched the second mate make his way to the compartment where Alric stowed his belongings. Cairell had no such piece.

"I had wondered last evening if we'd ever make landfall," Father Scanlan remarked, drawing her from her ponderings. "And now God's hand has been shown to us. It is only fit that we give God praise and glory for our deliverance. Will you join me, milady?"

"We are delivered into the hands of our pagan enemies," Deirdre reminded him.

"But alive, milady, with a marvelous opportunity to spread the Word."

"Perhaps *you* have the opportunity, but I have been shown nothing of a kind." Yet, she *was* alive, and that revealed a different opportunity. She might escape with Orna and the ransom. Perhaps, that was God's purpose for her.

"Aye, Father, I will join you in prayer and praise." Deirdre turned to Orna. The ship's stillness on shore seemed to have rid her complexion of the sickly green color. She would not be anxious to escape by boat, but the pampered lady-in-waiting was in no shape to affect a journey across a strange land.

Orna nodded, misreading what was really on Deirdre's mind, and bowed her head.

"Father of all heaven and earth," Scanlan began, already upon his knees in reverent fervor.

Deirdre knelt beside him, echoing his words in her mind.

"We thank Thee for our deliverance from the storm and for the civil treatment we have received from our enemies."

Civil? She stumbled over the thought. Her skin still burned from the scorch of Alric's unsolicited attention.

"For You have seen to our needs in their midst."

Aye, they'd been nourished and protected as much as was possible in such foul weather.

"We ask Your continued protection and strength as we struggle to do Thy will in this strange place."

Father, forgive me for my ingratitude. I don't mean it. I do appreciate surviving and having our meager needs met. The slit of her closed eye pried open by the distraction that too often frequented her prayers, and Deirdre spied the *Mell* docked near the village. If Alric intended to let her and Scanlan go as they will—*And forgive me, Lord, for my charade, but it's to Your purpose of saving your children from slavery*—then the ransom needed to be retrieved before it was discovered.

"Father, lead us as You did Your prophets of old, that we might reveal to the hearts of these people the light of Your Word and in it, the promise of salvation and hope in—"

Deirdre discreetly opened her other eye. There appeared to be only two men on watch. Surely after the scarcity of sleep last night, they'd succumb to it once darkness set in.

"—the precious blood of Your Son. We are not worthy, Lord, but we are willing."

Willing, Deirdre prayed, catching up. *Father, I am willing to try. Go with me, please. I cannot do this without Your blessing.* Deirdre made the sign of the cross, sealing her commitment to Cairell and her mission for God.

"Amen," she said in union with the priest.

Scanlan rose to his feet and Deirdre followed his example, brimming with excitement and a sense of purpose.

"Father," she announced, vying to keep from appearing too eager, "I have a plan."

SIX

God was surely with her. The arrogant pirate prince had inadvertently provided the means for their escape by having Wimmer ask if any boats would be headed to the island monastery off the Welsh coast. A woman who brought them a plain but delicious meal of fresh baked bread, cheese, and honey told him that her husband was taking her neighbor to visit kin at the monastery tomorrow and would be delighted to transport Prince Alric's holy friends.

While Wimmer had sent the woman away since Deirdre and the priest had decided to stay until Orna was well, Deirdre paid particular attention to which of the small stone-and-thatch huts along the beach the fishwife retired. After all, they could have a change of heart.

"Milady, are you certain this is wise?" Orna studied her, wide-eyed.

"I advise strongly against this," Scanlan said, reiterating his opinion of her escape plan.

"Father, you are convicted that this is where God has sent you. I am convinced that God sent that fisherman's wife to aid Orna and me. It's our lives and Cairell's at stake." Deirdre checked the breeches she'd taken from the captain's trunk to make certain they were secure enough not to hamper her in the water, as the voluminous gray robe had done. While the *Wulfshead* was beached, the *Mell* was not.

"Then let us pray that it's God's will you heed and not your own."

Why was her kinsman being so contrary? She understood his dedication to his mission, so why couldn't he understand hers? "That is why, if I am not back in time, Orna must leave in my borrowed robe before daylight."

Earlier, Deirdre had asked the obliging Wimmer if she might fetch Alric's cloak. Since the mate was still savoring the remainder of his honey-smeared bread and, more important, his flagon of wine, he'd given her leave without suspicion. Aware that she was still within sight, she'd reached into the trunk and dragged out whatever clothes she could, along with the bundled breeches and a shirt. With her hair braided and tucked inside the collar, she could easily pass as a boy...if she was detected at all.

"Milady, I do not think I can pass for you."

"Keep the hood over your head and say no more than you must. If you stuff your bedding well enough, it will look as if you are still ill and sleeping, should Wimmer check on you. Remember, it's this or slavery, Orna. If I do not make it back, you must get back to Gleannmara and tell Father what has happened."

"Oh, milady—"

"'Tis madness, fey as a swineherd, I still say," Scanlan fretted.

"'Tis a leap of faith, Scanlan." Deirdre was sorry instantly for her snapped response. She knew the priest objected out of concern. "I absolve you of responsibility. Orna, see that you make that plain to my father."

Orna looked as pale and frightened as Deirdre should have, except that something about the danger and thought of outwitting Alric of Galstead filled Deirdre with an excitement as heady as strong wine. "Now remember, lass, if I do not return by the first hint of light, go without me."

After their meal, she pretended to have second thoughts about remaining with Scanlan after dwelling more on the captain's warning. She told the mate that she would leave at daybreak with the fisherman's party, after all. He heartily agreed with her decision.

It *was* crazy. A second thought began to nibble like a worm at the grain of her confidence. Everything had to go just right...

"Father, I would pray before I leave."

This was the first thing Deirdre had asked the young priest that he was willing to do without reservation. She knelt with her companions in the stern of the grounded vessel and reached for their hands, as if she might draw strength and courage from their fellowship as well as from her Maker.

"Father of all heaven and earth, we beg that You surround Princess Deirdre with angels, that her mission be accomplished by Thy will and in Thy name and to Thy glory; that she and Orna escape the bonds of the heathen's slavery; that there be no blood shed, innocent or nay…"

Deirdre had never taken a life. Would she be able to spill blood rather than the stuffing of a practice dummy or hack flesh rather than the bark of the sparring poles?

At the end of the prayer, Deirdre's "Amen" came from the depths of her being.

Then, drawing to her feet, she scanned her surroundings one last time. Wimmer was asleep by the gangway. The *Wulfshead's* guards helped themselves to a wineskin.

Across the moonlit span of water, the *Mell* rocked in the cradle of the moving tide. Its watchmen were talking to someone who'd happened down the dock. They gestured wildly, as if to reenact a battle—most likely the very one that had led to this moment.

"Godspeed, child," Scanlan whispered as she climbed on the rail and viewed the distance between her and where the lap of the tide inched upon the sand. If she dangled first from the rail and then dropped beyond the water's edge, she stood a chance of going undetected and relatively unharmed by the steep jump.

"Do be careful," Orna whispered.

Deirdre managed a smiling nod over her shoulder and then twisted to ease her legs over the outer side. She arched her lower body away from the gentle curve of the side of the ship, swinging farther away each time as she counted to three. She let go, dropping hard to a crouched position, the sand muffling her fall. Holding her breath, she stayed low and waited, listening for any sign that she'd been found out.

There was no change in the cay's lullaby of nightbird song accompanied by the gentle slap of the tide and the hushed whistle of the breeze in the lines strung from the masts. She licked her dry lips. They tasted of the salt of life. Never had she felt so alive.

With a bracing breath, Deirdre crawled into the water until she could make her way just below the surface, stopping only to refill her lungs. Faith, it was cold. Her skin surely shriveled around her quivering bones, but the chill spurred her on.

Reaching the *Mell,* she treaded water on its harbor side, her discomfort no longer a concern. Climbing up its slick, tarred-leather side was. Fortunately, someone had dropped a trap of some sort into the water, for eel or some other sea delicacy. Perhaps one of God's angels had arranged it for her in answer to her prayer, for it certainly reduced the risk of her being seen by the ship's watch. All she needed to do was climb up the rope and pull herself over the side.

"Thank You, Father," she whispered, testing the rope one more time before starting up.

Deirdre had always thought of herself as slender, but her arms felt as if she carried the owner of her dripping clothing on her back as well as herself. With each successive handhold, she considered letting go, for not only were her hands tender and raw, but her muscles felt as if glowing coals were burning her alive from the inside out.

At last at the top, she rested, securing a foothold in the length of line below her. Even the night air scorched her aching lungs. Staring at the rail, her last hurdle, she fought against the despair hammering her resolve. She never dreamed it would be this hard. Her brother shot up a rope light as a jongleur's monkey.

Father, help me now. I don't think I can make it. She heard the beating of wings and pictured two strapping angels descending to take her up and over the sides, but none materialized. Instead, it was a heron making away with an ill-fated fish.

She rolled her forehead from side to side against the side of the ship. This close to Cairell's freedom and she was giving up? It wasn't her way to give up. Her father, and all of Gleannmara, counted on her to win her brother's freedom. Cairell had risked his life without hesitation to protect the church from Ecfrith's raid and had been taken. How could she save her own skin and not his?

Love for Cairell spurred her on. Recollections of her older brother carrying her on his shoulders, taking time to spar with her on the training field, making her a little wooden sword that looked like Kieran's, complete with painted gems…

"Father, with Your grace, I can do this," she said, clenching her jaw with determination.

With superhuman effort, Deirdre untangled her feet, taking the weight upon her arms again, and swung a long leg up, catching her foot on the edge of the ship's rail. With sheer determination, she hauled herself up until she lay lengthwise, panting shallow. If she was found now, she could not lift a cry for help, much less a finger to defend herself.

But God's grace was with her. The guards were still engaged in conversation with the stranger who'd wandered down to the dock earlier. The rest of the crew had gone ashore and were either drunk or working on it. With a silent groan, Deirdre slid off the rail and crouched in its shadow. Once certain all was clear, she crept to the grate and lifted it. The rough wood bit into her hands and the weight taxed her weary arms, but she managed to slip beneath it and find a rung on the ladder leading to the hold.

It was blacker than sin below deck. What little light the moon and the mast lantern afforded identified the location of the hatch from above but was of little use in her surroundings. Blindly, Deirdre oriented herself. The treasure chest had been straight ahead, but the kegs of wine were to her right. Feeling her way into the pitch darkness, she found some barrels of the right size, but something was wrong. They were stacked only two high, instead of taking up the span between the floor and the deck overhead. The Saxons had moved the cargo around maybe even unloading some of it.

Backing up till the ladder stopped her, Deirdre closed her eyes, crushed. There was no point in wasting more time. With a light, she'd have a hard enough time finding the right keg—

Something skittered across her bare foot. Clamping a hand over her nose and mouth, she stifled a scream. *Don't even* think *about rats…*

A sudden recollection stiffened her spine with renewed hope. She had rolled the keg between the beams supporting the upper deck, so chances were it had not been disturbed. If she crawled over the keg tops, she might find it lying on its side against the ribs of the ship. Rallying, Deirdre crawled on her belly on the top of the two layers of kegs, then wriggled toward the bulkhead. Ahead of her, she heard the scramble of her unsavory companions and shuddered but pressed on. If she could just—

Above her, the loud commotion of footsteps, laughter, and singing in that harsh Saxon tongue froze her in place even as her brain screamed for her to run. She breathed deeply, forcing herself to calmness and rational thought. Raucous feminine laughter provided the reason for the early return of the crew. Their celebration was in full blow and growing more debauched by the hour. Deirdre wrinkled her nose as one of the men grumbled, slurring the general sharpness of his foreign speech.

"Don't talk to me in that tongue, derling love," the female chided.

"He's lucky he can talk at all."

That voice. It couldn't be! What was Alric doing here? Deirdre refused to ponder the possibilities. The man was simply perverted.

"What I wish with you, my derling…" The other man paused. "What is your name again?"

"Raeda," Alric told him. "Our beautiful Raeda."

"Red will do," the woman said.

The wench must have red hair, Deirdre surmised inconsequentially. And she was likely of British stock, given her reluctance to use the Saxon language—a slave perhaps, sold to a brothel. *Father, deliver us from such a fate.*

"What I want has nothing to do with talking," the other man announced, eliciting a squeal of delight.

"Not here, silly boy. I'd not have the eyes of your men watching us."

"Go on, Gunnar," Alric conceded. "Take the cover. All I need is a blanket of stars and the moonlight for my pillow." Now that the Saxon prince waxed poetic, Deirdre knew the captain's friend was not the only one with an ale-sodden tongue.

They stumbled over the grate, shadows fluttering like Deirdre's chest through the light above. Someone fell with a loud thud.

"Frig's breath, man," Alric said. "Must I put you into bed and tuck you in?"

"Whoa, derling!" The woman giggled. "Get up now."

"A mane of fire, this one," Gunnar mumbled in drunken admiration of his lady friend.

"Just a few more steps, Gunnar," Alric encouraged.

"*He* won't last long," Red observed. "Then perhaps you and I—"

"Tempting as you are, lovely Raeda, the coin I gave you is for a full night with my friend. I have given him my promise, and he shall have it…even if he sleeps it away."

The Saxon prince dissolved into undignified amusement. Several bumps, scrapes, and grunts later, the sound of a single set of footsteps approached the grate.

Deirdre held her breath as they staggered, first forward, then back two, then forward three. All she had to do was wait. Gunnar and the woman were no threat. As for the captain, surely it was just a matter of time before the fool keeled over, senses dead to the world.

Something crashed loudly, as if the mast itself had fallen over. Deirdre gasped in spite of herself, staring overhead at the checkered openings in the grate. The fool prince had keeled over sure enough, blocking out all but a sliver of light above her—and with it, all hope of her escape.

SEVEN

"Move out, you drunken sot!"

A booming voice snatched Alric from the dreamless world in which he drifted with the speed of an assassin's blade. Towering above him, the mast with its trimmed sail loomed like one of those cloth-draped Christian crosses against the overbright sky. Frig's mercy, was he dead?

"Is *this* the fierce hero who captured this ship to his father's pride?" The voice boomed again, shaking the very rafters of his mind.

Whether in heaven or a heroes' hall, no one had the right to assail him so. Alric leaped to his feet, fist clenched, and swung at the bullish intruder. "Who dares—" His fists encountered only thin air as the man danced away with a speed that belied his size and erupted in laughter a safe distance away, the blinding light of the sun obliterating his face.

Alric's surroundings seemed to circle and close in upon him. He fought to keep his rebellious stomach down. Nay, he could not be dead, for no such agony plagued a spirit.

"Drink the tavern dry again, Brother?" another man, tall and thin compared to the robust build and paunch of the first, taunted.

Alric recognized his half brother's voice. Ricbert. Now Alric knew he wasn't dead. Unless this was the pit of torment Christians feared.

"'Twas well deserved," the larger of the two countered in Alric's defense.

And their father. Frig's mercy, what hour was it?

"The sun's halfway to its zenith, Son," Lambert answered, clearly reading the confusion on Alric's face, "and I could wait no longer to see our prize."

"Good thing we meant no harm to you," Ricbert observed dryly.

"The guards would have stopped you."

Alric's voice was strangled, as if his tongue were swollen and stuffed like a filthy stocking down his throat. He tried to swallow, but the acrid taste of stale beer refused to budge. Staggering, he made his unsteady way to a water barrel and dunked his head in up to his neck. The shock whipped his scrambled senses into an overwhelming state of awareness. A myriad of accusing voices thundered in his brain. What had he done to himself?

With a loud growl, Alric straightened and shook his head to be rid of them. Daggers of pain threatened to explode at his temples in retaliation, nearly bringing him to his knees.

"Hah, he couldn't even make it to his bed." Ricbert's chuckle was unpleasant.

Alric offered a vulgar suggestion as to what Ricbert might do to himself, almost hoping his elder might take offense. A good fight or another pitcher of ale were the only remedies for the raging revenge of the ale keg. Curse Gunnar and his red-haired companion! Alric cast a grudging glance to the canvas enclosure where his friend and the wench slept unmolested.

"This must be the richest cargo you've yet to capture, if the evidence of your celebration is any indication." His father clapped him heartily on the back and roared in merciless mirth at Alric's discomfort.

Were it any man but his father, he would be treading water by now. Alric cut a wary glance at his half brother. It was a shame the serpent mother's spawn was too sly to strike outright.

"We'll see," Alric answered, his second attempt to speak easier. "If the fight they put up is any sign, 'twill do Galstead's treasury well. There were no survivors, save a cleric's party of three."

He cleared his throat as if to clear the pang of guilt that assailed him from the depths of his pounding head. It had been the crew's choice to fight. Had they not, their lives would have been spared. Cupping a handful of water, he lifted it to his lips. The taste was not much better than the beer, but it was wet and felt good to his dry mouth.

"So where are they?" Ricbert looked about. "I want to see the women. Helewis is looking for a handmaid, now that the one she brought with her from her father's kingdom has wed. I do hope they're as comely as I've heard at the Boar's Head."

Alric narrowed his gaze at his half brother, not the least surprised at the lustful smile that grazed his lips. "Best mop the drool from your mouth before you step in it and slip, Brother. They are on the other ship."

"As if you have not already thought the same." Ricbert snorted. "Like as not, there's not a virgin between the two."

Lambert shook his head. "Stop your quibbling and open the hatch. Alric is not as susceptible to feminine charms as you are. Besides, if I heard right, one is a manless nun."

Alric hesitated for a moment before nodding, not because his father would give him a hard time over his setting Deirdre free, but because he still found her being a sister of the church, even disposed to such a fate, difficult to believe. No amount of the drink he indulged in during last night's celebration with the crew had dimmed his doubt. Her image was never far from his mind, even when the tavern wench threw herself at him. Curse the pious little vixen. The thought of her made his head thunder even more.

"Yes, you heard right." Hanging back by the water barrel, he pointed to the grate. "Have at it, Brother. If I lean down, my head may fall off."

He was too miserable to take exception to Ricbert's chuckle of delight at his agony. Let the grinning fool lift something heavier than a noggin of ale for a change. Besides, with luck, he'd fall facedown in the barrel and drown away his affliction.

At the first attempt, the grate slipped from his brother's hand. Alric might have laughed, but it would hurt too much. Impatient, Lambert reached down to help his eldest son. They tossed the grate back, where it thundered against the deck as though Thunor's hammer had struck. A startled shriek followed from within the hold.

"Well, well, what have we here?" Ricbert asked in a singsong voice.

"A wench…I think." Lambert glanced up at Alric for confirmation.

Stupified, Alric eased toward the open hatch and looked down at the bedraggled creature staring up at him. "You!"

It *was* the nun, wasn't it? Her fair face was red, eyes swollen as if she'd been born sobbing, and her carriage, normally proud and aloof, was as broken as a wounded bird's. She sat, legs dangling through the rung of the ladder, hands clenching it as if her life depended on it. What in Woden's world had happened to her? How did she come to be here instead of in the safety of the *Wulfshead?*

He doubted that he really wanted to know.

"There are rats down here, hundreds of them." Her lips quivered as though another tempest of sobbing teetered on them. The strangest urge to take her up in his arms as he would a frightened child crept like a thief into Alric's mind.

"Are you going to introduce us, Brother?"

Deaf and dumb with disbelief, Alric did not acknowledge Ricbert.

"Why couldn't you have wallowed with your cheap little trollop in the town like you said you would?" Deirdre sniffed loudly and wiped her upturned nose on her sleeve. No, that was *his* sleeve. He recognized the embroidery on it. Staring harder, he recognized his breeches as well.

"You are the snake's belly of debauchery," she went on, gathering strength with each condemnation she hurled at him. "I can only pray that your head feels like a swordmaker's anvil at fair time. That your stomach churns with the souring of your beer. That your legs feel like a willow's branch in the wind. That—"

"Enough!" Alric bellowed, condemning the vivid imagery of the truth. "How came you to be here?" Dropping to one knee, he reached down and gathered a handful of her shirt at the collar. With a grunt, he hauled her upward but fell back as he lost his grip, his buttocks striking the deck soundly.

"She's more bristly than she looks, Son." Lambert chuckled, leaning over to offer Alric a hand. "Seems you've underestimated your captive."

Alric snatched away from the extended hand, his humor turning blacker by the minute. "No, I've been deceived by a long-legged witch."

"Witch!"

The gasp from inside the hold brought a satisfied smirk to Alric's lips. He reached down again, this time dislodging the lady's hands from the rungs. He ignored her wince of pain without conscience as he hauled her up to her feet and gave her a head-snapping shake. "You lying little charlatan, I ought to—"

"Go ahead, rave like the beast you are." A hissing wildcat spat with no less fury. "You might outdo me with your muscle, but 'twas you who were outwitted in the end."

Her wan but nonetheless smug smile was as goading as a punch to his kidney. Who would have dreamed from his first sight of her dangling below, that she still had fight in her blood? But then, he never dreamed she'd steal his clothes and make her way to the *Mell*. Nor could he imagine how she—a woman—could spend a night with rats in a dank hold and not cry out. Even now, despite her red, swollen eyes, she exercised anger rather than horror, accusation rather than contrition.

Amazing. She was amazing.

"I was not the thief caught in a hold in the company of her four-footed kin," he reminded her gruffly.

"Aye, fortune turned against me at the last." Deirdre straightened her shoulders. "But not, I think, the lady Orna. She is on her way to a Welsh monastery with the fisherman you so thoughtfully provided."

Alric stiffened in alarm. "You there!" he barked at the guards watching warily from the dock. "See what has become of Wimmer and the other captives."

"So much for the worth of your guards," Ricbert jibed.

"I'll deal with *them* later." His head was a roar of hot blood and anger, mixing, boiling to the point of explosion. Or was that his stomach? Maybe both.

"That beguiling mix of fire and ice puts me in mind of your mother," Lambert observed with a contrary mix of melancholy for his loss and admiration for the captive.

"She's *nothing* like Orlaith." Alric's sharpness afflicted no one but himself. He pressed his fingers to the spot on each temple where blood and thunder were sure to erupt at any moment. He dared not give it sway, lest it embolden the rebellion in his gut.

"Gone!" one of the guards shouted from the deck of the *Wulfshead*.

"No one but the priest," the other chimed in.

Next to them, a sluggish Wimmer shook his head back and forth in disbelief.

Slashing a disparaging look at Deirdre, Alric was met with yet another twist of the knife to his pride.

"I told you as much," she gloated.

"So the wolf has been outwitted by the church's little dove," Ricbert chided. "And one who is far more fetching in that shirt than you ever were."

"This one is no dove." Alric was sorely torn between punching his half brother and shaking the satisfaction from his captive's face. With a low growl, he slung Deirdre at Ricbert. They deserved each other. "But she's yours if you have coin enough. *Guards!*" Humiliation did not sit well with his nature, and Alric had had his fill of it.

"Then *you* shall be dealt with," Alric added, his promise stopping the wash of relief on his men's faces.

Suddenly, a slap resounded, jerking Alric's attention to where Ricbert held his jaw in open astonishment.

"Touch me like that again, sir, and I will serve your liver to you on your own blade."

"Why you impudent—"

Alric caught Ricbert's fist a breath short of the defiant jaw Deirdre presented. She wouldn't last long. Life or that spirit, one of them would be beaten out of her. "Don't bruise the merchandise until you own it," he warned lowly.

Lambert raised a brow. "I wouldn't be too hasty, Son. She might be worth keeping for yourself."

"I'd rather keep this pounding head." Alric seized Deirdre by the arm and half-dragged her to the gangway, then shoved her into the custody of the guards rushing up to meet them. "Take her to the slave quarters. She'll serve in place of the other, even if she's God's own daughter, though I think she's more likely to be Lucifer's kin. Try to stay alert until she's under lock and key this time."

"Aye, Cap'n."

"I can walk without your help," Deirdre announced, surprising the guards by pulling away with more strength than they'd given her credit for.

Embarrassed, they looked to Alric for advice.

"Best bind her and keep her on a leash."

"That's a bit harsh, don't you think?"

Alric turned to his father. "Father, trust me. You have no idea. The sooner she's gone from Galstead, the better for the kingdom."

"I disagree." Ricbert's eyes glittered. "I'll buy her for my sweet wife tomorrow."

"Don't say I didn't warn you," Alric shot back in annoyance— annoyance at Ricbert and, perversely, at himself for hastily pronouncing her fate. The idea of Deirdre in his half brother's hands was worse than the thorn she'd be in Alric's side.

He clapped his father on the back, dismissing the thought before it obsessed him. "Come along, Father. Join me in breaking the fast, and then we'll see together just exactly what treasures await in the hold."

Gold wasn't nearly as troublesome as a woman.

EIGHT

I stopped by the Frisian's compound and had another look at your wily captive. I think I will purchase her on the morrow." Ricbert tossed the words at Alric as Lambert mounted for the return journey to Galstead.

Imagining Ricbert owning Deirdre was enough to make Alric cringe, but he simply shrugged. "Your money is as good as another's."

The inventorying of the *Mell's* cargo had gone smoothly. Lambert applauded Alric and his importance to Galstead as the value of the cargo mounted. Torn between satisfaction and a twinge of pity, Alric had watched Ricbert grow more dour by the moment. Eventually his half brother sulked off and rejoined Lambert only when they were ready to leave.

"She'll bring a high price, Ricbert, and she's clearly not accustomed to taking orders," Lambert objected. "Use your head, man. You can find a fine Saxon maid to do a better job."

Ricbert ignored his father's derision, looking beyond to where Alric's second in command recorded the number of kegs bound for Galstead—the king's portion of the privateer's take. "At least if she attends my wife, 'twill make Helewis's company more tolerable."

Gunnar turned and handed the log to Alric. "All there," he said flatly.

"Then I'll see you at the auction, *Brother.*" Alric smacked the flank of Ricbert's fine gelding, then offered his hand to his father. "Father, farewell and see if you can talk some sense into your son. We'll all profit if the Irish wench is sold in the Mediterranean. Her fair features are much in demand there."

"I might as well talk to my horse's hind end," Lambert muttered, nudging his steed after Ricbert's.

Watching the king drive his horse until he caught up with his eldest, Alric couldn't decide if the sick curl in his belly was due to the thought of Ricbert owning Deirdre or his pity for Gunnar and Helewis. Sent to escort the lady from Kent for the wedding to Galstead's heir, his friend had fallen in love with the princess bride. Usually an example of moderation, Gunnar drank himself into oblivion at the wedding festivities and had pretty much been that way since, at least in port.

"You're *not* going to let Ricbert have her, are you?" Gunnar broke his grudging silence as Lambert's entourage crossed the river bridge.

"She's nothing to me," Alric observed with typical pragmatism. It was more comfortable than the nagging twinge of guilt Gunnar played upon. "Besides, she'll bring a higher price than Ricbert can afford. You know his weakness for gambling."

"And his resourcefulness when he sees something he wants," Gunnar reminded him. If a woman he loved were subject to Ricbert's abuse, like as not, Alric might be as bitter. He wouldn't wish that on his worst enemy. Unbidden, the memory of his captive's rebellious face looking up at him from the hold rose to plague him. Surely someone would outbid Ricbert. And then what? Abuse by a stranger? With her temperament, she would invite more beatings than kindness.

Shaking her tear-stained, bedraggled image from his thoughts, Alric checked the total of the numbers he'd recorded and smiled. Gunnar had come within the price of an ox of determining the cargo's value just by estimation. "I don't know why I bother to do this."

"Because you are a heartless *and* distrusting son of Thunor." Gunnar clapped him on the back. "What say we open this keg, since it's already been tapped, and share it with these hearty fellows?"

Alric ignored the good-natured taunt. "Are you certain you are up to it?" He'd already put the keg aside for just that reason. It had been tapped, probably for use on the voyage, and his men deserved a respite after their hard work.

Gunnar took his cup from his belt and turned the tap. "Up to it, down to it, and ready for it." When nothing came out, he kicked the small barrel.

"That always works," Alric quipped wryly.

Grimacing, Gunnar put down his cup and lay the barrel on its side, shaking it. "It's heavy enough to be full, but I can vouch that there's no liquid in it, unless it's thick as grain."

Alric tested it himself and heard no friendly sloshing sound. Whatever was in the container had been packed solid. He stood back as Gunnar took a small axe and split the top.

The splintered wood gave way to a landslide of blue wool, followed by the jingling of coin and scatter of velvet purses. Gunnar shook the barrel more, eyes rounding as more spilled out.

"By Woden's eye, will you look at this!"

Alric *was* looking, but instead of the treasure consuming his mind, it was the face of his crafty captive that seized it. Now he knew why the ornate treasure chest had been empty.

Gunnar glanced up. "Our captive again?"

"The mistress of deceit." A mix of anger and admiration filled his voice as Alric picked up one of the pouches. Emptying into his palm were jewels enough to bedeck a royal family—assorted shades of red, blue, amber, and purple. "And I think 'tis *you* who owe me the round of drinks. This must be where she hid the treasure that had been in the chest."

"Resourceful little nun, isn't she?"

"If she's a nun, I'm Woden himself."

He helped Gunnar shove the coins back into the barrel. They'd count it in the warehouse, away from the curious onlookers who'd begun to gather about them. Carefully, he picked up the blue wool and shook the remaining coins out of its folds. A brilliant flash caught the sun and threw it in his eyes, nearly blinding him. It was a brooch...a lady's brooch.

He felt a blow in his chest—hard and without warning—as if his stallion had kicked him soundly. The sun beamed warmth onto his torso, yet ice surely formed in his veins as he stared down at the piece, his thumb tracing the shape and texture of it. Set in the pure gold, heart-shaped circlet were sapphires and rubies...

The arrangement—the large ruby followed by smaller tiny ones set in the tapered pin—crossed the sapphire-studded circlet in exactly the same pattern that was on his cloak.

"You look as if you've seen a ghost," Gunnar teased.

Alric shook himself. It couldn't be, but it was. "I'm not sure I haven't. Look at this closely. Where have you seen it before?"

Gunnar picked up the keg as if it weighed nothing, glanced at the cloak, and shrugged. "I haven't. Believe me, if I'd seen a piece of workmanship like this, I'd have remembered."

"Not in the gold and jewels themselves," Alric snapped, accompanying him into the warehouse. "It's the pattern on the cloak my mother made for me. I showed it to you once…never mind. You were probably too drunk to remember."

But Alric had not forgotten. The image and his mother's words were indelibly etched in his mind…

"God also revealed to me your earthly kingdom. Its colors are the royal blue of a sky lighted by the moon and its full consort of stars…and the gold of your hair."

Just like the cloak he now held. He examined it more closely, its royal soft weave and the gold fringe undoubtedly belonged to a noblewoman, perhaps a queen or princess—surely not the troublesome waif who posed as a nun? But then, hadn't he suspected as much from Deirdre's behavior? She was clearly accustomed to having her own way, to giving orders rather than receiving them. Humility was not part of her demeanor nor of her vocabulary.

"And the symbol on the cloak I made for you. You will know it by that."

It matched the brooch exactly. What were the odds of that happening by chance? He'd scoffed at such things…until now.

"And your earthly kingdom, Son, will be won by love."

Alric chuckled humorlessly. Therein lay the determining factor. He had no love for his captive; she was more worrisome than a gnat.

So it was all nonsense, and this similarity between brooch and cloak nothing more than coincidence. It had to be.

Yet…he traced the design of the brooch and heard his mother's words, heard the promise he had given her.

Another frisson of ice skimmed his spine, his scalp. Prophecy aside, was he willing to dishonor his mother by dismissing her beliefs?

His own doubts and lack of beliefs aside, was he willing to allow Ricbert to own Deirdre? To use her? To break her spirit, irritating though it was? He'd successfully ignored that question all day…until now. And now…

Now it was impossible.

"I knew you wouldn't let Ricbert have her," his friend called as Alric hastened out of the building.

NINE

The stockade was dusty and filled with the scent of the unwashed bodies of Britons captured during a border raid and of a few Saxon miscreants. The women, separated from the men by a wattled wall, were fewer in number. Deirdre learned that the majority of the females had been taken in retaliation for a cattle raid on Galstead's border.

"That's outrageous," she exclaimed to her talkative cellmates upon hearing what had transpired. Her opinion of her captors sank lower—something Deirdre hadn't thought possible.

"And that bloody Ecfrith claimin' to be a Christian." The young Welsh woman seated against the wall of the compound next to her swore, rolling her pale eyes heavenward. Ainwyn was typical of her people, with wild raven black hair, fair complexion, and fire in her heart. "'Twas not just unsportin', but outright heathenish."

Cattle raiding had been a way of life among the Celtic peoples since the earliest of times and was often considered an art form of wit and daring more than a crime. With the general peace in Erin—for there were always minor wars between this faction or that—such excitement helped keep the warriors in practice. But war or sport, no king worth his royal bench would tolerate the taking of the members of the offending clan as anything more than hostages to be held until the live-stock was returned. If blood was shed, which sometimes came to pass, then high justice promptly intervened to settle the matter according to the law.

"May the good Lord have mercy on us." Ainwyn crossed herself. "For all the churches they build, these men are no more Christian than the devil 'imself."

And this was the entrance to his world, Deirdre suspected. The auction was to take place on the morrow. Meanwhile, any prospective buyer had the right to inspect the captives ahead of time. Prisoners not sold to local lords would be transported by ship to Gaul, and then on to Rome. She closed her eyes. Had Cairell been treated any differently, since his captors knew he was a prince?

Deirdre prayed so. She'd seen swine fed better fare than the dried bread and sour wine passed to them during the noon repast. By focusing on the tantalizing scent of the food stalls nearby, she'd managed to take a few bites before the sight of something crawling in her portion did away with her appetite altogether.

Nearby, the door to the prison yard opened, and two of the Frisian guards entered. At least Deirdre thought they were. To her, Frisians and Saxons were no different, although they seemed to enjoy a friendly disdain for one another, like siblings from the same womb. They looked alike and spoke a similar if not the same language.

Ainwyn pulled herself to her feet. "Faith, here we go again." The woman inadvertently touched the bruise on her cheek, her punishment for rebelling against being examined and fondled. Deirdre had endured it with cold dignity, but if looks could kill, there were three less men who would exploit the plight of her sisters in bondage— including one Prince Ricbert.

Of all the vermin, it was he who made her feel the filthiest. His very touch felt like violation of the crudest manner. It was he who broke her silence.

"Crown a pig, it's still a pig."

But for the Frisian's intervention, she, too, would have been bruised. The trader warned the prince that one of the slaves had already been marked that day, and no more would be tolerated. Instead, Ricbert knocked the wind from Deirdre with a promise. "Consider this one sold, sir," he drawled, running the tip of his manicured finger along the curve of her face and down her neck to where her chest stilled. "Perhaps lying with a pig will teach the wench humility."

Deirdre shuddered as the words played again in her mind. *God spare me. I don't think I can bear this again.* She ached all over from the ordeals of the last few days. Lack of rest and an empty belly gave her body a loud voice of protest at any exertion.

But rather than a prospective buyer, it was Father Scanlan who approached with the guards. Surely Alric had not taken his ire out on the priest as well. Renewed by her ever ready hostility toward Alric of Galstead, she shoved herself upright against the wall and made her way toward the father.

"I thought the pirate captain's respect for his sainted mother forbade his enslaving a priest," she remarked dourly.

Scanlan was grim. "I am a visitor, not a prisoner, Prin—"

Deirdre put her finger to the priest's lips to silence him. "Give the thieving scoundrels no opportunity to increase their reward."

Cairell's ransom was lost. Now so was she...at least until the opportunity came to escape. The attempt could cost her her life, but better death than bondage to Alric's foul brother.

"I came as soon as I heard what happened."

She led the priest over to the wall, where Ainwyn moved away, affording a spot of privacy, although curious eyes followed their every move. Overwhelmed by the sight of Scanlan's familiar face, Deirdre abandoned her reserve and hugged him.

"Father, I am so glad to see you! Even if you remind me that you were right and I wrong in trying to retrieve Cairell's ransom."

"You did what you thought best."

It was better than an *I told you so*. She was so glad to have Scanlan's company, she'd take whatever he had to offer. "I honestly believed God was with me."

"He was, child."

This time she did not admonish Scanlan for calling a woman just a few years his junior *child*. He'd proved that he was many years more mature than she. That had to be the reason he saw what had happened through different eyes.

"Then why—" *Holy Father, don't let me cry now. I haven't a tear left.* "Then why did He allow me to be trapped in that filthy hold with rats running over my feet?"

Deirdre was wrong about the tears. Her eyes stung with a new supply of dismay. She blinked and looked away. She was a princess, not a simpering nitwit! She was schooled to affect composure in trying circumstances, though this was not one for which she'd been prepared.

And the rats. Nothing could have prepared her for that.

"They nibbled at my feet," she managed, her voice holding by a thread. Wrapping her arms about herself, she shuddered. "All night, they skittered about. I kicked at the vermin, but—"

"Let me tell the captain who you are," Scanlan interrupted. "I am certain I can arrange something through the church."

Deirdre squared her shoulders against the wave of panic spreading from the memory of the night's horror and stared at the faceless few across the compound until the image of gnawing monsters disappeared. "No. I forbid it. I'll not give the beggars the satisfaction…especially *him.*"

She turned to the priest when he made no reply. "You didn't!"

"I intended to but thought to seek your permission first," he admitted.

"Then I thank you. I will not have him benefit at Gleannmara's expense." It was war, and while she could not wage it with weapons, she still had her wit. A hint of humor tugged at the grim line of Deirdre's mouth as she recalled Alric's blank look of astonishment upon seeing her in the hold. God forgive her, that dumbfounded expression gave her a flash of satisfaction, in spite of his fearsome recovery. "I don't think he ever believed I was wed to the church. I've not an ounce of saint in me, I fear, and when I try my hardest, I fail the worse."

Scanlan shook his head. "You've the light of Christ in your heart, Deirdre. Yours is a common transgression, exercising our will over His. Not even the clergy are exempt from such tumbles in our spiritual walk."

"Then why can't I see what He wants? I prayed in earnest and saw signs that He wanted me to salvage the ransom and escape with Orna to see it delivered."

"What kind of signs?"

Deirdre told him of the episode during the storm, how she'd put it to God to either take her life and spare him and Orna to save Cairell or allow her to live. "Of course *he* interfered and thrust me to the deck," she added, leaving no doubt as to who *he* was. "And then everything seemed to fall into place with my plan." Until once again, the bane of her existence appeared, blocking her escape to freedom. "It's impossible to remain saintly around the likes of Alric. Can't you see why I thought God would have me make him the fool?"

Scanlan didn't answer at first. Deirdre leaned against the wall and slid down to a sitting position before her legs rebelled for lack of rest. In truth, she was feeling a bit queasy.

"Milady..." The priest appeared to weigh his words carefully. "We must listen to God with our hearts, for signs can be manipulated to suit our will rather than His."

Deirdre stared down at the dry earth before her. Had God's will been different from hers? The thought had occurred to her...after the fact. Most of the night she'd cried in confusion and anger, stifling her sobs with the back of her fist, lest she awaken the giant sprawled over her only route of escape. Was this to be her penance for not listening to Scanlan? After all, someone who'd given up the affluence of his home to live meagerly in the service of God was more attuned to God's will than a cosseted princess, no matter how noble her intention.

"I fear you're right, Father. I'm lost, to be sure—"

"Nonsense!"

Deirdre flinched at the uncharacteristic force in Scanlan's voice.

"You are not the first with a strong will and a love for God. One of His most favored saints struggled day by day with his pride, sometimes in victory, sometimes in defeat...our own Saint Columcille. Yet God used the man's princely pride to build his spiritual strength. Like the young Colum, you descend from a proud bloodline of warriors and kings. Rule comes more naturally to you than obedience. You do not retreat easily, but that is a virtue the Lord can refine into a glorious weapon for His Kingdom."

The comparison to the legendary Saint of Iona made Deirdre feel even more hopeless. "How can you mention Columcille's name in the same breath as—"

"He once interpreted a dream of a fellow saint who'd seen three chairs next to God's throne: one of gold, one of silver, and one of glass. Guess which he attributed to being his?"

"The glass?"

Scanlan nodded. "Aye, the glass. He granted the gold and silver to his contemporaries, acknowledging that his pride made his faith brittle like glass, more apt to shatter under pressure."

Deirdre pondered Scanlan's story but found no comfort in it. If a church saint's faith was like glass, then hers was like the wind, of little substance at all.

As if on cue, the door to the compound opened as though the Father of all winds was behind it, slamming against the wall of the compound. Her nerves at their most raw, Deirdre started before she even saw the tall Saxon prince storming toward her like thunder personified. Clenched in his hand was a blue cloak, not the one trimmed in ermine from his locker, but the one she'd stuffed into the keg while their ship was under attack.

So, he'd found the treasure with which she might have purchased freedom for her brother. She stiffened her body, refusing to tremble and crumple into a heap of despair, but stood riveted by the apparition of flesh, blood, and rage.

"Whose cloak is this?" he bellowed, waving it above his head as he strode straight for her. The muscles of his forearms bulged, as though knotted with the tenuous hold on the white-hot wrath that possessed him.

When Deirdre did not answer, he shook the garment at Father Scanlan. "Well, Priest?"

"It belongs to Lady Deirdre." Scanlan's answer was soft.

Deirdre gathered her scattered wits along with her voice. "Aye, 'tis mine." She didn't even try to keep the crossness from her voice. What could possibly be so upsetting about finding her *brat*? Unless he smarted from the fact that she'd nearly outwitted him a second time, causing him to miss yet more of the *Mell's* treasure.

"He doesn't take being bested by a woman well, does he, Father?"

"Tread softly, milady," Scanlan warned quietly.

"Milady…of what kingdom?" Alric fixed them with a glare. "For this is a royal brooch if ever there was one, as is the sword."

The priest gave Deirdre an apologetic look. "She is the princess of Gleannmara."

Alric snorted. "Never heard of it."

His annoyance was no less than Deirdre's. How *dare* he dismiss Gleannmara as inconsequential, when Cairell was being held for…for…

Unless Alric really hadn't been one of the plunderers.

"A princess," he reflected in disbelief, focusing his ire upon her. "Deirdre of Gleannmara, royal or nay, you are a vixen to the core. Is there no end to your deceit and trickery?"

She lifted her chin. "None, so long as I draw breath and must deal with your likes."

"Do you know what your name means?"

Her name? Deirdre frowned, thrown by the odd question. "Mother told me it was an ancient name that meant 'she who murmurs or chatters.' It was her favorite aunt's name as well." Deirdre preferred that explanation to the other one associated with the name.

"It also refers to the daughter of the DeDanan harper and storyteller at King Conchobar's court," Scanlan obliged when she paused. "Her beloved, along with his brothers, were lost to the hand of the man she despised."

Deirdre reflected a moment, struck by the irony of the second origin, for of late she chewed sorrow like a cow its cud. " Indeed, sir, I can now commiserate with the legendary Deirdre of sorrow, for she lost her freedom to love whom she pleased, as I have lost all my freedom because of you, black heart."

"Her namesake is sorrow, yet she will bring you great joy."

Had his mother's words referred to the old Celtic tale of Lady Deirdre, whose beauty was prophesied to bring so much sorrow to Ulster that its king had to prevent his subjects from putting her to death at birth? That much, Alric could well understand, for even in her state of dishevelment, Deirdre was a delight to the eye of any man with his natural sight—and she was enough trouble to douse a fool's painted smile.

"Hair of spun gold…eyes that shame the sky."

Her hair was ratty now, uncombed, yet glistening like the brooch. And her eyes…perhaps a shooting star aimed to skewer his heart better described them, for they were uncommonly bright with scorn.

"Her chatter will be like birdsong to your heart."

It simply could not be! *This* Deirdre made sorrow seem appealing, while her tongue wore like a stone in his shoe. The worrisome creature had nearly cheated him thrice—of a slave's worth, a king's ransom, and now that of a princess.

"Father Scanlan," Alric said, choosing the most reliable of the two conspirators, "I will have the whole truth, nothing less. Who is this woman, and what does this mean?" He showed the brooch to the priest.

"That is the brooch of Queen Riona. She and Lady Deirdre are descended from the southern Niall dynasty, which has ruled Gleannmara for two centuries. Milady's father, King Fergal, now sits upon Gleannmara's throne."

"Scanlan, I forbade you!" Deirdre cried out in frustration.

"I'm sorry, milady," Scanlan apologized, "but surely Prince Alric is preferable to an unknown master. He, at least, has shown us some sign of decency."

"He's a prince of thieves, a scoundrel in fine clothes."

If she were a man, Alric would break that stubborn jaw she flaunted at him and put out the lights in her flashing gaze. But since that was not a choice open to him and his conscience, he'd break her some other way. He lived on risk. Deirdre of Gleannmara would be no different. If this enigmatic creature was to be his fate, by the calluses on Thunor's hand, so be it. If she wasn't, he could certainly be rid of her later. For now, he needed time to think this through.

Alric seized Deirdre's wrist to pull her upright, only to have her try to twist away. Grimacing, he tightened his grasp. "Don't force me to hurt you, Deirdre. You are coming with me, one way or another."

"What do you think you're doing?" She dragged her feet.

"Claiming what is mine."

"I advise that you go calmly, mila—"

"Then *you* go calmly, Priest!" Deirdre's knees struck the soft dirt, plowing where her feet had left off. "I'll never be yours, you vile heathen spawn."

"Ho, there, Galstead. What is this?" The Frisian in charge of the slave quarters stepped into Alric's way. "You can't take her back now. You consigned her to me to sell. I've the documents and witness to prove it."

"I changed my mind." Alric's grip tightened as Deirdre struggled to stand.

"I don't want to go with him," Deirdre told the Frisian, still tugging.

"You have no say in the matter," he answered. "Nor do you, milord," the Frisian pointed out with a hint of apology. "Unless you wish to purchase her back."

Calculation fairly churned in the Frisian's eyes, and Alric knew his angry impatience was to blame. This situation was becoming more intolerable by the moment. If only he'd avoided the public confrontation. It wasn't like him to give anyone the advantage...but then he'd not been himself since crossing paths with the creature straining at his grasp.

"I'll offer the standard eight oxen. Trust me, a stubborn mule is all she's worth and that's—*argh!*"

Alric hopped aside before Deirdre had the chance to nail the top of his foot again with her lethal, slippered heel. With a sharp yank of her arm, he dove at her middle and hoisted her up on his shoulder.

"You brutish oaf!" She pommeled his back with her fists as he straightened.

"Your brother has already offered me twice that."

"What?" Alric grimaced as she elbowed the back of his head.

"I'll kill you. You have to sleep sometime, Galstead, and when you do I'll—"

Alric slapped her soundly across her bottom. "Silence, woman!"

"How *dare* you strike—"

He clapped her again with the flat of his hand. "I said silence, or I'll take you down and give you the thrashing you deserve."

"Will that make you feel like a big man, thrashing a helpless female half your—"

Helpless? He'd have laughed if he had the time or inclination. Alric lowered his shoulder as if to drop her to the ground so that he might carry out his threat.

"All right!" she conceded, breathless.

"That is better." With a smirk of satisfaction, he turned back to the Frisian. "What did Ricbert offer, Emo?" Ricbert would beat Deirdre into submission, which meant certain death, given her spirit. "And I would have the truth, not some of your exaggeration."

The heavyset trader shrugged, indifferent to the insult. "Your brother knows a prize when he sees one. He offered me sixteen head of oxen...and a cow."

"I could purchase a harem of women for that."

"Not if she's really a princess."

"Oh, she is certainly a princess," Scanlan offered from the sideline of onlookers.

Alric gave the priest a warning look, his displeasure rumbling deep within his chest. In truth, it was as much at himself as Scanlan and Emo. "Your ears are bigger than they look, you Frisian mule."

"Insult me with a higher bid, Saxon, otherwise unhand the female. She will be auctioned tomorrow."

"I *ought* to let Ricbert have her." Alric gave a snort of humorless amusement. "Then my half brother would be twice cursed with two women to please."

His captive grew so still, he glanced over his shoulder to see what knavery she was about until the reason dawned on him. It took no stretch of imagination to know how his half brother had treated her. Alric was struck with an urge to seek him out and cut off the hands that undoubtedly familiarized themselves with his captive. *His,* not Ricbert's.

The decision was made.

"Send for the port reeve then, while we work out a price." The lady was obviously no fonder of his half brother than he. Granted, it was a slim thread but nonetheless a common one. Matches were made on less.

Emo dispatched one of his men with all haste and motioned for

Alric to follow him. "I was thinking eighteen head of cattle and a horse."

Alric was so taken aback by the direction of his thoughts that he hardly heard Emo at first. "Wait," he called after the Frisian trader. "I'd have some lightweight shackles and hide to protect her ankles." The opportunity to escape, however small, was not something Alric was prepared to offer the resourceful lady of this Gleannmara.

"I have a pair here." The Frisian took a set of chains down from a peg.

Alric nodded. "I'll see to it." He glanced back at his now subdued prisoner. "Milady, I would have your word on your God's honor that if I put you down, you will cause no more travail for me or my friend here. Else, he can have you for the sale tomorrow, for my patience and purse are spent."

After a brief silence, Deirdre answered, "I promise, God's honor."

Shifting one side down, Alric let her slide off his shoulder, his arm encircling her waist until she was steady upon her feet.

"Must I wear chains?"

Gone was the fighting banshee, and in its place was a picture of forlorn innocence. That appealing, wounded look on her face called to a side of him he dared not recognize. To do so would be his undoing, delivering into her hands a weapon more powerful than any blade.

"Until you prove yourself trustworthy, you must."

The defiance that flashed on the luminous sea of her gaze told him he'd chosen wisely. Kneeling warily, he slipped the shackles around her slender ankles, cushioning them with the hide patches Emo provided.

Emo stopped him from dropping the key in his purse. "Not until we agree on a price."

Alric tugged a velvet pouch from inside his shirt and tossed it to the man. "My payment requires no expense for food or shelter and is worth the price you ask, even more to the right buyer."

Emo pried open the golden-tassled lacing that held the pouch closed and shook out the contents into the palm of his hand. A nearby witness gasped as a rainbow of gemstones glistened in the sunlight.

"No, *please!*" Deirdre tugged on Alric's arm, something akin to panic grazing her face.

"What is so special about a pouch of uncut gemstones?" They were part of the treasure she'd hidden away but hardly something of sentimental value such as the sword or brooch.

Instead of answering, she cast her gaze at the ground with a shaky little breath that plucked again at Alric's sense of pity.

He steeled himself against it and glanced at Emo. "Is it a deal?"

"We've been partners a long time, my friend." He motioned at the crowd around them. "We've witnesses enough to transact this bargain. I'll have the reeve sign the papers."

"Good. Then I'll be on my way." Alric started toward the deep-rutted street.

Deirdre held back. "May I say good-bye to Father Scanlan?"

He'd forgotten the priest. "Make it quick. I've business to see to."

Wary, he watched as Deirdre hugged the priest, whispering something into his ear. Pulling away, she faced Alric with grudging resolve. "I'm ready."

With the fortified gate facing the road to Wales to his back, Alric started toward the royal house his father kept on Governor Street. It had been built for the commander of the second Roman legion centuries before.

Even in chains and dirty, ill-fitted clothes, Deirdre possessed a regal presence as she kept up with his deliberately shortened steps. He should have seen it before. He *had* seen it. He simply hadn't recognized it for what it was. She'd been a puzzle since he'd laid eyes on her. Now she was even more so.

As they left the slave block and passed a string of food vendors hawking the remainder of the day's wares, she caught his sleeve, to ask for food, he thought. Again, he misjudged her.

"It will do you no good to seek ransom for me. The treasure in that barrel was meant to ransom my brother."

"Brother?" Alric stopped short, scowling. "Then there is already an heir to your father's throne."

"Cairell's been kidnapped, and father has been ill, so Gleannmara depends on me to arrange for his ransom."

Had he just spent a fortune on an old woman's ramblings and

nothing more? No, the emblem, the brooch, the name, even the description…it was all too much to be coincidence. And while he might not believe in visions or prophesies, he did believe in keeping the promise he'd made his mother on her deathbed. And he trusted the gut instinct that didn't balk when Emo had demanded such a high price.

What would happen, would happen, gods or no gods.

"I'm not sure your people would pay a ransom to get you back," he taunted.

She pulled back again, stopping him. "Then what do you plan?"

Riddled with irritation, he spun about. "I just might *marry* you!" He made the threat in an attempt to silence her. He needed to think without distraction. "A feisty wench like you could give me an army of warrior sons, enough to take and keep any kingdom I desire."

His ploy worked, but too well. Deirdre's mouth fell open, then clamped shut. Her lashes fluttered like dazed butterflies. But for Alric's quick reaction, the ghost-white female would have pitched headlong into the dusty street. Frig's breath, he groaned silently, gathering her limp body up in his arms.

He hoped his gut instinct wasn't indigestion.

TEN

N ow you be certain to sleep well, milady, and if you need anything, you call for Doda." The steward's wife plumped the
pillows on the bed, arranging them just so. Her fluent Latin
evidenced that she and her husband had been born on Albion. A
matronly soul, she also wore a small gold cross about her thick neck,
which surprised Deirdre, even though she knew not all Saxons were
heathen. She had to ask about it.

"Belrap and I are servants of Christ, in as much as weak mortals
can be," Doda told her. "When King Oswy declared Christianity the
faith of our country, everyone was supposed to change from the old
gods to the Only God, but old ways are hard to change for some." She
shrugged her rounded shoulders. "The constant border raids make it
difficult to take God's Word to heart, much less love thy neighbor,
especially when he's in spitting distance of your gate."

Deirdre understood what Doda meant. She had no love for the
man who'd dumped her like a trussed fowl on the bed of her quarters
and then abandoned her with a harsh "Stay!" as if she were a dog.

"So how do you feel about Christians taking others as slaves?"

Doda smiled at Deirdre's clearly peeved challenge. "No one is
exempt from slavery in war. It's just the way it is. But you needn't
worry. Prince Alric is a just man with a kind heart, just like his
mother."

"He's no Christian."

Doda waved her hand. "Ach, he is, he just doesn't know it yet. His
mama taught him the faith. The seeds are planted and someday love
will nurture them, I think. Such beautiful needlework," she exclaimed,
feeling the fine linen weave of Deirdre's night shift.

Seeds planted on barren ground if she ever saw it, Deirdre thought,
although the prince had told her he'd have her things delivered from
the ship and, true to his word, they'd arrived while she was bathing. "I

believe he did mention something about his mother being a Christian," she acknowledged purely to be polite.

"And a slave." Doda let loose the smooth material. "Yet, even in such a menial position, she softened the hearts of all who knew her toward her God...all save the queen and that...well, Prince Ricbert."

"Are you saying Alric's father is a Christian?" From what she'd observed of the man before Alric had ordered her removed from the *Mell,* he hadn't appeared pious toward anything save the riches aboard the ship.

"King Lambert allowed Orlaith to keep a small altar in the same temple with the queen's gods, so that the kingdom might be blessed by them all. As soon as Orlaith died, though, Ethlinda disposed of it. Her husband didn't care. He'd lost all he cared about, poor soul."

Doda tutted as she opened the window of the room overlooking the courtyard, revealing an ironwork of twisted vines that provided fresh air, ornamentation, and security. There were no windows on the opposite wall, it being part of the overall perimeter of the house.

"What about the queen?" Deirdre asked. "Surely it must have distressed her not to have her husband's heart."

"She was a *freou-webbe*...a peace weaver, the daughter of one of Lambert's father's Mercian enemies. Love was not an issue in the marriage, alliance was."

Nor would love be an issue in hers, if Deirdre was to believe Alric's mad threat that he might marry her rather than ransom or sell her. Her head still spun with possible reasons for the wild words, but none made sense. Marrying her would not bring Gleannmara under his control, at least not while her father lived. Then there was Cairell's claim, should her brother find a way out of his captivity. She'd not only failed to aid him in that, but she failed miserably. She shuddered to think how this would affect her ailing father.

Heavenly Father, please, please be with us in this hour of our trial, especially Father, who does not have Cairell's and my youth to sustain him against this Saxon scourge.

"Well!" Doda slapped her hands on ample hips. "I am thinking you must be looking forward to that nice plump bed, yes?"

"Oh, yes." Deirdre let her gaze wander to the bed. How wonderful it would be after the foul cell she'd been sleeping in. Seated on the bench at its foot, she continued to brush her freshly washed hair. "And thank you for having me released from those bonds." Alric had put the fear of retribution in his steward if he permitted Deirdre to escape, but once Belrap had turned the princess over to his wife, Doda would not tolerate her *guest* being trussed like a goose.

And thank You, Father, that even in the midst of my tribulation, You send blessings like Doda to make it easier on me. I pray that Cairell is equally well blessed.

"Men! Where are you going to go, even if you wanted to escape?" Doda chuckled. "Though, if I were a pretty young woman, I would not run from a man such as our Alric."

Yes, well, Doda didn't have a mission to accomplish, nor had she seen her chances of success dissolve in captivity. "Even were you a slave and not a lawful wife in God's eyes?"

"Even the Hebrew kings David and Solomon had wives and concubines and slaves, just like the bretwalda, and they *still* got in trouble with women." The servant chuckled at her jest, then sobered when Deirdre did not share it. "Besides, Tor will not let you pass."

"Alric's dog." Deirdre recalled the gnashing teeth of the great wolfhound that bounded out of nowhere upon hers and Alric's arrival.

"Alric raised him from a pup, though he's bare grown. Tor will not tolerate anyone threatening his master."

"But you won't let him in *here,*" Deirdre clarified, her hairbrush frozen in midstroke.

She had never met a dog she could not ingratiate, but she and Tor had not met under friendly circumstances. The memory of the wolfhound's ferocious snarl still lifted gooseflesh on her arm. The prince's sharp command stopped the dog from leaping wholeheartedly into the fray between Deirdre and its master. Fearful of tempting the animal into further aggression, Deirdre ceased to protest—and to breathe—until Alric deposited her behind the closed door of her quarters.

"Tor knows he is not to sleep in Alric's bed…unless the prince is here," Doda stipulated.

Alric's bed? "This is…*Alric's* room?" Faith, she'd almost rather have the dog in here than that Saxon. And why had Alric put her in *his* room? The obvious answer would have taken out Deirdre's knees had she not been seated. Would he ravage her without so much as the loveless marriage he mentioned?

Heavenly Father, please no.

"The prince has gone for the night," Doda reassured her, having read Deirdre's unguarded panic.

The knot of breath and anxiety lodged in her throat unraveled. "Everyone calls him a prince, but…I thought he was illegitimate…a bastard."

"A wishful title on the people's part, perhaps." The housemistress lifted her shoulders. "Lambert would have no son of his a slave, so when Alric was a babe scarcely a week old, there was a grand manumission ceremony to declare the child a free man. And a greater one still when the prince turned his thirteenth year to recognize him as a *thane* in the king's highest regard. In place of land, he has a fleet of ships, which contribute as much to Galstead as any thane's lands. Many wish Lambert would acknowledge his youngest son as heir. From the king down to the lowest slave, Ricbert is not so well thought of as Alric."

Sometimes the role of monarch was as constraining as that of the slave. Raised in a politically conscious atmosphere, Deirdre realized that Lambert's naming the son of his concubine as heir would break the alliance made with the marriage to Ethlinda. At least she was beginning to understand something of the man who'd taken her captive.

"Now, I will take your dress and make it fit for the journey tomorrow to Galstead's court. Our prince would have his lady companion look her best when she is presented."

"Journey?" Deirdre felt the blood leave her face. She needed more time.

"That is our Alric." Doda's words were as fond as her smile. "He's a man of action, not words."

That much Deirdre agreed with, but—

"This color will look lovely with those blue eyes." Doda gave Deirdre's hand a quick squeeze. "Who is to say? If I know our Alric, he will marry you sooner than see you treated as his mother was. And you'll give our prince handsome, strapping sons."

An army of them, she thought, recalling Alric's words. Deirdre felt sick. This couldn't be happening. Surely he was trying to frighten her into submission.

"It would be wonderful to have little ones here." Doda flitted toward the door, Deirdre's dress slung over her arm. After giving the room one last, critical perusal, she stepped out in the covered colonnade, where the gray wolfhound climbed to its feet.

"Move, you big flea breeder."

Tor obeyed instantly, but not in the manner Doda had in mind. With a deep-throated bark and a bound, he bolted into the room. With a strangling terror, Deirdre threw up her arms to protect her throat, but the dog leaped past her and bounded up on the just-turned bed.

Clucking like a wet hen, Doda made straight after it. "Oh, no you don't! Your master is not here, and the lady does not want a mongrel's company."

Hairbrush clutched to her chest, Deirdre watched warily as Doda coaxed the animal off the bed.

The wolfhound, which, even *bare grown* could stand on his hindquarters and look Doda squarely in the eye, yapped at the woman, tail wagging in excitement. His moods seemed as varied as his master's, for it cavorted now like an overgrown pup, happily rumpling the bed covers.

"I'm going to get the broom, Tor," Doda threatened, mouth set in determination.

Whether the dog recognized the word or simply interpreted the warning in her voice, his tail ceased to thrash the bed. Statue still, his dark eyes followed Doda to the tiled hearth in the corner of the room. With a yelp that suggested he'd known the thrash of straw, Tor retreated outside the chamber and sat down with a short bark of protest.

"You big baby." Doda chuckled. "As big as he is, I think the broom scares him more than it hurts." She returned it to the hearth and shook her finger at the animal in triumph as she shuffled toward the bed. "Outside the house, you are in charge. Inside, *I* am." She gave Deirdre a sheepish grin. "At least when Master Alric is away, he spoils this animal like a baby." She fussed over the mussed bed. "Men and their dogs!"

"I can do that, Doda." The sooner the door was closed between her and the gray beast eyeing her with a mutual distrust, the better.

Doda kept on working until the bed was in perfect order. "Now, you sleep well, milady. And call for me if you need anything more. Perhaps some custard or—"

"I couldn't eat another thing." She'd already made a pig of herself, cleaning off the plate Doda had brought her earlier. Now all she wanted was peace and time to think about her next move with regard to Alric of Galstead. "Thank you again."

"It is my pleasure, Lady Deirdre." Outside the room, Doda gave Tor a rough pat on the head and cooed, "Doda will bring you a nice, big bone, eh?" The latch clicked into place behind the retreating housemistress.

Putting the brush on a table, Deirdre listened to determine if the hard-headed animal remained at his station. Although she had no intention of trying to escape, at least for now, his presence made her nervous. The door rattled a little, the only sign that Tor had resumed his watch.

Now that she was alone, Deirdre took time to study her surroundings. The room itself was part of a group of buildings that formed a square around the inner yard. The Saxons had done a decent job of repairing the Roman ruin, but there still might be a weak place in the outside wall, which could lead to freedom. Just in case, Deirdre peered behind the tapestry of a stag hunt hung over the bed. In the light that slipped in, she saw what appeared to be a faded mural on the wall. More than likely the artist had been dead for at least two centuries, the same as the builder who'd completed the stone enclosure. She sighed in disappointment. Like as not, it was at least three or more feet thick.

Allowing the hanging to fall back in place, Deirdre studied the covering itself, curious about its depiction of life across the North Sea from whence the heathen had come. Instead of the circular symmetry so prominent in Celtic stitchery, the Saxon embroidresses had worked bizarre animal representations into their patterns. Gods or pets, she wondered, scholarly curiosity overcoming her disdain toward her captors.

Her gaze fell upon her sea chest. She'd stored her dining dagger there shortly after they'd embarked at Wicklow. The story of a lady who'd fallen upon her dining knife during a rough sea crossing had made it seem prudent at the time.

Taking heart, she hastened to the leather-hinged trunk and began to dig through her belongings. Everything was there, including her jewels and coin, but the knife was nowhere to be found.

With a grunt of disgust, she sat back on her heels. Oh, how Alric had smiled just prior to leaving her in Belrap's care. He'd likely mistaken the luxury of her surroundings as the source of her stunned acquiescence rather than the dog nudging his thigh to get his attention. She should have known he'd search the chest before having it brought to her.

Closing the lid, she rose and walked over to the window, her voluminous night shift swirling around her body. In the light of the rising moon and the lanterns hung round the square promenade, she saw a fountain at the center of the courtyard. She knew such remnants of the old Roman world were still in existence but had never seen one. This villa must have belonged to a Roman general or governor. A pity it was wasted on Saxons.

Soft breezes blew through the window, toying with Deirdre's damp hair and stirring the spice scent of the soap Doda had provided her. Would that she was safe in that antiquated great hall tonight, listening to the bards sing of the glory days of her ancestors or of some romantic tale of star-crossed lovers. She might even play along on the harp and do a verse or so herself, for she'd memorized all of Gleannmara's past as part of her scholarly and musical accomplishments. How her father beamed with pride to hear her sing...

The blade that formed in Deirdre's throat was sharp enough to cleave song from it forever. A sob worked it loose, along with the despair that had piled upon despair since she'd left her ailing father.

Tearing away from the window, Deirdre crossed the room, bare feet padding on the tiled floor, and flung herself across the bed. The royal restraint ingrained in her by her tutors gave way to tears of shame and desperation. Anguish wrung them from her eyes until no more would come. Snatches of her trembling breath became less and less frequent, and the emotional scald of her face cooled against the arms in which she buried it. She was spent—physically, emotionally, and spiritually.

Why, Father? Why have You allowed this to happen to me...to Cairell...to Gleannmara? What possible good can come of this? Cairell is lost. Surely You'd not have me marry a heathen and bear his little demons. What am I supposed to do now?

Lost in a black sea of hopelessness, Deirdre rolled on her back against the plush pillows, her arm over her eyes, when a pitiful wail, not of her own making, sounded next to her. Turning her face toward it with a gasp, she stared straight into a pair of bright, dark canine eyes—Tor! Deirdre's heart slammed against her throat as she tried to read his disposition in the way he cocked his head at her, ears perked as much as the breed allowed. A furtive glance at the door revealed it to be open, but there was no sign that anyone had let the animal in. Had he mastered the latch without Doda's knowledge?

A dog his size could take down a wolf, so she would not fare well against him, not weaponless as she was. Deirdre lay motionless, trying to steady her breath, but emotion had yet to give up its grip. Her attempt to swallow a hiccough turned into a pitiful squeak that set the wolfhound into motion.

As its front feet struck the bed, she pulled one of the pillows over her face and neck and braced for the attack. But no sharp teeth assaulted her bare arm. Instead, a wet tongue lapped at it—once, twice, three times. Dogs didn't taste their food; they just wolfed it down. Only slightly less fearful with the realization, Deirdre lay as still as she could. Her hair pulled beneath the weight of one of Tor's paws as he lightly nuzzled her locked fingers.

Dare she cry out for help? No, that might provoke the beast. Suddenly the bed shook with the full weight of the animal. His feet brushed against Deirdre as he picked his way to her other side. She flinched as a wet nose pried under her elbow, as if to ease under the pillow in a stubborn yet surprisingly gentle manner. When that didn't work, the dog whined and pawed at it. Remembering the sight of his snarling teeth, Deirdre held it fast.

Perhaps if she remained still long enough, he'd lose interest and leave her alone. The thought had barely formed, when the wolfhound plopped down and stretched out lazily against her. Ever so slowly, Deirdre lifted one corner of the pillow to see exactly what the situation was and came face-to-face with a gray furry muzzle. As Tor raised his head, she pulled the pillow over her face again.

Heavenly Father, she prayed, afraid to so much as breathe until the beast rearranged himself and settled once more. His big paw brushed against her rib and suddenly the weight of his head dropped upon her stomach. She could not suppress a pitiful whine of her own.

It was going to be a long, long night.

ELEVEN

Alric, the night is yet young. You have had much on your mind."

"Don't touch me, woman." Alric pulled away from Aelfled's touch and sprang from the bed, but his humiliation followed. Never had he failed to pleasure a female, not even his first, much less an enchantress like Aelfled.

She wrapped a sheet about her and padded across the straw-covered dirt floor toward him. "If you will only listen, I think I can explain why—"

"Which time, out at the pool or just now?" he growled as he pulled on his clothes. At her patient silence, he acquiesced. He certainly had no idea what was wrong and he was desperate for answers. "Is this permanent?"

"Don't be absurd. It is not the natural order, only a temporary disturbance designed, perhaps, to get the attention of a bull-headed man."

"Disturbance?" Alric raised a finger at her. "Aelfled, I am more than disturbed."

"You belong to another, one of golden hair and blue eyes—"

Alric shook his head. "*She* belongs to *me*. Besides, you heard that from the Frisian's wife." He pulled his shirt over his shoulders. Women and their self-proclaimed ability to know and see all.

"You love her."

"Hah! If this is what love does to a man, I might as well be gelded."

"Your destinies are matched by fate...or your mother's God." Aelfled put her hand on his arm and motioned him to the bench at her table. "Now sit, and I will share *my* vision."

He stiffened. "What you've actually seen, or the gossip carried on the wind of the Frisian's wife?"

Aelfled took up a small bag of smooth, flat stones from the table and cast them before Alric. "Choose."

"All?"

"I will tell you when to stop."

Alric swept half aside with his hand. "There. Satisfied?"

"Put three back."

When he'd shoved the first three closest to the remainder aside, she began to turn his chosen stones, one at a time. "I saw her in the water at the pool. She wore a blue gown with golden braid and seeds of pearl, fit for a princess, because she is royal. Her throne is not ripe and when it becomes so, it comes with a blight."

"Do you talk thrones or apples?" Still, Aelfled had his interest.

"It is a throne protected by a sword." She continued to turn over the rune stones. "A king's sword."

His elfinlike friend was very good at her craft, but whether her vision was real craft or simply conjecture eluded him. "Do you see the sword in those stones?"

"I saw it in the water, a long blade with a hilt of gold inlaid with silver and jewels...sapphires and three small, red stones." She flipped three stones. "A scholar, a warrior, and a priest."

"And the sapphires?"

"Thanes, I think, who support the king of the sword." She smiled. "A wealthy king."

Anyone could have described Deirdre, but few had seen the sword close enough to describe it in such detail. Still... "Do you also see that the king is alive and has an heir?"

Aelfled shook her head. "I only saw the blight on the water, like evil fingers tearing your destiny apart. Not only yours, but hers."

Alric laughed. "Galstead is filled with evil fingers, complete with hands and arms and bodies to back them."

"Her kindness will make many enemies."

"I am not familiar with any kind streak in her."

"Because you have not looked beyond her physical attributes."

"I didn't need to. They flew at me like a swarm of bees, stinging my pride, my purse, *and*—" he held up his wounded hand—"my hide."

"I speak of her heart."

"She cloaks it in deceit."

Aelfled gathered up the stones and returned them to her pouch. "I will be glad to help you and your lady when the time comes." Her tone clearly pronounced the session finished. "The stones and water agree with your mother. Believe them or not, it is your destiny, not mine."

Alric stood, spurred by frustration, and strode to the door. Destiny, indeed!

"Do not hesitate to send for me when the time is right. Even a stubborn mule as you will know when," she called as he reached the doorway.

Alric turned. He didn't want to hurt Aelfled. She was the only refuge he had, but if she was so intuitive, surely she knew how he suffered this very moment. He knew neither his mind nor his body.

"Go to her, Alric." A smile warm and sweet as a summer morn lighted on her lips…but it wasn't Aelfled who spoke. It was Orlaith.

Alric blinked in disbelief and looked again. Nay, his mind vied with his body for fiendish trickery. It was Aelfled—small, beautiful, and more seductive than he'd ever seen her. And to his horror, he felt nothing. He fled from the place that had always been his refuge as though driven by Woden's own fire.

Although Aelfled's glen was tucked into the forested landscape a good walk from Chesreton, Alric had no idea of the time when he greeted the night watchman at the royal villa's gate. The opening of the iron hinges split the quiet of the night with a hair-raising creak. No foe would ever slip quietly through this entrance.

"We wasn't expecting you back tonight, milord," one of the men told him.

Neither was he, Alric thought morosely. He started across the courtyard, making straight for his quarters, his thoughts tumbling like a rockslide into a bottomless pit of indecision and bewilderment. Even if his heart had chosen another path, what connection did this destiny of love women were so enamored with have with his inability to satiate his desire? Desire and love need not go hand in hand. It would take more than a pile of stones to convince him he was in love, much less the visions his friend told him about.

Granted, it did *seem* as if all the gods, Christian and pagan alike, had sent Deirdre to him. A sign from one or the other was one matter, but the same sign from both was enough to make even the most skeptical of cynics pay heed. The king's sword with its stones was intriguing, but this talk of scholars, warriors, priests and black fingers... Frig's breath, it made no sense! All he knew was that both mind and body now failed him. He knew not what to think of the first and the second was unbearable. What good was a king who could not sire an heir? This was no *disturbance,* as Aelfled had said, but a disaster. He was no longer a man. Perhaps he was ill.

Alric paused by the fountain in the courtyard of the villa. His hands were steady. His skin was cool to the touch. His stomach was satisfied by the food and ale from Aelfled's table. All he felt was frustration, nay panic, that his body had failed him with no excuse.

A faint light slipping through the cracked door of his room drew Alric's attention from himself. Surely that woman had not escaped again. And where the blazes was Tor?

A myriad of curses vied for expression as Alric reached the door...and spied both the female and the dog on the bed. Tor's head bobbed up from the flat of Deirdre's abdomen. Tail wagging proudly, he barked.

The still figure beside the dog cringed. The toes of her bare feet curled tight against their pink soles, and her arms clutched the pillow over her face even tighter.

Alric had forgotten that the old latch to his quarters was no match for the wolfhound. If he wanted to keep Tor out, he had to use the bolt on the inside. Given the trouble the wench had caused him, Tor's mischief was well deserved. A slow smile came to Alric's face.

Tor gave another short bark as Alric approached the bed. Shushing the dog, Alric leaned over the bench at the foot of the bed and ran a finger up the center of Deirdre's foot. Predictably, she recoiled. Put out that it was not he receiving Alric's attention, Tor climbed to his feet and rubbed against Alric's arm. As Alric ran his finger up the center of Deirdre's other foot, the dog began to lap at his hand, as well as the sole of Deirdre's foot.

With a shriek, she rolled off the bed, pillow and all. Tor would have bounded after her, if not for Alric's restraining hand on his collar. By the time the animal was in check, Alric caught a glimpse of a night shift disappearing under the bed.

"Ho, Tor. Easy, boy," Alric cooed, settling the excited animal. "You can come out, milady." He laughed shortly. "This playful beast is under control."

Silence was his only answer at first. Then a dainty foot ventured out. Wriggle by wriggle, the rest of his captive appeared, her shift twisted about the curves of her feminine figure. As she gathered herself to her feet, she still hugged the pillow in front of her. Modestly shaking out her garment, Deirdre raised her face to him.

Guilt edged out Alric's humor at the sight of her tear-ravaged eyes, now shifting in wide terror to the dog. The proud chin that had given him thunder trembled above the edge of the pillow. Fear of the dog had broken her spirit where neither he nor a hold full of rats could. He was not the least gratified by the victory.

"Tor won't harm you, I promise," he said softly.

As if to prove Alric right, Tor barked, wagging his tail. With a jump, Deirdre backed against the wall. "I hate you for leaving me with that beast," she cried into the pillow drawn over her face. "I hate you for ruining my life and my brother's chances of freedom. I hate you."

Her utter despair clawed at Alric's conscience, and her avowal of hatred unaccountably ripped at his pride just as her fingers did at the last barrier of defense between them. Alric caught Tor's eye and motioned the dog out of the room with a jerk of his head. When that didn't work, he snapped at the wolfhound. "Out, Tor. *Now!*"

At the last command, the dog leaped off the bed and ran into the courtyard as Alric closed the door and bolted it from the inside.

He removed his sword belt and hung it on a large peg near the large bed, then turned toward Deirdre, who was still quivering in the corner. The guilt that assaulted him suited him less than his previous humiliation with Aelfled. Women, it seemed, were a ripe source for both. "I am sorry about your brother." He drew a deep breath, searching for some words of comfort. "I guess I'd hate me, too, if I were in your shoes."

Frig's mercy, how could he make her understand *his* side of this when he wasn't certain himself? It behooved him to have the brother out of the way, although he was loathe to benefit from Ecfrith's brief madness. Brotherly love was something he'd never known. He'd been raised on brotherly rivalry and outright dislike, if not hate.

"I let my father and Cairell—all of Gleannmara down." She sniffed wretchedly into the pillow.

But it wasn't *his* fault. He hadn't intentionally set out to ruin this young woman's life. "Why in blazes did they send a woman in the first place?"

Deirdre rallied brokenly, glaring over the pillow. "My father is ill. Time was of the essence and…and I don't have to explain anything to you! I was perfectly capable of negotiating the exchange. I am a princess. I have been trained for such things."

"Then why are you here in this situation now?"

"Because I was trained to deal with honorable men, not scoundrels."

The broken blade in her voice cut Alric in two. A nobler part of him wanted to throttle his lesser self and protect her from himself. But what was done was done. He couldn't undo it. This was war. Deirdre and her brother were casualties.

"Maybe I can ask around to see what might have become of your brother—"

"Prince Cairell of Gleannmara."

"I'll see what can be done." Alric had no idea what exactly that was, but the brightening of hope in her gaze peeping over the pillow's edge might just be worth the effort. At least *one* of them would have some relief. He certainly preferred the role of comforter to that of scoundrel.

"You don't need this now," he told her, gently taking the pillow from her.

Childlike in her fear, she drew in a fragile breath. "I thought the dog would—"

"I know." Alric put his finger to her lips. "I'd forgotten how Tor could open a latch when it suited him. I'm sorry, but he'd never hurt you."

She shook her head as if to contradict him.

"He only threatened you at first because he thought you intended me harm." Alric kept his tone gentle. "Frankly, I am surprised he didn't try to roll you out of the bed, since you were in his rightful place. He's pushed me out before, during a sound sleep."

Doubt reined in her gaze, but a slight twitch of her mouth encouraged him to go on. He couldn't help but run coaxing hands down the cold flesh of her arms, moving her stiff body into the intended comfort of his embrace. She neither resisted nor cooperated. "Come here, sweetling. I promise you are safe now."

Her breath was warm against the front of his shirt as he pressed her face to his chest. It was uneven, riddled with the terror that had held her at bay for the last few hours. Alric could well imagine the warrior queen he'd seen brandish a sword against Gunnar struggling with the terrified child within. The first would draw his blood; the latter, his compassion. He inhaled the scent of the golden hair falling in disarray about her shoulders. His soap had never been so appealing. For all its masculinity, it could not detract from Deirdre's softness. If anything, it enhanced his awareness of her femininity, stirring instincts that had failed him earlier.

Alric's mind and body reeled. Was there merit to Aelfled's talk about love and his mother's musings of his destiny? Everything stacked like a *cromlech* upon his mind.

"Come, let's put you to bed before you take a chill." With sheer will he turned her toward the bed, breaking the close contact between them before his body betrayed him. The renewal was sheer relief and pure torture at the same time.

Alric tugged back the covers and held them as Deirdre obediently slipped between them. Gathering them in her hands, she pulled them tightly under her chin, watching him warily.

"You will have to move over, milady. I sleep on this side, next to my sword."

He watched as she absorbed his meaning.

"Here?" Her voice was little more than a rasp.

"There's no other bed in the room." Alric's pragmatism was not shared.

"There's the bench at the end."

The plea in her eyes was almost impossible to ignore. Besides, Alric was too tired and weary for another confrontation. It was easier to drag the bench around to the side on which he customarily slept, grab a pillow and blanket from it, and settle on the thin cushion.

She watched him, doubt furrowing her brow. "What about Tor?"

"I bolted the door so that he will not join us," he said gruffly.

Us. The concept ran through Alric like a bolt of lightning, but he weathered it behind a mask of reassurance. Despite the distance between them, the room itself made her nearness inescapable. Desire played havoc with him, denying him a female he might enjoy with a free mind and placing him with one his conscience forbade him to touch in intimacy. His mother had been such a maid of privilege, snatched from her home and thrown into the bed of her captor.

Alric shuddered inwardly, turning away from the bed. Why, after all these years, he wondered as he stripped off his shirt, did he ponder such things? He'd accepted his parents' relationship as it was, never thinking of how it came to be…until now.

As he reached for the laces of his breeches, he heard a small gasp behind him. With a pull of a smile, he turned out the lamp before he finished undressing and settled in on the bench. He'd slept on harder surfaces, but not with a large, plump mattress and a warm wench a turn away.

"You *are* still abed, aren't you?" he said, tugging the blanket up to his shoulders. She'd grown so quiet, it sounded as though he were alone.

"I…I have nowhere to go."

Alric flinched as though the doleful words had been hurled like barbed arrows and almost wished they had. Fighting her defiance had been far easier than resisting the compelling lure of her vulnerability. He tried to shed his conscience—and any other finer emotions she had the knack of bringing out in him. He was a prince and a warrior doing his duty in taking the *Mell* and its passengers. It was his right and her misfortune. All in all, he'd been gracious and honest toward her, which was more than he could say on her part. And if he kept her, he would not do what his father had done. She would be his wife, not a slave. That should count for something, shouldn't it?

He caught his breath as the thought settled like a blanket upon his confusion. Had this many advantages pointed toward claiming a prize ship, he'd have taken it by now and cursed the risk. It was a tactical decision. In doing so, he gained not just the prospect of his birthright, but his manhood as well, for he was suddenly overripe with it in her presence. Gritting his teeth, he closed his eyes.

Surely this was the beginning assault of the dark powers Aelfled warned him about. If indeed Deirdre was his destiny, it was so close— and yet too far away.

TWELVE

Morning broke on the horizon, the first rays of light streaming through the iron grate in the villa window. With bright fingers it pried through the layers of slumber in which Deirdre had found refuge. She cracked open one eye, then closed it quickly as the direct sun assaulted it. Turning on her side, she prayed instinctively.

Thank You, Father, for another glorious day.

Her nose registered the scent of bread baking and some sort of meat frying, which produced a small growl in her stomach and launched moisture to her tongue. Flexing her feet she stretched lazily, hands extended to the head of the bed.

Her fingers contacted warm flesh instead of the cool wood that should have been there, waking the memory of where she was…and with whom.

Recoiling, Deirdre opened her eyes to find herself staring face-to-face with the sleeping prince of Galstead. Somehow, during the night she'd crossed to the side where he'd placed his bench and lay poised on the edge as if to watch him sleep—indeed as she was doing now.

Motionless, Deirdre studied the chiseled square of his jaw, almost soft in repose. The morning light made the stubble of his beard glisten like gilded dew. With his long, narrow nose buried into the pillow and lips puckered like a round-cheeked swain for his first kiss, he looked deceptively boyish and sweet.

Except she knew Alric of Galstead was no boy when it came to kissing. Faith, he might have invented the art, the way he'd claimed not just her lips but all her senses. Caught in the embrace of the sinewy arms now holding the blanket against his broad chest, there'd been no escape from the farewell warning he'd given her on the deck of the *Wulfshead*…

She shook herself from the thought. How could the memory linger through all that had happened since? Deirdre caught her breath at the shiver of excitement kindled by the memory. With a low grunt, the man turned with a short snatching motion onto his back. The arm that had been stretched under his pillow was now flung across his face, but there was much more to her strapping captor than his face. Deirdre had seen the bared chests of many warriors, but never close enough to touch. Even at rest, the lines of muscle looked as firm as those of a statue. Hanging about his neck, on a black leather thong, was some sort of medallion, turned so that its wooden back faced away from him.

Strange, she'd never noticed it before. It was probably a wolf, like the one on his belt buckle. Her gaze shifted to the wall where Alric had hung his scramasax before turning out the light the night before. Dare she take it while the man slept?

A few days ago, she'd not have hesitated, but the more she crossed this man, the worse her situation became. She no longer trusted her instincts, much less her interpretation of God's will. Even the answers to her prayers left her wary. Last night she'd prayed fervently that someone save her from the wolfhound and the prayer was answered, although the Almighty once again chose His own way of going about it.

Should I have told the truth from the start and made it easier for him to ruin my life and that of my loved ones?

Deirdre clutched the golden cross she wore on a fine chain round her neck as if she might squeeze the answer from it. *Father, I do not mean to be disobedient or disrespectful, but surely You never intended me to marry a heathen...even if he might pass as one of Your golden warriors.*

She cut a sheepish glance at the sleeping Saxon, her cheeks warming. What a sight that would be, Alric brandishing his sword for God, with her at his side much like her ancestors Kieran and Riona or Rowan and Maire. Beyond the flat plain of the man's stomach, the garnet eyes of the wolf's-head belt buckle hanging on the wall glittered in mockery of her foolish notion. A chill swept through her, lifting the hair on her arms. The predatory creature looked as though it stood guard over its master and his weapon, daring her to even think of possessing either. Indeed, was that low rumble Alric's snoring, or was it a feral growl she imagined that came from the beast engraved in silver just beyond him?

Of course, it was all an illusion. Satan toyed with her mind, playing on the accounts of demons, which the priests reputedly exorcized from the unsaved. Even if it was a demon, she had nothing to fear. She wore the armor of her faith…even if the wolf peered right through it to where her heart fluttered unevenly at its brutish challenge.

In the name of Jesus, I have nothing to fear. Slowly, so as not to awaken her Alric, Deirdre slipped out from beneath the covers and up on her knees. The garnet eyes of the silver image seemed to grow wide at her impudence. All she had to do was turn the buckle away from the sunlight and the eyes would dim. Holding on to her cross with one hand, Deirdre reached for the buckle with her other, lips moving silently. *Neither demons, nor Satan himself can harm me for I am washed in the—*

"Blo…*ood!*" she screamed as an unseen hand locked in the thick of her hair and yanked her away from the hanging weapon.

"Frig's—" Alric began as she fell across him, cutting short his breath as well as her own. He gave a pained grunt as her elbow dug into his ribs.

Suddenly she was falling, the impact of striking the floor knocked the wind from her startled shriek.

Deirdre struggled to escape as Alric rolled off her, but the now fully alert warrior had wound her hair in one hand, grunting broken oaths and warnings as he pinned her to the floor. Outside the window, Tor barked and lunged at the ornate grill as if to come through it.

She seized a fist full of Alric's hair with her free hand and yanked vengefully. "Hurts, doesn't it?" she panted.

"I wasn't about to let you…*ach!*" He grunted, pinning the knee she raised between his with a shift of his body. "Slit my throat with my own blade."

"I…" She could hardly breathe, much less speak beneath the full weight of his torso. "I wasn't; I swear it."

"Then what were you about?" He snarled the question, eyes glowing molten with fury like those of the wolf, golden and death dealing.

"I only wanted to look at the wolf's head."

He narrowed his gaze. "Swear on it."

"Swear on *what?*"

To Deirdre's disbelief and horror, the Saxon bared his teeth and lunged at her throat. Where she found the air to scream, she had no idea, but scream she did until there was nothing left to fuel it.

"*Dis,*" Alric growled, lifting something with his teeth.

Her cross. Somewhere within her chest, the blood that had stilled there thawed with relief. Alric wasn't going to tear out her throat like a bloodthirsty hound. *Really he wasn't,* reason scolded. Deirdre moved her lips to swear, but her throat would not give up the words. In truth, relief made her head swim so that she lost them amid the heaving of their chests and the frantic barking of the dog in the distance.

A sharp pounding at the door burst the bubble of confusion pressing at Deirdre's temples. "Milord Alric?" Belrap shouted.

Above her, Alric spat out the necklace. "Everything is fine, Belrap. Just take that blasted hound and feed him to shut him up."

"Shall I send Doda for the lady, sir?"

"No!" the prince roared. "All the lady and I need is privacy."

Privacy. Deirdre blanched, her strength waning away as she stared at her captor and realized what was happening. He barked his orders in that savage tongue of his...yet she understood *every* word—

She stared, terror sweeping her. His image blurred, changing from the hairy face of the wolf on the belt to the golden warrior until darkness edged in from all corners of her mind to take him away.

"Deirdre? Deirdre!" Alric shook her face from side to side as he faded from her view. "What is wrong with you?"

Gradually he came into focus—the man, not the animal. "I..." Deirdre hesitated, adrift in a fog of recollection. He thought she'd meant to kill him. His brow rose in impatience, his eyes dark with distrust.

"On the cross, I swear I meant no harm. I did think about it," she admitted, "but...but God wants me here." What else could it be? Emotion welled in her voice as well as her eyes. "I just don't know *why.*"

She stared into Alric's face, as if the answer might lie behind his guarded gaze. Something incredible was happening to her and it frightened her. Had she inadvertently tempted a Saxon demon? How else could she suddenly understand this heathen tongue?

Father God, save—

Alric dipped down, catching a renegade tear with a kiss so tender her prayer stalled.

"Don't cry, sweetling. I swear by *all* the gods, I will not dishonor you." His deep-pitched croon was velvet enough to make the marble nymph of the fountain outside swoon in his arms. "On my mother's grave, I promise I will make you my wife before your God and His priest."

Priest. The very mention kindled hope. Yes, she needed a priest. "I want to see Father Scanlan. I—" He caught yet another tear, this one dangerously close to her lips. The thought of Alric, particularly this gentle Alric, staking claim on them warmed her body like a wildfire, despite the cold floor beneath her. Her heightened senses could almost discern the perspiration forcing its way through each pore, making her tremble with anticipation. Though of what, she had no idea. All she knew was that the demon inside her wanted it.

"You need not fear for your soul," he whispered against her lips, "for I shall respect your faith."

Her soul. She had to think of her soul. The heady nuzzle of Alric's cheek, rough and manly against her face, combined with his long, relentless kiss would only lead to its destruction. If she gave in, the hands that wormed their way behind her would weave chains she could never break away from, for the demon hacked away at her control, one heartbeat at a time.

"Jesus save me, for I cannot save myself." Even as she prayed, she clasped Alric's face between her folded hands. Lucifer himself was the most beautiful of all the angels. If she gave herself to Alric— "Deliver me, Lord, else I am lost. Take away this demon, I beg you—"

"Demon!" Alric pulled away, looking at her as though she'd driven his scramasax through his chest. "Is that what you see in me?" He held her by the shoulders at arm's length.

Alric's wounded gray gaze faded from view as the medallion he wore swung back and forth between them. The eyes of the wolf's head mounted on the wooden disc glowed with unnatural fire. Deirdre turned her head, but there was no escaping as its snarl gave way to gaping jaws that opened wider with each pass until all she could see was a pair of red eyes in the blackness. And when they closed, not even the scream propelled from the last thread of her consciousness could find a way out.

"She's burning up with fever!" Doda cast a reproving look at Alric as she tucked Deirdre in. "This poor girl has been through so much, it's no wonder her constitution has weakened."

Alric stopped pacing beside the bed. Try as he might, he could not shake Deirdre back into consciousness. Perhaps if he'd seen what had struck such stark terror on her ashen face, he might be able to explain.

"So what is it?" he demanded as Doda poured water from a pitcher into a bathing pan. "The plague? Some female malady? What?"

"A protected princess and likely a virgin." Doda snorted. "Maybe it was the sight of a hot-blooded man who scared her witless with his—"

Alric held up his hand. "You know me better than that. I did no more than subdue her when she tried to turn my sword on me."

"That is not my business." The housemistress turned to soak a clean towel in the water.

"No, it is not." All the same, he'd done nothing to frighten Deirdre except defend himself. As for his kisses…

Alric plowed his hands through his hair. She'd been warmed by his attentions until she panicked. "If I'd an inkling of the ill wind waiting on that cursed ship of hers, I'd have retreated in the opposite direction as fast I could make sail. She's been near the death of me." Was his destiny to never have peace of mind again?

"Looks to me, it's the other way around. It's sure you look hale and hearty as the day you came squalling from your sainted mother's womb."

Alric groaned inwardly. When old crones started running on about knowing him since the day of his birth, a stern lecture was in the making. "Doda, I have heard all I will hear on this. Whatever is wrong with that woman, it's not of my making."

She looked up at him, her brow raised. "Did I say it was?"

Frig's mercy. "I'm going to find the priest she asked for." He turned to the wall where his sword belt still hung.

"She asked for a priest, and you refused her?"

Alric swung the belt around his waist, patience exhausted. "Of course I did! But only after I ravaged her until she fainted."

Doda swelled like a toad, not even deigning to look Alric's way as she switched the towels on Deirdre's forehead. "Utter nonsense! Don't think that I don't know my princeling better than that," she muttered as he rolled his eyes and stalked out of the room.

Alric fetched Tor from the chain Belrap used to restrain the dog when he became unmanageable. The animal jumped up on Alric, lavishing him without censure. That was the good thing about a dog. It never judged, just gave unconditional affection and, at times, concern when it sensed something was amiss with its owner. Or maybe it was wishful thinking that suggested such affinity.

"Come along, friend. We've some hunting to do," he told the hound, shoving him down as he tried to jump at him. "Now, *stand guard!*"

Obediently, Tor dropped behind Alric and sat down, waiting with a puppylike wriggle for him to move on. Grinning, Alric petted the coarse ruff of Tor's neck, working his fingers under the leather collar to the dog's ecstasy. "Good dog. Good dog."

Since the rest of Alric's world had been turned upside down by Deirdre's entry into his life, he'd wondered if Tor had been affected as well. He took a short leash and tucked it under his belt, in the event that it was needed. Perhaps that was what *he* needed, Alric thought, flushing with the memory of kissing Deirdre. When she was in his arms, the discipline he prided himself on was as elusive as the reason for such loss of control.

Tor's impatient bark tore Alric from his quandary. With a lopsided grin, he nodded. "You are absolutely right, my friend. What we need is action. Let's go to the *Wulfshead*."

Tor vaulted ahead of Alric at the word *go*, but in midgait, he seemed to recall his training and dropped to heel again. With a comical yelp that seemed to say "oops," he showed Alric his teeth. To someone who didn't know the animal, it might have appeared a threat, but Alric knew it as a grin and returned it halfheartedly. At least someone still remembered who he really was and loved him for it.

A demon. The cursed woman thought him a demon!

Struck with an overwhelming urge, Alric kneeled down and gathered the eager wolfhound in his arms, hugging it to him tightly. Not since he was a callow youth at his mother's knee had the need for understanding and acceptance weighed so heavily upon his heart.

THIRTEEN

Deirdre struggled to open her eyes, her mind as blurred as her vision until she made out Father Scanlan sitting on a bench at her bedside, where he'd nodded off against the wall. It took a moment for her to piece together where she was. A lamp burned on the table at the far side of the mattress and the day waned beyond the open window. Frowning, she raised her arm to wipe the dampness from her forehead and was shocked by its weight, more like stone than flesh, as if she'd been bled of strength, although she saw no sign of a leech's pan. Was she dying?

Deirdre closed her eyes, trying to remember. As she searched through the mire of recollections, it was difficult to separate what was real and what was illusion. She saw herself tiptoeing past a sleeping Alric—how boyishly handsome he looked in slumber, despite the golden shadow of manhood upon his cheek. But it was his scramasax that called to her. No, not the blade. It was the belt buckle, with the red-eyed wolf, mocking her with its glowing gaze. Even as she'd reached for it, she felt foolish to think its demonic glow was anything more than morning sun lending its fire to the stones, then—

Deirdre shot up with a gasp, clutching her chest.

Beside her, Father Scanlan started. "Oh…you're awake."

Yes, she was awake, but the fright Alric had given her, grabbing her and wrestling her to the floor managed even now to wedge her heart in her throat. Deirdre hardly noticed the priest as a steady flood of memories swept into her mind. Alric had lunged at her throat with bared teeth…then the wolf's head swinging between them ever closer to her, its eyes—

"Lady Deirdre?" Scanlan watched as she clutched her neck. It was damp but without wound.

Nay, it was an illusion. She saw it clearly now, a cross, not a wolf's head. Alric had wanted her cross, wanted her to swear upon it that she had not thought to cut his throat with his own weapon. The recollection drained the stiffness from her shoulders as tears of humiliation and relief stung Deirdre's cheeks. Still, she heard again Alric ordering Belrap to take Tor away, the syllables of his pagan words as harsh to the ear as the wolfhound's bark. The thunderous prince had wanted to be left alone with her…

She'd understood his baffling language! So how could she swear that she hadn't seen the garnet eyes of the graven wolf's head open and close?

Deirdre grabbed the golden cross between fingers of flesh as invisible ones cold as the grave raked up her spine. "Holy Father," she whispered, trembling.

"You're safe, milady." Scanlan's voice seemed as far away as God, beyond the black fear congealing about her.

"I'm lost," she protested with a wail. "Possessed to be sure." At the touch of Scanlan's hands upon her shoulders, Deirdre threw herself at him, clinging to him to keep the gaping, snarling demon from taking her over completely.

"You've a fever, child, nothing more."

"It was real. Father, a demon gave me the Saxon tongue. I heard it and I understood it."

"Feverish babbling, Deirdre. Perhaps the same malady that sickened Orna on the journey over."

"It was real, as God is my witness." Deirdre clamped her hand over her mouth, but she could not take back the sharp-edged foreign syllables she spat at the priest. Horror clutched at her throat. *"God save me, it still possesses me!"*

Scanlan backed away from Deirdre, crossing himself. "Father of Holies, Son of man, Spirit of the flesh, be with us." He might as well have wrenched Deirdre's heart from her chest, that not even a priest dared touch her. Clearly he was shaken by what he'd heard.

It had to be the work of a demon. "I'm lost, aren't I?"

Scanlan shook his head, gathering himself from the initial shock. "No one is lost who cries for the Christ."

A change came over the man. What Deirdre had always thought a soft cherubic cheek squared with the fierce set of a warrior. She'd always seen Scanlan as meek, the sort who would inherit the earth, not take it with a sword of fire. Yet his eyes blazed as though forging a weapon for battle beyond the scope of mortal sensibilities. As he approached Deirdre and folded her hands in his, the power of his presence encompassed her.

"Pray to Saint Michael, the Victorious, with me. Thou, Michael the Victorious…" Awkward at first, he proceeded in the language he'd studied in order to save the lost of Albion.

"I make my circuit under thy shield," Deirdre chimed in. Could they pray the demon out in its own tongue? "Conqueror of the dragon, be at my back…ranger of the heavens…thou warrior of the King of all…" Though one of her favorites, how foreign the ancient hymn sounded to her ear now. "Though I should travel ocean and the hard globe of the world, no harm can e'er befall me near the shelter of thy shield…"

"Believe it, Deirdre," Scanlan interjected, drawing her head to his chest. His cross of wood and bone burned cool against her flushed cheek.

"Be the sacred Three of glory, aye at peace with me…"

Peace. The word cleared the knot that throttled the previous lines. *"In every thing on high or low."* The age-old melody to which she'd sung the hymn many times found its way *into* her voice, lifting it and the darkness with hands that, though unseen, bore the marks of driven nails. "Every furnishing and flock, belong to the holy Triune of Glory…"

"As do you, child," Scanlan said.

He raised his hand. "I invoke the Trinity, that you may rise from your bed, Deirdre of Gleannmara." The priest threw aside the coverlet and backed away.

A prick of panic assailed Deirdre, for she recalled how leaden her limbs were.

Scanlan saw it and his smile was reassuring. "Sing, milady. Take neither your eyes nor your heart from the Almighty."

Or she'd sink back into despair, just like Saint Peter into the water.

Although her legs protested, she swung them off the bed and finished the hymn.

"And to Michael…"

She stood, wavering with uncertainty as her gown fell around her ankles. The early evening air rushed to her skin, as if to scour the damp remains of her weakness with its cool breath. Eyes widening, Deirdre felt she might float above the floor, as though she were weightless in body and spirit.

"…the victorious!"

"By virture of the Christ's birth and baptism…"

"By virture of the Christ's birth and baptism…" So why did she still speak in this vile tongue as though weened on it?

"Crucifixion, burial, and resurrection…"

Her entire body felt lighter than the arm she'd lifted only moments ago, making it impossible to dwell on the doubt, had she wanted to. Which she didn't. "Crucifixion, burial, and resurrection…"

"Return and descend to the last judgment…"

Deirdre echoed Scanlan's prayer, finishing with him, "Christ be with me, in front of me, behind me, above me, below me, and within me. Amen."

Like a vulture hovering in wait for a soul to surrender to death, doubt circled around again. Aside from the last word, the entire sequence had been in a language she'd never studied as Scanlan had. Yet the demon had to be gone. Were she any more light of heart, she'd hover at the beamed ceiling like a sun-bright cloud.

"What does it mean?" she whispered, afraid of sounding ungrateful for her deliverance from the black clutches of the wolf—or whatever she'd seen.

Scanlan fell to his knees and embraced her ankles, placing a kiss on her feet.

Startled, Deirdre danced away. "What *are* you doing?"

The priest looked up at her and smiled. The round-faced cherub had returned, ever cheerful, ever full of praise. "Milady, 'twas no demon that came upon your tongue, but the fire of God Almighty. The same fire that came upon the apostles at Pentecost—"

Deirdre recoiled in disbelief. This was blasphemy, to be sure. "Father, bite your tongue!"

"You've been blessed, milady. You were right. God has a great mission for you." Scanlan looked at her in awe worthy only of a holy relic. It drew her into his misguided madness, but she wanted no part of it. "I studied for years and haven't your ease with the Saxon language."

"Well, it must be an accident. Surely the miracle was meant for yourself…or some other priest or a sister of God." Deirdre turned away, flesh crawling in rebellion against the very notion. "And I'm certainly neither, nor have I any wish to serve God in that capacity."

"God makes no mistakes, child."

"Nor could I serve Him so, even if I did suffer such delusion! I've a fearsome temper—"

"As did Moses, if you recall."

"Moses? Listen to yourself, man! 'Twas you yourself who warned me that pride would be my downfall." She threw up her hands. Her wolf demon had shape-changed into a mule and kicked the holy man soundly in the head. If Deirdre was born to champion God, it would be on the strength of her troops and influence, not her faith. Look what she'd done with her efforts to interpret God's will to date! She'd misunderstood everything. Now she was bound for slavery—or worse, marriage to Alric.

"I'm not that strong, Scanlan."

"God knew you when you were in the womb, just as He knew your great-great-aunt. Look at what Kieran's and Riona's foster daughter overcame, even as a child."

Scanlan's reference to their common ancestor, the abbess Leila, was not entirely lost on Deirdre, but it was not convincing either. "Her miracles died with her; they were not passed along to me. I've too much of the Niall blood for a holy calling."

"Jonah was consumed thrice. Once by his prejudice against sinners, once physically by a whale, and again by his sheer stubbornness to avoid the path the Lord had chosen for him."

A priest had no end of scriptural riddles. Surely they would be the end of her. "Father, I could be wrong in labeling all Saxons not worth saving, for Doda and Belrap have been most kind to me. But God might as well give this heathen tongue to a turnip for all the good it will do."

"A turnip would do neither your brother nor Gleannmara's interest any good, but the wife of a Saxon prince might use her influence and her *gift* to solicit help in finding Cairell."

"Besides, I never said I'd marry the—" Deirdre stopped midrant. The embroidered hem of her gown lagged behind her sharp pivot. "Brigid's fire!" She could scarce take in the practical side of his suggestion. "Do you really think that is God's purpose?"

"'For I know the thoughts that I think toward you, saith the LORD, thoughts of peace, and not of evil, to give you an expected end,'" the priest quoted solemnly. "Do you think your despair is greater than that of Jeremiah, or any of God's chosen? He has plans for each of us, for our welfare, not harm, that we will have hope. He does not promise us ease, only His support." Scanlan motioned for Deirdre to take a seat. "I've also done my share of seeking out the spiritual condition of Galstead. The kingdom teeters between the queen's old pagan ways and those of our Lord."

As she perched on the edge of the bed, he began to pace.

"Because of Lambert's love for Alric's mother, the faith had a tenuous advantage, but since her death, the queen has gained more sway." Scanlan pivoted and dropped to the bench in front of Deirdre. "I prayed for a miracle, and *you,* milady—" he clasped her hands in his fervor—"received it. There is no doubt in my mind. You have been chosen to shift the spiritual tide away from the Ethlinda's influence, just as the bretwalda's Christian wives have done for all Northumbria. I am only your servant."

Deirdre was aware of how Oswy, the father of the current bret-walda, the Saxon high king, proclaimed Christianity as the new faith at the Synod of Whitby when she had been a fosterling with her mother's clan. Oswy's Christian queen and the influence of Bishop Wilfred had swayed the bretwalda toward the Roman doctrine, as opposed to that of the Celtic saints like Patrick, Columcille, and Aidan. It had sounded petty to her at the time.

"We must make history repeat itself…and perhaps help our church brethren as well," Scanlan added grimly.

How her marriage to Alric, the illegitimate prince, would further God's cause was beyond her. Ricbert seemed to be the one with the influence and, from what Deirdre had seen of him, he was his mother's son—base to the soul. Scanlan was desperate, though earnestly so, to save souls, but he'd been prepared for this. She was not.

"But, Father, 'twill be *me* sharing the marriage bed with a heathen, not you."

Her candor disconcerted not just her companion, but Deirdre as well. Her will was not always her own around Alric, particularly in his arms. And when he played the tender heart, will danced away, mocking her as she reached out for it. She remembered vividly now…Alric had not shape-shifted. That part was the illusion of her fevered mind. But his kisses, butterfly light upon her cheek…the drum play of their hearts…the heady closeness that heightened her senses to a devastating awareness had been all too—

"You may not have to," Scanlan reported with no lack of confidence. "There is a precedent in the Saxons' own court…"

She heard Scanlan's answer, indiscernible, like a ghostly whisper in the recesses of her mind. Deirdre gave herself a mental shake, but Alric's spell would not let her go. She crossed her arms across her chest, as if to erase all trace of the Saxon's spell. In truth, no demon had possessed her, but something twice as dangerous had.

She hadn't been afraid because she couldn't stop Alric. She was frightened because she didn't *want* to.

"God has to have made a mistake!" The words blurted out. "I'm not strong enough—" Scanlan's last words caught up with Deirdre at last. She cocked her head at him. "I may not *have* to share his bed?"

"Stop thinking about what you can't do and consider what you *can* do." Scanlan gave her a conspiratorial wink. "I have learned much in the last few days. Just lean in and listen."

FOURTEEN

The salon in the royal seaside villa at Chesreton had been furnished like a mead hall, with trencher tables and benches rather than the cushioned lounges depicted in the mural on the wall. In the mural, robust Roman men lazed in their togas while half-clad serving wenches, their hair coiled like springy serpents off their heads, fed their masters fruit. Peacocks strutted about in full plumage while a poet plied the lyre. Alric studied the picture as he had not since he was knee high, squirming on the bench next to his mother.

If all Romans lived such lethargic existences, it was no wonder the empire fell, he thought with a smirk. Of course, he knew better. He'd studied history and especially anything he could find regarding the great armies of the past. Still, as he'd remarked once to his mother, it was a wonder the Romans hadn't lost more emperors to choking on a grape, with this practice of eating while lying down, than to the sword. Of course, the little prince hadn't told Orlaith that he'd tried it and very nearly met that end.

There were good memories here; ones he missed sorely. Alric helped himself to another cup of ale. Belrap had seen food enough for four men placed on the table before the prince dismissed the staff. But Alric was too preoccupied to do it justice, much less entertain as he usually did when in port.

How long would this strange fever of Deirdre's last? What had he done to her to make her recoil from his attentions, accusing him of being a demon? Nothing had made sense since he met the enigmatic princess. Certainly not her actions...nor his own, for that matter.

He scowled at the empty places round the room. Maybe he should have invited Gunnar after the two of them had verified the value of the cargo taken from the *Mell*. But no, he instead returned to the villa to see if the priest had fared better than Doda in helping the delirious bride to be. Alone, he'd waited, grinding his teeth like a man braced to have an arrow wrenched from his chest. Even Lambert and Ricbert, with all their thanes and servants, would be better than this. Although since Orlaith's death, the king of Galstead was loathe to stay in his beloved mistress's favorite retreat.

Having spent more of his life here than at the decidedly more rustic royal seat of Galstead, Alric preferred Chesreton, the kingdom's chief port, as well. It was here, watching the ships come and go, that he'd become enamored with the sea. He'd built his first working vessel—large enough to carry him and his mother—when he was no more than ten. He'd sailed her up and down the banks of the protected river, armed with a small sword and ready for any foe who dared cross his path. Orlaith had made him feel like the fiercest champion to ever sail the sea. Even then, the water was his kingdom, a place far away from Galstead's dark undercurrents of envy and greed.

Lost in melancholy, Alric took a small loaf of bread and began to carve it with his dining dagger. With the top crust removed, he hollowed it out, munching on the soft pieces of interior as it began to take shape. At least Deirdre had not suffered seasickness as the other woman had. That resilience was part of her charm, which was why this fever worried him so. She wasn't the sort to swoon without serious cause. The warrior bred into that Celtic blood of hers would go down fighting, not in the terror he'd seen in her eyes.

Swearing off the tenacious concern with an oath that would have gotten him soundly smacked had he uttered it before his mother, Alric took a chunk of cheese and began to cut small rowing benches from it until the vessel was lined on both sides. Belrap's father, a shipbuilder and waterman, had amused the small prince just so many times. Thin slices of Doda's special sausages served as shields, which he placed ever so carefully upon the inward roll of the crust—an enforced rail—

The gruff clearing of a masculine throat drew Alric from his idyll. At the arched entrance to the room, the priest, whom he'd found earlier at the stone hovel of what served as a village chapel for transient Christians, stood, obviously uneasy.

"How is she?" he asked, motioning Scanlan in. His abdomen tightened from within as he awaited the news. Frig's mercy, what manner of malady had the woman brought upon him? First, he lost his ability to please Aelfled, though it had returned mightily when he'd least needed it that morning with his captive. Now she robbed him of appetite and peace of mind.

Scanlan approached the table. "The fever is quite remarkably gone." Curious, he peered into the bread boat and smiled. "And she's hungry."

Alric got up instantly. "Then I will have Belrap take—"

His guest raised his hand to stop him. "Lady Deirdre is dressing for supper and will join you shortly. She vows she's been abed enough. She is ever the restless one."

"You speak as though you've known her a while." Alric motioned for a servant.

There was always someone nearby, making himself scarce but ready if needed. The young lad who helped bring food from the kitchen, which was removed from the main structure of the dwelling, rushed over from a corner, tucking something behind his back. Given the bulge of his hairless cheek, it was part of his evening meal.

"Pauls, tell Belrap the lady guest will be joining me for supper. See if the cook can stir up something warm and bracing." Alric had told them previously that summer that cold meat was enough for him, but a guest was another matter…particularly this guest.

"Begging your leave, milord, but what you have is a feast in itself," Scanlan protested. "I would recommend a mild wine in lieu of your stout Saxon ale, or a Rhenish import for her delicate condition, perhaps a warm broth, but—"

"Given a choice, you clerics starve yourselves with all your fasting. I believe a hearty meal makes a hearty heart."

"For a warrior, mayhaps, but for a young woman just risen from a fever, that is my recommendation. The final decision is yours."

"Milord?" The lad glanced anxiously from the priest to Alric.

Scanlan made sense, of course. Most priests were healers to some degree. Alric merely wanted to show Deirdre that he was not as heathen and unschooled in social graces as she believed. Orlaith had seen to that.

"Have the cook prepare a broth and ask Doda if we've a mild wine."

Young Pauls's Adam's apple bobbed as he swallowed his mouthful. "Aye, milord. Right away."

Alric shoved the platter of food toward Scanlan. "Help yourself, sir. I am indebted to you for coming so graciously in the lady's time of need and much relieved that her condition was not as serious as it first appeared."

Perhaps the fever coupled with virginal panic at his attentions had brought about the disturbing reaction and accusation. Undoubtedly, she was one of those women taught to fear sexuality rather than enjoy it as Aelfled did.

Well he remembered how it had been with Tor and Dustan, the Arabian foal he'd captured on its way to Argyll on his first sea quest. The training to demonstrate who was master had been a slow process. He'd had to gain their trust first. So it would be with Deirdre, although the marriage bed promised mutual reward for them both.

Instead of taking the seat Alric indicated, Father Scanlan helped himself to one of the sausages, which he wrapped in the discarded crust Alric intended for a sail. His thoughts so absorbed him, that he could not stop the priest before it was too late.

"This is more than enough for me, milord, and I thank the heavenly Father and you for your hospitality."

"You're not staying?" Alric made a pretense at being disappointed. The truth of the matter was, Father Scanlan made him uncomfortable. Most priests did. They were so quick to judge souls as lost who did not subscribe to their beliefs. Some said as much in words, others with their eyes. "I'd hoped you might tell me more about Lady Deirdre."

"If you truly intend to marry her, I imagine you do." Scanlan chuckled, as though privy to some jest that Alric was not. "I grew up at Gleannmara, her father's tuath." He settled back on his seat. "Her mother and I are of the same clan, distant cousins." He shook his head. "I have seen the princess transform from a bright child into a remarkable young woman. She knows her mind and has never been afraid to speak it. Some men find her intelligence combined with her will intimidating. Deirdre puts more stock in books than in suitors."

This surprised Alric. "The princess is a scholar?"

"She is gifted beyond the imagination." Scanlan paused, resting in the cloud of his admiration. "Although her zeal is exasperating at times. Her fancy is to rule in a scholarly world, not her father's kingdom."

"A teacher." Had his bards looked like Lady Deirdre, Alric might have enjoyed his study far more.

The smug quirk of the priest's lips indicated that Alric might qualify as the lady's first student. It was gone as quickly as it appeared. "I do hope you will keep all this in mind when you take her to wife…if that is your intention."

His intention? Frig's mercy, his mind was in a spin of doubt and befuddlement that shamed the worst hangover, though the questions were not so different. What had he done? What would be the consequence? Was he certain he wanted to stand by his actions? Could he afford not to?

Despite these vexing thoughts, his answer was firm. "It is."

"She is a prize worth cherishing. A gift from God."

Alric stiffened. Not another prophet! They surrounded him, he who had sought none of them. "I recognize her for her beauty and her station, Father. That will have to do for now."

"Of course. Love must be nurtured for a lifetime to keep it fruitful."

Riddles again. "So I have heard," Alric replied, uncertain as to whether he was agreeing figuratively or literally. "But rest assured, she will not suffer the shame that my mother did but retain all the rights of a proper wife under the law."

"Under God's law as well?"

Alric hesitated. "I make no commitment to that with which I do not completely agree."

"Then perhaps you do not understand them, for I take you to be a decent man on the whole. We should speak before you make your vows."

Alric grunted in reluctant agreement. He had enough to wrestle with now without the priest adding more to the weight on his shoulders. A marriage of the law was enough for him.

"Well, I must be off." Scanlan brushed crumbs from his robe and stood. "While I would love to speak on the matter and enjoy your fine table, I wish to return to the protection of Saint Peter's before the full pitch of night has fallen."

Rankled, Alric was tempted to engage in a game of riddles to prove he had no need for tutelage of a scholarly or clerical nature. His mother had seen to his education in both spheres. Instead, he gave the man leave to go. "I'll have someone accompany you," he offered, ignoring his ingrained obligation to offer the hospitality of a bed for the night. He assuaged his conscience with the knowledge that travelers and a few local Christians enjoyed sitting in that damp little pile of stones, sharing their faith and fellowship as much as his men enjoyed the camaraderie of the mead halls. He'd been dragged there enough as a boy.

Alric stood at the small open foyer of the villa watching Pauls lead Father Scanlan toward the east gate.

"Scanlan didn't stay."

Turning, Alric saw Deirdre standing in the tiled entrance. She bore no resemblance to the ashen, frail creature he'd left with Doda and the priest earlier. Indeed, her priest was a miracle worker.

"Milady." Alric cleared hoarseness from his throat and offered his arm to the stunning vision in blue and gold. "You are…recovered."

"Aye." A half smile graced the rose curves of her lips, as if she was fully aware of her disconcerting effect upon him.

Ears growing hot at her silent amusement, Alric hardly noticed Belrap and Doda's efforts until he'd helped the princess arrange her royal robe on the bench so as not to crush the rich fabric. As pale as the lighter shade of her eyes, it was hard to discern if the velvet shot with gold threads was blue or a soft pearl gray. A matching cap crowning the golden cascade of her hair was of the same fabric and flocked with tiny seed pearls, as was the modestly dipped bodice. Where the small cross had graced the creamy flesh of her neck, a twisted ribbon of gold now sparkled—a torque worthy of a princess.

Though what he longed to finger most, the gold or the living satin against which it was displayed, Alric would not admit.

"My apologies, milady, for such a mean repast, but your priest suggested that I...er...rather that you would—" What the blazes was he saying? "He said you wanted broth."

Alric resumed his place at the head of the long table and pretended to assess his servants' efforts. The lavish silver candelabra cast dancing shadows on the ceiling as unfettered flames reflected in the gaze she raised to his.

"Broth will be excellent, milord."

The filigree of her lashes dipped fanlike upon cheeks ripe with vitality. Alric's insides mimicked the motion with such effect that he was grateful for the seat beneath him. He'd felt this sensation before, just before the unbroken Dustan sent him airborne on his first attempt to ride the stallion. He had to take charge of the situation before he struck the ground hard.

"Will you have wine, milady?" His leather drinking cup had been removed, and glassware from the Rhineland put in its place. As Alric reached for a decanter, Doda rushed in with another.

"No, no, milord. This is the milder wine you asked for. That is a Rhenish one for—" Upon seeing Deirdre, the housemistress broke off, her mouth dropping open. "Look at you, my pretty girl." The servant put down the wine bottle and clapped her hands to her round cheeks. "Oh, I am wishing the prince's mama were here to see you."

"You're making the princess blush, Doda," Alric observed, futilely resisting the enchantment swirling around him. How could this lovely creature possibly be the bane of his existence?

Doda placed a matronly hand on Deirdre's forehead, crushing the comely fringe of hair that spilled upon it. Like its owner, it sprung back as the housemistress withdrew her palm and tested her own brow. "It is cooler than my own. Praise God!"

"Indeed," Deirdre agreed softly. "He is ever my protector and benefactor." She cut Alric a sideways glance. "Even in this captivity."

Ah, the beguiling rose still had her thorns. Alric wanted to argue that this luxury was hardly *captivity* but could not. Were he to offer her the freedom to leave, he had no doubt that she would.

"Belrap must see this—"

"That won't be necessary," Alric interrupted, his guard raised by the prick of reality. The sharpness in his tone drew a bemused look from Doda. "I would like privacy with my bride to be."

Alric met his servant's critical gaze steadily. The silence in the room grew until Doda acquiesced to his will. At the open portal, she hesitated. Alric braced, expecting the beloved servant to exercise the privilege of having witnessed his birth to offer further objection, but instead, she stalked away in a self-righteous huff.

"She was of great comfort to me," Deirdre told him, a prompting hand resting on the gilded stem of her empty glass.

"Doda and Belrap were among my mother's favorites." Alric cursed the tremble of his hand as he poured the dark wine. He was the master of this situation, yet he felt like a toy boat caught in the tide, swept away by a force he couldn't see.

"Your mother must have been a gracious noblewoman, even though she was a slave."

"Aye, that she was. Which is why I take you not as a slave, milady, but as a wife, with all the rights accorded you by the law."

Instead of sampling the broth steaming in the glazed porringer, Deirdre focused on Alric's makeshift bread boat, which had been inadvertently left behind by the servants.

"May I?" She asked the question with the innocence of an angel.

"By all means." Pleased that she was intrigued by his handiwork, Alric reached across the silver platter of meat and cheeses and handed it to her. Pride vied with sheepishness, the latter heating his neck and face as she peered inside the outfitted rig.

"How clever," she murmured, taking out one of the little cheese benches and popping it into her mouth. "Now, about this *possible* marriage," she said, taking time to swallow daintily. Distracted and dumb, Alric watched as Deirdre broke the bread craft in half and dunked it into the broth. As it took on the liquid, the hair lifted at the back of his neck. Frig's mercy, the priest had destroyed his sail, and now this revived enchantress sank his ship!

He was no saintly prophet nor mystery-cloaked seer, but even he had a queasy premonition that this somehow was a portent of his future.

FIFTEEN

Deirdre was no prophet, but Jeremiah had been. By the time she was dressed and ready to face Alric of Galstead, she'd committed God's assurance to His chosen to memory. It was her armor, and the bizarre fact that she now miraculously spoke the Saxon language, her secret weapon.

At first Alric's almost boyish awkwardness upon seeing her had been as engaging as it was reassuring. She'd had not just a renewed confidence but the upper hand of surprise. Still, as she dunked his little bread boat in her broth, one would have thought it was the *Wulfshead* itself from his expression. Yet how could that be? Surely the cook or someone in the kitchens had filled an idle moment by carving the bread and cheese. Surely, it was meant to be consumed...

The candlelight seemed to become brittle in his gaze as he clenched the very blood from his knuckles.

"For I know the thoughts that I think toward you, saith the LORD, thoughts of peace, and not of evil..."

Thus girded, Deirdre spoke. "Since there is no one to speak for me regarding the marriage negotiations, I shall have to do so for myself."

"Indeed?" A slight pull of his upper lip hinted at a snarl. "I said that *if* I did marry you, milady. I offer you more than any slave can expect."

"I am not *any* slave, and you know it." Faith, had she gone through this agony of accepting marriage as God's plan for naught? Thankfully, the glass she lifted to her lips did not betray her bravado. The man was still as dangerous as the predator portrayed on his belt. She took her time, recouping from the unexpected blow. "Well, *if* you do decide to marry me—and trust me when I say I'd as soon raise swine in a mud hole—I expect what a bride of my station deserves."

Alric took the glassware from her hand and put it aside, leaning forward. "And what would that be?"

Deirdre remained steady beneath the intimidation of his glare. "A bride-price is the custom of my people."

"I paid for you already, and dearly, I would add."

"But some filthy Frisian has my bride-price, not I, nor any of my family. And that, sir—" she took the wine back—"is unacceptable. Without it, your family would consider me no more than it did your mother, a purchased slave."

Deirdre cut a piece of the broth-sodden bread with her spoon and focused on getting it past the knot threatening to trip her tongue. Her nemesis watched her every move like a wolf, watching for the advantage through a seemingly indifferent slant of mercurial eyes, though the remark regarding his mother seemed to set him back.

"I do not wish that on any woman," he admitted, "although a little humility might do you well." He considered her as though searching for her very thoughts. "And just what would that bride-price be, milady?"

"My brother's ransom—the contents of the barrel in which you found my cloak and brooch, the trunk, and, of course, Kieran's sword."

"The king's sword belongs to this Kieran and not your father?"

"The sword is a family heirloom, handed down from one of our great kings." Pride filled her voice. "Kieran dedicated it to the altar of the church he built on Gleannmara, vowing it would never draw innocent blood and be used only for God and Gleannmara. It was part of the ransom, which shows how desperately we wish to save Cairell."

Alric took the decanter of the stronger wine, removed the stopper, and drank straight from it. Slamming it on the table after he'd lowered the level by a good third, he tapped on the top as if counting. The more he counted, the more Deirdre noticed the veins beginning to swell in his neck and temples.

"If you were your brother," he murmured, like the low, distant rumble of an approaching storm, "I would slit your throat and leave you for the hounds, thus relieving myself of the trouble you have caused me."

She refused to let the raw comment rattle her. God was on *her* side, not this heathen's. "If I were my brother, you would not wish to marry me." Deirdre glanced at his empty plate. "You aren't going to eat?"

"I'm not sure I can afford to."

"May I use your dining knife then? I'd like one of those sausages."
She added with wide-eyed innocence, "Someone took mine."

"I'm not sure I can afford *that* either." Alric speared a sausage with
his knife and placed it on Deirdre's plate. As he chopped it into bite-
sized pieces, she thought he'd hack the design on the tableware into
oblivion.

"Thank you," she said as sweetly as she could manage.

With equally oafish disregard for the fine dining table, he buried
the tip of the knife in the wood on the far side. "You are most welcome."

"Actually, I took the liberty of writing out the contract. Doda provided me with the materials," she explained at the lift of his brow. "And
Father Scanlan helped me get it all down. If you sign it, then he will
post the banns…in case someone has cause to protest the marriage."

She withdrew the document from the pocket of her dress and
handed it to him.

"I'm beginning to think *I* may protest myself." Alric snatched the
folded parchment from her hand and opened it.

"Would you like me to read it to you?"

"I'll *struggle* through."

The cryptic note of his voice made it hard to smother a smile, but
Deirdre managed. Gaining confidence by the moment, she finished the
bread and broth, while he studied the words she'd penned earlier. She
hadn't realized just how hungry she was. Besides, she would need to
build herself up for her bridal fast. Fasting wasn't one of her strengths,
but if she were to convince Alric that she was meant to dedicate her virginity to the church as the bretwalda's pious Queen Aethelreda had
done, it was necessary. Ecfrith had needed the alliance, so he'd agreed to
a platonic marriage. If Alric wanted this wedding enough, so would he.

"For a sickling, you've surpassed yourself."

Deirdre lowered her gaze. "The Lord God gave me a miracle. I am
not the same person you left this morning."

"I believe that is the first truth you have actually admitted since we met. You are not the same woman. That's plain to any eye, save a blind one." This time when he took more wine, Alric poured it into the glass before him with deliberation in every movement. After a sip, he tapped the parchment with his finger. "This reeks of the priest's hand. So he is to be your mentor."

"It would make my life more bearable to have a man of God to confide in."

"Does he suspect your soul will consume his time such that he'll have no time to save other souls?"

"Scanlan has known me since I was a child…and he was witness to my miracle," she answered, as Alric returned to reading.

He smacked the parchment with his finger. "You *really do* expect me to give you a king's ransom and use my influence to find your brother and rescue him with it?"

"That is what the agreement says."

"Woman, I'd have to purchase back my men's share of the booty, not to mention the king's."

"Perhaps your father would give it to you as a wedding gift."

"'Tis blackmail!" The timbre of Alric's anger echoed like a war drum in her ears.

"Your proposal of marriage or mine, milord?"

Alric rocked forward as if to get up and and then sat back, apparently reining in his fiendish fury. He chewed his lips as though to draw blood, a feral glower in his gaze. Surely if he so much as spoke or moved, the beast would be unleashed upon her. The hallucination of the wolfman came to her mind and would not be banished.

"For I know I think thoughts that are best for you—"

No, that wasn't it. Deirdre scurried for the right wording as if it were a weapon knocked beyond reach. Scanlan thought she might handle the negotiation best, but now she wished he'd stayed. She braced for the final explosion, but when Alric reached her last condition, he spoke so quietly, she could hardly hear him for the pulse thrashing in her ears.

"And I'm to believe that you, a deceiver among deceivers, have suddenly become as pure and pious as our bretwalda's queen?" He sounded almost amused, were she not aware that the beast strained at his last tether.

"As suddenly as I was healed." Her equally deceptive calm was heaven sent. If God had truly chosen her, she *wanted* to be worthy, to be pure and pious. "I told you, it was a miracle. And remember that Northumbria's queen is winning souls for His kingdom. Your people worship her for her purity and devotion, I've heard."

"Those I know mock Ecfrith behind his back."

"If I must live in this heathen land, I might at least have that comfort—that I am not merely one of your peace weavers but a servant of God." This had to work! Scanlan assured her it would.

The leash snapped.

"Servant of *God?*" With a bellow, the beast leaped from his seat, overturning it behind him. Cynicism laced his reply. "My *mother* served her God well enough...*and* my father, too."

"She had no choice."

"Neither do you."

"For the Lord knows what He thinks—"

Deirdre willed down the rise of panic and exasperation undermining her task. Whatever God said, He meant it for her, even if Alric was bullying the exact words from her mind. God was with her, she told herself, leveling an affirmed gaze at the outraged incredulity flashing in his.

"You told me you would never harm me, that you never took a woman against her will. Did you lie, milord?"

"Not nearly as much as you have, milady," he sneered. "What manner of fool do you take me for?"

"One who wishes me to marry him when there is nothing to be gained from it." Daring to turn away, Deirdre washed her fingers in the laver and dried them on the napkin. Still clasping it, she rose in a leisurely fashion. "Even if Cairell is lost forever to Gleannmara, my hand is of no use to you regarding my father's kingdom. My people will not accept a Saxon king. One of my cousins will succeed him when the time comes."

She placed the linen back on the table, signaling the end of the evening's hospitality with forced control.

"It is not your *hand* that interests me, Lady Deirdre."

The insolent rake of his gaze down the length of her and back left a smoldering trail, despite the distance between them.

"Nonetheless, milord," she rallied, "that is all you will have...*if* you wish this marriage to take place."

Neither she nor Scanlan could guess Alric's reason for this mad course he'd set, though now he cast doubt on that. If it was not to be, she could only guess that ransom was the motive. She supposed her father would find the money to save at least one of his children. Cairell would be lost as his ransom was far higher than hers would be. And Gleannmara's coffers would be empty.

Love was out of the question as the prince's motive for wedlock, ambition ill founded, and desire unlikely. Given his good looks and money, he could have any female he wanted to satiate the baseness kindling in his gaze. Deirdre only prayed that the peculiar brand of honor he professed was real. Slavery or marriage—she might as well choose which hand she'd like severed, the right or the left.

"Now 'tis you who play false, Alric of Galstead. A man such as yourself would not enter marriage for physical satisfaction alone."

"What does the pious virgin know of a man like myself?"

Deirdre braced as he reached out and traced the curve of her neck, from the glittering *torque* to her chin. The senses at the nape of her neck tingled, awakening others behind the defenses she'd thought in place. Stepping closer, he cupped her chin and tilted her face. The predator had shed his princely skin and now smelled the blood catapulting through her veins and hammering at her throat. He would settle for nothing less than a kill.

"Much less of *physical* satisfaction." Alric's throaty seduction taunted places the hand could not, exacting tiny shudders that threatened to unravel mind, body and, heaven forgive her, soul.

"For I know the thoughts that I think toward you, saith the LORD, *thoughts of peace, and not of evil, to give you an expected end."*

Returning his bone-melting gaze with the steel of God's promise, Deirdre drew to her full height. "I know only what God will have me do," she replied steadily. "And that is plainly written for you to accept or reject. The decision is yours." Gathering her skirts in hand, she stepped around Alric. "I bid you good evening, milord."

Fully expecting the beast dwelling beyond her companion's civilized facade to leap upon her back at any moment, Deirdre walked out of the room and beneath the cover of the inner colonnade. She had to concentrate to place one foot in front of the other as she made her way back to the room, gaining speed with each step. By the time she was inside and slid the bolt into place, her heart seemed to pound against the back of her throat. Ear pressed to the plank door, she listened for any sign that Alric had followed her, but all she heard was the peaceful patter of the fountain.

Exactly how long she waited, frozen in the same spot, she had no idea, but her breathing had returned to normal and her pulse slowed to a cautious rate. She'd held her own against the Saxon's temper and his devilish seduction. A smile lighted on Deirdre's lips as she closed her eyes in prayer. "This unworthy but willing servant thanks You, Father!"

For the first time since her capture, she giggled outright, intoxicated not by the fruit of the heath but the fruit of faith. She prayed it would sustain her through the night ahead.

Christians and their miracles!

It was a notion such as this that had put Alric in this untenable position to start with. His course was as unpredictable as the *Wulfshead*'s had been that first night away from Erin's coast. The contract in his shirt burned like a fireball lodged in the hold of his ship, fueled by the frustration and fury of this battle of wills. How could someone so fragile one moment be so formidable the next?

A white burst of pain increased the blankness of Alric's wit as he broke off the low-hanging tree limb that assaulted him on the moonlit path to Aelfled's glen. Rending it in two over his knee, Alric found slight relief that it was not a certain princess's soft white neck. She dismissed him like some underling and then dared to lock him out of his own room. Yet, had he indulged in the luxury of breaking in the door, he might not have stopped there. He threw away the broken branch and plunged deeper into the trees, as though daring another to test his humor.

The exotic scent of Aelfled's incense wafted out to greet him before the wooded path to the glen widened at the ivy-draped entrance. Moonlight bathed the small cottage in an ethereal glow, almost as otherworldly as the laughter that haunted it. But it was the more masculine accompaniment that stopped Alric in his tracks. Aelfled had company.

The might of the realization struck a blow no less harsh than that which had taken Woden's eye. Oddly, the pain was not that of jealousy, for he had no more claim upon Aelfled than she on him, but more of disappointment. Where was his elfin beauty's premonition when he needed it most?

He swore, making his silent way around the edge of the clearing to the spring path in the back. Curse the Irish wench! She tossed this contract at him, making it clear that no power or monetary gain could be had in their marriage, not even conjugal bliss. And now, the fact that Aelfled was not available when he needed her made him feel as alone as the day Orlaith went to the other side.

Had he fooled himself? Allowed the promise of what he deemed illusion to distract him to the point of recklessness and indecision? What was the point in marriage at all?

Because you will not take a woman as a slave the way your mother was taken, a nagging voice reminded him. So why, he asked the voice, did he have to take the princess at all? Because of a prophecy he didn't believe in?

"Frig take it all—women *and* gold!" He swore, angry at Deirdre for plaguing him, at Aelfled for not being here for him, and at his father for leaving him such a legacy of guilt.

Without taking time to strip off his shirt and breeches, Alric waded into the healing waters of the shaded pool as though they were his last hope for relief. Since it wasn't expansive enough for him to work out his exasperation by swimming, Alric sought out the hot spring. Staring up at the starlit ceiling of the night, he rested upon a slab of rock just beneath the water's surface, alone in the mystical glen for the first time.

God, if that be Your name, or whatever power rules over man and earth, I need help, not the assurance of others, but from You, that I will know what I must do.

Shocked at the cry of his innermost being, Alric moved to where the water from the hill swirled with that of the hot spring. He lay back so that it flowed around his neck and over his shoulders. Resting his head on the rocky ledge, he listened. God had spoken to his mother. The water stones had spoken to Aelfled.

Would anyone speak to him?

A pair of night birds hailed each other. The breeze whispered in the canopy of the trees. The water babbled, but Alric heard no words of wisdom or condemnation. Nothing.

With a sigh, he closed his eyes. A panorama of memories began to play across his mind, pleasant and plentiful enough to keep him company and distract him from the quagmire of the present. Muscle by muscle, the healing waters worked their magic until he felt his muscles give up the burden his mind had piled upon them. The numbing effect lulled him into an almost druglike state of rest, just as a night of Aelfled's potions and bed had done, except that this was the result of neither drug nor a charmed mortal.

Had he been wrong when he'd insisted to his mother that he needed Aelfled's charms? He returned from one of his first sea battles, badly wounded. While Orlaith had seen to his wounds and prayed over him, his healing had not progressed as quickly as his impatience to recover. He ordered servants to help him to Aelfled, where the forest beauty saw him immersed in the healing spring daily. Improved, he returned to his mother to gloat over the superior powers of his elfinlike enchantress.

His mother's answer was as serene as the setting about him: "She was but the star who guided you to the healing well, muirnait. 'Twas God who placed the star in your path and created the waters."

And tonight, beloved, your star failed you, but He did not.

Alric's eyes flew open at the invasion of his mother's voice upon his recollection. The night was as still as the moon in the cloudless sky.

Frig's mercy, now the Irish vixen had driven him to hallucination.

"I thought I'd find you here."

Startled out of his skin by the velvet stroke of words behind him, Alric leaped to his feet.

The voice and the petite figure outlined by the moon belonged to his friend, not his mother. All was suddenly alive again, the water flow, the birdsong, the rustle of leaves. Had he fallen asleep?

"Aelfled," Alric managed, looking beyond her for her companion. Yes, he must have dreamed it. "Where is your…guest?"

"He left." Aelfled offered no more. Alric would not ask for it. "You wear your clothes?"

"Aye." His humor darkened at being the source of hers. "And if what I have been through these last few days is love, as you suggest, then it agrees no more with me than green apples and sour grapes."

Aelfled had the nerve to laugh, despite Alric's drilling glare.

"Spare me." He stepped out of the pond to make his way to where she stood. "I've no second sight, but I've seen things this night ominous enough to curl your nails like a crone's."

His companion sobered instantly. "Then you must tell me." Producing a towel from behind her back, she handed it to him.

Less than ready to give absolution, Alric left her to hold it while he stripped off his shirt and wrung it dry. As he repeated the same procedure with the balance of his clothes, he summarized the gist of what had happened since he'd left the glen—of Deirdre's miraculous rebound from her fevered delirium and of her marriage contract.

"And then she ate my ship," he finished, as he wrapped the dry towel around him in a huff. "Now tell me, what do you make of *that?*"

At Aelfled's uncommon silence, Alric looked at her, thinking the ramification even worse than he feared.

"Perhaps she was hungry?" A chuckle nearly strangled her suggestion.

Without a word, Alric picked up his wet clothes and left her to catch up with him…if she dared.

"Oh, Alric, wait!"

Too angry to share his other *revelation,* Alric ignored the plea, just as he did the water that shot out of his sodden footwear as he made his way along the path. His mother had been right about one thing at least. The worth of Aelfled's powers had been an illusion, nothing more.

"Alric of Galstead, you need a friend, not a seer. Now come to your senses and wait, or stew in your own juice alone."

Astonished at the size of voice coming from such a tiny figure, Alric stopped and turned to make certain it was indeed Aelfled who spoke. There she stood, hands fixed on practically nonexistent hips, her foot tapping with the same impatience that magnified her presence. It was rare that Aelfled resorted to threat, yet even then, she was charming.

Where would he go? Back to Deirdre, who twisted him in knots and wrung him out like he'd done his wet clothes? Frig spare him! Alric laughed shortly and extended the crook of his arm.

"Aye, I suppose a man can always use a friend…even if it is a halfling." Besides, no seaman worth his salt turned away from an offer of a star to guide him, be it hung by God or by fickle fate.

SIXTEEN

D eirdre awakened in a startled daze at the sound of Tor's excited bark, the panic subsiding as she realized it was morning. The night had passed without incident. Stunned, she threw aside the covers and padded across the floor to peer out into the courtyard. Aside from the diligent water nymph, there was no sign of activity; although the dog's barking was evidence that someone was up and about. The tantalizing scent of baking bread confirmed it.

Her stomach growled, but she ignored it, recalling that for the next three days until the Sabbath, she was to fast and pray regarding her marriage to Alric. Although the more she considered what had happened to her the day before, the more convinced she was that Scanlan was right, that it was God's will. Why she had to fast when she'd already agreed to the marriage in writing eluded her, but since she'd made such a bungle of things, Deirdre was inclined to rely more on Scanlan to interpret heaven's intent. Perhaps it would prepare her better for what lay ahead.

If Alric signed the contract, Father Scanlan would post the banns. To date her prayers had been answered, for the door and lock were still intact. Alric had not even tried to follow her, much less force his way into the room.

Stirred by the swirling hem of her gown, something moved at her feet and skittered across the cool tiled floor. The contract! Slowly, she knelt and picked up the parchment, rumpled as if Alric had literally slept on it. On the back was a pristine seal with the impression of a wolf's head in wax.

"Father, let his signature be on it," she whispered as she broke it open. That was what she wanted, wasn't it…to follow God's lead? *Yes.* She could do more as a prince's wife than as a slave.

The first thing that struck her as she opened it fully were the bold strokes that edited her delicate script. His was a clear, strong hand, more suited to a scholar than a warrior. Some sections of the proposal had been altered, others deleted altogether. The addendum at the bottom drew her immediate attention.

> *I place my signature upon this contract, as witnessed below by my oath helper—the shire's reeve—and as amended by my hand with the following pledge: That my contracted bride will be afforded the freedom of a lady of her noble station, both in my home and country, based upon her oath upon her Christian God; that she will make no effort to avoid honoring this agreement to its full extent as recorded above. With her signature, witnessed by Father Scanlan of the church, let our agents post the banns; that one month from now our lives as husband and wife will commence accordingly with the wedding at Lambert's court in Galstead.*
>
> *Alric, Prince of Galstead, Northumbria*

"'The freedom of a lady of her station,'" Deirdre whispered, as though to convince herself that it was really there, signed and witnessed for all to see.

Taking a deep breath, she perched on the edge of the bed to scrutinize the amendments. She was to have her bride-price as her own. Gleannmara's treasure was safe, praise God! Alric agreed to inquire as to the whereabouts of her brother for her; God was using the enemy to help her find Cairell. Why hadn't she listened to Scanlan before?

Father, thank—

Deirdre stopped in midthought as she saw the line struck through her proposal to publicly dedicate her virginity to the church. It had been replaced with another.

With trepidation, she read the new terms. Alric would privately honor her wish to remain a virgin wife for as long as it was her will, as he would allow her to practice her faith freely in his home, provided this was known only to the oath helpers assigned below—Scanlan and the reeve. Their silence was pledged by their signatures as well, except should they have to act on the behalf of an injured party.

Deirdre scowled as she read and reread the clause. It *appeared* fair, but this was the one term she was not at peace with…although Alric had kept his word thus far. She folded the parchment, reluctant to give into the exhilaration welling in her chest. Nay, she'd not celebrate with a free mind until Father Scanlan approved of every word.

A sharp knock on her door brought her up from the mattress with a quick intake of breath. But before she could answer it, Doda called out. "Good morning, milady. Will you take your breakfast in your room or shall I serve it in the salon?"

"Where is Alric taking his meal?" Deirdre tensed for the answer.

"He has been away all night, milady, and not yet returned. I cannot speak for him."

Her shoulders dropped with relief. "Thank you, Doda, but I will not be having breakfast. I'll be going out as soon as I'm dressed."

"Do you need help?"

The servant didn't even question her. Alric must have sent a message to his staff advising them of her new freedom. Thrilled, Deirdre rushed over to the door and unbolted it.

"That would be lovely, Doda. Thank you for offering."

Before Deirdre knew what she was about, Doda embraced her warmly and gave her a loud buss on the cheek. "You are going to marry the prince, no?"

"Possibly…" How much more of their agreement had Alric shared with the steward and his wife? "I would go to the chapel and discuss our contract with Father Scanlan."

"But you should eat—"

"I fast, Doda. By fasting and prayer, God shall confirm that I have made the right decision."

"Orlaith fasted," Doda observed, not entirely put off by the idea but clearly not impressed either. "I sometimes believe it made her weak."

"My mother was not as pious as my bride to be."

Deirdre didn't need to look to know who'd joined the conversation. Ignoring Alric as he strode in through the open door, she took the housemistress's hand between hers and gave it a squeeze. "You see, I must be certain that this is the man with whom I'd spend the rest of my life. Surely you, as a woman, understand the importance of being certain."

"But I already *am*," Doda assured her with a wide grin. "And so will you be pretty soon."

"Nonetheless, I will go to the chapel daily and fast to be certain."

"And I shall accompany you for the same reason," Alric announced, dropping down onto the bench at the end of the bed. "To be *certain*." With a grunt of effort, he pulled off one of his boots.

Doda looked from the prince to Deirdre and back to her master again. "But it is not fit that you should share this room with your bride to be, milord."

"I did so the night before," he pointed out, tugging at the other boot.

"Then she was your slave." Deirdre started at the housekeeper's boldness. "I do not think your mama would approve of this."

"I don't think my *father* would approve of your meddling." Alric rose and kicked his boots beneath the bench. "But I'm in such a good mood, I will humor the two of you."

After digging through a trunk and retrieving fresh clothes, he made a sweeping bow before Doda. Then, brandishing a roguish grin, he approached Deirdre and slipped his arm behind her before she had the chance to slip away.

She stiffened as he pulled her against him, those disarming lips worked their magic without even touching her own. "Ah, milady," he said, nuzzling the tip of her nose with his. "I shall await your readiness with most hearty anticipation."

Wary, Deirdre dug her toes into the cool tile under her feet. How did the saying go? Beware the hoof of a horse, the horn of a bull, and the smile of a Saxon?

"Well, the longer you stay, milord, the longer you'll have to wait." Doda snorted, oblivious to the skillfully disguised threat behind his adoring declaration.

The twin edge of Alric's parrying words was not, however, lost to Deirdre. The caress of his fingers through the linen of her night shift;

the warm prison of his arm—strong enough to protect her or break her in half; the rising temperature of the mercurial pool of his eyes told her that Alric of Galstead was not speaking of today, or tomorrow, but of a time no less inevitable.

An hour later, Deirdre stepped out onto the seaport's dry, rutted street on the arm of her pirate captor and soon-to-be husband. Alric was well known in the town and obviously as well liked. At every corner, someone stopped to engage him in conversation. Men and women alike eyed Deirdre with outright curiosity. The story of Alric's plucking her from the slave compound only increased their intrigue and disdain. Deirdre endured their bad manners with a sweet smile, even though she understood every remark they made. Men not in the company of their wives made lewd suggestions as to Alric's motivation, while the women could not possibly understand why the prince didn't choose a buxom Saxon bride.

Deirdre almost hoped he might reveal his true reason, but instead, he cordially put most of them in their places regarding his business being his own and needing no explanation to anyone. He even steered the conversation toward Latin for her sake, but the little said directly to her was stiff with condescension.

The smells met them before they turned into the square, where vendors hawked everything from produce to livestock to freshly prepared foods for the visitors. The scent of roasted sausages and meat pies blended with that of the rounds of cheeses and baked breads on display.

"I think I'll have one of those pies. Hilda makes the best in the market," Alric said, pointing to a short, round-figured woman carrying a tray of pure temptation resting against her aproned belly. "Will you have one?"

Deirdre shook her head, grateful that the general noise drowned out the rumbling protest of her stomach.

"Ah, I forgot. You will fill your belly with the Holy Spirit until Sunday." Switching to Saxon, he asked the jovial lady for two of her meat pies.

"Only two?" Hilda asked, glancing at Deirdre. "What about your lady?"

"I tried to tempt her, but she declined."

"A voman shouldn't have no sharp edges, derling."

"She said a woman shouldn't have sharp edges," Alric translated. "And she's not even heard that well-hewn tongue of yours," he added with a chuckle as he handed over a coin in exchange for the pies. "Thank you, Hilda, but you will never make enough pies to take the edge off my companion's disposition."

Hilda looked at Deirdre and burst into laughter. "*Ja, ja,* you enjoy now."

"Oh, I will; I'm sure of it."

Quite smug in his conviction that Deirdre had no clue what he'd said, Alric bit into the sealed crust envelope. Eyes growing round in alarm, he tried to breathe in air to cool the hot mouthful without choking.

There was justice, Deirdre thought, responding with a genuine smile this time. "Milord enjoys it overmuch, I think." His answering scowl had no edge to it at all, diluted as it was with the water streaming from his eyes. She couldn't help but giggle, appeased that his discomfort made her own easier to bear.

"I could have choked, you know," Alric grumbled, when the food in his mouth was cool enough to swallow. "Then what would you have done?"

"I'd have been free." Deirdre heaved a dreamy sigh and walked slightly ahead of him to where a dog, clad in shirt and breeches like a little boy, sat. She glanced back at her disgruntled escort with an impish twinkle in her eye. "Or at least had the pleasure of beating it out of you."

Adding insult to injury, she pinched off a piece of Alric's pie, and, after cooling it with her lips, she gave it to the animal, cooing, "Even you know not to bite off more than you can chew, don't you, little—"

Suddenly, Deirdre stumbled as she was blindsided by a running figure. Grabbing for Alric, she barely escaped being knocked against the dog and its owner. A young girl dropped to her knees behind them, where a handful of stones she'd apparently been carrying had scattered. Her wild, raven hair spilled over her small shoulders as she dug in the loose dirt trying to retrieve them.

"Here, let me help you." Holding her skirts to the side, Deirdre stooped down to pick the smooth-marked pebbles up. They were tokens of some kind, perhaps part of a game.

"I'm sorry, milady. I was running," the girl babbled, struggling to toss her wild tresses behind her shoulders.

"It's all right, I—"

The girl's hand shot out, seizing Deirdre's wrist. "No, that's enough," she declared sharply, reaching for those Deirdre had already collected. As quickly, her tone softened again. "Thank you, milady. I can get the rest."

"Best watch your step, milady," Alric sternly advised, taking her arm with his free hand and ushering her away as though the market were afire.

"It was just an accident," Deirdre protested, looking back as the strange little girl straightened and realizing that it wasn't a child but a petite woman with eyes dark as her hair. She met Deirdre's stare with brazen curiosity, although the princess sensed none of the hostility or disdain she'd experienced with some of the other Saxon women.

Alric tightened his grip on her arm and stepped up his pace.

"The chapel is on the next street over."

A smile lit up the enigmatic woman's face, as though she'd seen something that pleased her. At the same moment, Deirdre stumbled over the raised root of a sprawling oak. By the time she recovered and looked back again, only the dog and its owner were still there. The woman was nowhere to be found.

"That's the Water Gate," Alric informed her, pointing ahead to the entrance from the harbor through the thick city wall. "The Romans built the wall to keep the *Irish* pirates at bay."

"Irish what?" Deirdre asked, still distracted by the encounter.

"Pirates," he repeated. "You know, like me."

The mischief in his eyes was utterly charming. It was a shame he'd opened his mouth and spoiled the effect. "But unlike you, *we've* become civilized in the last two or three centuries."

"War is not civilized, no matter how advanced the civilizations are that wage it."

Unable to refute his point, Deirdre marveled at the myriad of people who meandered in and out of the city. From heavy leather and fur to bright silks and wools, the costumes were as varied as the accents and languages echoing around. More amazing, she understood three of them perfectly—her native Irish, her scholarly Latin, and Alric's Saxon. It was as exciting as it was overwhelming.

"On the yon side of the wall is where clay pipe was made and exported for the Roman engineers," Alric said, pointing north. "There is still a large store of it, buried in overgrowth. As a boy, I'd tunnel through the larger ones. It was a great kingdom of caves."

What had launched Alric into this uncommon talkative state was beyond Deirdre, but it piqued her interest. "Is the bridge I saw down-river from the harbor a Roman one?"

"The stone foundation is. It's been built and rebuilt. We'll cross it when we leave for Galstead on Monday."

"Monday?" Deirdre stopped short and waited while Alric finished the first of his now tolerably cooled pies. At least the steamy scent no longer taunted her nose and stomach.

"We need to plan the wedding so that once the waiting period for the banns is met, we can get on with it," he explained. "Then I must return to the sea to make the most of the good weather."

"And where will I go?" She'd had enough of the sea for a lifetime after those storms.

"You'll remain with my family, like a good Saxon sailor's wife, until I secure some land and build a proper home."

"You mean *conquer?*"

"I mean *purchase*…at least for the time being," he added mischievously. "So long as our neighbors remain allies and our enemies respect our boundaries, I've no desire to start another war. The one we wage against the Scots and the Picts is—"

"And the Irish," Deirdre reminded him.

Alric stopped short. "No, I do not make war against the Irish, only on ships bound for my enemies' coastline with supplies for them to wage war against Northumbria. No Irish ship bound southward of the Scottish coastline has ever been molested by my hand." That settled, at least to his satisfaction, he retrieved the other pie from the bag at his waist and took a bite.

"You made the mistake of traveling on one of those bound for Argyll." He brushed the light flakes of crust from his mouth. "An innocent victim of war."

"Like the priests and nuns attacked and slaughtered by your king on our own coast?"

All trace of Alric's earlier lightheartedness vanished with the mention of Ecfrith's raid. "Northumbria's king made a grave mistake, milady. Not all of his thanes agree with his cause against the Celtic church. Many of them were saved, even tutored by men like Cuthbert and Wilfred…at least on the surface. I make no claim to a holy cause. I admit that I am a warrior who profits from war in the name of politics and greed, not under the guise of God's will."

Red hot fingers of guilt crept up Deirdre's neck to her face. Was he talking about the bretwalda or her? But she *was* following God's will. Wasn't she doing what Scanlan instructed?

"Not that there are not sincere Christians. My mother was one, for all the good it did her."

"So you believe there are those of us earnest in our faith." This was somewhat reassuring. If only her faith in herself was as strong as her faith in God.

"Aye, some…" His gaze lingered, seeming to search her own for something. He still didn't believe in her. Well, how could she blame him when she doubted herself. *Father, I need Your help. I can't do this on my own.*

Alric looked away, pointing to a small hovel of stone in a row of poorly maintained dwellings. "There, milady, is my mother's chapel. Lambert allowed a missionary from Lindisfarne to establish it here for Orlaith and Christian merchants and travelers. It's the only one in all of Galstead."

Wedged against the thick city wall, the corbeled stone dwelling looked out of place next to the two-story, timber-framed rowhouses and the A-framed shacks of the poor. Standing in front of the low entrance of the beehive structure, Father Scanlan and an older priest were engaged in a lively conversation with a pair of men.

Deirdre watched the priest infect his listeners with his enthusiasm and knew that, no matter what Scanlan told her, she was not the only one with a gift. Alric's comment flashed through her mind: *"The only one in all of Galstead."* Something told her that was soon to change, and she'd been chosen to somehow play a part in it.

Alric finished his breakfast and licked the remainder of the pie off his fingers.

"That was the best batch Hilda ever made." He clearly took no sly delight in his belief that she was hungry and caught in a trap of her own making. "She grinds a mixture of venison, rabbit, and goose, with a hint of honey...and her crust almost melts in your mouth."

"You mean melts your mouth, don't you?"

His conciliatory grin was enough to melt far more, but it was mostly lost to Deirdre. Her hunger was gone! The gnawing in her stomach, which had tempted her to wrestle Alric for that first pie, had been sated, not with nourishment of flesh or land but of the *spirit*. As her hunger had vanished, so did Deirdre's doubt. Though she knew not the nature of it, God indeed had a plan—and if it was His, *it was good*.

Scanlan called out to her. "Lady Deirdre, you are looking most well this day."

She knew an inner radiance fit to rival that of the sun, whether it showed or nay. "I am *good*, Father," she told him in a voice that reflected the brightness. "I truly am."

SEVENTEEN

The improvised livestock cart carrying Deirdre and Father Scanlan stirred dust on the well-traveled road leading from the port of Chesreton to Galstead's royal court. Deirdre wished, not for the first time, that Alric's mother's transport was not disabled. Walking would be preferable. The grit invaded her mouth and covered her cloak as she clung to the rails and was jounced like sheep being carried to slaughter.

Under her bench was the treasure chest Alric had filled and returned to her according to their contract. Missing was Kieran's sword. Alric had cleverly deleted her list and replaced it with one of his own, omitting that detail. In her excitement that she was getting back the treasure, she'd not detected it and, if Scanlan had, he hadn't mentioned it. That morning when she noticed Alric wearing the sword, Scanlan tried to placate her, saying that it wasn't essential to their mission.

But it was to hers, Deirdre thought, staring at the jewels glistening on its scabbard as the prize hung from Alric's waist. It was part of her heritage, and the Saxon had tricked her out of it. She should have caught the ploy, but he had stood with a possessive arm about her as she penned her name to the document.

She was lucky not to have scattered the ink in the quill in her nervous scrawl.

The peacock wore Kieran's sword like a ribbon of honor for his triumph, although she had to admit it was a fitting addition to his princely procession. His stallion was a magnificent steed, reminding Deirdre of those bred on Gleannmara since King Rowan introduced the first pair two hundred years ago. The black and silver trappings on the tack showed well against the horse's glossy butternut coat and matched its dark mane and tail. Trotting happily at its heels, Tor seemed uncaring of the dust cast on his already gray coat by Alric and Gunnar. The rest of his men rode behind the wagon, all armed and ready for a possible attack.

Next to her, Scanlan handled the reins of the cart horse and sang hymns to his heart's content in both Latin and Saxon. His was a booming, clear voice that carried as if on the wind. It ran in the family, according to his uncle. He referred to the Abbess Leila, whose voice had been taken and then given back to her that all might know the glory of God. Deirdre wondered that Scanlan's mouth didn't fill with the grit of the road till he couldn't sing at all. Taking up a small skin of ale, she washed her mouth out and then handed the skin to the priest.

"Bless you, milady." He helped himself to a swig, then, with a wink, handed it back to her. "Thank God that Galstead is only a day's ride. Still, have you ever seen such a peaceful day?"

"Peaceful? We're being hauled like livestock into the heathen lair."

"Ah, Deirdre, feel the embrace of the sun. Hear the birdsong. Peace does not come with the absence of trial but with the presence of God."

Deirdre forced a smile and stowed the refreshment away, wondering how her companion managed to find particles of hope in this heap of despair. Where Scanlan saw beauty, she looked at the backside of her captors' horse and choked on the dust they kicked up. And while Galstead's court was only a day's ride, what awaited them there was another matter. The first part of the marriage was complete, once Lambert approved it as fulfilled. The second half, the ceremonial giving of the bride and celebration, remained to be planned.

Meanwhile, she rode to her destiny in a livestock cart, like an animal—a possession, not a bride. And certainly not a princess. Surely, if his mother's tranport had been damaged, Alric could have found a steed for his bride to be if he'd wanted. His men, most of them seamen, had mounts.

Father, I don't want to seem ungrateful, but given all the humiliation this man has heaped upon me, I would have him pay dearly. Surely that is not too much to ask? And if it is, then surely I am not fit for this purpose Scanlan proposes. I'm willing, mind You, Father, but just feel inadequate—

The wood-planked wheel of the cart struck a stone, suddenly lifting Deirdre's side up in the air. Just as fast, it slammed down again, jarring her teeth with the impact on the hard road.

"Brigid's fire!" she gasped, all thought of prayer shattered.

Alric turned at her oath to see the nature of her distress. Discerning no real threat, he broke into a grin. "Is there something I might do to make milady more comfortable?"

"Aye, you can give me the luxury of your horse."

"He's mighty spirited."

"So am I."

"Fortunately, the journey is not a long one," Alric observed with seeming indifference.

Deirdre bit her tongue to keep from giving him a piece of her mind. But his time would come, she resolved, brandishing a honey-sweet smile in return. Not even Scanlan's low "tut-tut" could dampen the pleasure she found at the prospect.

The noonday meal was taken in the shade of the green wood, beneath the spreading branches of majestic oak and yew, with a spotting here and there of evergreen conifers. Glad to be done with her fast, Deirdre ate with relish, ignoring echoes of her mother's cautions against having an unladylike appetite.

Scanlan had been her earthly mainstay during the last three days without food while God managed her spiritual support. A fast did bring one spiritually closer to God, if for no other reason than praying that He keep the hounds of hunger at bay—and prevent her from choking Alric as he helped himself to all manner of tasties in front of her. The scoundrel had even fed the treats to Tor!

"Are you ready to make way, milady?" Alric asked, approaching from a short distance away where his men had eaten.

Deirdre made a face but nodded. Her backside felt as if it had been flayed with the oak bench instead of sitting on it. Tor nuzzled her hand as she approached the cart, no doubt in hopes she had more tasty morsels. To think this overgrown pup had frightened her so that first night was almost laughable.

Deirdre lifted her russet skirts, resigned to climbing into the back of the vehicle, when Alric stopped her. "Sir Dustan awaits." He pointed to where the stallion pawed impatiently. An extra blanket had been added for her comfort. "You wished to ride my horse."

She struggled to unknot her tongue. There was surely something amiss, given that treacherous Saxon smile of his. It infected his men as well, but not until he'd lifted her onto Dustan's back was its nature clear. With a single bound, he leaped up behind her and, circling her waist with his arms, gathered the reins.

"This is *not* what I meant, and well you know it. Would that *your* bottom be flattened by a bouncing oak plank."

Alric laughed, and the vibration of it against her back was far more distracting than a lifeless board. "Milady, I speak with the authority of a scholar, having studied the very matter whilst you wandered to and fro along yon stream. You have my word that such sore fate has not fallen upon your person."

"But *sore,* nonetheless, milord, for I speak on the authority of experience," she averred quickly. Too quickly, for the sniggers Alric's remark evoked gave way to raucous huzzahs, all at her expense.

Brigid's fire! Her thought kindled instantly, spreading like the real thing upon her face and neck. Hot and fueled as she was by her humiliation—and by the distracting presence of Alric's body against and around her—there should at least have been smoke.

"I must say, you make a striking couple." Gunnar's brown eyes danced with ill-suppressed delight. "Such fire you kindle between you."

Deirdre looked at him, aghast that her thoughts were so transparent.

"Careful, lest you feel the scorch, friend," Alric warned. Whether he bantered in good humor or nay, the threat glanced off Gunnar's wide shoulders without effect.

As the cart squeaked into action behind them, Scanlan broke from the traditional hymns in favor of an old bardic tune expounding on the omnipotent power of love.

"Frig save us from a priest playing the romantic buffoon," Alric muttered. Were it not a sacrilege, Deirdre would have chimed in with a hearty amen.

Oh, heavenly Father, help! I cannot feel the least bit holy with Alric so close. Indeed, she wasn't the least bit sure this man and the word *holy* should even be in the same prayer.

By late afternoon, the enveloping shade of the forest gave way to the gentle rise of sun-blanched fields and heathered meadows laid off in long rectangles divided by low stone walls or hedges. Beyond lay a yellow and stone backdrop of gorse-splashed hills rising toward the skyline. The farmsteads boasted humble A-framed dwellings and, occasionally, separate structures to shelter the livestock. Now and then the ruins of a villa or the more familiar corbeled stone huts, left behind by the displaced Britons and now taken over by their Saxon conquerors, appeared.

Unfamiliar to Deirdre was the parched look of the land. What wasn't yellowed was a sickly green bled by the sun. She had heard of the drought during her pilgrimages to the Water Gate Church during her prayer fast and now understood why the people in Chesreton spoke of nothing else.

The field workers lacked the friendly zeal of Gleannmara's people, as though the sun had bled them, too, of life. Either that, or they were an unfriendly lot…or perhaps they simply had nothing to offer in hospitality. The idea would have been unthinkable at Gleannmara.

These men and women toiled with lackluster indifference to the travelers until Alric was recognized. Only then did they stop what they were doing and wave, inviting him to join them for refreshment. In a hurry to reach Galstead by nightfall, the prince graciously declined, but the story the people approached to share with him during his polite stop was always the same. If their gardens and corn crop did not survive, they and their livestock would starve come winter. Only those whose hides of land lay along the riverbank expressed any hope.

"My wife lost the child she was carryin' tryin' to tote water to her garden, so that we could feed the rest of the babes. I'm thinkin' the old gods were kinder to us," one farmer complained. Dressed in rags and covered with the dirt and sweat from his labor behind the ox-pulled plow, he was a study of hopelessness and anger. He cast an accusing look at Scanlan and repeated his sentiment in tattered Latin for the priest's benefit. "We could protect ourselves from invadin' enemy, but not this. Never were our fields suffering for lack of water."

"It is when we are weakest that God Almighty is strongest," Scanlan replied. "But I shall pray on your behalf and suggest that you do so as well."

"I'm not much at this prayin'. That's best left to you priests. You speak your God's language better."

"God created the languages as well as the men who speak them, sir." Scanlan turned to Alric. "Milord, would you allow me some time to—"

"If this man has a mind to pray, I welcome him come to Galstead to learn how. You can teach him there." With that, Alric gave Dustan a nudge, starting the procession forward again.

"Wait!" Deirdre drew back on the stallion's reins, halting it. Hastily she took off the golden cross from her neck. "Sometimes we need to feel something that reminds us of God and how present He is with us, even though we can't see or hear Him." She cast an apologetic look at Scanlan. "I know it helps me sometimes, even though it isn't really necessary for Him to hear me and answer my prayers." She held it out to the farmer. "Just hold on to this and share your troubles with Him as you would your closest friend, because that is what He wants to be."

Skepticism furrowing his dirt-and-sweat-smeared brow like the plow he'd been working, the man hesitated, glancing at Alric.

"Go on, it's the lady's to give," Alric assured him. He tightened his grip about Deirdre's waist as she leaned down to bestow the token.

"Milady is generous," the man mumbled, backing away from Dustan, his head down.

"Come see our priest at Galstead and learn how God is even more so," Deirdre invited. She'd never championed God in such a manner before. While a believer, she preferred to debate the essence of the Word and His nature. The resulting sense of reward seemed to glow within like the filigree chain dangling from the peasant's callused hand—pure, without the tarnish of recrimination or second thought. "Better yet, come to our wedding and bring your family. Milord will set a table bountiful enough to fill our bellies, while Father Scanlan fills our souls."

The man nodded and waved, still avoiding her gaze. It wasn't until

Dustan led the party forward again that she realized the man had been too overwhelmed to speak. She'd given things away before, but somehow it had never felt like this.

"I couldn't have said it as well, Princess," Scanlan called out to her as she rested without thought against Alric.

"What possessed you to give away your jewelry?" Alric whispered in her ear, his lips not touching her yet still evoking a tingling sensation.

Was that mockery or wonder she heard? Regardless, her thoughts scrambled, unable to settle on the answer. Indeed, all she knew was that it had been a good thing, at least for her and hopefully for that wretched soul with hope-shallow eyes. "God led me to do it. Does that bother you?"

"No, milady. I saw my mother give away half the gifts Lambert bestowed upon her. It seemed to give her pleasure."

"If someone saved your life one day and on another you saw the opportunity to come to the aid of His Son, wouldn't you do so?" Deirdre could sense her companion's wariness in the way he stiffened behind her.

"Were it in my power."

"God saved me, and I have tried to help one of His children."

"Ah, *that.*" Alric had obviously heard the message before. "Well, if the prayer doesn't work, the jewelry will purchase him some food, I suppose."

Instead of anger, she felt as sorry for the heathen as she had for the discouraged farmer. While she'd always championed the downtrodden, this felt different. After all, Alric and his people were her enemy, her captors...

Lost in her own thoughts, she left Alric to his, riding on without really seeing the passing farmsteads and common pastures until they crossed a planked bridge over a dry, overgrown ditch between some properties. After they'd crossed two more like it, she inquired as to their purpose, aside from a division in the land.

"It's left from the Roman legion that used to be stationed here years before. There is a network of them branching out from the outpost at Galstead. Maybe for defensive purposes," Alric suggested.

"Or irrigation," Deirdre said. "You know, like the Egyptians used."

"The nearby creek is no Nile," Gunnar scoffed.

"But it's continuously fed from somewhere. If it could be channeled into the ditches, there would be that much more hope for the crops."

"For the Egyptians, drought was the normal circumstance," Gunnar replied.

"Yes, but this is not ordinary for Galstead. I have never seen it so dry." Alric looked about them.

"Besides," Gunnar pointed out, "by the time we clear the ditches of the brush and fill that has washed in them, the rain will have returned. Left alone, they'll make fine hedgerows."

"You may not have seen such a drought as this, but I'll wager the men who dug these ditches have. Nature works in cycles." Surely, Deirdre thought, everyone knew that. "Clearing and digging a series of ditches with dams for when the water is not needed would be a practical solution. Perhaps one of the mills on the running water might be modified with buckets to fill them."

"Hah, she speaks like an engineer!" Gunnar grinned at Alric. "What manner of female are you marrying?"

"One who will never allow me to waste away with boredom, of that I'm certain."

"Surely you've mills here." Deirdre wished she could see Alric's face. "And think, if this land is sufficient to produce clay for piping, why—"

She broke off at the sharp, silencing raise of Alric's hand. With the other on the reins, he stopped Dustan. Gunnar reined in his own steed. Deirdre looked at the crossroad beyond and below the hill they'd just breeched, where a number of armed soldiers surrounded what appeared to be a funeral procession. A following of peasants escorted a two-wheeled farm cart bearing a wooden coffin draped in a pall. Angry voices rose from where men waved their arms at the troops, who apparently harassed them, while two women and a child held back behind the vehicle.

"Bandits?" Deirdre whispered.

"Hardly." Gunnar snorted. "Isn't that Hinderk's banner?"

"Aye, but what is the bretwalda's horse thane doing here instead of up at the wall with Ecfrith?" Alric said.

Gunnar tilted his head. "Collecting tribute?"

"'Tis bad enough to tax the living, but the dead?" Alric put his hands at Deirdre's waist. "Your place is here, milady."

With that he lifted her from her seat and dropped her on her feet next to the horse. Just as startled as Deirdre, Dustan sidestepped and snorted. Tossing the extra cushion after her, the prince gained control of the animal as he slid forward onto the saddle. In a flash, his scramasax was drawn. The others followed suit.

"Ready, friend?" he asked Gunnar, rising in the saddle to address the men behind them. "You will proceed cautiously with the lady. If there is any sign of trouble, take her to Galstead."

Without waiting for acknowledgment, the prince gave Dustan a hearty prod and started down toward the crossroad at full gallop, Gunnar less than a length behind him. With a loud bark, Tor covered their flank.

The men left behind closed in around the wagon as efficiently as they'd manned the ship—proficient warriors on land or sea. One could not help but admire the cohesion and discipline their leader inspired in them. Just from the way they spoke and looked at Alric, it was clear they'd follow him to their deaths, not out of fear but out of loyalty and respect.

"If nothing else, we can praise the Almighty that our journey has not been a boring one." Scanlan seemed unconcerned that battle might erupt at any moment.

Taking his offered hand, Deirdre climbed up on the wagon seat again. "How can you be so calm at the prospect of bloodshed?" In truth her pulse pounded with an excitement as shameful as the priest's lack of concern.

"God is in charge, milady," Scanlan reminded her as she strained to look through the protective barrier of horseflesh at what transpired below them.

EIGHTEEN

Father Scanlan's saintly focus robbed Deirdre of her former feeling of benevolent obedience. It wasn't as if she wanted to see another bloodbath like that on the *Mell*. Like any red-blooded Irishman, though, combat in games and sport stirred her like nothing else. She loved the whistle and percussion of the sword song to a breath-for-breath cadence. With his animal-like grace, Alric undoubtedly would present a fine spectacle of skill, no matter his spiritual deficiency.

Whatever the armed party was below, the leader rode out ahead of his standard bearers to greet Alric with the friendly wave of a hand once the prince hailed him and identified himself, so her quandary was moot. "The prince should have a standard made," she remarked to Scanlan.

"His standard is a sail, milady," one of the guards informed her, "belonging only to the wind."

And his kingdom the sea, Deirdre recalled. It was hard to imagine never having a place where she felt at home—a concept she'd find unbearable. No matter where she was forced to live, her home would always be Gleannmara. Mist and glen, forest and fall, mountainside and sea sand—she would always be its daughter.

Below, Alric signaled his men to join them. On a downhill slope, Deirdre's party made good time while Alric, Gunnar, and the thick-bodied leader of the troops continued to speak to one of the mourners—a scrawny, yellow-haired man in a ragged shirt and trousers. The rest were gathered around the cart bearing the coffin, as though to protect it. From what?

She watched as two of the armed troopers dismounted. Handing their painted shields to companions, they approached the wagon.

"I'd last heard that you were with the bretwalda in the north, Hinderk," Alric said to the commander.

While thicker than Alric at the waist, Hinderk was undoubtedly as hard as the prince beneath his leather tunic and armor. Like good horses, some men were built for the race, others for endurance. His armor and his long, brown hair spoke not just of command but of affluence.

He shoved a polished helmet back off his forehead, wiping perspiration away with the back of his hand. "The death rate from Saltersford has been uncommonly high. I've been sent to investigate."

"Since when has it been against the law to die?" The low, wolflike rumble still raised the hair on Deirdre's arms. Conflict didn't seem out of the question yet. "Or do you seek to take over my father's duties as king of Galstead? I believe it is up to his aldermen to collect tribute from his people for the bretwalda." Alric clearly was not pleased at this infraction on Lambert's rights. His hand rested on the hilt of his scramasax, ready to either sheath or use it.

"It isn't against the law to die," Hinderk answered. "But if the corpse is packed in salt, there is a tax due. Considering the drop in revenues from Galstead, Ecfrith asked me to investigate."

"Investigate Lambert?" Alric's bellow made Deirdre flinch. "You dare—"

"I dare nothing more than to look for something your *loyal* father may have overlooked."

On the edge of her seat, Deirdre glanced around anxiously. Hinderk's men numbered the same as Alric's. Whether they were as seasoned as the prince's warriors remained to be seen.

"Well, milord?" The mourner who'd been speaking for the rest looked anxiously at the prince. "Will ye have him disturb my cousin in his own grave box?"

"I'm sorry, Dak, but let the king's thane see the man so that you and your good family might see him properly buried before sundown."

"But—"

The prince cut the churl off. "Unless you've something to hide in there? I'd hope my father's salters have more respect for the law than to embarrass him by resorting to such a morbid charade."

"And our bretwalda as well," the armed leader added.

"Your loyalty to Northumbria would do you honor, Hinderk, were it not for that Mercian in your ranks." Gunnar glared at one of the men beside the banner carriers. Clearly Alric knew the bearer, for the man looked no different than the others to Deirdre.

"Your queen is a Mercian," Hinderk reminded Alric's friend smoothly. "Besides, he is an envoy to Ecfrith's court, sent on behalf of our neighbors. He has a proposition that is of interest to all Saxon shires bordering Welsh land."

Whatever Gunnar had been about to say, the loud thud of the coffin lid against the side of the cart as it broke loose headed it off. The two guards reached inside and scooped out handfuls of gray-white crystals and allowed it to pour back into the box between their fingers.

"By cracky, milords, the salt's done eat up the body," one of them derided.

"Not a bone left of the dear departed," the other said, digging through the salt.

Alric looked down at the salter, his expression grave. "This was a foolish thing, friend."

Dak lowered his head while the others drew together in a knot.

"What would ye have us do?" one of the women cried out. "All we wanted was to put aside a little to buy food for the winter. The fields about us are gone already."

"What is it the Christians say? Ashes to ashes and dust to *salt?*" Hinderk's derisive laugh fell off abruptly. "Arrest the lot of them."

"Hold a moment!" Alric gigged Dustan forward with his heels, blocking Hinderk's men. Gunnar joined him. The *Wulfshead's* crew tightened the circle around Deirdre's cart.

"You dare defend them?" Hinderk's glare spoke volumes.

"Nay, but they are men of Galstead, and I will arrest them in the name of King Lambert," Alric declared. "He is the authority here, not you or your men. Let our king decide their punishment."

Neither of the Saxon lords were the sort to back down. Alric sat upon Dustan cool as a statue, but the kindling in his eyes betrayed his readiness to fight. Like the motionless scramasax he held, cool did not mean less deadly. Hinderk bristled before the prince's look, but Deirdre sensed his experience and discipline held the anger flaring from his nostrils in check.

Even the soft breeze, which had made the sun's heat bearable, seemed to hold its breath as the silent battle of wills continued.

The commander finally gave in. "Let this would-be king have his knaves," he said, with a slow-spreading warp of a smile. "Besides—" he selected a more subtle weapon from his arsenal—"it wouldn't do to make him appear more of a fool than he already has to his bride to be." Hinderk shifted in his saddle and looked straight at Deirdre. "Milady, I would be honored to offer you my steed, since we are all bound for Lambert's court."

The blow landed at the weakest link in Alric's armor. The prince leaned forward, resting his weapon across his lap. His manner suggested a leisurely exchange of words, but his voice was lethal. "She'll ride with you over my dead body, Hinderk."

Deirdre had no doubt that Alric meant it.

Hinderk recognized it as well. He feigned being wounded, hand clutching his chest, and let the beast out of its corner rather than tangle with it. "I would ride with one of my men, milord."

Deirdre brightened at the prospect to save her backside and put a thorn in Alric's for subjecting her to her misery. "So there *are* gentlemen among you." Not that she believed it for a moment. She considered one as bad as the other, but Alric needn't know that.

"If your definition of *gentlemen* include those who raided Ireland with Ecfrith."

Deirdre staggered under the weight of the revelation. Alric might as well have smitten her across the chest with the flat of his blade, for the wind left her lungs and blood congealed in her still-struck heart. This was one of the murderers, the bloodletters who'd raped the monasteries along the coast and left a trail of mutilation and bodies in their wake? Nay, she wanted nothing of this man, save one thing—his blood.

Above the beating drums of her rising indignation, Scanlan tossed another fagot into the fire, knocking it down with one word. "Cairell."

Cairell! If she was this close to one of the blackguards, then Deirdre was close to finding her brother. God *was* in charge. Mastering her spontaneous lust for the bearded leader's blood with newfound hope, she lifted an imperious chin. "I am Princess Deirdre of Gleannmara. But then, I imagine you've heard of our fair land."

Was Hinderk the name of the Saxon who sent the ransom letter to the Northumbrian monastery where Gleannmara was to have sent the ransom? She didn't know, or even if Cairell's captor had been mentioned specifically.

The dark-haired Saxon snorted after a moment's contemplation. "No, milady, but if I had, rest assured that I'd not have let Alric claim you first."

She had learned one thing if nothing else since her capture: All Saxons were not alike. Alric was a prince among men, and, despite her annoyance with him, he grew more so in her estimation all the while. Deirdre focused on her mission. "Surely, you've heard of my brother, Prince Cairell, heir to Gleannmara's throne."

Hinderk scowled, apparently nonplussed. "No, I never heard of him. But then we didn't go there to socialize." His men joined him in mocking laughter. "We took gold and some peach-faced scholars, who fancied themselves warriors. Like as not, those fair lads are on their way to Rome for the sport of some—"

"How *dare* you—!"

Scanlan caught her by the arm, stopping her. "Milady, I am certain Lord Hinderk means no affront to you directly. What is done is done. Our purpose is to forgive."

In no humor for priestly serenity or conscience, Deirdre continued to glare at Hinderk.

The thane brought his horse about, looking past her at Scanlan, as if noticing the young man for the first time. "Ho, what have we here? Be you druid or priest?"

Well Deirdre knew that Scanlan wore the same tonsure as those Hinderk and his kind had mutilated. His thick, brown hair grew lionlike from his shaven forehead in the style of the ancient druids who'd embraced Christianity, giving up the prestige of their station to serve the One God who they believed lived in the sun.

"I suppose both, milord." Scanlan's reply was soft. "As our sainted Columcille once said, 'Christ is my druid.' He is my Master and Teacher too."

Feeling helpless, Deirdre cast a frantic look at Alric. His mother was a Christian. Would he do nothing?

Hinderk started round the cart to Scanlan's side, his hand resting on the hilt of a sheathed dagger. "Have you Irish priests not learned your lesson yet?"

"We are always learning, milord. The school of life has many lessons, but the Word of God has more." Scanlan smiled, his philosophical posture smacking of either courage or lunacy.

"Keep your religious war to yourself, Hinderk," Alric spoke up, as though tiring of the game of wills holding them all suspended. "It has no place here. The priest is my betrothed's companion, just arrived and under Galstead's protection."

The Saxon dog was not pleased to have such an easy bone snatched from his reach. Whipping his horse's head about, he sneered at the one who'd taken it. "You assume a lot of responsibility for the son of a slave."

"Nonetheless, I wield the power of a king's son…and this." Alric drew Kieran's sword with his free hand. Dustan moved at the click of his tongue and, with a single leap, brought his master within sword's length of the slanderer.

Deirdre's heart mimicked the steed, taking her with it. "Enough!" She pulled out of Scanlan's hold and jumped from the cart before he could stop her. With no idea of what she intended to do, she shoved through her circle of defenders. "There is no doubt that each of you fine warriors are capable of inflicting untold damage to the other," she blurted as she lifted her shoulders, throwing up her hands in an exaggerated shrug that caused Dustan and the other steed to rear back their heads at the sudden movement. "Who's to say that a slash or puncture might benefit you, given your grossly overblown estimation of yourselves. I've seen dogs fight with more dignity."

Tor, who'd been at Dustan's heel, got up and trotted to her, tail wagging. Ignoring the beast, Deirdre boldly marched between the dumbstruck prince and his nemesis. They might run her through, but one way or the other, she'd have relief from this web of anxiety.

"As entertaining at that might be for me, who has no great love for either of you—" She ducked under the extended blade of her ancestor's sword, somehow emboldened by its touch—"I am weary of travel, hunger, and this verbal chest beating. So if your beloved mothers ever instilled in you a wisp of gallantry, for their memory's sake—" The mother's guilt was a stroke of genius. She'd seen fierce men wither at the mention of their mother—"Let's be on our way. Your men and I long for the hospitality at Galstead."

Not a soul moved. They just stared at her, Alric included. Seizing at the last strand of her nerve before it snapped, she stomped her foot and shouted. "Now sheath your weapons!"

It sounded like her voice, but it was much bigger than she felt at the moment, now that her insanity had run its course. From the corner of her eye, Deirdre saw Scanlan cross himself, lips moving, no doubt in a prayer of exorcism, for even she did not recognize the woman in her memory's replay of the last few moments. Her knees grew watery, requiring all her effort to keep her upright. She not only risked her life, but Scanlan's as well. *Father in heaven, help us now...or Scanlan at least.*

A soft, sliding sound drew her gaze to where Alric returned Kieran's sword to its sheath. "My apologies, milady. Lord Hinderk," he said, his gaze never leaving her, "I invite you and your men to accompany us to Galstead. Gunnar, see to these smugglers and their goods."

She glanced at Hinderk as he nodded and proceeded to give corresponding orders to his own troops, but Alric would not release her from the shackling silver of his gaze. Prodded by some silent command, Dustan carried him toward her, stopping abreast of her. Was he going to cut out her tongue with the scramasax still in his hand?

Without a word, Alric slid off the stallion's back and lifted Deirdre up in his place. She flinched as he leaped up behind her and took the reins. Only when he took the lead did he whisper in her ear. "How long, milady, have you spoken our language so fluently?"

How could the same voice warm and chill her at the same time? Why was her life a clash of opposite feelings and sensations where this man was involved? Through bombardment of sense and sensibilities, the meaning of Alric's words sunk in. She'd spoken Saxon? Deirdre sought out Scanlan in disbelief, but he was busy coaxing the cart horse back onto the road. They'd agreed she not do so until...

No wonder the priest prayed. When had she switched from Latin? How could she explain, when she didn't understand herself.

Behind them, Hinderk chuckled, not as much at Deirdre as to himself. "Your betrothed certainly has command of our tongue, milord. She not only wields it as artfully as my mother, but with like comfort and authority."

"There seems no end to her accomplishments," Alric agreed. "I continue to be overwhelmed by my good fortune in finding her."

Caught up in her own quandary, Deirdre let the blunted barb slide.

NINETEEN

Galstead had been an old legion fortress situated in the mineral-rich hills and river valley that had fallen into ruin until Lambert and his thanes were awarded it as sword land, claimed by their fierce scramasaxes and spears. Upon realizing its strategic location on the crest of a natural hill, Lambert established his settlement there. Like most of the Saxon towns, it came together a piece at a time. First there were soldiers, then farms, and then tradesmen to support the increasing center of population.

In lieu of the usual Saxon stockade and earthen work, Galstead's walls were of block, repaired to their original strength and thick enough to afford a walk behind the bastions. The ditch around its perimeter was filled with water from a natural spring that would provide a good water supply in the event of siege. Skirting the hilltop settlement were the neatly arranged rectangles of farms and commons, fading green in the waning sun.

Alric waited for Deirdre to show some sign of being impressed, but she'd not said a word since her rant. The way she acted, one would think *she* had been as surprised as he by her ability to speak his native tongue. He would have wagered his sword arm that she could not speak Saxon aside from a few words. That she boldly stepped between him and Hinderk in the first place to stop what might have escalated into a physical confrontation had set both Alric and his adversary back. But when she proceeded to scold them in their own mother tongue, Alric could have been knocked off his horse with a feather. Fortunately, Hinderk had been affected as well...or at least intrigued by her beauty and courage.

But then, his captive had that effect on men. Even the peasant hadn't been certain how to react to her. Alric glanced down at the golden crown of her head resting against his shoulder. She looked like an angel and fought like a devil for what she believed in, making her a formidable opponent full of surprises. And this last one she'd explain to him before the night was out.

The noise of the market spilled over from inside to out of the city proper, rousing the subject of Alric's introspection as they rode through the main gate.

"Welcome to Galstead, milady," he whispered, unable to suppress his pleasure that she'd drifted off to sleep in his arms. As with Tor and Dustan, time and patience were proving the key to winning her trust.

She gave him an embarrassed glance, a blush creeping to her cheeks. It flushed Alric as well, but not in his face. Frig's mercy, he felt like a love-struck pup, bombarded by so many urges that all he could do was grin like a simpleton.

"Welcome back, milord," one of the guards in the elevated block-house of Lambert's royal compound shouted down as they passed through the gate.

Pulling himself together with military discipline, Alric returned the wave. By the time the stable hands took over the horses, Lambert himself emerged with a following of thanes and servants from the great timber-framed hall.

"Father," Alric greeted him, stepping stiffly into the open arms the man extended to him. Lambert was not usually open with his affections in the public eye, especially to Orlaith or Alric. Had the queen and Ricbert left the country?

"Tell me it's true," Lambert exclaimed, holding Alric at arm's length. His jowled, round face beamed. "I've heard that you're taking a wife."

So that was it. "News travels fast." Alric was unable to control his smile any longer. He motioned Deirdre over. "You remember the waif we found in the hold of the captured ship?"

Lambert squinted in the dimming light as she approached them. "My word, it *is* her. Something told me there was more between you two than you admitted. I almost stopped you from sending her off to the slave market, the way you reacted to her."

Alric lifted one eyebrow but held back his question as to exactly what his father observed. He wasn't ready for Deirdre to know the extent of the advantage she held over him. He wasn't exactly sure *he* knew.

"Father, I present Princess Deirdre of Gleannmara, my betrothed as soon as you signify the contract is in order."

Deirdre bent her knee in polite deference but not her head. "Milord." Now that she was fully awake, the cuddlesome kitten had again become the aloof cat.

To Alric's astonishment, Lambert chuckled. "Ach, it's the same wench all right. I've only seen fire burn on water twice—once in your mother's gaze and then in this one's. I commend you on having wit enough to recognize such a diamond in the rough. Betrothed to her, no less," the king marveled.

"I mean no disrespect, milord, but this marriage is not one of love, my being here is not of my choice, and I am filthy and weary of the travel and this company."

Eye's wide, mouth gaping, Alric stared at Deirdre. She spoke in flawless Saxon yet again. Lambert was no different from anyone else who'd heard the Irishwoman. It took him a moment to recover, but he did so with an uncommon grace and patience for his nature.

"Then I shall have my retainer—"

"I'll see her to Abina's house," Alric interrupted. "Then I'll join you and these good thanes in the hall to wash the dust from my throat. Meanwhile—" he reached into the bag slung over his shoulder—"here is the contract. The payment is in that jeweled trunk and is hers to either send to her father or use as she sees fit."

Lambert took the parchment and held it to his chest. "I have long waited for this," he said to his thanes. "Mayhap I'll soon have an heir in the making with one son or the other."

The retinue laughed, some more heartily than others. Alric's attention shifted, shocked from his intent to get Deirdre to himself by his father's quip. Could it be *this* was what Orlaith meant by her prophecy? After all, Deirdre had made it clear Gleannmara would never accept him as king. Frig's breath, had he given away his birthright with his word not to take her as his wife in every sense of the term?

Humor souring, Alric took Deirdre by the arm. "Come, *beloved*, I would see you to your temporary quarters until we can officially enter Lambert's contest for the throne."

"And what of my things and Scanlan? I'd see him—"

"My father's retainer is capable of that, but you, my derling, I prefer to deal with personally."

In his eagerness, Alric seized her arm a little rougher than he'd intended and was startled by Tor's fierce bark. He'd forgotten the wolfhound was even there. In the moment of Alric's hesitation, the dog clamped a warning mouth over his wrist.

"That's *your* pup, isn't it?" Lambert's brows arched, as taken aback as Alric.

"What's the matter with you, dog?" Alric ruffled the animal's head with his free hand. Tor's tail wagged, but he did not let go of Alric's wrist until he released Deirdre's arm, at which point, the wolfhound immediately licked the hand he just released. "It seems you've betrayed me for a few morsels of food, you fickle mule." Alric slipped his arm around Deirdre, softening his voice. "If you would come with me, milady, I'll show you and your newest conquest to your quarters."

Uneasy with both master and dog, although the latter did shadow her for leftover morsels, Deirdre accompanied Alric through an orderly gathering of lodges, miniatures of the massive timber hall. It wasn't much different from Gleannmara, except that these were rectangular while her people's homes were usually round, with walls of wattle and mud rather than planking.

Men, women, and children, fair-featured like Alric, paused in their tasks or conversations, watching as the prince rushed her with determined gait toward an elderly woman sitting in the sun on a bench by the door. The woman looked up from her stitchery as though sensing something amiss, but upon seeing Alric, her wrinkled face took on a glow of welcome.

"Muirnait!" she exclaimed in delight, hastily putting aside her needlework.

"Sit, Abina. I have someone I want you to meet," Alric answered in the same Irish. It was to no avail. With the stiffness of her age, the woman struggled to her feet and opened her arms to him. For that brief embrace, the annoyance on the prince's face gave way to tenderness.

"Abina, this is Princess Deirdre of Gleannmara, my bride to be." The old woman looked at Deirdre, seeming distracted at first. Then wonder filled her pale blue-gray eyes. "'Her name means sorrow, but she will bring you great happiness,'" she murmured as though reciting a verse. She reached out to finger Deirdre's hair. "You are as lovely as Orlaith said you'd be."

Orlaith? Alric's mother? Deirdre glanced at the man beside her, fully expecting him to give her some sort of signal that the old woman had gone dotty, but his features had become unreadable.

"I would have Deirdre stay with you until our wedding, if you don't mind," Alric said.

"Ach, I tended your mama and you, how could I not want to care for your pretty bride?"

So that was why the old woman greeted Alric in Irish, calling him beloved. She was the servant captured with his mother and had also been his nurse. Somehow the picture wouldn't come together of Alric, now towering head and shoulders above the woman, in her arms.

Abina clasped her hands together. "I praise God that I have lived to see her delivered to you at last."

"Delivered?" Deirdre could not help herself. Just when she thought she understood what was going on, this strange conversation took another turn. "Milady, I was—"

"Abina," the woman interrupted. "I am Alric's Abina, and now I am yours." She put her hands up. "But look at me babbling like a witless hag when you must be exhausted. I'll have a bath drawn for you and—"

"Excellent idea, Abina. And while you make the arrangements, I would speak privately with my betrothed inside."

Abina's eyes twinkled, framed with laugh lines of a lifetime. "Of course you would. I'll be back momentarily, milady, to see you properly cared for." With another childlike clap of excitement, the small woman hustled away.

"What a dear soul," Deirdre said, relieved that she once more had been blessed with a Christian caretaker and a kinswoman of a kind. "But she shouldn't be carrying water—"

"Abina will give orders only," Alric assured her. "She has a special place here." Stepping back, he motioned for her to step inside. "'Tis time we spoke."

It took a moment for Deirdre to adjust her eyes to the dimmer light of the cottage. The banked embers in the hearth filled the room with a homey scent, keeping the air dry for its mistress's old joints but not affecting the pleasant summer temperature warming it from without. An old loom hung on one wall, along with other weaving paraphernalia. Baskets lined the shelves above. A cot was arranged on the far side of the fire. Deirdre glanced about in search of another, but a table and two stump benches were the only other furnishings.

"I would have expected her to remain at the seaside villa," Deirdre observed, "since that is where Orlaith spent most of her time."

"I think the memories are as painful for her as they are for my father, and she says the constant nearness to the water reminds her of the danger I'm in at sea."

"I certainly don't wish to take her only bed—"

"I'll have another brought in." Alric blocked Tor from following them inside, edging the dog's head out with his knee so that he could close the door. "I said *privacy*," he answered when the wolfhound offered a bark of protest. When he turned, a hint of a smile curled at one corner of his mouth. "It seems even my hound is not impervious to your charms."

Deirdre took the remark as a compliment, even if it was delivered in a dubious tone. "He's not as fearsome as I first thought, though I'd not care to test his disposition."

Alric motioned her to a seat on one of the table benches, studying her every movement until she settled. "You *are* different," he said at length, as though trying to convince himself. "What happened to you, Deirdre? How is it that you speak Saxon like a native now? What made Hinderk humor you when you stepped uninvited into the midst of our quarrel? It isn't his nature, trust me." Alric nodded toward the door. "Even Tor treats you differently, and believe me when I say that no amount of tasty treats can account for his threatening me when I laid my hand upon you."

Deirdre shook her head, not sure exactly what to say as she watched Alric approach and drop on one knee, gathering her hand in his. If she didn't know better, he looked about to pledge his suit.

"You have been a mystery to me since my mother told me of you, and now that I have you, you puzzle me even more."

Now that he had her… A mix of anxiety and anticipation tripped up her spine.

"Perhaps if I knew what your mother said about me, how she even *knew* of me…" Deirdre shrugged, certain Alric was no more confused than she. It was as if each of them had different pieces of a puzzle that somehow fit together, but the other pieces still eluded them. Could they find them together? Was that also in God's plan?

"Believe me, Alric," she said in all earnest, "you are not the only one confused by all this. The only thing I know is that God is in charge and has a plan for me…for both of us."

"God has plans for one who questions His existence?"

"God uses saint and sinner alike, but you'd best ask Scanlan to explain it, for I scarce can grasp any sense in what happened myself."

"*What* happened? Tell me, Deirdre." Alric squeezed her hand, lifting it to his lips so that they brushed across her fingertips.

This was the last sort of interrogation she anticipated. Were he angry and demanding, she could stand up to him, but this was not a fair play. The man wielded charm as proficiently as his scramasax.

"What is this *gift* you and the priest allude to?"

Who could not be drawn into the silvery sea of warmth affixed upon her, reaching beyond her defenses to coax her to speak her heart, not her mind? "I thought in my fever that a Saxon demon possessed me, and that was how I understood what you and Belrap said when you spoke in Saxon." She shouldn't tell him. It was to be her secret to use against him, even if she had unintentionally let part of it out. "But I prayed and prayed with Scanlan, and no demon would pray, much less call on the One who could purge it from its hold upon me. All I know is that I suddenly knew your language as if it were my own. That's how we knew—Scanlan and I—that it was a gift from God." Even now she trembled with awe.

"To what purpose, woman?" Alric studied her with a wary yet attentive look.

Deirdre shifted the conversation. "Tell me about Orlaith. I've told you my secret. What is yours, Alric of Galstead?"

He let go her hand and rose to take a seat at the table across from her. For a moment, he was no longer in the room with her but somewhere far off in his memory. He was neither disbelieving nor mocking as she'd expected him—or anyone—to be at what she said. His profile, silhouetted against the light of a small window by the door, was a solemn, noble one, like that of a Roman statue. Only in his distant gaze did the myriad of emotions churning within show themselves.

Sure, Deirdre had one to match each of his as she listened to the account of Orlaith's last moments—how a loving mother poured out her heart's desire for her son—with a detail that challenged doubt.

"Mother believes those visions came from God," he finished, looking at her, eyes wide. "She said I would win my birthright by love, not the sword, and that you are the key. She described you... I thought it was her illness, but after hearing of your feverish experience, I am not so sure." He took a deep breath and continued. "It was either God or some omnipotent power that transcends all man's understanding, for it controls even the water and the stones. Even Aelfled believes our paths have crossed for a purpose."

"Who?"

"A friend...with certain gifts of her own."

"Your mistress, perhaps?" The green words were out before she could stop them.

"Not *now.*"

Deirdre did not miss his implication, but as she wondered as to its veracity, a flashback of the childlike creature who ran into her at the marketplace came to her. "She was the woman at the market, the little one, with the stones."

"Aye, and she concurs with Orlaith's prediction. Even the stones you picked up say that our destinies are entwined."

"God created them, so of course He controls them," Deirdre pointed out, struggling as hard as her companion to grasp the nature of what had planned out their merging destinies. "He uses saints and sinners alike," she murmured, repeating what she'd told Alric earlier.

"What?"

"That night on the ship, when I was nearly swept over the rail, you stopped me. I'd given myself to God's will to be taken into the arms of the sea—but it was your arms I wound up in."

Alric watched her as she rubbed the gooseflesh on her arms into submission.

Instead of rebelling against her opinion or scoffing, he gave a wistful smile. "You remind me of my mother in so many ways."

He reached across the small table and, taking her hands, drew her to her feet and to where he rose. Deirdre could not resist the gentle force that brought her into his embrace, nor did it seem, could he resist the urge to bring her there.

"Would it be so wrong to yield to that which we cannot understand? No logic I know stands up to the right feeling of you in my arms."

She echoed the very notion in her mind. Feelings definitely had the advantage over reason. Something bigger than both of them rendered thought useless. But that Alric felt exactly the same as she gave her the flutters, as if hundreds of butterflies beat their wings upon her heart and senses.

"It's hard to recall how you vex me when I can feel your heart beating against mine." He nuzzled the top of her head. "Or the downy softness of your hair tickling my nose…" Lifting her chin, he gazed down at her face as though caught in the same trancelike state as she. "Or the satin warmth of your lips. If this is God's plan, milady, it is a heavenly one, do you not agree?"

A sweet fever engulfed her as he lightly brushed her mouth with his. Deirdre couldn't talk. Faith, she could hardly breathe, and when she did, she shared it with Alric. Yet it was oneness of spirit and emotion that sprang from the physical intimacy, as though divined by something greater than the both of them.

She nodded and became lost in his gaze, only vaguely aware that her own secrets were exposed to the same search of the soul.

"Out of the way, you big puppy!"

Abina's order came from the outreaches of Deirdre's awareness, and the latch on the door lifted with the sharp click of bar, shattering the ethereal sphere that had captured the two of them. They broke away from each other abruptly, but their gazes would not give up the enchantment.

"Ooh," Abina gasped from the periphery of the union. "I am sorry. I—"

"I was just going, Abina," Alric said, drawing away with one last searching look at Deirdre. "You'll be in good hands," he assured her as he gathered himself with a square of his shoulders and a clearing of his throat.

Deirdre nodded wordlessly, watching as he spun about and retreated toward the door. She had not let go of him as easily, for surely he took a part of her with him.

TWENTY

T he great hall was a cacophony of celebration over the announcement of Alric's wedding to Deirdre. The first part of the procedure had been fulfilled according to Lambert's pronouncement. Immensely pleased, the king of Galstead announced that his wedding gift was to be the royal villa in Chesreton.

Refreshed from a bath and wearing her pearl-adorned, blue smocked gown and cap, Deirdre endured the toasts of congratulations, still lost in the mysteries in which she and Alric found themselves. His mother had described her and Gleannmara so distinctly, how could Deirdre not believe that God was involved? Orlaith had been a saintly woman, devoutly believing until her last breath that Alric would receive his birthright on earth and in heaven because of her.

After the arrival of Abina and the servants earlier, Deirdre had been so distracted by the new revelations and the spell that compelled the baring of their souls to one another that she'd hardly paid attention to Abina's fussing over her like a mother hen.

"Orlaith could not have picked a more perfect mate for our Alric than you, milady. What glorious hair…said it was like spun gold and it is."

Alric had left, no less affected than Deirdre with the notion that there was a master purpose in their match. Yet how else could the coincidences be explained when the only common element was God? Granted, Alric did not say he believed it was God, but he did concede that some master power seemed at work. Even now she could feel it, as though they each possessed some part of the other that forged a common bond, despite all their other differences.

"Perhaps, once my seafaring son discovers the attraction of remaining on land," Lambert proposed, after a round-cheeked maid had refilled all the glasses at the royal table, "the surrounding shires may become part of his domain as well."

If only she'd had time to share all this with Scanlan. As it was, the priest was living outside the city walls so as not to stir Ethlinda's ire against him. The moment Orlaith had died, all traces of Christianity had been forbidden inside the gates. Only Abina was unaffected by the queen's edict.

"And who will fulfill our naval obligations to the bretwalda?" Ricbert's drawl was rank with cynicism.

"Your brother has built an admirable fleet of ships, and all but the *Wulfshead* fare well without him," his father answered, pride swelling his chest. "His captains on the water are as able as my thanes on land. Take Cedric's second born, here."

"Gunnar is a better warrior than I," Cedric snorted. "I'm not one for battle on footing that bobs and dips at whim."

"I'd wage my life and the *Wulfshead* on the abilities of the man." Alric lifted his glass, first to Gunnar's father and then to Gunnar himself.

Now that the relationship between the two had been pointed out, Deirdre could see the resemblance, especially in those devilish eyes. Except that Gunnar didn't seem his usual carefree self.

"Milords are all generous," he replied with courtly grace.

"Just don't wager your bride, eh, my dear?" Ricbert sneered under his breath to his wife beside him. His voice carried nonetheless, just as he intended.

Gunnar slammed down his cup, glaring at the prince.

Next to Ricbert, the Princess Helewis reddened but continued to pick at her food with downcast gaze.

"Ricbert, shame on you!" On a floating cloud of silver and black silk, a tall stately woman with the same sharp features as the dark-haired prince swept into the hall from a side entrance and took the empty seat next to Lambert. "Your teasing makes your young wife nervous, which forces her to eat like a horse." Queen Ethlinda smiled at the plump princess. "Which we all know is to her detriment."

Aware that all eyes were now fixed upon her, Helewis pushed aside the food before her. "If milords and ladies will excuse me," she said in a barely audible voice, "I'm not feeling well."

Deirdre was mortified for the young woman. She was about to abandon courtly etiquette and run after a complete stranger, but Gunnar lost control first.

"Begging your pardon, Your Majesties, but Lord Ricbert's insinuation—"

"*Prince* Ricbert," the queen reminded the man.

"He acts like neither," Lambert grumbled.

"The *prince's* insinuation," Gunnar resumed, "is unfounded and an affront, not just to my honor, but to that of Lady Helewis. Your princess was pure as the first snow of winter when he took her to the bridal bed, and he well knows it. I demand he apologize."

Ethlinda laughed. "You champion Helewis?"

Deirdre disliked the woman already. "It seems someone should, when genteel manners so sorely elude some members of this court."

Ethlinda slowly turned toward Deirdre, the chevron of a painted eyebrow exaggerated by her surprise. Placing a long, curled fingernail upon her cheek, she gave Deirdre a pointed look. "How dare a slave address me in such a manner?"

"Enough!" Lambert slammed both fists on the table with such force that Tor leaped to his feet behind Alric's chair.

Alric seized his collar, calming him. "Welcome to my happy home," he whispered in a sarcastic aside to Deirdre.

"So help me, woman, I'll have you served a bowl of cream, if you don't draw back your claws and curb that viperish tongue."

"I will not be chided by a slave, husband."

"But you will be chided by your king, Ethlinda, and I say *enough*."

"Is it any wonder I built my first boat as a pup and set out to sea?" Alric mumbled, leaning over Deirdre's shoulder to offer Tor a beef rib to calm him down.

She smothered a giggle, one of the first genuinely pleasant reactions since her capture. Having Alric as an ally was an engaging novelty. Cutting a sidewise glance at him as he turned back to the assembly, she caught a devilish wink that made her pulse stumble. Perhaps God's plan for her was not as gloomy as she'd first estimated. She *had* to share this with Scanlan.

When his guests were well satiated with food and wine, Lambert summoned his chief musician and storyteller. "Hengist, herald us with the great tales of our ancestors that our guests might know the noble bloodline of their hosts."

It was noble, Deirdre acknowledged, but also brutal, with gods as savage and fickle as the mankind with which they mingled. Somehow the ancient tales she'd heard in song did not seem nearly so heathen now, even though they were spawned before the coming of the faith. Perhaps the clerics who'd preserved them had softened their harshness, although meddling with the lyrics would have been a challenge. They'd been handed down from generation to generation in rhyme, just to prevent such tampering.

Although she had to fight exhaustion to keep from yawning, the Saxon tales gave her insight into the people she was to live with.

"Lady Deirdre," Lambert said, after beating his cup upon the table in approval with the rest, "a dear companion of mine used to sing a haunting melody for me. 'Twas in Irish, but the tune alone was enough to soothe the most troubled spirit."

He started to hum a line of it but the combination of food and drink—or the lack of ability—so distorted it, that Deirdre could not identify it. With a half-laugh, half-curse, he gave up. "She said it had to do with a sword-carrying angel who protected those who sang it."

Deirdre felt the color leave her face. Surely it couldn't be the same song she'd called upon to pray away her demon. "Was it the angel Michael?"

"Yes!" Lambert winced, as though his booming enthusiasm had been pierced by the same sword meant to protect him. He rubbed his temples and then shook off his discomfort with kingly discipline. "I thought that since you are so well versed in our language, you would share it."

Deirdre's pulse accelerated, pumping the blood back into her face. She knew it by heart in Irish, but without Scanlan, could she translate as she sang? *Father, You have not failed me yet, and if this is indeed Thy course, then—*

"Have you a harp, Hengist?"

"By all means, fetch it for the lady," Lambert commanded. "You know the one."

It was difficult to tell whether the musician was intrigued or insulted by the king's request, but he snapped his fingers and one of his students left immediately.

Nervous, Deirdre rose from the bench, aware that every eye in the hall rested upon her. "As you may know, Michael is one of God's archangels, the messengers and protectors God sends to His faithful."

"Do you know of this Michael, Juist?" Queen Ethlinda addressed one of the white-robed men seated at the head of a table next to the royal one.

"I am still acquainting myself with the personalities of Oswy's choice," Juist replied. "Perhaps His Majesty would like me to fetch a powder to ease his head."

"I am not infirm, witan," Lambert snapped. "I wish to hear a song that I enjoy in my own language. Besides, those powders of yours dim a man's wit as well as his pain."

"They are naught but the ground bark of a healing tree, milord."

"And bitter as venom," Lambert reminded the queen. "To hear you and your witan, these people will think I'm an invalid. Ah," he said upon seeing the apprentice musician return, "that is the one. It is in tune, is it not, friend?"

Hengist nodded. "I tend it daily."

"It belonged to Orlaith," Alric whispered to Deirdre.

His mother's harp, an audience of his people. *Heavenly Father.* With no time for more plaint, Deirdre took the harp and walked to the bench Hengist vacated for her. A quick strum of the instrument's bright strings confirmed that it had indeed been well kept by an experienced hand, but her throat had gone dry. She tried clearing it, but it felt as if every word she attempted was coated in lint. "In this song, Michael is appealed to by a peasant for his everyday troubles and cares with regard to his cottage and farm."

"A peasant's plea?" Ethlinda let her disapproval be known. "You are enchanted by the song of a peasant?"

Deirdre bristled. "My father, the king of Gleannmara, finds it fit for any man, royal *and* common, for what man does not care for his home and his land…and what good king does not care for his people's homes and land? If they do not prosper, then neither does their king."

"Your future bride is not only pious but argues with the skilled tongue of a politician." Lambert smiled at Alric.

"I argue with the Word of God, Your Majesty," Deirdre said humbly. "For it is the guide for king and commoner alike, as Christ is the example."

"Then why appeal to Michael? Why not to God Himself?" Ethlinda challenged.

"Any appeal to heaven is to God, for not even Michael can act without God's blessing."

"So he is a thane," Lambert suggested. "Like my own, they come to me on behalf of their people but do not act without my approval."

Deirdre nodded, watching as her frantic debate registered between Lambert and his council. "And if I may be so bold, Your Majesty, given the threats I have seen in and around your kingdom, it is fitting to seek the protection of God's own."

"Sing it, child." Lambert inclined his head. "No man here will find objection with the protection of his land and people."

As her fingers took to the strings, years of practice possessed them.

"Thou Michael the victorious, I make my circuit under thy shield…"

Her mouth grew moist with the sweetest nectar, sent undoubtedly from heaven. The Saxon, like the drink, came as a gift. Focusing on a cross beam, she let the prize flow, not from her voice or her mind, but from the spirit that filled them.

That Michael was a dragon conqueror would appeal to the Saxons' warrior pride; that he might also care for the humble soul enough to protect him, not just in the fields but away from his home, would surely touch those who had left their homes across the sea to find new ones; that he protected not only the man but his property—the sheep in his pastures and crops in his fields, his home and furnishings— clearly found a place for consideration in their minds.

They pondered it in a deafening silence, even as she finished and handed the harp back to Hengist.

Lambert shook himself from the invisible hand that stilled them all. "Nay, milady, keep it. It is my gift to you for your gift to us."

The hold broken, his guests stomped their feet and beat their cups on the table, though Ethlinda and Ricbert, along with a minority of others, withheld their approval.

"Well!" The queen took up her goblet and lifted it to Deirdre as she returned to Alric's side. "Since our seafaring prince's captive bride seems to have taken our court as prize instead, I propose a toast to hasten our plans."

"And what plans are those, Ethlinda?" Alric drew Deirdre into the protective circle of his arm.

Feigning a wounded look at the suspicion in the prince's gaze, the cold beauty smiled—for even at her age, the queen's comely features retained the deceptive youth of a sculpture. It was such an unnatural expression, Deirdre almost expected it to shatter the regal mask the lady wore. "Why, the wedding plans, of course. What else?"

"I have no qualms with that," Alric admitted, giving Deirdre a toe-curling grin.

"I will help your bride on the morrow, since her own mother is not here."

"Excellent," Lambert agreed. "Most excellent." He lifted his cup. "To my son and the charming bride to be who captured him."

Deirdre blushed, not from the toast, but from the intimate appraisal her betrothed gave her. She was on a downhill run toward fire and feared she could not stop, even if she wanted to. Congratulations echoed from one end of the hall to the other. It would have been gratifying, even reassuring—but for the exchanged looks between the queen of Galstead and the Mercian visitor. They seemed to be drinking to an entirely different proposal.

A chill razed Deirdre's spine, lifting the hairs on the back of her neck. Mistaking the source of her shiver as cold, Alric drew her closer so that her body shared the warmth of his, but the cold would not yield, not even to him.

TWENTY-ONE

Abina was still asleep when Deirdre rose the following morning and made her way through the waking village. Tor's absence must have meant that the wolfhound followed Alric after he'd seen her safely to his nurse's lodge the night before.

"You not only remind me of Orlaith with your faith and melodious voice," he'd told her when they reached Abina's door, "but you've managed to stir as much trouble as she on your first day here." He leaned over and kissed her lightly on the lips. Abina had opened the door just then, clad in her nightdress and squinting at them in the glow of the candle she held.

Alric gave Deirdre a peck on the tip of her nose. "Later, my sweetling…"

Deirdre held her hand against her chest as if to stay the starstruck swelling within. She had so much to tell Scanlan, and it would wait no longer. After finding her bearings as best she could, she followed some of the workers on their way out into the surrounding fields through the gatehouses. Beyond, vendors were assembling at the market, filling the air with the tempting fragrance of fresh-baked goods.

Deirdre stopped to ask directions to the visitor's chapel. No one seemed to know what she was talking about, until she spoke to a weaver setting up a display of her handiwork.

"It is not used," the woman said as if proud to make that point. "But I heard a priest was sent there. How do you know him?"

"He is my companion," Deirdre explained.

The woman's eyes widened. "Ach, you must be the prince's betrothed!" She clasped her hands together in a mix of delight and dismay. "I am sorry, milady. Allow me to show you."

Deirdre declined politely, wondering if this strange language would ever sound right to her, no matter how well she understood and spoke it.

Following the woman's directions, she came to a common pasture where the village livestock was kept. There, at its edge, was the small hut of wattle and thatch. Some of the mud coating on the walls had broken away, exposing the frame. A wisp of smoke wormed its way out of one of the three depressions in the roof.

"Scanlan," she called out at the half-hinged door.

"Deirdre?" The priest wrestled the rickety door open. "What is it?" he asked as she grinned broadly at him. "Are you well?"

"Well *and* happy." She gave her companion a hug. "Oh, Scanlan, it was just as you said. I didn't believe it, but the Holy Spirit came over me and...even Alric and his father and—"

"Slow down." Scanlan chuckled, and his initial frown faded into a smile. "Come in, come in. I've just finished scraping this bristle off my jaw."

"Shouldn't you use some kind of soap?" She ran a finger along his smooth but abraded cheeks.

He propped the door against the outside wall and motioned her inside. "Soap is a luxury."

Deirdre had never understood the Celtic clerics' penchant for doing without what she considered creature comforts. Surely there had to be some meeting point between their vow of poverty and their Roman brothers' pomp and circumstance.

She looked at the drapes of cobwebs and the coating of dust covering the two benches in the room. "Well, this lodging is not."

There wasn't even a table or altar. She supposed the shelf on the front wall sufficed. The symbol of a cross had been carved in rough fashion into the wooden support behind it. Now it was highlighted by a thin shaft of sunlight battling through a hole worn in the roof by neglect.

"I have slept in better, but it is fit enough for my needs." Scanlan reached into a sack and drew out a crust of bread left over from a previous meal. "Will you join me for breakfast?"

Deirdre shook her head and waited while he gave thanks, not just for the stale bread, but for the shamble of a dwelling.

"Once I am renewed," he told her upon finishing, "I shall set to work to repair those holes and shore up the walls. The foundation is sound and that is all that counts."

Deirdre sensed a sermon in the making, but Scanlan surprised her.

"So tell me about last night. I take it something has gone wonderfully right, given the sparkle and flush of your demeanor."

"Something has changed in Alric." She gripped her hands together. "Once we spoke, heart to heart, he became different. He's actually quite charming and intellectual." Not to mention romantic. Deirdre withheld her latter thought, lest the priest think her moon addled.

Scanlan hesitated from popping the piece of crust he'd broken off into his mouth. "You told him all about the gift?"

"It's not just that. There is even more than we realized. You said God ordained all that has happened, but I never dared to believe it with all my heart." She made the admission in a flash of contrition. "Until now." Deirdre went on to tell Scanlan about Orlaith's prophecy and Aelfled's concurrence. "Alric was not convinced by faith, but the combination of all these things…well, it's changed him. It is as though I am allied with a different man. He is—"

"To what do you attribute the change?"

How could Scanlan be so calm? Wasn't this what he said was to happen? "To his believing that our union is meant to be. It's obvious, isn't it?"

"So he has not confessed to God."

"Well, no, but…" Deirdre groped for what she wanted to say. No, he hadn't confessed to God or admitted to believing, but he was going along with God's plan. "I think he is like I was, giving his will to God…but surely his heart will follow."

"Because God's will suits his purpose, not because it suits God's," Scanlan thought aloud. "Remember, dearest, for now you are his key to power and prestige, not salvation. Undoubtedly one can follow the other, so you are on the right track. God can use all manner of earthly motivations to accomplish the heavenly, but there is a difference between love and greed."

"Like my pride?" Deirdre couldn't help the sting in her reply. This was not what she'd expected. Had she made a mistake?

Scanlan put aside his meager breakfast and took her hands, his face awash with contrition. "Deirdre, though not much your senior, I have watched you grow up like a little sister. Yours is a noble heart and a willing faith, although both can be impetuous."

"I don't understand. The harder I try, the more mistakes I make."

"Muirnait, know that God finds you all the dearer, for it is your willingness and not your failures that are important."

Deirdre did not object when Scanlan hugged her. She needed grounding. What had come over her, acting like a smitten maid just come of age? She was a scholar, well into her prime, as Orna had so pointedly reminded her, and certainly not new to the workings of man's deceit.

"I thought God had changed him, as He changed me." She sniffed. "How could I have been so blind?"

"While I believe Alric is a noble-hearted being, he cannot offer a suit of love, for he doesn't know the meaning of it without knowing God. Do not pick an unripe apple too soon."

Deirdre's spirit sagged beneath this new worrisome weight. "'Twas you who said I should marry him." Was it greed that motivated this change in Alric?

"Because as his wife, you will have the opportunity to put your gift to the most use."

"But he knows Father rules Gleannmara—"

"And that your brother is out of the way."

"But he signed the contract—"

"Can the parchment force him to earnestly seek Cairell's freedom?"

"I told him Gleannmara would never accept a Saxon as king, that a distant cousin, perhaps our champion, would be elected instead."

At Scanlan's silence, Deirdre pulled away. A half smile tugged at the priest's lips. "You should have been a *brehon,* for I believe you could hold your own with the stoutest of lawmakers and judges." He sighed. "My only point is that to do God's will when it suits is easy. To follow it when it goes against one's own, as you are doing, is the truest test of faith. I have every belief that you will know when your Alric is motivated by God and not his own plan."

"Father, I need you in Galstead with me."

Scanlan shook his head. "You have God with you, and He is using your gift."

"Oh," Deirdre said, recalling the rest of her news. She told Scanlan how the very hymn they'd sung together to root out her alleged demon happened to be one of Lambert's favorites. "Alric's mother used to sing it to him to soothe his nerves, but he'd never heard it in Saxon, so he only knew the gist of it. And then I had to explain what I could about Michael and God and—I really think the thanes were intrigued. Of course, Ethlinda scoffed at it, but…that woman sends chills up my spine." Deirdre paused to catch her breath. "I wish you'd been there."

Scanlan chuckled. "It sounds like you managed quite well without me."

"I feel I'm rushing blindly into something I'm not prepared for."

Scanlan grabbed her hands again, folding them in his. "Milady, sometimes we must act without understanding. Perhaps your freshness is reaching where my training cannot. Your example will do more than I can ever do."

If Scanlan thought to console her, it wasn't working. She was confused, nay, exasperated—or perhaps both. Tears stung her eyes, but she held them back. "Will you pray with me?"

"Of course, muirnait."

Together they knelt on Scanlan's makeshift pallet on the floor before the barren, grime-covered shelf. "Isn't it reassuring that no place is too low or too high for God's presence?" he said, folding his hands. When Deirdre didn't answer, he bowed his head. "Heavenly Father, hear us, Your children, as we call on—"

A loud bark cut off the priest in midsentence. Before either Deirdre or Scanlan could react, Tor bounded into the chapel and wedged himself between them, his tail lashing from side to side. Knocked off balance by the wolfhound's enthusiastic welcome, Deirdre sprawled sideways with a startled cry, only to have Tor proceed to smother her in kisses while assaulting her person with his heavy paws.

"Tor," she complained, shoving the dog aside.

"So there you are." Alric ducked under the low door frame, filling it with his broad shoulders as he stood up inside the dwelling.

"I…I came to pray with Father Scanlan."

Alric gave the priest a drilling look and then stepped forward, offering Deirdre his hand. "I did not give you permission to leave Abina's lodge. She was frantic when she awakened to find you gone. Do you know what the penalty is for attempting to escape? Flogging at the least, hanging at the most."

Taken aback at his blustering accusation, Deirdre drew away from him and rose to her feet unassisted. "I am not a slave; I am your betrothed. And I told you, I came to pray with Scanlan, *not* run away."

"Father, do you mind?" Alric ordered Scanlan out with a jerk of his head.

"*I* mind." Deirdre grabbed Scanlan's sleeve as he started to comply. "We are in God's house, and I came to pray. If you would speak to me, then you will wait outside—" She caught Scanlan's warning look and added sweetly, "Please."

She didn't mean it. Alric knew she didn't. But she had given him a way to salvage his pride. Instead of going outside to wait, he took a seat on the split-log bench near the door, arms folded against his chest. Tor followed him and sat at Alric's quiet command.

He has no respect for the church or my prayers, Deirdre thought, resuming her kneeling position. *Heavenly Father, what a mistake I have nearly made.*

"Give us Thy Spirit. We fall on bended knee in the eye of the Father who created us, the Son who purchased us, and the Spirit who cleansed us…" Scanlan chanted. "Bless us with fullness in our need that our love for God is met with His affection for us, His smile upon us, His wisdom shared with us, and His grace surrounding us."

"In shade and light," Deirdre chimed in. *Heavenly Father, I so need Your Spirit.* "In day and night…" *Fill me, Father, that I might do what You will.* "All with Thy kindness, Lord, give us Thy Spirit." *That I might meet anger with serenity and scowl with smile.* "Amen."

There should have been more to the prayer, more specifics to ease Deirdre's troubled mind, but with Alric listening, Scanlan resorted to a prayer that covered all her concerns. He rose beside her and walked out of the enclosure. Behind her, she heard Alric rise. She smiled and imagined her anxiety draining away with each breath. Tor nudged her, impossible to ignore. With a little laugh, she grabbed his ears and scratched them.

"You have no more reverence than your master," she scolded lightly. With a sparkle of renewal in her heart, she turned and extended her hand to Alric. After he helped her up, she did the same to his ears, taking him by surprise, not only with her action, but her playful laugh. "I am sorry I frightened Abina," she said, "but she was sleeping so peacefully, and I hated to bother her."

"Abina wasn't the only one you frightened."

It was Deirdre's turn for shock. He was as earnest as she.

"It isn't safe for you to wander about as you will in this den of wolves. You have made enemies in the queen and her followers. I would put nothing past my half brother on any account. I have my own men guard even my horse and dog when I am not about."

Alric's protectiveness made Deirdre wonder at his childhood—how horrible it must have been. "Someone would wish harm to your pets?"

"Jealousy and resentment have run rabid within these walls since my earliest recollection. It's why my mother preferred the villa by the sea."

Deirdre recalled her thoughts regarding Ethlinda's and the Mercian envoy's exchange of glances but could find no real grounds, save intuition, to share it. Nonetheless she intended to keep an eye on the queen, a decision that did not need Alric's counsel.

"Then I shall go nowhere without you or Tor or—"

"I will be leaving in a few days, but Gunnar is to be at your disposal, and you are safe with my father. He is quite taken with you."

"Where will you go? Won't you need to help with the wedding plans?"

Alric looked around inside the chamber. "We have the church and your priest. As far as I am concerned, that is all we need. Father, on the other hand, would like to impress his neighbors and thanes with a bit more." He gave her a lopsided smile. "He's waited for me to take a bride for so long, I feel as though I should indulge him this much. The only thing good about his waning health is that we will not have the betrothal period extended."

"But he looks well," Deirdre said.

"His headaches are becoming more severe and requiring more medication, according to Abina."

"Why can't I go back to the villa with you?" The moment Deirdre expressed her wish she regretted it. Her work was here with Scanlan, at least until he was accepted.

"I want to see the *Wulfshead*'s new mast installed and try her out for a few days at sea."

"You go to plunder again," she accused him.

"I patrol the coast, looking for ships carrying supplies to my enemy."

"The Dalraidi."

"The same," he admitted. "Now, will you join me for breakfast?"

"I shall come here every day," Deirdre warned him. Faith, the idea of remaining in Galstead without Alric raised the hair on her arms.

"I'll make certain Gunnar brings you. Meanwhile, the women will help prepare whatever it is the women prepare. You'll like Helewis."

"Ricbert's wife?" At Alric's nod, Deirdre grimaced. "At least I have something in common with her. Neither of us likes the queen."

"Neither of you likes Ricbert either."

At Deirdre's startled look, Alric laughed. "Come along, milady, 'tis a long story I will share on our ride this afternoon."

"Ride?" Deirdre blinked as she stepped out into the bright sunlight. "But I have no horse."

Alric crooked his arm and brushed Tor aside. "You do now, muirnait," he told her, folding his hand over hers as she placed it on his forearm. "And it's fit for a princess."

Twenty-two

I 've never seen anything like it," Ricbert said, watching as Alric rode away from the town enclosure with his bride to be. The horses were the best that could be had, the wolfhound trotting along beside them of the finest stock, and the woman a lovely, fiery princess rather than the meek, little cow Ricbert had wed. But it was the sword hanging from Alric's waist that the elder prince coveted most.

"I have to have that sword."

"You will, Son. The weapon of a king shall belong to a king."

Ricbert turned to Ethlinda, who'd denied him nothing since birth. "He will not sell it."

"Dead men have no claims, save the right to rot."

A rush of excitement whetted his waning humor. He'd waited a lifetime for the rule of Galstead, and now that it was within sight, it consumed him day and night. "What if he isn't here?"

"As long as she is here, he'll return."

"How can you be sure?"

"He cannot take his eyes off her. No one can, for that matter."

Ricbert arched his brow at the cryptic turn of speech. He wondered if the fair-haired lass had any idea of how dangerous an enemy she'd made. His mother, like her mother before her, was a high priestess of the earth mother.

"But after the wedding, she'll move to the villa."

He preferred the luxury of the seaside estate to Lambert's austere fortress, but his father had set it aside for his whore and her whelp. Had Ethlinda and Ricbert taken up residence there, his coffers would be running over with treasures like his half brother's. Ricbert would have built a fleet of ships and milked the seas like a fatted cow. Instead, he inherited a land of ungrateful peasants. Collecting the king's portion from them was like squeezing blood from a stone.

The peasants continued to devise ways to cheat their protectors of the luxuries due them, and what did his father do? He fined the salters, gave the leader a few token flogs, and totally ignored Ricbert's suggestion that they hang the men as an example, as well as fine their kin. But nay, Lambert would jump off the cliff protecting Galstead's back if his illegitimate son advised it. If Ricbert never ruled Galstead, just to run a blade through Alric's beating heart would be enough to appease a lifetime of hatred he felt toward his younger sibling.

His muttering drew Ethlinda from her own thoughts. "Don't concern yourself so, derling. Your half brother is the least of our problems."

"Our problems?" Ricbert watched as his mother ran a painted fingernail along the flawlessly chiseled taper of her chin. She was so beautiful—in a cold, brutal way that made his flesh crawl and his blood boil. No maid he'd ever seen excited or frightened him so, certainly not his simpering Helewis. The only satisfaction he received from his marriage was denying Alric's best friend what he so desperately coveted. Were Ethlinda not his mother—

"That Irish princess and her priest," she said, "*they* are our problem."

"We can kill the priest. I'll do it myself." With pleasure. "The female as well," he added, with an intoxicating tingle of anticipation.

Curse Alric for claiming her first. Taming her would have provided more thrill than he'd had since capturing that little Welsh firebrand a year ago. Ethlinda's laugh defied the pitch of the smallest of harp strings. Ricbert fancied it stemmed, like her knowledge of magic, from elfin blood infused into the line in a generation long forgotten.

"You may have her as well...*after* the wedding," she stipulated. "But for now, this new development suits us perfectly. What better excuse to invite my brothers than to a *family* affair." She pulled her dark, rouged lips into a pout. "My husband has made a grave error in not accepting the Mercian's offer of protection. He is not the warrior he used to be, and his main force is on the northern border. While he gawks at Alric's bride and frets about dying in his winter season, his enemies ally against him."

"From without and within." Ricbert savored the fantasy of taking Lambert's kingdom from him by force, thus making the pie all the sweeter.

Ethlinda lifted his chin, peering into his eyes with a delicious wickedness. "You will not be so foolish, will you, my sweet?"

"Friends and enemies are of little consequence, aside from their use to me."

"Come, derling." The queen opened her arms to him.

As Ricbert stepped into his mother's embrace, his heart rate quickened. If she only knew how she tormented him. Ethlinda hugged him and, drawing back that she might see his face, ran her long nails through his dark curls.

"You are your father's son." Admiration turned to venom as she added, "*Not* his Northumbrian murderer's."

Since his sixteenth year, Ricbert had known the truth. It was a Mercian thane who'd fathered him, a man who died by Lambert's sword just before the marriage contract sealed the peace between their kingdoms. It had been with revenge on her mind that Ethlinda came to Lambert's court and bed.

What would Lambert say if he knew the son and heir she delivered was not his?

What a cunning beauty she must have been then, for even now Ricbert's breath grew short at the perfection in his embrace. That his feelings were forbidden only fanned his want. He ought to hate her for this torture, for it had anything but a motherly effect upon him.

Ricbert drew away and crossed him arms. "So when, Mother. *When?*"

Stepping up behind him, she spread her long, jeweled fingers on his shoulders.

"Patience, derling, makes the victory all the sweeter." She massaged the tension there, but her ethereal titter of laughter worked against her purpose with a sweet torture. "I have waited for this revenge for thirty long years. You can surely endure a few more weeks."

Ninga was a beautiful dappled gray with a dark mane and tail. While not as solid of build as Alric's Dustan, the mare's sleek lines were more suited to the racecourse than the battlefield. Deirdre proved as much, racing the two to a nose-to-nose finish on the return from their ride. For just a few wild moments, they'd been free of the concerns that both kept them apart and united them with the same tether.

Deirdre constantly reminded herself that this heady suit of Alric's was born of greed and nothing more. She was a gamble to him. If he won with her, he would keep her. If not, she would be divorced, discarded like used clothing. For that reason alone, she had to keep him to his promise regarding a conjugal relationship.

"Have you given any thought as to how you might find my brother?" she asked, loosening the reins so that Ninga might drink in the shallow stream.

"I have made some inquiries. Things like this take time, but Hinderk gave me his word that he would try to find out where the prince was sent. I've made it worth his while."

"You did?" She could not hide the fact that she was pleasantly surprised.

"Did I not give my word?"

"Of course, but I thought…well, I didn't think you would act upon it until we were officially wed."

"If I am to make my word good in this case, prompt action is called for. Although…"

Her heart dipped. "Although what?"

"Hinderk thought all the captives were sold. Not one admitted he was of royal lineage. So if your brother is being held for ransom, it's without knowledge of Ecfrith and his thanes."

"Can you trust Hinderk to tell you the truth?"

"Ecfrith values the support of my fleet more than a prince's ransom." The dryness of his comment told her she'd once again pricked at his pride.

"Well, I thank you for trying. It means a lot to me."

"Having a king for a brother-in-law cannot hurt a man."

Having such an attitude surely hurt a woman, Deirdre thought. Scanlan was so right. Alric didn't want her but whatever influence or power he could derive from the match. That was all that whetted his appetite for marriage.

"What say we let the horses graze for a while and walk along the streambed? 'Tis a perfect day to spend with a beautiful lady."

Deirdre raised her hand to her temple. "I fear the sun has been overmuch for me, milord. Would it be untoward to ask that we return so I might sleep off this pain in my head?"

"You're ill? Why didn't you say something?" To her surprise, his scowl was not one of anger but of concern. "By all means, milady, let's return at once." He leaned across the short space between them and cupped her chin, a perfectly rakish grin tipping his lips. "Although I have a perfectly sound remedy to restore your humor."

It felt as if the brightly colored butterflies flitting about the meadow had found their way to her belly and clamored for escape. The lady in her tried not to think what he might mean, but the vixen was beguiled. "I had no idea you were a healer as well, sir. What manner of concoction do you recommend?"

"No concoction, only tender, sweet care enough to make a woman forget her woes."

"How sweet," she managed, her throat dry as the pasture grass that yellowed a distance away from the stream. "Handed down from your mother, no doubt."

Without waiting for a reply, Deirdre nudged Ninga forward. A retreat was often the best line of defense when one's own guard deserted one. Behind, she heard Alric laugh shortly and then click his tongue for Dustan to catch up.

Ninga strained at the bit, eager to return to the care of the stable hands and a feed bag. Much as she longed to let the mare have her rein, Deirdre knew her headache would hardly be convincing if she launched into a full gallop. The painfully slow walk would simply have to do. Perhaps if she kept moving, temptation would not be able to keep up the pace.

Deirdre managed to keep Alric at bay that evening, despite his considerable charm and eagerness to please her, by conversing with Princess Helewis. Without Ethlinda's presence, the mood in the hall was festive and the princess was more at ease. She commiserated with

Deirdre as a bride far away from home in a strange court.

"But it is the duty for which I was trained," Helewis said. "I fear I have enjoyed the food here more than the company." The more nervous Helewis was, the more she munched. With all the political and personal undercurrents in the hall, Deirdre wondered Helewis wasn't big as a horse rather than nicely rounded. In view of the story Alric told Deirdre about Gunnar and Helewis's ill-fated attraction, Deirdre wasn't certain she'd have done as well.

While duty and honor had been placed ahead of love, it had not put out its light. Ignored by Ricbert, Helewis slanted more than one longing look to where Gunnar sat with the *Wulfshead*'s men.

"I am so glad that you have come to Galstead, for now I shall have a sister, yes?"

"Yes, you shall. We'll go riding together. You do ride, don't you?" Deirdre asked, already regretting Alric's impending departure.

The Saxon court was crude in comparison to Gleannmara's. The joviality was a glossy surface for backstabbing and envy everywhere she looked. Thanes and their retinues sat like chessmen of different colors, grouped for the start of an undeclared game. Deirdre distinguished their ladies from the raucous serving wenches by their dress and their stations at the tables. Their behavior was hardly distinguishable—aside from their disdain for the lower classes.

"Oh yes," Helewis answered, upon swallowing the chunk of lamb she'd just bitten off a section of leg. "I love to escape from these walls into the countryside."

Escape. Yes, they were sisters of the same heart, trapped in loveless matches. "Then we'll have to schedule a ride every day. Gunnar is to see me to the chapel and back daily. Afterward, we'll ride."

"I would like to see the chapel, too," Helewis exclaimed, brightening for a moment. Just as suddenly, she faded back to her customary meekness. "That is, if it is no intrusion. It is our new faith, yet I know little about it."

"God's house is open to all," Deirdre answered, although she wondered at the sincerity of Helewis's motivation to really be with her.

More likely it was Gunnar's company she sought.

God can use all manner of earthly motivations to accomplish the heavenly...

Perhaps this was some minute part in a grand heavenly scheme. Regardless, she certainly was not one to judge them.

Glancing to where Gunnar and Alric drank with the *Wulfshead's* crew, she met the dark-haired first mate's gaze. He smiled, color rising to his face as he acknowledged her, but Deirdre knew he had not been looking to catch her eye. She returned the gesture, somehow reassured that she would have at least two allies in the enemy camp besides sweet Abina.

A third made himself known later that evening. Lambert, stricken with yet another headache, refused the witan's medicine and asked Deirdre to sing before he retired. Nervous at first, she took up the harp Hengist gave her. This time the chief musician didn't seem as offended that the king chose someone else to play for him.

"Sing more than one," Lambert encouraged.

Alric looked up from where he'd been speaking to Gunnar. What he thought about his father's request was impossible to tell, for he promptly schooled his features to polite interest.

Deirdre sang the song of Michael the Victorious, drawing a sense of assurance from it herself. The king pressed his head against the small silk pillow a servant brought him and closed his eyes, listening. Some of the thanes at his table continued to speak, but most were content to hear the farmer's humble plea for heaven's messenger to protect him and his family and his land.

"That song speaks to me." Lambert sighed, never opening his eyes. "You mustn't take her far away, Alric," he cautioned, half in jest. "She has a gift."

Alric yielded to a discerning study of her. "Aye, that she must, but be assured that neither I nor my lady will be so far removed that you cannot avail yourself of our support." Alric gave Ricbert a pointed look. Like two rival dogs, one watched the other with equal distrust. And like a ringmaster, Lambert egged them on in a game of his own.

Deirdre wondered that one or the other hadn't killed his brother by now, for murder haunted Ricbert's glare, contempt Alric's, and calculation worked in their father's. She began to understand why Alric believed in so little. Nothing was as it seemed in Galstead.

"Your gifts will put all of Galstead at your feet, milady, including myself," Alric said later as he walked her back to Abina's lodge. Admiration filled his voice. It appeared genuine, but this was the Sodom and Gomorrah of deception.

"You ride as well as any man," he elaborated. "But for Dustan's longer gait, you and Ninga would have won the day. You sing like an angel…" He stopped before Abina's door and turned her face so that the moon glow fell upon it. "And you look like one."

Leaning toward her, he started to brush her lips, but Deirdre turned away. She knew Alric's suit was born of greed, not love. But if she let him kiss her, what she knew and what she felt would have at each other—and she feared which would prevail.

"What are you doing?" His brow furrowed as she dropped to her knees on the ground.

"Praying."

"Now?" Crossness added backbone to his demand.

Hands folded beneath her chin, she looked up at him. "I pray that someday you will believe that we were matched by God's hand and not that of fate."

"Does it really matter?"

"It does to me." She chewed her bottom lip at the scowl claiming Alric's brow. "I'm not pretending to be holier than thou. I don't even know why God chose me to give this gift to, but I know that He did. And so I mustn't take any risk that would distract me from His will."

"And I distract you?" With a cocky air, Alric leaned against the side of the building, arms folded across his chest. "Since our marriage is to be blessed by both His presence and His priest, how is that distracting you from His will?"

"If your motivation for that marriage is anything but love, it will."

"Do you even know what love is, my pampered, virgin princess?"

"I know there is a difference between love and lust. Lust is temporal. Animals can lust, but they cannot love."

"Tell that to Tor."

Upon hearing his name, the dog shoved his head against Alric's thigh.

Deirdre petted the wolfhound, earning a generous lick. "Love is eternal."

"Do you believe in fairies as well?"

Ignoring the jibe, Deirdre slipped into the past for memories of her mother and father. "Love can overcome anything. It's strong, able to weather differences and allow for forgiveness, because each one knows the other is not perfect. It's unselfish, putting another ahead of one's self...enough to be willing to die for that loved one. It's unconditional."

"You mean like our marriage contract?" Kicking away from the building, Alric mimicked a bow. "Milady, I think you'd best consider your own advice before handing it out to others. Good night."

Stunned, Deirdre stared after Alric's retreating figure. "You cannot contract the heart," she called after him as she recouped her thoughts. But it was too late. The shadows of the buildings swallowed him up as if he'd never existed. She sat back against her legs, deflated with dismay.

Oh, heavenly Father, he's making sense to me. Please, please show me what to do. And if that fails, for I know I am thick witted at times, tell Scanlan so that he can explain it to me. Otherwise, I fear my heart and soul are in danger from a golden heathen with a silver tongue.

TWENTY-THREE

Aside from fittings, there was little for Deirdre to do in Galstead. Ethlinda insisted on overseeing the wedding plans and, considering the circumstances of the marriage, Deirdre's input was hardly needed anyway. The highlight of her days were the rides she took on Ninga. Helewis, who took to Deirdre as a sister, accompanied her, as well as Gunnar—Alric's watchdog. Ironically, Gunnar's eyes were more on Helewis than on Deirdre, and vice versa.

The second week of her stay, Deirdre was astonished to have the king himself join their daily exercise. He vowed that her song accounted for his remarkable recovery from his headaches, although Deirdre suspected his not taking the powders his wife and witan had been giving him was more likely. Regardless, his company proved surprisingly stimulating.

With Gunnar and Helewis hanging back, allegedly out of respect, Deirdre spoke her mind on many matters, from Galstead's drought to her views on astrology and Scripture.

"By thunder, diverting the river to the fields through those ditches makes more sense than just sitting here twiddling our thumbs," Lambert exclaimed, adding dourly, "or sacrificing good livestock to a tree."

"Mind you, we cannot possibly irrigate every hide of land in the shire." She offered him a smile. "Only God, who sends the rain, can save them all."

Gunnar's voice called to them from the rear. "I told Your Majesty that Alric has caught himself a scholar *and* a beauty."

Deirdre didn't think he was even listening, but then the shy Helewis wasn't much of a conversationalist, and there was only so much they could discuss in the king's company without blatantly flaunting their affections for one another.

"Tell His Majesty of your theory on the sun and stars as the first timepiece."

"A timepiece?" Lambert turned to Deirdre for an explanation.

"When God created heaven and earth and hung the sun and the moon, He made the first measure of time. Their cycles mark off our hours, days, months, and years. By observing them, the earliest of man could mark off time."

The king's brow furrowed. "And this is in the Scriptures you are always referring to?"

"The creation part is," Deirdre said, "but the theory of the timepiece is a humble theory of mine as to why He created them so. All things were created for mankind. The Scriptures are written as instructions for us, whether we are kings or peasants, warriors or wives..."

"Instructions for kings and warriors?" Lambert's interest was piqued now.

"The greatest and most-loved warrior kings in history followed them. In fact—" Deirdre felt a burst of inspiration not of her own making—"many of them face the same trials you do, Sire, both as a king and a father."

Daily afterward, Scanlan was called upon to bless the thanes and shire reeve before they were sent out to supervise the clearing of the ditches and swales. Lambert heard the stories of King David—the problems among his sons, his women, and his court with a new fascination. From what Deirdre could ascertain, Orlaith had shared them from a salvation standpoint but not from the perspective of royal rule and all its pitfalls and glory. While neither the priest nor Deirdre took this as a sign of Lambert's acceptance of faith, the king's interest kindled his thanes' interest—as well as that of his people.

At the end of the second week, Alric's ship put in at Chesreton with a sizeable cargo seized from the Dalraidi trade route. While it was only grain, the ship that carried it was the real prize, which would increase the prince's fleet by one more, once a few repairs were done. Deirdre made certain to look her best in anticipation of her betrothed's arrival, but instead of coming to Galstead to visit his bride to be, the captain of the *Wulfshead* put out to sea again for one more venture.

If he thought to punish Deirdre for spurning his affections, it worked. She called him all manner of names in her mind, and when he did show his face again, she was determined to repay him with as good as he gave. Her days spent with the king and Scanlan were full enough, but during the nightly feasting in the hall, she never felt more alone.

Gunnar did his best to keep her company, but it was Helewis he truly sought. It was heartbreaking to see the unrequited love light in their gazes doused by one of Ricbert's snide remarks. It was only Helewis's pleading looks that kept Gunnar from calling the malicious heir apparent out.

"My life will never be complete without Lady Helewis, and it is sheer torture to see such a pure, sweet maid so mistreated and maligned," Gunnar confessed one day as he and Deirdre meandered through their market on the way to visit Scanlan. "What, then, is there to live for? Save the satisfaction of serving Ricbert his noxious tongue on the tip of a blade." The lovesick pirate drew his dagger and buried it in a tongue of an ox on display in front of the butcher's shop.

"I vow, I've never felt so hopeless." He sighed, dismay piling upon dismay, and kicked at the straw-strewn ground.

"God will sustain you, Gunnar." Deirdre was certain it was true, but uncertain as to how. Ahead of them, a thatcher waved from the roof of the chapel. Below, his apprentice trimmed a bundle of thatching straw before handing it up to him. "I have personally seen Him accomplish some impossible things," she murmured as Scanlan stepped out of the lodge, grinning. He swung the newly hung door back and forth, admiring the handiwork of the carpenter who was fitting the top of an altar table on its base. Deirdre indicated the building before them. "God rebuilds our shattered lives through our faith, even as He has done this little church, one piece at a time."

"Isn't it wonderful?" Scanlan encompassed the whole of Galstead with a sweep of his arms. "We have to assemble on the commons because there is not enough room for my flock here."

"Did someone contribute to the chapel?" Deirdre asked. Surely the cost of thatching and repairing the building was no small sum.

"I spoke on Colossians last week—doing all as one would do for the Lord—and these good men showed up this morning to work for

God." The brightness in Scanlan's eyes stung Deirdre's own. "I have seen miracles abound, more than even I believed possible. If ever there was a place ripe for God's message of hope, it is this one—from the king to the peasant, they thirst for spiritual water as the land does for rain. Had we made our journey uninterrupted—"

"Pardon me, Father, but could ye have a look at this?" the carpenter called out.

Scanlan didn't have to finish. Deirdre knew exactly what he meant. Their capture was no accident but part of a plan. Alric, Gunnar—they were merely unwitting instruments. But what of Cairell? Had Alric found out anything?

Chances were that he hadn't, as he'd been at sea practically the entire month. Even now tents were being set up on the common for the arrival of wedding guests. She'd had her last fitting in Helewis's beautiful gown of lavender damask just that morning.

"If you don't mind, milady, I saw a lady selling ribbons a while back. I'd like to purchase a blue one to match Helewis's eyes."

It was a sweet thought, no doubt sincere, but Deirdre had not missed the young man's interest in a friendly wrestling match between some strapping youths near the livestock pens.

"Go," Deirdre told Gunnar. When she came to visit the chapel, he was as restless as a dog on a leash. "Why don't I meet you back at the court? Scanlan can escort me."

The young warrior needed no further absolution. He was off in a flash. Left to her own devices, she walked past Scanlan, who was holding a piece of molding in place, and into the chapel.

Seated on one of the aged benches, Deirdre bowed her head. *Father, You have indeed worked miracles these last weeks, and I believe—I have to believe—that You are caring for my brother as You have seen to my needs and comfort. Lead Alric to him, I pray, that at least Cairell might return to Gleannmara and our father. I do not think father's health could bear the loss of our mother and both his children.*

Straw dust from above sprinkling her hair and clothes, Deirdre kept her quiet vigil in the midst of the work going on outside and above her. The enemy who held her captive had faces now—and troubled hearts, where she once thought none beat at all. How inadequate she felt to be chosen to speak to them of God's love, when, like Jonah, she was prepared to condemn her Nineveh rather than seek to save it.

Forgive me my pride and prejudice. Perhaps she'd learned as much of God's love in the last few weeks as those she'd been chosen to teach. Christ's plea to forgive those who tormented Him because they knew not what they did had never seemed so befitting, not just in Galstead, but in Deirdre herself. So many verses she'd studied had taken on a new light since her captivity.

"Excuse me, milady."

Deirdre turned at Scanlan's hesitant intrusion.

"I must go to the common now. Will you come with me or will Gunnar return for you?"

"I sent him on without me," she admitted, "but I'd like to remain here for a little while longer, if you don't mind." Scanlan usually spoke for an hour to the men and women coming in from the fields near the day's end. In increasing numbers, they stopped and listened as time or interest afforded. "I'll wait for you to return."

Scanlan pointed to his plain wooden traveling chest. "I've books in there, if you wish."

"Thank you, dear heart." She'd known the man a lifetime, yet it was only in the past weeks that she realized just how dear a heart her clansman was. "I'll take a look, though mostly I'll just enjoy the quiet."

Deirdre closed the door behind him to shut out as much noise as she could. The door no longer creaked in a spine-raking manner on its one hinge but moved silently on two new ones. She was surprised that among her kinsman's few precious books was a favorite of her own: *Mythology of Ancient Man.* She chuckled at the idea of a priest fascinated by mythology, and she made herself comfortable on the bench against the wall. Aside from being thrown together to work God's will these last weeks, it seemed they had yet another interest in common.

Deirdre found one of her favorite myths—on how the changing of the seasons came to be—and began to read by the sunlight pouring through the open window. It was warm on her shoulder and, combined with the solitude, relaxing. Breathing a sigh of contentment, she was drawn into the story of the maid who'd been carried off by her rakish abductor to his dark world. His loneliness and torment in his own kingdom softened her heart toward him, as she softened his, and they fell in love. Deirdre blinked sleepily.

Love. It was always the one thing in both myth and reality that overcame all obstacles. If only…

What startled Deirdre from her inadvertent nap, she had no idea. Perhaps it was the jar of her head as it dropped to her chest. She straightened and folded the book shut. In the midst of a most unladylike yawn, a passing shadow shuttered off the sun outside the window, yet upon listening, she heard nothing. Heavens, how long had she slept?

"Scanlan?" She jumped to her feet, stirring a cloud of dust in the streaming sunlight.

Goodness, she was covered in it. Deirdre shook her skirts and brushed her shoulders and arms, walking toward the door. The market must be closed or closing, she thought. No more had her fingers brushed the door when it opened.

But instead of Scanlan, Ricbert of Galstead stood agape at the entrance.

"Well, well, if it's not our *perfectly, pious, princess,*" he said, with punctuated mockery.

Alarm snuffed Deirdre's peace as completely as the man before her blocked the doorway. "What are *you* doing here?"

There were more shops near the chapel than homes. This late in the day, the market was usually closed, now that Scanlan held services on the common. The stories Helewis shared about Ricbert made Deirdre's skin crawl, exactly as it was now.

"I've come to be saved."

She stepped back as Ricbert ducked under the low header and straightened inside.

"Well, then, I wish you the best." Deirdre made to move around him, but he planted his hand against the frame, thwarting her.

"You've used those sweet lips with such heart to save my father," the man drawled. "Surely you might spare a word—or a taste—for me."

"Milord, you will step aside now, please." The door bumped against the outside wall as Deirdre's heart struck her throat. How she spoke, she couldn't imagine, but her voice projected a deadly calm she did not possess.

Undaunted, Ricbert laughed. "Hah, you seem to forget which court you find yourself in. 'Tis *mine,* not yours, my feisty little princess, and I have a wedding present for you."

Deirdre drew away when he reached for her face, but he lunged after her, seizing her roughly. Stitches in her dress ripped on the shoulder he sought to expose. The sound grazed her spine like a cold spike of steel, but instead of rendering her weak with panic, it fortified her.

"This is *not* your court!" she ground out, turning her face as he tried again to kiss her mouth. "'Tis *God's.*"

She drove the heel of her foot hard into the top of his, eliciting a yelp. His hold loosened, and she elbowed Ricbert's stomach. With all her strength, she shoved her hand against his sharp, bearded chin, driving his head against the low frame over the door with a nasty crack. As he dropped, dazed and cursing to his knees, she barreled past him and broke into a dead run down the row of abandoned stalls and around the tinsmith's shop on the main avenue to the gate.

"Milady?"

A man stepped out as she turned the corner toward the town proper. Deirdre glanced over her shoulder to where the bemused shopkeeper followed for a split second. Suddenly, Deirdre slammed hard against a wall of living flesh, just as hard and unyielding as any made of stone. With a startled grunt, she bounced backward, her feet scrambling for footing in the dry, rutted thoroughfare.

"Deirdre!" Developing hands, the living wall caught her before she sprawled on the ground.

Stunned and half hanging in its grasp, Deirdre looked up. It had a face as well, and the face belonged to Alric. She made some sort of sound, half laugh, half cry. Then, winded and mad with relief, she threw her arms about his neck and held on in case her wobbly knees gave way completely. She was safe at last.

"Frig's breath, you look like you've been rolling in the hay!" He picked at the straw in her hair.

Frig's breath. Alric's familiar curse had never sounded so sweet to the ear.

"And his teeth and eyes," she chimed in, a bit hysterical.

"Hers," he corrected, neither hysterical, nor amused.

"What?" Deirdre tilted her head back to judge the nature of his humor and blinked as he pulled another bit of straw from the hair clinging to her forehead.

"Where in Woden's world is Gunnar?" The thunder in Alric's voice sobered her giddy relief. "I forbade you to go anywhere without him."

She had nearly paid dearly for her disobedience. "I was supposed to wait for Scanlan," she blurted out, glancing back to see if Ricbert had been foolish enough to follow her. Just as she thought, there was no sign of him. The man was a coward hiding behind a bully's mask.

"He left me in Scanlan's care," she explained, her thoughts tripping ahead of her. All she had to do was tell Alric what had just happened and, in this humor, he'd kill not only Ricbert, but her and Gunnar as well.

"What happened to your dress?" Alric fingered the shoulder seam that Ricbert had ripped.

Father, forgive me, but I'm trying to prevent bloodshed. "I ripped it in the chapel," she answered, leaning as close to the truth as she could. "The thatcher was working on the roof while I was inside—you know what a shambles it was—and Scanlan wasn't back yet, so I left without him to bathe and dress for the evening."

It really wasn't a lie…just not the entire truth.

"Alone."

"Until I ran into you." At Alric's scowl, she added, "And I'm sorry. I just forgot."

"I gave you an order, woman," Alric's angry snap sent the tinker back into his lodge.

Deirdre bristled at the very idea. "An *order?*"

"You gave me your word," he said in a softer tone.

"As you forgot me, I forgot all about you…just as I forgot for a minute that I was angry at you." She thumped an accusing finger at the vee of his shirtfront. "You left me here the whole four weeks while you were off having a grand time on your boat."

"Ship."

"Toy," she countered, gathering up her skirts in a building huff. "That's no way to treat a bride to be, even if she is a bride to be against her will."

No less filled with righteous indignation, Alric folded his arms across his chest as if to keep them from reaching for her throat. Like two storm fronts about to clash on the horizon, they stood immobile, each waiting for the other to move. Intuition told her there would be no winning with Alric if she took him on as she had Ricbert. The pirate knew her too well.

There was only one thing to do—the unexpected. Abandoning her haughty stance, Deirdre ducked around the broad width of Alric's shoulders to make a mad dash for the city gates. The cheers of the guards warned her that she was being chased.

She heard only one loud thud that was not of her making, and Alric was upon her. His vicelike grip on her arm nearly yanked it from its socket. The momentum of her interrupted flight carrying her in a circle, and she smashed into his embrace, her cry of protest smothered by the harsh kiss he planted upon her lips.

Nostrils flaring with what wind she had left, Deirdre pushed against his uncompromising hold. Above the roar of the bloodrush in her ears, she made out laughter and crude jests coming from more people than she had seen in her hasty retreat. They seemed to whet Alric's appetite for a long, torturous revenge, just as it provoked a riot of its own upon her senses.

Deirdre tried to stomp his foot as she had Ricbert's but only skimmed it, spurring Alric to lift her off the ground in defense. The more she railed against him, the tighter his arms closed around her, until she grew lightheaded from the effort. Only when she surrendered—outmanned, outmuscled, and out of breath—did he offer her quarter.

A hero's cheer went up as he let her go and stepped back, pleased as a pig in lavender at his victory. "Is that the way my bride to be wished to be treated?"

Scarlet burning her face, Deirdre squared her shoulders with the dignity he'd so ravaged. "Unlike your townspeople, milord, *I* am unimpressed," she declared, once she was certain her knees had regained their worthiness. "Pity you won't be wed to *them.*"

With that, Deirdre turned and walked, head held high, through the city gates. Curse his black heart! Nearly four long weeks she'd felt as though she'd grown spiritually. And in four short minutes with Alric of Galstead, she was right back where she started—ready to send at least one Saxon to perdition.

No. Make that *two.* They deserved an eternity with each other.

TWENTY-FOUR

First she upsets his personal world, Alric fumed as he marched through the vendors' row, and now all of Galstead. The closer he had come to his father's town fortress, the more evident it became. Instead of working in the fields, churl and serf alike cleared the ditch banks. In the closest hides of land, water seeped into those ditches already open. While it was no more than knee-deep, it was enough that the crops on those long, rectangular pieces had begun to lose their wilted, dying look. Women and children filled pails from the ditches and carried the precious commodity inland in an attempt to revive even more. Although it looked like futile attempt to him, it seemed to have given something to the people that had not been there the last time he passed this way—heart.

What his idealistic bride to be didn't seem to realize was just how dangerous that could be in a place where a man was always a friend in fair weather, and with the coming of a shower—or the lack of one—he would become just as quickly one's deadliest enemy. This wasn't her safe haven of Gleannmara, though judging from the panic that drove her round the corner earlier, she'd found that out.

Her fear had become his the moment he saw it, stark and white upon her face. Her torn dress and disheveled state slashed at him like an enemy's blade, and he reacted accordingly, ready to exact revenge. He had every right to be upset that Gunnar and Deirdre had ignored his orders and worse, that she seemed bent on protecting whoever or whatever had frightened her.

Most of the vendors had gone to their homes for the day, and the chapel wedged in their midst seemed abandoned also. He stepped inside and saw nothing but an abandoned book lying on the bench near the window. It was still open, face down, which meant whatever had frightened Deirdre must have interrupted her reading.

He picked it up. Instantly he recognized the myth of Demeter and

Persephone. It had been part of his Latin studies. He supposed Deirdre might well feel like Persephone, carried off by hades' lord to a dark place. Like his mother, she had to miss her home.

Alric put the book down and shook off his twinge of guilt. He had his reasons, he thought, glancing inadvertently at the cross carved over the altar shelf. Even his mother's God approved, if Orlaith's vision was to be believed, and with each passing day he found it more difficult to explain recent events in any other way. He heaved a breath of frustration and stepped outside before the quiet sanctuary provoked too many memories of the peace and security he'd felt as a child kneeling beside his mother in that very place. Clearing the blade of grief in his throat, he stepped out into the open air, retreating...

From what? an inner voice challenged. *From peace and security? Why?*

Because it wasn't real. As he reached back to close the door, he heard a muffled thud inside. Bemused, since there was nowhere to hide in the single room, he glanced back. The book he'd returned to the bench lay on the floor. Ignoring the ripple of awareness tickling his spine, Alric put it back squarely.

Frig's breath, soon he'd be having visions himself. As he made certain the door was soundly latched behind him, his own observations turned upon him. *There is nowhere to hide...from God.* The sooner this wedding was over and he was out to sea, the better he'd be. Alric brushed off some of the fleck from the new roof, as if to rid himself of something deeper and more troubling, when he saw a crowd approaching from the commons. To his astonishment, his father's standards flew over it.

Heading out to meet the procession, Alric recognized Lambert walking beside Father Scanlan, both heartily engaged in conversation. His father without a horse and, more incredibly, speaking in earnest to a cleric after refusing to hear even Orlaith's testimony.

"Well, well, the bridegroom cometh." Lambert's call was utterly cheerful! The man was *never* cheerful, unless he was enjoying someone else's discomfiture. "But it's too late. All of Galstead has fallen in love with your bride. You may have to fight us all for her."

Alric's face grew hot, as though the sun were at its peak rather than completing its downswing for the day. Frig's breath, but she had a tick's way of working under one's skin and bleeding him dry of sanity.

"Hah, look at him, Scanlan! He stands on his tongue like a gaping fool."

That was more like his father. "Well, this fool has news for you, news that can be verified," Alric said with a pointed look at Father Scanlan. "I'd speak with you in private."

It wasn't wise to discuss affairs of the kingdom in public, but when Lambert insisted that Scanlan accompany him and his thanes to the private chamber of the hall, Alric nearly forgot what he had to tell them. Deirdre obviously was not the only tick on the hound.

"Well, let's have it," Lambert instructed, after the men had been served mead.

"One of my captains informed me that the Welsh are gathering forces near the border, more than is needed for one of their cattle raids."

"How many?" one of the thanes asked.

"Somewhere around five hundred men when he was there. More were en route."

"Those infernal Welsh are a wart on the hind of the earth."

Gunnar's father snorted at Lambert's vehemence. "I can take my men and fortify Chesreton."

"And leave Galstead itself short of men, Cedric?" Lambert said.

"Short of men for what?"

Alric turned to spy Ricbert at the entrance to the chamber.

"You call a counsel, Father, and leave me out?"

Alric bore the scorch of his half brother's look without effect. "The Welsh are gathering an army on the border. We are discussing what to do."

"Ricbert, what happened to your lip?" Lambert demanded curiously.

"I bit it," he snapped. "Most annoying." He took a cup of mead from the maidservant with a smile.

"Most of our army is with Ecfrith," Lambert said, returning to the subject at hand. "But thanks to Alric's wedding, a good number of neighbors will be attending and can supply us with men."

"If you ask me, you should have paid the Mercians their protection money." Ricbert took a deep draught of the brew.

"I didn't and I won't," the indignant king replied. "Alric, can we count on manpower from your ships to defend Chesreton?"

"Absolutely. There is one ship in port. More are due within the next two weeks."

"Excellent, Son, excellent." Lambert rose from the table. "Cedric, you know what you need to do. I'll send messages to our wedding guests advising them of the situation. If Galstead is threatened, so are they." Those seated around the council table rose, following the king's suit, when Lambert stopped them. "Father Scanlan, a prayer, if you will."

"A prayer?" Ricbert's words dripped with contempt. "You offend Mother's gods?" A few of the men at the table mumbled agreement.

"Let it not be said that I am not a fair ruler," the king said firmly. "I will treat no one's god greater than another."

Scanlan flinched. It was barely perceptible, but Alric did not miss it. How often he'd seen his mother do the same thing.

"Now, Scanlan, if you will." Leaning toward Alric, the king whispered in a none-too-quiet voice. "The man has something in his book for every occasion."

And Lambert was listening to it, Alric marveled. Granted, it was not the whole acceptance required by the Christian God, but just to get the king to listen was a major step. Alric waited, head bowed from an ingrained respect regardless of his belief. A few awkwardly followed his example. Lambert was not one of them. He looked at the priest in anticipation, as if he'd presented the cleric with a test and awaited the answer.

"In the book of Isaiah the Lord says, 'When thou passest through the waters, I will be with thee; and through the rivers, they shall not overflow thee: when thou walkest through the fire, thou shalt not be burned; neither shall the flame kindle upon thee.' And in the book of Acts, Jesus Himself said of His followers meant to spread the Word of

God, that 'Ye shall receive power, after that the Holy Ghost is come upon you: and ye shall be witnesses unto me...unto the uttermost part of the earth."

Alric glanced around the table through half-lidded eyes. Did these men understand what Scanlan really said? Power certainly appealed to this lot, if nothing else did. They feared weakness more than death itself. And what Scanlan spoke of was a contract, as well constructed as the one the priest had contrived for the wedding. If all went well, it was valid. If not, it would be an excuse for failure.

But whose failure...yours or God's?

If Alric could lay hands on the voice that crept upon him seemingly from nowhere, he'd squash it as he would an insect.

The hush seemed to intensify as Father Scanlan continued his prayer. "Father, we lean upon Your Word and its truth as You look into our hearts for our earnest confession and belief. These people have not known You long, Lord, and some not at all, but their ears are open to You. They ask that Yours be open to them and their petition for water of the sky and of the living Spirit, that their people might be fed the same. We ask all this in the name of He who sacrificed Himself for us, so no other sacrifice need suffice in His stead. Amen."

The scent of a summer meadow ablaze with wildflowers filled the lodge as Deirdre stripped and stepped into the wooden tub of water boiled with Abina's own selection of dried herbs and flowers. Because Lambert's guests were being attended to at the bathhouse, where a larger tub was in service, her own bath had been delayed, but she didn't mind. Deirdre asked Abina to tell the king that she would attend his table later. For now, she would enjoy the luxury of the warm, scented water without hurry, even if her legs were drawn up to her chin in its confinement.

Besides, given Alric's mood, she hardly felt like celebrating her upcoming marriage to the man. How could she possibly have pined for his fiendish humor? It would serve him right to squirm alone at the head table after treating her like one of his underlings. It was a fine line that separated Alric from his half brother. Both were beasts. One she had no trouble fending off.

Alric, however…

Deirdre furiously worked Abina's soap into her hair, as though ridding herself of both the snake and the strutting peacock who'd claimed her lips so triumphantly before his men. Had she been able to collect her wits as she had with Ricbert, she'd have at least bitten Alric's lip.

Eventually, her frustrations succumbed to the water's restful spell as she rinsed her hair and leaned back against the tub, using one of the raised handles as a neck rest. Too soon for her liking, the water became uncomfortably cool, so Deirdre hastily dried off and pulled on a thin, embroidered undershift of fine linen.

Two more days and she'd leave Abina's cozy little abode and cheerful company to share Alric's lodge. Tingles of anxiety and excitement raised the gooseflesh on her skin at the thought. Though theirs was not to be an intimate relationship, just being near Alric plunged her into a tizzy of mixed feelings. While he was away, she'd blindly followed her instincts—God's direction—with the king and the people of Galstead. But with Alric, logic fled, and she became as moon addled as her father with her stepmother.

Deirdre's hand stopped the hairbrush in midstroke. Heaven forbid, was *that* what was wrong with her?

"You look as though you've seen a ghost."

A poke with a hayfork wouldn't have brought Deirdre to her feet any faster than the male voice behind her. She turned to face the very source of her madness. "You…well…I…" There was not a single coherent thought to emerge from the quagmire of her brain.

"The door was…uh…" Alric pulled his sweeping gaze away from her and pointed to the door. "Ajar," he said triumphantly.

"*Moonlight passion fades in the light of the sun.*" Deirdre's words to Orna on the deck of the *Mell* flashed back to her.

"I came to see what was keeping you." Alric's smile was almost sheepish, out of character but most beguiling. "There are many who would like to meet my bride to be."

"I sent Abina to explain that I'd be late." She knew she was immodestly clothed, yet she could not move…could not think beyond the burn of his gaze. *Father in heaven, spare me this. Help me to remember I'm angry and that it will take more than a winsome smile to…*

"And I wanted to speak to you…to apologize…at least explain my behavior earlier." He turned his gaze away, yet it returned to her seemingly of its own accord. "I'd appreciate it if you put something more on so that I can concentrate on what I need to say instead of the enticing form you present in front of the window."

Deirdre stood frozen, blank for a moment until the sense of his statement sank in. With a gasp, she scrambled to don the blue dress Abina had laid out on the bed. It fought her at every pull and tug, but eventually afforded her decency. At the same time, Alric turned his back to her.

Faith, if he never said another word, that consideration alone was a winning one. She stared at his wide shoulders, fascinated by the manly taper to the narrow of his waist. "I…um…I'm decent now." Deirdre smoothed the nonexistent wrinkles of her dress. If her heart beat any faster, it would leave her chest.

Alric cleared his throat and turned, speaking quickly as if he would lose the words if he did not use them immediately. "Deirdre, when I saw how frightened you were, I was afraid that someone had threatened or harmed you. If I was unreasonable, it was because of my concern for you."

Again he cleared his throat. "Everything I have ever had, I've had to fight for and then fight to hold on to." He scuffed aside a wet towel with his foot. "And as for the kiss…well, you challenged my authority in front of my men. I can't permit that. Frig's mercy!" He ran his hands through his hair. "You would drive a saint insane, and I am no saint. I used to think I was logical, but no logic I know applies when it comes to you."

Deirdre's heart did a dizzy little dance within her chest. "You feel moon addled?"

Alric turned, dumbstruck. "Yes, that's exactly it."

"I also. You bring out the worst in me because I'm not accustomed to it."

"The very worst." He stepped up to her and clasped her shoulders with gentle fingers. "And something quite pleasant as well, like a fine wine."

Leaning over, he caressed her mouth with his. His fingers wound through her damp hair, but Deirdre was too intoxicated by the wine of his affections to notice the pull. His thumbs moved the curls away from her forehead, clearing it for another worshipful brush of his lips.

"Wine treats one well when treated well—" He slipped his hands off her shoulders and swept her into his embrace—"and exacts a terrible vengeance when abused."

"Like love." Deirdre nestled her head against his shoulder with a giddy sigh, her face buried in the hollow of his neck. She felt him nuzzle the top of her head.

"Then if this is what I am pledging to, I shall mean every word of our vows."

Were she not loathe to miss a heartbeat of what was transpiring between them, Deirdre would have swooned with joy. "I, also."

They hardly spoke poetry, yet the muse that held them translated their words into magic, and magic into feelings that carried their hearts beyond the limitations of their bodies.

"I want you as my wife in every sense of the word, muirnait," Alric whispered, as he tilted her face away and kissed her from her forehead to her chin. "*Every* sense."

His lips found hers, kindling a wildfire that melded her body against his. Echoes of sweet surrender assaulted her thoughts, like sirens drawing her toward fulfillment of every sense.

Every sense. It sounded wonderful—and terrifying. Was *this* why her father had given in to her stepmother and compromised his integrity and good judgment?

Every sense. Now Deirdre understood. Temptation was the heart's worst enemy, for it made fools of both man and woman.

"There you are," Abina exclaimed from the doorway. Upon seeing how untimely her intrusion was, she laughed, unabashed. "Look at the two lovebirds." She clasped her hands together. "But you must wait just two more nights."

Alric at long last gave Deirdre reprieve, stepping away reluctantly. "Abina, your sense of timing has not faltered with age." The good-natured complaint was for his elderly nurse, but his eyes—those silver fountains of intoxication—were for Deirdre alone, to drink from as much as she wished. But she dared not. He knew nothing of love, only lust.

"Yes, it was perfect," Deirdre chimed in. What might she have agreed to in the state of honeyed bliss he conjured in her? "We were just agreeing that nothing is going to make us change our marriage contract, weren't we, *muirnait?*"

At the Irish endearment, Abina's face brightened enough to illuminate the room in the waning light of day. "I praise God that I have lived to see it."

"Nothing?" Alric repeated, disbelief registering on his face.

Deirdre rallied. "Nothing." *Thank You, Father in heaven, for stopping me from making a terrible mistake. This wolf could charm the wool off an innocent lamb.*

The wolf frowned. "I thought—"

"You thought wrong."

"This is that priest's fault."

"I made the terms. Scanlan only approved them."

"You'll change your mind."

"When you prove that you are a husband in the scriptural sense, I shall be a biblical wife."

"I just said I did…" Alric groaned in exasperation. "I mean, I am…or am willing to be."

"You must love me as you love Christ, and since you cannot love Christ, you cannot love me."

"I never heard such a thing." Alric marched toward the door.

"Ask Scanlan. You're no real husband until you do."

Alric stopped, casting a formidable look over his shoulder. "I will," he vowed. "Trust me, Deirdre, I *will.*"

TWENTY-FIVE

Alric listened halfheartedly to the conversation of the guests at his father's table. Conspicuously absent were the royal ladies. Both Deirdre and Helewis had sent word of indisposition, which Lambert attributed to prewedding dithers. As for the queen, she was about the business of a sacrifice to her gods for the sake of Galstead's safety against the building Welsh forces at their border.

"While our new priest, Scanlan—" the king motioned to where the priest sat among the remaining witans in the hall—"is teaching us the ways of Northumbria's Christian God, I believe in protecting both flanks."

The priest winced at the comment, one that was likely missed by the multitudes but not by Alric, who watched him like a hawk. He would have a word with the meddlesome holy man before the night was out and settle this ridiculous notion of a marriage without conjugal rights. Alric would never have agreed to such an absurdity if he hadn't believed that he could change Deirdre's mind by playing upon her natural-born desires. The wedding was upon them, and while Deirdre the woman had responded to him, Deirdre the maid, who'd been so browbeaten with piety by this priest, held her back. He should have addressed the issue with Scanlan right away, but since Deirdre had come into his life, reason had fled.

Through the thin haze of smoke from the central fire, Alric watched Scanlan converse with the witans of the court, who had changed with the times. Like their predecessor, the pagan priest Coifi of Edwin's court, had nearly a half century before, they felt the new Christian faith held something more certain beyond man's fleeting existence in time. Others, like Juist, continued to travel the old path.

Those championing the past gathered to the king's right, where Ricbert entertained most of his mother's Mercian relatives. On the king's left were those who had yielded to the new ways. In his glory,

Lambert played one side against the other. Regard for the rule of the king's peace—and the fact that all weapons save dining daggers had been left outside the hall—ensured the lively debates did not turn violent.

Alric had to admit that Scanlan was persuasive. He not only spoke the Word, but lived it, which was why so many paid him heed. Unlike the Roman priests who'd come to Chesreton in the past, Scanlan had taken the time to learn the Saxon language and customs. He lived humbly, asking nothing for himself save meager hospitality afforded to anyone. Even in the king's hall, the priest had hardly eaten enough to fill a child's plate, much less that of his lean, tall frame.

When at long last Scanlan rose and graciously excused himself, Alric was ready for him.

"Ho, priest," he called out from the door to the great hall. "I'd have a word with you, if I may."

"By all means, milord." Scanlan waited for Alric to catch up with him. "What can I do for you?"

Alric fell in step with him, whispering so that others milling around the large building could not hear. "I want you to talk Deirdre out of this nonsense of not being my wife in every sense."

Scanlan paused, casting a surprised glance Alric's way, and then started forward again. "I thought you and the lady had settled on this issue. Based on my assurance to her that you were a man of your word, she agreed to sign the contract without its inclusion."

As they passed through the gate, Alric returned the wave of the guards. "I *am* a man of my word, but I didn't think she understood…that is to say…Frig's breath! You're a man. You know full well what I mean, unless they gelded you before you came of age."

To Alric's further annoyance, the priest chuckled. "Deirdre would beguile the hardest heart," he admitted, a little too dreamily to Alric's notion.

"Sir, I—" Alric broke off as Gunnar rounded the corner of vendors' row.

"Where in Woden's world have you been?" Alric demanded. "I left you to stay with Deirdre, not take your leisure as you see fit."

Gunnar was taken aback at Alric's foul humor. "You did, and I saw her safely into *his* care." He nodded to the priest.

Alric started to reply that his friend shouldn't be so sure of that, but the matter of his bride to be was between him and Scanlan for now.

"The lady is well, isn't she?" Gunnar asked, glancing from Alric to Scanlan and back.

"She would beguile the hardest heart," Alric mimicked with a glare at the priest.

There was a moment's awkward silence before Scanlan broke it. "The prince and I were about to discuss the wedding plans, and he rides the edge of his humor. I recommend you hasten to the hall before you miss the meal altogether."

"Yes, well…" Gunnar rubbed his stomach. "I could eat the whole bullock I saw Juist choosing earlier for his sacrifice."

"Waste of good beef."

Alric and Scanlan exchanged surprised looks at their simultaneous remarks. It was difficult to dislike the man, but no one meddled in his personal life without invitation, no matter who sent him, God or man.

"Then I'm off. A pleasant evening to you, gentlemen, and my apologies, Alric, if I have caused you or your lady any distress. It was obviously a misunderstanding on my part."

Ordinarily, Alric would have questioned his subordinate more, but his mind was on other things as he and Scanlan walked the rest of the way to where the chapel stood, its newly thatched roof standing at attention against the starlit sky.

"That's odd." Scanlan put the small lantern he carried on a shelf inside the door. "It smells as if someone has just doused a candle. You don't suppose your Gunnar—"

"Not likely." God had too many taboos to suit his friend.

"Perhaps one of my new listeners." The idea pleased the priest. "I say *listeners,* for as yet, most are like your father, intrigued and accepting of God but afraid to let go of their old ones. Until one does so, he is not reborn. Like the flowers that bloom each spring, they must shed the old completely and become new."

"I didn't come to discuss flowers or my father." Alric dropped on a bench and folded his arms across his chest. "I want to know what your relationship is with my bride to be, for I'm thinking your interest in her is more than that of a priest."

"Deirdre and I come from the same bloodlines, one blessed with miracles. I have been trained for such things in the hope that God would continue those blessings through me. Instead, the gift fell to the princess. It's only natural that I would mentor and protect her—"

"Curse it, man, are you in love with Deirdre or not?"

Scanlan's mouth fell open, as though his chin were weighted with stone.

"I had to ask." Alric felt the fool at Scanlan's shock.

The priest was too kind to take advantage of Alric's embarrassment. "At least now I understand your sudden hostility. Rest assured that I protect Deirdre as her closest male relative and in the name of God."

Satisfied, Alric switched to his original purpose. Scanlan might not be interested in Deirdre as a woman, but he would still make a martyr of her at Alric's expense.

"I read in your Scripture that God warns a wife against withholding her body from her husband." Alric smiled at the lift of the priest's brow. "Aye, I have my mother's Bible and have read bits of it, enough to know that you have no right to put ideas to the contrary in Deirdre's head."

"That admonishment is in there," the priest admitted. "But the key word here is *husband.*"

"I will be that, before the laws of God and man, when I take the vows."

"But will you follow all the admonishments God gives to the husband?"

"'Tis wordplay! I can't love her as I love Christ because I have no regard for Christ."

"You want the princess *completely* as your wife before God, yet you do not wish to commit *completely* as her husband."

"I will not be like Lambert and use this God for my own means, if that is what you imply." Alric jumped to his feet and paced across the room. "Not when I still have doubts."

"Then what are you doing about those doubts?"

Alric turned. "What do you mean?"

"Are you seeking the truth or resolution of your doubts, or are you simply content to disbelieve?"

"I would...have the truth." Alric hadn't been seeking any sort of spiritual truth. He didn't feel spiritual, never had—

No, that wasn't true. Right here in this little room, he'd once thought he felt God, back when he was a child and believed. But then he'd fought imaginary dragons, too.

"God is an understanding God who wants you to know Him as closely as an earthly anmchara," Scanlan said softly, as though he knew he was treading upon private ground.

God as a soul mate? Alric supposed He'd been such to Orlaith, for often, especially in later years, she spoke of keeping His company in the long and lonely hours.

"If you earnestly seek the truth with a heart and mind open to His Spirit," Scanlan went on, "that is, if you seek only what you *can* accept rather than what you cannot, He will reveal His truth to you. No man, not even I, can reveal it to you so that you know it is God. That is between the Lord and you alone."

Alric had never heard a priest say not to take his word on something. He was an anomaly. "Then what good are you priests?"

Scanlan sighed. "Sometimes, I wonder...like when I hear your father say that he will worship all gods, so as not to honor one over another."

"Father is more political than spiritual."

"And when he truly accepts God, the Holy Spirit will guide his politics, not greed or power."

Alric snorted. The priest had a lot more talking to do, although Scanlan had at least gotten Lambert to listen to him. Or Deirdre had convinced the king to listen to the priest.

"A man changes when he accepts Christ as his savior and guide."

The statement fell between them like a sword cast in the ground. Alric stared at the invisible weapon quivering. It wasn't his nature to walk away from a challenge and he wasn't about to do so now.

"I'd have to weigh the cost," he answered cautiously.

Scanlan's gaze dove into Alric's like a gull after a fat fish.

A desperation razed the back of Alric's neck as though he perched on *Wulfshead*'s rail, about to leap into a life-or-death fray, senses sharpened beyond the physical realm.

"The cost—" the priest's words broke the ethereal silence of the chapel like new wood on a fire—"is your soul."

TWENTY-SIX

Alric rode into the starlit night as though pursued by spirits.
Well, perhaps he was…not by dark ones, but by the One
Scanlan told him would reveal itself when the time was right.
If it did, then it would find him in the one place where he was truly at
home—the villa on the river running from Chesreton to the sea. Tor
was as winded and wet with perspiration as Dustan when Alric handed
the animals over to the stable hand at the villa. Belrap stirred in the
predawn hour to see what was amiss, but Alric assured him all was
well. Alone in his room, Alric dug out the books of Scripture that had
been so precious to his mother.

"Father God," he said, his voice almost haunting the room, "if
You've a message for me, then I would have it." He winced at the terse
note in his voice. Impatient with the confusion that had descended
upon him the moment he'd laid eyes on Deirdre, he would have his
answers. But it would serve no purpose to provoke God if He indeed
existed. "I listen, though I don't understand. I am willing, but I am
wary. This is Your chance…if You would seize it," Alric added, more
humbly.

Unfolding the list of references that Scanlan had scribbled down for
him to consider, he pulled the oil lamp closer and began to search for
them. With each illuminated page Alric turned, reverence seeped into
him as surely as the scent of burning oil infiltrated his nostrils, not
with offense, but with comfort. It went beyond the present to the past,
from his surroundings to his mother, for so many of the words were
familiar—words she'd read to him or quoted; words she'd chided him
with; words she'd leaned upon in her darkest hours; words that had
made her what she'd been in Alric's heart: an earthly angel.

The miracles of Christ were a wonder and not new to Alric, but it
was Jesus Himself that intrigued him—the man, the motivation, the
discipline, the compassion. Here was the model, not just for a hus-

band, but for a warrior and a king. Here were strengths that Alric had contemptuously looked upon as weaknesses. When had the story changed? he wondered, turning page after page.

Or perhaps it wasn't the story at all…

The morning of the wedding, Galstead brimmed with guests and their retinues. Those who could not be lodged within the walls of the fortress were housed on the common without: a meadow alive with tents and banners fluttering in the breeze. Aromas of roasting meats and wood smoke shouted welcome as loudly as Lambert's heralds.

Deirdre, clad in Helewis's remade gown, nervously awaited the hour of noon. Abina clucked and fussed over her hair, which had been woven with gold-shot ribbons of deep blue and strings of pearls into a single braid. On the bed lay a cloud-thin mantle of silk, embroidered by Alric's late mother.

"How I wish Orlaith were here to see you." Abina sniffed, as she draped the ivory mantle over Deirdre's head.

"I am sure she smiles down from heaven as we speak." Deirdre placed a hand over Abina's drawn and wrinkled one. A blade of emotion rose to her throat. "And my mother, too."

But would Banba be as pleased, seeing her daughter forced into a loveless marriage with a heathen prince? *Heavenly Father, give me strength to do what I must.* How could Scanlan possibly be so enthusiastic, knowing what lay ahead of her? His assurance to trust in God floated somewhere in a sea of second thoughts and fear.

"For I know the thoughts that I think toward you, saith the LORD, thoughts of peace, and not of evil, to give you an expected end…" It was the answer she dwelled upon each time her anxiety threatened to overwhelm her with the urge to steal a horse and make way for the Welsh border at breakneck speed.

"I just wish Alric were here already," Abina fretted.

He'd left for Chesreton sometime in the night after Deirdre sent him away, angry over her insistence of holding him to his word regarding the marriage bed. Lambert had sent Gunnar for him as soon as the king heard the news and was in a dreadful humor over his son's disregard for their guests. When Gunnar returned after a full day's gallop there and back, he reported that Alric had taken a small boat downriver but assured the king that Alric would arrive in time for the wedding. Many crude jests were made by the men about the nervous groom spending his last nights sowing wild seeds, while the women looked at Deirdre with a mix of curiosity and pity.

"But if he says he will be here, he will be," the old nurse assured herself when no comfort came from Deirdre. "He may look dirty and ragged as a Pict," she stipulated with a voice of experience, "and if he does, his mother will haunt him the rest of his days, and so will I." Abina bristled at her image in the mirror. "But Alric never breaks his word. Never. He has a heart of gold, my pretty muirnait—a little tarnished by life here at Galstead, but nothing your kind and loving heart cannot polish to a bright sheen."

Outside Abina's lodge, a syncopated rustle of skirts and hurried footsteps approached, followed by the entrance of Helewis, pretty in a rose gown smocked with green thread about the yoke. "Alric is here!"

Deirdre's heart dropped to the floor and sprang back just as quickly, where it beat from her chest with every emotion from fear to anticipation.

"Did I not tell you so?" Abina's face glowed with triumph, as well as relief.

"Even more peasants have gathered outside the walls," Helewis said between gasps. "They cheered Alric all the way to the gates. Never have I seen such a—" With a stricken look, she weaved dizzily. Abina and Deirdre both rushed to grab her before she fell.

"What is it?" Deirdre fought back alarm. "Are you ill?"

"Come, dear, sit down. You have overwrought yourself, running in this dry summer heat. If it doesn't rain soon..." the nurse trailed off rather than address that possibility. Never had Albion seen such a spell of dry weather.

Helewis trembled as Abina mopped her face with a wet cloth.

"I...I think it's the excitement," the princess said in a quivering voice. "To have a sister and a friend and..." She leaned against Abina.

"It's making me awfully sick. I lost my breakfast."

Deirdre met Abina's sharp glance over Helewis's head. "It could be the heat and all those layers of dress," the nurse said. "I'll fetch you some mint to chew."

If it wasn't the heat, it could be serious trouble, Deirdre thought. By Helewis's own admission, Ricbert had not visited her bed since Yule. Perhaps Deirdre's pity for the unrequited love between Gunnar and the princess had been for naught. If so, she feared for them. "When came your last season?"

Helewis looked up startled. "I don't know...I mean, I don't remember. I've had no reason to account for it." Meeting Deirdre's compassionate look in the mirror, she dropped her head. "But I think it was before you came to Galstead." She bit her lip as the reality gripped her and fear stirred the creamy flesh of her brow. "Oh, my!"

"Your secret is safe with me," Deirdre pledged. But it could only be kept so long.

"But what can I do?"

"Have faith." That seemed to be the message of the day, she thought wryly. "'For I know the thoughts that I think toward you, saith the LORD, thoughts of peace, and not of evil, to give you an expected end,'" Deirdre quoted. "That promise of hope has carried me through, and it will do the same for you, Helewis. I don't know how. I just know that it will."

And she prayed that it was an all-encompassing promise, one that covered human weaknesses as well as faith's strength, for Ricbert would leap at the chance to rid himself of the marriage and demand a terrible blood price, mutilation at best. Faith, she'd seen women with their noses split for committing adultery. Helewis would never survive such humiliation, considering that Ethlinda and Ricbert had already driven her to despair over her round figure and plain looks.

Abina returned to the lodge with fresh mint from her garden. "I don't know what is going on, but Alric insists that Lambert and his guests meet him in the meadow beyond the town or there is to be no wedding. That boy has a will of his own, and it'll be the death of me." She looked apologetically at Deirdre. "I'm afraid he wants you and the priest, too. Imagine, hauling us all out and it nearly midday. I hope your dress isn't ruined by the dust and dirt."

Reeling from one shock to the next, Deirdre pulled Helewis to her feet and hugged her. "You help me through today, derling, and I promise to stand by you tomorrow."

As they joined the royal ensemble gathering outside the gate, Deirdre was taken aback at the number of peasants being restrained by the guards. Helewis was right. It was as crowded as a fairground. Was *she* to be the entertainment?

"What do you know of this, young woman?" Lambert demanded upon seeing her.

Ethlinda fixed an icy, onyx gaze at Deirdre. "I suspect, milord, that you should be wary of insurrection. Your Christian pet and bastard stir your own people against you."

Deirdre flushed with anger. "Don't be ridiculous. These people have come to see the wedding."

As if to back her word, a yeoman called out to Deirdre from just beyond the gate. "Princess! You said to come and here I am...along with my good wife."

Deirdre looked hard at the man, trying to place him.

"How the devil are we to feed them? We hadn't prepared to feed so many," Ricbert complained.

Lambert sweated profusely in his purple and scarlet robes under the peaking sun. "I'm cursed if I know. We'd have one more bullock, if your mother hadn't set it afire and nearly all of Galstead with it."

"Someone must have spilled oil in the temple," the queen rallied in her own defense.

"Maybe it was the gods saying they've had their fill of beef," Lambert derided.

The queen held her burned hand to her side as though it were nothing. By all accounts, the fire had flared up when an altar lamp overturned. Just as quickly, it was beaten out, but not without causing a panic.

Alric's leaving, the temple fire, Helewis, and now the crowds... Deirdre shuddered to think what was next as she kept looking at the friendly peasant. Suddenly she recognized him as the man who'd stopped them on their way to Galstead, the woeful farmer whose wife had lost a child by carrying water into the fields so late in her term. She'd given him her cross.

Ricbert scowled. "I don't think it's wise to go among them."

"'Twould do you well to listen, husband," Ethlinda chimed in. "Juist and I saw an uprising in the entrails of the slain bullock."

"Before or after you fried them?"

"Nonsense!" Deirdre ignored the king's ready quip. He had the gift of the trouble-making Brichriu's tongue, though according to Abina, it had not always been so. The king had turned most bitter, with a penchant for stirring conflict between his associates, after Orlaith passed away.

No matter how tempted, Deirdre resisted showing her humor at Ethlinda's expense. While she did not understand the queen's beliefs, she respected her right to them. Scanlan's admonishment to love the sinner and hate the sin was far more of a challenge.

Deirdre marched ahead of the royal family without guard or escort through the gates and straight to where the farmer held up the necklace she'd given him. As she did a trill of excited chatter—"There she is…it's the princess,"—flowed through the crowd. Her single invitation had multiplied a hundredfold, she thought, disconcerted.

"It was good of you to come—" she spoke first to the farmer, then to the rest—"*all* of you."

Presenting her hand to the man brought about a collective gasp among the onlookers. Surely he was not fit to kiss the feet of a princess, much less her hand.

"We are all equal in God's eyes," she assured him when he hesitated.

Awkwardly, the yeoman kissed it.

"And you, mistress," Deirdre said to his wife. "I pray your strength has returned, as your husband told me of your misfortune."

"Well enough, milady," the woman answered, her raw-boned features giving way to a smile that took years off her life-hardened face.

"I told ye I knew the princess," the man boasted to his surrounding fellows.

"I, my husband to be, and the king of Galstead welcome you all," Deirdre shouted for the sake of being heard. "We are overwhelmed by your numbers but will share what we have prepared with all, thane and serf alike."

A hearty cheer went up in increments throughout the gathering. "Long live the king!"

"And Princess Deirdre!"

"And Prince Alric!"

Ushered by the cheering throng, the royal assembly proceeded to the meadow beyond the village. There, astride his stallion prancing back and forth along the stream that trickled through Galstead from the mother cliff at its back, Alric sat. With the sun dancing on his hair and playing upon the gold threads and trim of his tunic he looked like a young god. Even Dustan looked as though he could take flight, like the legendary Pegasus in gilded tack, with his black mane and tail flying like banners.

Thick muscled arms dazzling rich in splendor, Alric rode to meet the royal entourage. With a graceful leap, he dismounted and bowed low before his father. "Milord."

"What in the name of Woden is all this about?" Lambert clapped him on the shoulder. "Where have you been?"

"Learning what it takes to be a good husband." Alric rose and turned to Deirdre. Kneeling, he took her hand to his lips. "Milady."

Deirdre said nothing. How could she with her heart quivering in her throat and her belly doing a giddy little jig?

"You spent the last two days on that?" Ricbert's sneer was incredulous. "You were born with that, I thought."

Alric allowed the crowd its laugh. "I said a *good* husband. Anything worth doing is worth doing well."

A riot of humor spread from where they stood to the outreaches of the assemblage, turning Ricbert as scarlet as Deirdre felt.

Ethlinda stepped forward. "And this involves routing our guests to the meadow like so many bullock?"

"I decided to choose a ceremony involving water rather than fire. It's safer." As Alric spoke, Father Scanlan broke through the circle of the guards. "Ah, there you are, priest. Now we can begin."

"Here...now?" Lambert stammered.

Alric grinned. "Aye, Father. There's too many to fit in the chapel."

Deirdre grabbed Helewis's arm and felt her new friend return her anxious squeeze. "Trust," the young princess whispered in her ear.

Aye, Deirdre told herself sternly. Except that trusting in God wasn't the problem at the moment. Her knees were of more concern. How could she marry a man who was as unpredictable as the wind?

TWENTY-SEVEN

When Alric remounted Dustan, every eye was upon him, every ear strained to hear. Deirdre thought sure she could hear the heartbeat of the wind itself. It, too, awaited with bated breath.

"The priest issued me a challenge the other night." Alric's voice rang loud and clear. "He said to sift through the Christian law and Scripture for the things I was willing to believe, instead of picking through it for that which I cannot accept."

"We came for a wedding, not Christian rhetoric," one of the queen's brothers shouted.

"And a wedding you shall have, sir," Alric replied, "*when* the bridegroom has had his say. If that offends you, you are free to await us back at the hall."

When no man made a move to leave, Alric resumed. "It was a fair challenge, and this is what I found. The Christian God tolerates doubt, if we accept that challenge. So a man is no hypocrite if he is earnestly searching the Word for what he can believe. Rather, that man is a student. Our priest here, or Christ's example, is the teacher."

"How wonderful." Ricbert was openly jeering his half brother. "We can learn how to die."

Alric nailed Ricbert with a steely gaze. "Exactly." Princely armbands cast their brilliance in all directions, as though God in heaven ordered the sun lend its weight to Alric's words as he swept his arm over the crowd. "You all are living. That you know how to do. But who among you does not cower at the thought, not of death itself, but of what lies beyond?"

Around Deirdre, a few nodded their heads. Others exchanged whispers of speculation.

Lambert studied his son. "And this Christian God tells us that in His book?"

"Aye, Father, that and more. But today, I have more pressing matters on my mind." He grinned at Deirdre. "Like vowing to be a godly husband."

Dustan snorted, tossing his head, a reflection of the restlessness of the crowd.

"It's warm and I'd have you back to the hall soon, but first I want to make certain I understand what I am about to promise. Father Scanlan, correct me if I am wrong. If I am not, then let these witnesses be my oath helpers."

Scanlan nodded and waved. Unlike Deirdre, this did not seem a surprise to him at all. She wondered what the priest told Alric to bring this about.

"I am supposed to love my wife as Christ loved the church," Alric announced. "How is that, you might ask? I know I did. Christ was willing to die for the church, that its believers might live forever, even after death." Alric looked at Deirdre. "I would die for my bride, even if death were the end. What man among you would not sacrifice your life for the ones you love?"

Ayes and other echoes of assent rose around her, accelerating Deirdre's tumble of emotions. Was ever there such a prelude as this to a wedding? Had a proud man such as Alric ever humbled himself so before noble and peasant alike? She wasn't certain she was hearing him aright, yet she held her breath, a strange anticipation gripping her, thrilling her…frightening her.

The multitude was his, even a few of the queen's followers. Juist strained, attentive, at her side.

"Christ forgives the church when it makes mistakes and is truly repentant. He even forgave the ones who betrayed Him as He hung on the tree, when 'twas more natural to curse and condemn."

Ricbert snorted. "Evidence of a fool."

"Evidence of how much He loved mankind that He excused their ignorance of who He was. I daresay there's no one among us who hasn't made a mistake and wrongfully condemned someone, at least in his mind. Only a real man or a noblehearted woman would admit to it."

The reason settled well among the listeners, tightening the rein on their attention as Alric addressed Deirdre.

"Given our stubborn natures, milady, we will both make mistakes, but you have my word that I will try to forgive you, in trust that you will do the same for me. 'Tis no more than I'd ask of any man here."

"'Tis only fair," someone behind Deirdre agreed. Who could refuse the earnest simmer in Alric's gaze, as though the pledge kindled in the soul itself?

"Lastly," the prince went on, "Christ was a king and a leader—not a dictator. He asks that His church give no more, to suffer no more, or do any more than He did Himself. I can live with this lady according to that rule, if she will."

Alric's conviction could have lifted her straight off the ground. "No man nor woman could expect a fairer treatment, milord." Her answer spread through the crowd like wildfire in brown grass. Part of the world retreated beyond herself and Alric, leaving them alone, their gazes cleaving to one another.

Next to Deirdre, Abina broke with a sob. "Surely the sun this day is a reflection of your sainted mother's smile."

Deirdre and Helewis hugged the happily distraught woman.

Clearing a rare emotion from his throat, Lambert wisecracked, "Stay on this course and you'll have the whole lot wed to you, Son."

Alric hesitated, not to allow the amused reaction to his father's remark to die down, but because he was obviously moved by Abina's observation. Even Deirdre, who'd never known Orlaith, was touched.

"That said, good fellows and ladies," Alric recovered after clearing his throat, "I personally have found this God and His Son to be just and reasonable. And I ask Father Scanlan as Their representative, to perform the water ceremony, that I might pledge my life to studying and following Their example to the best of my ability, for I could not promise more. Is that fair, priest?"

The water ceremony? Alric wished to be *baptized?* Deirdre could scarce wrap her mind around the miracle, for it was surely that.

"Aye, milord, it's fair and welcome in the eyes of the Lord, but…" Scanlan glanced at the stream, shrunken by drought in its wide-cracked bed. "There's hardly enough water to baptize you properly."

At that moment, a loud crack of thunder echoed above them. As startled as the others, Deirdre looked up at the sunlit sky. Incredibly, a droplet of water struck her face, then two, then more. From out of nowhere, a smattering of soft gray clouds stole upon them like late arrivals to God's chapel. Rimmed in gilt by the sun, they gently shed their water on the thirsty meadow below.

Scanlan's bellowing laugh rivaled the thunder itself as he looked up, arms reaching toward the heavens. His loose sleeves fell away from them, revealing a sinew that belied a calling of words alone. "Never mind, lad. I see God Himself has decided to baptize, not only you, but the entire assembly, ready or nay. No water I bless could ever be so holy as that straight from heaven's hand."

Alric dismounted and approached the spot where the priest stood. "Then let's be about it, man, before the ladies stampede in distress at wetting their lovely gowns and hair." Suddenly, as if by second thought, he turned to Lambert. "Milord, would you care to join your son in the Christian God's own baptism?"

Amazed as she was by what was unfolding before her very eyes, Deirdre felt sorry for hesitant Lambert. The king was truly beside himself as to what to do.

"Perhaps the king is not ready," she suggested. "This must be a decision he reaches in his own heart, not because you prompt it. You, Alric, have had time to deliberate."

"Orlaith waits for you, milord." Abina's brightness took wrinkles from her aged face. "She waits for you to be with her again."

Ethlinda dragged the older nurse away from the king and slung her aside. "Be gone, you babbling old fool!"

Like quicksilver, Alric caught Abina before she fell, glaring over her head at his stepmother. "Royal or nay, I will cut off the hand that harms one hair of this lady's head," he growled.

The wolf had not completely surrendered to the lamb, Deirdre mused, but surely the Lord used His wolf to protect His own.

Whether it was to please Alric's late mother or to vex the queen, Lambert came to a decision. "Very well then, but let it be known that I bow only to the bretwalda of Northumbria and the Christian God in the heavens, no other."

The soft rain that dropped upon their shoulders as Scanlan sang the baptismal rite in Saxon created a havoc of joy rather than distress. As father and son knelt to be blessed by the priest, only those closest heard their confession and commitment to Christ. Deirdre struggled between laughter and tears when her husband to be rose along with the king, forgiven and free of their past transgressions. Truly all things *were* possible in God's name, for had someone foreseen this, she would have disbelieved, even disdained the idea.

And if this was possible, then her brother was not yet lost.

The only black cloud in their midst hovered over the queen and her guests, who drew away as if fearful that whatever madness had affected the king and his son might be catching. Indeed, Ethlinda's lips never ceased to move as Lambert and Alric admitted to being sinners and lost in this world. It was as though she sought to undermine what was taking place, but the rain—the glorious, prayed for rain—would not allow it.

"Milady," Alric asked upon rising, "will you take me as your husband here, before God and all nature, before that darkening on the horizon sets upon us?"

Deirdre was struck by the sun that shone straight from the silvery bright mirror of his soul. Or was it the Son? At that moment, there was no one else in the universe but the three of them and a truth she could scarce credit: God had used her in this miracle. She could not doubt it. And she could not doubt that this was not the only surprise she would know this day.

"But it's raining." Once again Alric had won Lambert's favor and Ricbert's whine did little to belie the unadulterated hatred he bore toward his fairer sibling.

"I'll not stand here like a gaping turkey and drown in the rain." Queen Ethlinda swirled her cloak about her shoulders, enshrouding her humiliation at Lambert's betrayal, and marched off toward the gate.

Some of the guests followed, more ladies than men, and nearly all of the queen's countrymen. The rest surged forward, besieging Scanlan with questions and requests for the same absolution. Both men and women, noble and poor, had listened attentively to Alric's declarations and agreed with the prince that if God was willing to accept them with their faults, that they were willing to accept Him.

The rain—so long denied—was a sign no one could ignore. Surely, this God was not only real and reasonable, but He answered prayer.

"Wait your turn, good people!"

Alric's exuberance was enough to lift him off his feet. He was weightless, if human words could possibly describe how he felt. He was drunk, intoxicated with a joy he'd not know since the innocence of childhood. So often he'd heard his mother say that he needed to lay his burdens down at the Lord's feet, and it had made no sense to him…until now. He glanced at his father, wondering—hoping—that Lambert knew the same carefree exhilaration, as if he could slay dragons with laughter.

"I am sure the priest would tell you more, but please, my wedding first. I'd have it done before the weather, or my bride's mind, changes."

Surrounded by an unprecedented and nearly crushing gaiety for Galstead, Lambert, his most trusted thanes, and the main of Alric's men from the *Wulfshead* formed a barrier to protect the bride and groom from being overrun by good intentions.

"Now *this* is more to my liking," Gunnar whispered none too quietly to his friend. "The old crow and her flock have flown."

Alric gave Gunnar a hearty pat on the back as he stepped up beside the lady Helewis. Clad in her gown of rose, the shy princess bloomed in the radiance of the young seaman's smile. Alric owed Gunnar much for staying behind with Deirdre, knowing how it tortured him to see Helewis at Ricbert's mercy. Gunnar deserved his own ship and a chance to make his own fortune as Alric had. The ship they'd taken a few weeks ago was exactly what Alric had in mind for his best friend.

Although wealth was not everything, he thought with a twinge of pity for his friend as Scanlan placed Deirdre's hand in his. Joy struck Alric again, so fresh he nearly laughed out loud. Time was, it was himself he'd pitied.

His mother was right yet again: Love changes everything. He felt giddy as a wet-eared pup.

He loved Deirdre. The certainty removed more weight from him rather than adding to his earthly burdens. And he loved her God. It did not weaken him as he'd believed it might but gave him strength. More strength than any mortal could wield.

God's strength.

"Dearly beloved—" the priest looked about them, eyes both solemn and joyful—"our prince has declared this day not only his love for his bride, but for our Lord. Be there any man or woman among you who has reason that these two, Alric of Galstead and Deirdre of Gleannmara, should not be wed?"

"No one would dare," Lambert blustered, casting a hawklike gaze around him. Taking their example from Galstead's king, Gunnar's father, Cedric, whose troops now fortified Chesreton, and the other thanes did the same.

"Very well then," Scanlan resolved, turning to Alric. "Alric of Galstead, wilt thou take Deirdre of Gleannmara as your lawfully wedded wife before God and these witnesses, keeping only unto her, wilt thou honor, protect, and love her as Christ loved the church, unconditionally, till death do you part?"

Alric delved into Deirdre's upturned gaze with his own. "I said as much before and state it again now. Yea, I will." Deirdre would be like Orlaith was to Lambert, but with all the honor that Alric could afford her. "And should I die first, I will wait for you, for to live without love is to exist like the earth without rain."

Without the priest's blessing, Alric lifted her hand to his lips. Her own quivered as he spoke against it. "May I never take you for granted, lest I discover what it is to be without you again."

He'd taken his mother for granted. Not until he met Deirdre and saw Orlaith's goodness reflected in her had he realized how much he missed that good in his life. Like the creek bed, he'd shriveled spiritually and emotionally. And as he'd talked to the priest and then taken up Orlaith's books of Scripture, it all flooded back. Why God cared enough about a cynical pirate to send Deirdre and the priest into his path had to be part of that unconditional love.

"I, Deirdre of Gleannmara, promise you, Alric of Galstead, to keep only unto you, to love, honor, and obey you as my lord and husband *in every sense…*" Deirdre paused, as if torn between surprise that she uttered the promise she'd thought to withhold and sudden certainty that she meant it. The smile that lit her features was like God's own sun shining forth from the heavens. "According to God's Word, until death do us part."

Alric felt the promise at the core of his senses. His undoubted physical desire for Deirdre had given way to spiritual attraction in the course of the last day or so of soul-searching, but now it blindsided him like a traitorous dog. Body flushing and tensing all at once, Alric hardly heard Scanlan's prayer above the cacophony within himself. His breath was short and mouth too dry to add his "amen." Were her words just a turn of phrase, or did she mean…?

"You may kiss the bride."

Although the priest spoke passable Saxon, Alric stared at Scanlan, trying to make out the meaning of his words.

"Well, go on, Son! We're not getting any drier!" Lambert waved his arm. "'Tis a curious time for shyness now."

It wasn't until Deirdre snickered beside him that Alric's wits returned, riding high on a wave of embarrassment.

"Her chatter will bring you delight."

With a perfectly wicked quirk of his lips, Alric gathered his precocious bride in his arms. Ignoring the heady sway of her figure against him, he steeled himself for his attack. First a feign, a brush of lips to belie the desire she'd stirred…

A disjointed cheer rose around them.

Then a peck on the forehead where her gold-threaded veil folded back.

The cheer gained voice again, only to fade as Alric bestowed another and another, first on one cheek, then the other. As he eyed her chin, it hung uncertainly in the air. Gently, he left a peck of homage there as well.

Deirdre's eyes were wide open, swimming with uneasiness and anticipation. Surrounded by a collective holding of breath, Alric swept in and laid his claim upon her lips. When he at last offered her reprieve, she gasped with shortened breath, and he grinned at her flushed cheeks and dazed demeanor.

For the moment, he'd caught her off balance—but a lifetime lay ahead of them in which she would undoubtedly even the score.

TWENTY-EIGHT

T he first son to produce a grandson will become my heir," Lambert proclaimed, lifting his goblet first to Alric and then Ricbert. The red wine sloshed over the king's fingers, but well into his cups, he was beyond caring. He not only celebrated Alric's wedding, but the fact that Alric finally accepted his wedding gift—the villa in Chesreton.

It wasn't the first time it had been offered, but, until now, Alric needed no home, nor the ties that went hand in hand with such a gift. But a proper bridegroom prepared a house for his bride, and Alric was determined to be that, despite his reluctance to be beholden to anyone, particularly his father. Much as Alric tried to love the king, Lambert's penchant for stirring strife, especially between his two sons, troubled him. While Alric could fend well enough for himself with Ethlinda and her offspring, he now had a wife to be concerned about—one who'd been separated from him by the endless stream of well-wishers.

He looked to where Deirdre sat next to Helewis, her cheeks as flushed as the other woman's were pale—like a red rose and a white one. Frig's breath, had this new faith made a poet of him?

"The sooner we leave this place, the better." The grumbled comment came from Gunnar to his left. Rather than the mischief it spawned in Lambert, the heath fruit worked a morose spell on his friend. "I'll not bear it another moment, knowing your weasel of a half brother is back in her bed after *that* little announcement."

It would suit Ricbert's nature to drag poor Helewis off on the instant, but Gunner's familiarity with the loneliness of the princess's bed set Alric on his heels. "Back?"

Gunnar apparently pulled his wits together and cleared his throat. "Everyone knows your dear brother prefers any bed but that of his wife. Until now, at least things were tolerable."

This was all Alric needed—his best friend drinking himself into a confrontation with his half brother over a woman lost to him.

"Lambert just toys with our minds," Alric disdained. "Ricbert is heir, always was, always will be."

He would not allow himself to even entertain the thought that he might become ruler of Galstead in lieu of his half brother. Although a second thought niggled. If Gleannmara—with its present king on the throne and its heir still alive somewhere between Britain and Rome—was not to be his kingdom, that left only one other to fulfill Orlaith's vision.

Not that even kingdoms mattered to Alric's love-besotted mind. It had to be love. What else could turn a man's head so that he hardly knew himself? He had wealth enough accumulated to live with his bride in ease, even if he never made another trip to sea.

"Unless the *heir* should happen to topple off a cliff," Gunnar mumbled under his breath.

The wistful remark brought Alric's wandering thoughts back to the present. Thankfully, the merriment threatening to raise the roof from its planked walls kept Gunnar's words from carrying. Alric was in full sympathy, knowing, perhaps for the first time, just how deeply his friend felt about Helewis. Were their positions reversed, he'd have made off with Ricbert's bride before—

He caught himself. He hadn't exactly rushed into this union with Deirdre. He allowed that it was his mother's prayers and God's grace that moved him in time to keep from losing her forever.

"You ask too much of me." Gunnar laid his head upon folded arms on the table.

Aye, Alric commiserated with his friend's plight, but Deirdre came first. Gunnar was needed here with her, while Alric followed up on Hinderk's lead regarding Cairell of Gleannmara.

Just where the prince was depended on which source one believed. A short conversation and a tidy reward of gold revealed that Deirdre's brother had been taken to Gaul—or he'd escaped—either one conveniently at the moment Hinderk began his discreet inquiries around the bretwalda's court. There was no doubt in Alric's mind now that the bretwalda knew nothing about Cairell, for Ecfrith would hide nothing.

One of his thanes had been bitten by greed and now hastened to cover his subterfuge. Regardless, Alric was obliged to at least try to find Cairell.

"You ask too much of me." Clearly, Gunnar was too far gone on heath fruit to know he repeated himself.

"I know, but—" Alric broke off and nudged his dazed companion. With a short nod, he motioned to where Ricbert and Ethlinda spoke in dead earnest with the Mercian envoy and several thanes, mostly relatives. Alric suffered their company on too many occasions. For all its benefits, the kingship carried curse as well.

"Snakes like to coil and huddle together."

"I thought Hinderk's companion had left for the Mercian court upon our refusal to pay their blood protection." It was bad enough having his stepmother's relatives slithering about…

"Another toast to the cap'n," Wimmer chortled from his table with Wulfshead's crew a few yards away. "Come on over, ye lucky dog, and have a last drink with us as a free man."

"More likely he sent a messenger. That way he can keep an eye on us." Gunnar rose unsteadily and, seizing Alric's arm, steered him toward the Wulfshead's faction.

Alric dismissed the notion that something was amiss. The queen and her son always kept to their own at such occasions. It was normal to gather with long-missed kin.

Instinctively, he cast a protective eye to Deirdre's last whereabouts and was vexed to see that the princess was no longer at the head table. But then, neither was Helewis, he noted, taking a measure of comfort in the notion that the two women had retired momentarily from the king's hospitality. Females never left in solitary number but in packs. He supposed it was either because they were schooled by their mothers to take comfort in numbers, being the weaker sex, or nature mysteriously called them by instinct all at once.

The imported ale glittering in the sterling and gilt goblets Lambert had specially crafted for the bride and groom was no better for taste, nor for the way it settled in Alric's gullet. He suffered an uneasiness that would not abate, yet he could not pinpoint the source.

He endured his crew's jibes and more serious comments, process-ing them on a separate track of attention from which he focused on his bride's whereabouts. From the moment he'd laid eyes on her, Deirdre of Gleannmara had commandeered a permanent block of his attention that none other could erase. She was with him, wherever he was, if not in physical presence, certainly in his mind.

Some of the guests got up to indulge in a dance, which kindled a plan in Alric's mind. He'd suffered court etiquette enough to try the patience of a saint, much less that of a bridegroom. He'd have his bride to himself with no more of this nonsense.

Taking up his discarded cloak, he leaned over and whispered in Gunnar's ear, "Play the fool for me, friend, and we'll both escape this drudgery." With that, he threw the blue garment over Gunnar's head and shouted good-naturedly, "That's it; enough is enough for you, mate. Time you walk this off."

For a moment, Alric wondered if Gunnar was drunker than he thought, for the man stood still as a statue. Then, of a sudden, he came to life, struggling and cursing fit to singe a smith's ears.

"We have him, Cedric," Alric called to Gunnar's father, who rose upon hearing the ensuing ruckus. "We'll tuck him in and be back anon."

With a conspiratorial wink at Wimmer, Alric steered his rowdy friend toward the door and out into the night air and freedom.

The cook fires at Galstead continued to put forth food for all the guests, including the unexpected ones who camped beneath the makeshift shelters of vendors' row or shared such shelter as could be had among the townsfolk. There was enough, no more, no less. Truly God's handiwork was everywhere this day, in the heart of the town and, increasingly, in its people.

Scanlan, who'd remained outside in the baptizing rain for as long as there was someone to come forward to claim God's redemption, walked on air. Thrice he embraced Deirdre as his partner in triumph—how her faith had changed the man she married! And he, then, led others to accept Christ. Then there was the rain, the long-prayed-for rain, falling still, yet soft enough that it did not dampen the spirit of the celebration.

Caught up in God's spell of wonder, Deirdre shared Scripture's accounts with the cooks and their assistants of a wedding at Cana, where Jesus turned water into wine, and when He fed five thousand using five loaves and two fish, then she slipped out with Helewis to be certain that none be turned away without food. The king's steward had matters well in hand, but her friend had been on the verge of hysteria ever since Lambert made that ridiculous announcement regarding Galstead's heir.

"Would that God would deliver me from this life, for I haven't the courage to take it myself," Helewis said woodenly as they passed a wagon under which some dogs and children had taken shelter from the wet mist.

The smile on Deirdre's face at the sight of a waif and a hound gnawing on opposite ends of a rib of beef faded. "You mustn't give up, Helewis. Surely your situation is no more hopeless than mine was when I was captured by Alric and forced into this marriage."

"But you love the man you are married to."

"Only by God's grace and answer to my prayers…not what I prayed for, mind you, but for what was best for me." How far she had come in the last weeks, not in understanding, but in faith. Alric was not the only one who'd changed. "God has brought about the impossible for me—"

"Ricbert will kill me when he finds out I'm with child." The poor soul was deaf to anything but her own despair. "Which is the worse fate, I don't know—being killed outright or having that animal return to my bed."

Deirdre shuddered, not wanting to even imagine what her friend experienced at Ricbert's hands. "'For I know the thoughts that I think toward you, saith the LORD, thoughts of peace, and not of evil, to give you an expected end,'" she said with conviction. "You must believe that. You mustn't lose hope."

"God does not reward sin, and I am an adulteress." Helewis fell to her knees in the light rain, sobbing.

"Helewis, your gown!" Deirdre struggled to raise the distraught soul to her feet. "Come with me to Abina's lodge. You must hold together, if not for your sake, for the sake of the babe you carry."

"Father, save us!" Helewis pushed Deirdre into the shadows, fear displacing despair on her face. "It's Ethlinda! She spies upon us."

Deirdre watched as the queen made her way toward the kitchens, snapping her fingers to summon the wine steward and admonishing servants who did not move fast enough to suit her. "It appears she's doing what we did, checking on the kitchen to be certain her guests are being well fed and their cups remain filled. Our extra guests put her into a tizzy," she pointed out. "But God's taken care of them, just as He will you and your baby. Now come along. I doubt she's even noticed our absence."

The lodge was pitch black, save one of the lanterns strung about for the sake of the celebration and Galstead's guests. Deirdre lit a small candle lamp inside the shelter, all the while searching her mind for words of comfort.

"You are right," she said, still pensive as she put the lamp on a shelf near Abina's bed. "God does not reward sin. He forgives it. David was an adulterer and a murderer, and yet God forgave him."

"This is your wedding day. We mustn't stay—"

"We'll join the others just as soon as you are fit." Deirdre took a cloth and wet it with water from a pitcher. "Hold this on your eyes to take the redness and swelling down while we pray."

Father, give me the words, for I am barely saved myself, but by Your grace. Even as her plea formed in Deirdre's mind, her scramble of thought cleared. His Word was all she needed.

"God, we know You have plans for us, and they are for our good, not our harm, but Father, we are surrounded by darkness and fear, knowing we have not been as faithful and upright as You would have us be."

Helewis began to sob again. Deirdre hugged her friend to her.

"But Father, You know our circumstances, our pain, and our remorse for our weaknesses. You do not expect us to be perfect, for only Your Son was without weakness or flaw. You have said ask and ye shall receive, and so we are asking God, for Your forgiveness and Your support as we deal with the earthly consequences of our sins. Be with Your child Helewis now. May she know Your presence and peace—the peace of Your forgiveness and hope in Your Word. Amen."

Deirdre held Helewis away, looking the overwrought woman in the eye. "He keeps His Word, Helewis. It may not be in the way you expect, but He will not forsake you or your baby."

"Deirdre?"

She turned toward the door as Abina opened it. "Aye, Abina, I'm here with—" She broke off upon seeing Alric duck under the doorway after his nurse.

"I was about to send my men looking for you." His brow knitted. "Helewis?"

"I...I'm fine, Alric. I was just more emotional than I thought. I'll miss Deirdre when you take her from the court to your villa. She's been grand company." She sniffed loudly. "But I'm fine now. Just a headache."

"Come with me, little one." Abina drew Helewis to her. "I have just the tea for you. A cup of that, then I'll tuck you in and give your regrets to the king. He's so happy among his guests now, that you'll not be missed."

Deirdre started toward them. "Perhaps I should—"

"Come with your husband," Alric interrupted, slipping his arm about her waist. "It's all arranged."

She cast a wide, questioning look at him and then Abina.

"Listen to your husband," the old nurse said, her eyes twinkling beneath the wrinkled shed of her brow.

Her husband. Sure, the term hadn't escaped Deirdre's thoughts since that day Alric threatened her with marriage on the street before the villa. Except now, the idea warmed her rather than shot her through with dread. Indeed, blood heated her face and neck as though she stood over a hot fire instead of walking under the protection of Alric's arm toward his lodge. The uncertainty, the anticipation—they were all but behind her now. Their union was sealed by words and spirit. All that was left to commit was that of the flesh.

She had made the commitment without knowing how she'd come to that decision. She had only a vague awareness of why, yet it seemed right and proper for her to forsake her earlier vow to remain chaste.

"What of the others?" She glanced toward the great hall as they bypassed it.

"Let them find their own brides." Alric stopped and gathered Deirdre up in his arms. "I've waited overlong for mine."

"But shouldn't we at least excuse ourselves from the guests?"

"The way the wine and music are flowing, I doubt we'll even be missed." He smiled down at her. "Unless milady would rather rejoin the king's table."

"Faith, *no!*"

Deirdre covered her mouth, too late to stifle the fervor of her denial. One would think her a wanton hussy rather than the blushing bride. At Alric's chuckle, she relaxed against him.

Gunnar and Wimmer awaited outside the lodge. Unsteady on his feet, Gunnar leaned against the door and practically fell in with his attempt to open it for the newlyweds. Tor, who'd been locked within during the celebration, bounded for Alric and Deirdre, taking Gunnar's wobbly knees out in the process.

Gunnar grumbled as he pulled himself upright. "You can rest assured, milord bridegroom, that no one has made mischief about the nuptial lodge, save this barking horse."

"As for His Majesty Lambert," Wimmer said, helping his comrade, "he grins from ear to ear that an heir might be in the—"

Alric cut him off abruptly. "We thank you both," he said, turning his back to the jumping, tail-wagging dog in order to put Deirdre down unmolested. "Now, one last favor…" He seized Tor's collar before the animal succeeded in placing his front paws on Deirdre's shoulders and wrestled him back through the open door. "Take this mongrel and—nay, I'll see to him and give the lady time to…do whatever it is ladies do," Alric finished. "I'll return momentarily," he called to her in a louder voice.

"Thank you, milord," Deirdre answered as politely as her flustered mind allowed.

Left to her own devices, she studied her decidedly masculine surroundings. A number of tapestries as well as a few weapons hung on the
walls. Judging from their small proportion, they'd been Alric's at different
stages of his growth. His scramasax hung from the wolf's head belt. Below
it, the bright enameled shield he'd carried when she first saw him hovering, bigger than life, over the hold of the *Mell* rested against the wall.

The trunk with his belongings, the one she'd riffled through to find
clothes for her ill-fated mission to steal back Cairell's ransom, lay at the
foot of a large bed. Next to it was her own.

Her heart skipped a beat as her gaze moved to the bed, where her
nightdress had been carefully laid out. On a table beside it was a
decanter of wine and two goblets fashioned of green glass. Abina's
handiwork? At home, her stepmother and friends would have helped
her undress and don her nightshift, but with Helewis ill and Abina
attending her, Deirdre was on her own.

Since Alric sounded no more certain of nuptial etiquette than she,
Deirdre promptly set to work on the laces on either side of her gown.
No sooner had it struck the floor than she pulled her nightshift over her
head and tugged the bodice of her underdress loose. As the first came
down, the latter dropped about her ankles, preserving all modesty.

A log fell on the hearth at the center of the room where Alric's men
had built up the fire. With a tiny gasp, she pivoted to see the scattering
sparks drift with the draft toward the opening in the thatched roof
when a knock sounded on the door.

"Yes?"

"'Tis your husband, milady."

"A moment more," she pleaded, rushing to put out the lamps on
either side of the large bed. The men had struck enough light to
embroider by. "Very well, you may come in."

Ducking inside, Alric closed the door behind him and leaned
against it, feasting his eyes upon her. The fire leaped up, revealing the
silver weld of his gaze as it raked over her from head to toe.

"Finally." Alric's one word reached across the room and touched her
with a thousand fingers.

"I forgot my shoes and stockings," she blurted out, dropping on the bed with the grace of a cow to see to them.

"Allow me." Alric knelt in front of her before she could gather wit enough to object.

"I would imagine you have plenty of clothing to remove without—" Deirdre broke off at the cock-eyed slant of his brow.

The twitch at the corner of his mouth ground against her raw nerves. "You wish me to undress first?"

"I don't care what you do, if you make light of…" She exhaled in frustration, for lack of the appropriate word. "If you cannot be serious."

"Milady, I assure you I am most serious—" He eased the hem of her shift up to her knee—"about your muddy shoes and stockings in my bed."

"I…I can get them from here." Deirdre covered the hands at her knee with her own. As they locked gazes, her hands fell away.

Affording her all modesty, Alric unlaced her slippers and slid off the silky soft linen trappings, taking the shoes with them. Self-conscious, Deirdre curled her toes and drew them primly beneath the hem that fell back in place.

Alric placed the shoes beneath the oaken frame supporting the mattress and rose. "Would you like to help me undress or will milady await me in bed?"

"What?"

With an indulgent smile, Alric took her hands and drew her to her feet.

"Don't be afraid, muirnait. I would only please you, nothing more." He tipped her face toward his with his finger and leaned down, pressing his forehead to hers. "Trust me."

She did. She truly trusted him. It was herself she feared, as if some vital test lay before her and she wasn't prepared.

"Perhaps a glass of wine," Alric suggested, breaking away.

Deirdre shook her head. She needed what little wit that hadn't already abandoned her. "But by all means, you have some."

"Milady is all the intoxication I need this night."

Faith, his words were more heady than any heath fruit, going straight from her ear to the nethermost reaches of her awareness…except her knees. Surely they belonged to one infirm, unreliable as they seemed.

"Come to me, muirnait." It was not a command but the most convincing of pleas.

Alric bracketed her shoulders with his hands, coaxing her closer. As he ran them down the curve of her back, someone in her body sealed the space between them. His warmth was comforting and wildly disturbing at the same time. She felt his breath hot against her cheek, waiting...but for what? As she drew away in question, he answered with a kiss.

How could something so sweet, so tender, raze her awareness with fierceness enough to take her breath, nay, all resistance away? The woman, that other female who dwelled within Deirdre, shed her demure mask altogether with a brazen show of surrender. She ran trembling fingers up Alric's neck and wove them into his thick mane of hair, holding to him, lest she be dismissed as in times past. She returned his kiss, caress for caress, breath for breath, until even their hearts thundered in union between them.

Suddenly Alric tore away with a ragged groan, staring at Deirdre as though the fires of all his ancestors raged within. The wolf on his belt buckle—the red-eyed beast that had terrified her—looked tame compared to what she saw now. Yet she was not afraid, not any longer.

"Milady..." His Adam's apple struggled up and down amid the taut sinew of his neck as he swallowed. "If you would stop this, say so now, for fleeting seconds remain that I might retreat."

It took a moment for his meaning to register. The full measure of the sacrifice he was still willing to make for her sake was driven home by the echo of his declaration before God and all witnesses: *"I would die for my bride, even if death were the end."*

In the light cast from the fire, the chiseled frame of his face blurred. He would give up all for her—exactly as a husband ordained by God would do. If Deirdre only thought she loved the man, she now knew it, not just with her heart, but with her soul.

Gently she framed his face with her hands, answering with her all. "There is no reason to stop, milord. No reason here on this earth or in the heavens."

TWENTY-NINE

R icbert unsheathed Alric's sword, his hand shaking with excitement at the feel of the gilded weapon in his hand. It was heavier than he thought. So it would take two hands to take his half brother's head off. He ran a bloodied hand down the hard steel—not his blood, but that of the murdered thanes in the hall.

By his mother's gods, he'd waited overlong for this moment. It had been so easy. Those who'd been slow in succumbing to Juist's concoction were easy prey for the secretly armed Mercian contingent. Walking among the unconscious wedding guests and selectively slitting their throats was as refreshing as a walk after a spring rain, one where blood ran underfoot. But the best was yet to come.

"You are supposed to gather the Welsh weapons and standards from your father's armory to give to my brother's troops, not stand fawning over that sword."

He looked to see Ethlinda, the twisted dagger in her hand dripping with blood. In her other was a swatch of dark human hair.

"The priest has a new tonsure?" Ricbert queried.

His mother smiled. A bloodrush made her lovelier than ever. "I couldn't resist. I left him to Juist and the guards to finish."

"The Welsh wouldn't do that to their own kind," he pointed out. "If we'd have Ecfrith think the Welsh—"

"The *animals* that did this would do anything." The reply was barren of concern, save a sinister smack of humor when she added, "Why, they've even slaughtered children." Upon seeing the shocked lift of Ricbert's brow, Ethlinda hurried to assure him. "Some of the freemen's nits, silly boy. I won't bite the hand that belongs to me…much."

The plan was ingenious. Ecfrith would think the Welsh took advantage of the wedding celebration and massacred Lambert's court and guests while they slept. Only Ricbert survived and, with a few others, turned the blackguards on their heels. It would make for a splendid story for years to come in Galstead's hall.

"What of those who left the celebration early?" They'd waited intentionally until the celebration was well underway before introducing the wine the queen and her witans had prepared to drug the attendees, although the unexpected show of Alric's adoring common horde had taxed the plan momentarily.

"If anyone awakens, my brothers' men will kill them. If you mean our newlyweds, I left a decanter of wine just for them. I may even have saved your brother's bride for you."

Ethlinda sauntered up to him and traced the sharp line of his trimmed beard to the point of his chin. Ricbert watched her tongue as she moistened her lips, savoring her undoubtedly craven thoughts. No ordinary female could make molten fire run through his veins like this—certainly not his bride, who'd pled another of her endless stream of headaches. He ought to despise his mother for spoiling him for other women, but he couldn't. He worshiped her.

"I've had your father removed to his lodge. I shall revive him enough for a *private* farewell." Her laugh shattered the air like icicles upon stone, but to Ricbert's ear, it was nothing short of music. "Then we'll visit the lovebirds' nest." As quickly as it came, the fancy in his mother's voice gave way to harshness. "Now take your uncles' men to the armory, so that they can arm our 'attackers' with Welsh weapons. The sooner our work is done, the sooner we can play."

When the servants who'd not been killed outright came to their senses amid the bloodbath and discovered the foul play too late to defend their lords, they'd rally only to find Ricbert and his uncles driving the Welsh assassins off. The Welsh army conveniently camped at Chesreton's gates provided the perfect scapegoat. The few banners and weapons captured from Saxon retaliatory raids across the border would add weight to the survivors' story of the surprise attack during the wedding feast.

Ecfrith would expect no less, what with Lambert ignoring the bretwalda's suggestion that they pay the *wergild* for Mercian protection. Galsted was his at last, and the lords who would help him keep it were Ethlinda's kin.

"But the sooner we are prepared for the morning, the sooner we can toy with that whore's whelp and the pious little virgin he vows to die for."

Ricbert felt as if the same heat that drew Ethlinda's lips to a ruby smile now drew fast every muscle in his body.

"Now off with you, while I break the news to Lambert that his first-born isn't even his."

"You can wake him?"

"I saw to his drink personally. I want him to feel every prick and quiver of my revenge."

"And if that doesn't finish him?"

Mesmerized, Ricbert watched as his mother dabbed an idle finger in the blood that had congealed on the blade of her dagger and rubbed it over her lips like a pomade of rue. Slanting her painted eyes at him, she smiled.

"Then, my pet," she said, slowly drawing it across his mouth, "*I will.*"

In mortal form or nay, Alric had glimpsed heaven with the woman in his arms, and the journey took its sweet toll. He wanted to pray, to thank the God who'd blessed their union and set Deirdre aside for him in Orlaith's vision. No more had he begun when a sweet lethargy dragged him into a deep sleep, a dreamless one, for no dream could rival the glory of the reality he'd shared with Deirdre.

So sound was its hold on him that not even the cold, lethal press of metal against his neck could penetrate it at first. Only when the serene thrum of his pulse echoed against the blade did the possessive slumber shatter. Each muscle, one by one, tensed as awareness of danger swept through him, moving him to action's edge and no further. If the intruder meant to kill him outright, the deed would have been done by now.

Cracking his eyelids open without so much as missing a breath, Alric barely made out the figure of a man crouched by the side of the bed.

"I know you are awake, Galstead."

The intruder's broken Saxon burst like hot thunder in Alric's ear, increasing the pressure of the blade until its edge stung, a heartbeat from Alric's life's blood.

"I would have you know who your executioner is before you die."

Roused by the angry rumble, Deirdre lifted her head from the cradle of Alric's shoulder and rose on one arm. "Alric?" she queried sleepily.

His other arm freed, Alric took advantage of the distraction and seized the wrist of the hand about the handle of the dagger, twisting it away from his neck and kicking at the intruder.

"Alric!"

The man fell back off his haunches, and Alric threw himself after him.

"Run, wo—" He grunted as his opponent caught him full in the stomach with a ready boot. Confused and unprepared, he should have rolled away and regrouped, but that would give the brigand time to harm Deirdre. Alric grappled instinctively for the man, catching a foot with a vicious twist.

"Get out—" Dark as the room was, a white light burst in Alric's vision as the villain's other foot caught him on the side of the head.

"No, *wait!*" The intruder spoke to Deirdre, scrambling next to Alric.

Alric willed himself to block the man, but his limbs refused to obey. With an angry growl, he rolled to his feet when a loud crack resounded.

"Deirdre?" he rasped, heart stilling at the sound of a body striking the hard floor.

"Alric, I got him." The triumph in Deirdre's voice wavered as she added, "I think."

Alric crawled blindly toward the groans of his dazed assailant when his knee came down on the handle of the man's dagger. With a curse, he seized it.

Deirdre rushed past, the fold of her voluminous nightshift fanning the scent of her perfume in her wake. "I'll light a candle."

"Who the devil are you?" Alric demanded, as he found the intruder's neck with the weapon.

The man moaned unintelligibly, but Alric was in no humor for compassion. "Speak now, or I'll slit your throat and pull your tongue through it."

Behind him, a light flickered from the hearth, growing stronger with each quiver until it drove the pitch from the room. Alric had never seen the senseless man sprawled beneath him, although the split flesh on his forehead masked his features in blood. While peasant by his dress, he had the build of a warrior. Had Deirdre not intervened, the element of surprise might have delivered the upper hand to the villain.

Alric's shield dragging in one hand, Deirdre approached her fallen foe, a candle raised. Eyes still fierce with the fight and hair falling in a wild tangle over her shoulders, she reminded Alric of the northman's Valkrie. Frig's mercy, he'd married a harem of women in this one creature, and each incarnation stirred him more than the last.

"Milady, I owe—"

The stricken look that suddenly claimed Deirdre's face silenced him.

"Oh, heavenly Father!" She threw aside his shield and dropped to her knees in a puff of linen.

Thinking her on the verge of a swoon, Alric tried to catch her with his free hand, but to his astonishment, she stuck the candle in it, very much in command of herself. Before he could react, she tugged the knife away from the stunned man's throat, as though to protect him.

"Oh, Alric, we've killed my brother!"

"What?"

No more cognizant of what had happened, much less how Cairell came to be here in the bedchamber, Deirdre gathered her brother's head into her lap and wiped frantically at the blood covering his face.

"Get some water...quick!" She pried at the wound where a stud on Alric's shield had split Cairell's forehead. "And for heaven's sake, put on some clothes."

A thousand questions mingled with the stark fear that she might have seriously injured, if not killed, the brother she'd tried so hard to rescue. Cairell moved and moaned, but he was far from coherent. Deirdre raised his hand to her lips.

"I'm so sorry, love!" She sniffed, turning impatiently to where a disconcerted Alric struggled into his trousers. "Water, Alric. I need water."

"You call *him* love, when he attacks *me* with a dagger?" Glowering, her husband hopped over to the wash table and grabbed the pitcher. Laces still undone from an earlier urgency, he marched to where Deirdre held her brother and slung the full contents in Cairell's face.

"Alric!" She cradled her brother as he struggled upright, caught somewhere between shock and awareness. "Cairell, it's me…Deirdre," she said, as her brother fumbled for the empty sheath at his belt. "You're safe."

"He's lucky you got to him before I did. 'Tis *he* who is the villain here, milady, not I."

"Dee." Cairell winced, as though the mention of her name pained him. "I…I came as soon as I could."

Deirdre tried to help him sit up, but his weight was all but dead in her arms. "Alric, help me put him on the bed."

"No…" Cairell protested, seemingly repelled by the idea.

"*No!*" Alric jerked the laces of his trousers tight and secured them, never taking his gaze from the man on the floor. "Not till he explains himself."

"I thought you were trying to kill us," Deirdre apologized. "I never—"

"I *was* trying to kill that—"

Deirdre clamped her hand over Cairell's mouth, but the vile name he called Alric had already struck its mark.

"Alric, no—"

Seizing Cairell by the shoulders, Alric hauled the young prince upright and slung him on the bed. "That's where you wanted him, wasn't it?" His glare challenged Deirdre.

Cairell caught himself and bounced back, swinging clumsily. Before the two men could clash, Deirdre shoved the shield between them. The force of their punches wrung it from her tenuous hold and sent it crashing to the floor. Singed by oaths of accusation from both sides, she climbed to her feet and wiped her hands on her bloodied nightshift.

"Stop it!" She stepped between the two angry bucks before they went at each other again. "I'll not let either of you harm someone I love."

"*Love?*" Cairell cast a grudging look at Alric over her shoulder. "Him?"

"Aye, *him!* He's my husband, Cairell. Why wouldn't I love him?"

"You willingly married this Saxon—"

"Sure, I'll strike you again if you say it!" Deirdre drew back her fist.

Cairell knew her well enough not to call her bluff. With a grimace, he dropped down on the edge of the bed and mopped his head with the back of his arm.

Assuaged by her defense, Alric snorted. "A fine way to treat a man who's spent a small fortune trying to save your thankless hide."

"I'll bite off my tongue before I thank the man who abducted my sister and forced her to marry him against her will."

Deirdre gaped in surprise. "How…who told you that?"

"It's true isn't it?"

"It was—" Deirdre felt the heat of her blush as she glanced at Alric—"but it isn't now. At first I only married him so that he'd help me rescue you, but…but he does have this certain irascible charm."

Faith, if she grew any warmer, her gown would catch fire. When Alric stepped up beside her and claimed her waist with a possessive arm, she leaned into him.

"I've had people searching for your whereabouts since our banns were posted. Where have you been?"

Cairell shoved his hair off his face and behind his ears, as if that might clear away some of the confusion. "It's a long story, one neither of us have time for. As we speak, this place crawls with Mercian assassins, and a small army gathers outside. I sneaked into the city to rescue my sister before they attack at dawn and found no guards at the walls and a bloodbath in the hall—everyone is either drugged, dead, or drinking till their comrades arrive with the sun."

With an oath, Alric pulled away and marched to where his scramasax hung. "Then you must take Deirdre away from here and quickly," he said as he strapped the belt on.

She reeled with the implication of his words. "What are you going to do?"

"Get dressed." Ignoring her question, he turned to Cairell with a skeptical arch of his brow. Indeed, her brother was ghastly pale. "Are you up to the task?"

"Only because my sister didn't get her hands on that." Her brother pointed to the short but lethal length of sword. "But even that will only kill so many before they get you."

Seemingly undaunted, Alric took up a strip of stocking and handed it to him. "Wrap this about that wound for now. It won't do to have you blinded."

This couldn't be happening, Deirdre told herself, as Cairell took the wide linen strip and secured it around his forehead. This was all some horrible dream and any moment she'd awaken in her new husband's arms, safe and secure.

"All I ask is that you take my old nurse with you," Alric went on. "Tell her to show you the druid's cave I used to play in when I was a lad. It will take you out of Galstead without detection. As often as Abina hunted me down there, she'll remember where it is."

"No."

Startled by Deirdre's flat denial, both men turned to her.

"I'm not leaving, Alric." Dream or not, she wasn't about to stand by and have her future decided as if she weren't even there.

Alric frowned but said nothing as he handed Cairell his dagger and marched to a tapestried wall. With a jerk, he tore away the artful covering, revealing weapons of all manner, from spears to axes and swords to knives.

"I don't care if you're an expert with every one of those," Cairell observed, "you're outnumbered."

"I marked exactly how many villains supped at my wedding table," Alric answered, donning a leather vest from the wall. "But 'twas no more than had shared my father's hospitality in the past. God forgive me, I ignored my instincts."

Alric's contrition was enough to break her heart.

Cairell turned to Deirdre. "If you care anything about the fool, you'll come with me."

Resolute as her husband, Deirdre grabbed her wedding dress. "I pledged till death do us part," she said, stepping into it. "And I meant it."

She hauled it up over her bloodied gown. Facing the wall, she slipped the nightshift off and finished putting the dress on. By the time she finished lacing it and turned back to the men, Alric the pirate straightened from pulling on his boots. Blades of all description nested handily in the leather trappings of his vest. The handle of the ax on his back was equally within easy reach.

"Frig's breath, woman, stop your gawking and put on your slippers while I see if the way is clear."

Jarred from her stupor, Deirdre hurriedly found her shoes and laced them on.

"A few walk about in twos and threes," Cairell volunteered. "Obviously, they're pretty sure of their control." He glanced from Deirdre to Alric. "Look, I'm not inviting your company, but she's not going to go with me if you don't."

Given what her brother had told them, Cairell did speak sense.

"Alric, please," Deirdre said.

He pierced Cairell with his gaze. "Would you leave in my stead?"

Her heart sunk as Cairell answered honestly with a shake of his head. Men and their confounded honor at all cost! "There is no dishonor in retreating against insurmountable odds to fight another day."

"I'm no fool, sir," Alric assured him, turning to Deirdre. "That is what I hope to do...but I have to see to any survivors—my father, my men—"

"But Cairell says they're dead."

"If they are in the hall," Alric pointed out. "And what of Helewis and Scanlan? Would you have me leave them, wondering if I could have saved them? Sweetling, I am trusting Abina to you and your brother. Those I find, I will send to the safety of the cave." He took her by the shoulders gently. "Trust me."

The very same words he'd used a few ecstatic hours past loomed even larger this time. Yet he'd yielded better than his promise.

"Deirdre, I will take no unnecessary risk that will keep me from you, I swear before God. Do you understand?"

She did. She didn't want to, but she did. Still, she couldn't say it. All she could do was nod. His face—his grim, ever-so-handsome face—blurred before her.

Relief rode high in his voice as he went on. "There's a forest to cloak your escape. If by some chance, I do not join you by dawn, make for the Chesreton road to Wales. I'll catch up with you."

"Promise me," she said.

"I promise." Alric seized her and sealed the vow most convincingly with a kiss.

THIRTY

I t was eerily silent, save for the occasional bark of a wary hound. No birdsong or insect chorus—not even the air stirred around the glow of the lanterns that had been placed around and about for the guests. Even Tor seemed to sense the urgency, for it was unlike him not to answer one of his own, much less be led away from Alric without protest. The wolfhound would be protection, as well as a keen pair of ears, should trouble approach.

Alric held the troubled gaze Deirdre cast over her shoulder as she followed Abina and her brother until the heavy mist swallowed them all. He knew now beyond a doubt that he and his wife were one, for he ached as though part of him had been wrenched from his chest when she pulled away from his parting embrace. It was as though all that was good and righteous left with her.

The rest, this terrible blackness that filled the void, his enemies would have to deal with.

"Don't let your taste for revenge keep you from your bride and birthright, Son."

Abina's parting caution surfaced and sank like a graze of oil upon a sea of emotion. He could taste the blood he would spill, not that of many, but that of anyone who stood between him and the two serpents responsible for this. They'd bitten both him and his father soundly in the Achilles' heel, seizing upon Alric's love-smitten distraction and Lambert's predilection for showing off to friends and kin.

The shadowy cover worked like a partner in his mission, making it easy to sneak up on the guards drinking outside the hall. A slash to one's throat with a dagger and a blow to the other with his scramasax silenced them before they could sound an alarm. As a precaution, Alric donned one of their bright tunics. An enemy close enough to tell he was not one of them would not live long enough to share his knowledge.

Steeled as he was for battle, Alric was not prepared for the senseless carnage that met him inside the great hall. His stomach pitched at the sight of his guests lying in their makeshift beds on the rush-strewn floor, their blankets and clothes soaked in blood. Servants lay where they fell. Mostly men, he noticed, as he stepped over and around the bodies, had been slaughtered like swine, throats slashed from ear to ear.

It was no wonder the villains took so little precaution. The two guards left behind would have no trouble keeping this assembly in order. Keeping an ear open for anyone returning, he made his way to the head table, his nostrils filling with wood smoke tinged with meat drippings and the piquant bouquet of the imported ales and wines—the scents of warmth and hospitality now tainted with that of death.

Lambert was not among the dead…but Gunnar's father was, as well as all of the king's most trusted thanes, the Christian witans Alric had last seen Scanlan with…

He scoured the great room for any sign of the coarse, gray robe the priest wore, then approached the table where he'd shared a drink with his crew earlier. Perhaps like Alric and Deirdre, Scanlan had left before the massacre.

If only the *Wulfshead*'s crew had done the same, he thought as he closed the sightless eyes of his helmsman. This had to be the work of Ethlinda's herbs. That Gunnar and Wimmer were not among the dead offered small comfort. Ironically, the drunkenness that threatened violence had protected rather than endangered Gunnar by forcing him and Wimmer to leave early. A few others were missing, at least from the crew's table. By God's grace, they were sleeping in the barn with their steeds. Still, the roar of anguish building in Alric's chest at those lost wedged like a battle mace in his throat, refusing quarter.

Alric stumbled away from the corpses of the men he'd drunk with, fought with, lived with, and laughed with. *God!* The silent scream rose from his chest, half protest, half plea—all pain. Blinded by it, Alric broke into a run toward the connecting corridor to the king's lodge, his weapon clenched so hard in his fist that his fingers throbbed. Fate kept the passage clear ahead of him as he rushed the entrance past two guards who lay slain where they'd stood.

Like a tormented bull, Alric charged into the large room. "Father!"

The queen crouching over the writhing form of King Lambert leaped away from the bed. The way the black silk of her gown billowed, she looked like a startled vulture. The round astonishment of her gaze strained against the pronounced slant of the paint she used to dramatize her eyes.

"What have you done, witch?" Alric snarled, his scramasax balanced before him as he approached his father's bed.

"P…poisoned me," Lambert moaned from the bed. "The witch has—" The man rolled on his side, retching to no avail, but the room reeked of his previous success.

"How come you to be about at this hour?" Fully recovered, Ethlinda asked the question as though he were a visitor—unexpected but strangely welcome.

"Kill her, Son…and kill her bastard. They plan to rule my kingdom as heroes for turning away their own army posing as the Welsh."

"Don't be absurd, Lambert," Ethlinda taunted. "This boy is a child of God now, a champion of justice…and justice is exactly what I give you for the murder of my son's father."

"*What?*" Alric couldn't believe his ears. Ricbert wasn't the legitimate heir?

"Ricbert is the son of Elwid, the champion your father slew when he attacked my father's burgh and offered peace by accepting my hand." The queen glared at the weak, gasping man on the bed. "And I have waited nearly thirty years to see him avenged. How does it feel, Lambert, to know your enemy's son will rule Galstead?"

Alric shook himself before Ethlinda's evil aura trapped him like a helpless fly in a web of death. He started for her, one deliberate step at a time. There was no escaping his blade, unless she turned to smoke and vanished.

"If you die, Father, then die knowing you are avenged."

"Alric!"

The flicker of brightness in Ethlinda's onyx gaze alerted Alric of danger behind him ahead of his father's gasp. Dropping low to a squat,

Alric heard the air slice over his head. The wind of the passing blade blew cool against his cheek. He sprang up, quick and hard, driving his scramasax into his assailant's side, which was left unprotected by the momentum of the heavy, long sword in his hands.

With a howl of agony, Ricbert stumbled, legs twisted beneath him. Beyond them the sword of Gleannmara clattered to the stone floor. Ricbert stared at Alric with disbelief, and when his knees gave way, Alric instinctively tried to steady him. Ricbert's weight rested on the hilt of Alric's blade, which had entered just under the rib cage and upward, skewering all in its path.

"Mother!" The prince's wail waned along with his strength as Alric wrestled him to the floor. "I'm slain."

With no time to savor the moment, Alric withdrew his blade with a mighty pull. Ricbert screamed and curled on his side, no longer a threat, as Alric spun to face a very deadly one...the queen.

She was nowhere to be seen, as if she *had* turned to vapor and risen through the smoke hole in the roof over them.

His father lay clutching the hilt of the dagger she'd plunged into him. "Never felt...felt like he was mine." Bile and blood trickled down the king's thick beard. His breath was labored and pained.

Alric knelt by the royal bed. "I will track her down and give her the death she deserves."

Lambert snorted, as if he saw humor in this most dire of circumstances. "I won."

The blood that rose in his mouth choked him. Alric lifted him by his shoulders to a sitting position. Clearly Lambert was out of his senses.

"Don't try to talk." Alric wiped his father's mouth tenderly, but the action felt awkward. To his recollection, the closest thing to affection Lambert had ever shown him was praise—a clap on the back at best. Life had forged a formidable wall of social and political taboo between them.

"Look at 'im..."

Struck by the pity he thought he heard in the king's voice, Alric looked at where Ricbert wriggled toward the sword of Gleannmara.

"Not fit to carry a king's sword," Lambert disdained. He coughed, his grip tightening on Ethlinda's dagger as though that alone held his spirit within his dying frame. Having seen more than one man spend his last breath with the removal of a fatal blade, Alric let the weapon stay where it was.

"He couldn't swing it straight with both hands."

Ricbert moaned, collapsing with the verbal stab the king thrust at him. Tears spilled as freely down his cheeks as the blood seeping through his fingers.

"You are my heir, Alric, always were…in my heart."

Alric tightened his embrace, stumbling for a reply. "That's because of Mother."

"Yes, derling, the best of us both."

Derling? Alric tensed uneasily. His father couldn't be speaking to him. He'd never called anyone *derling* but Orlaith.

"I've done many—" Lambert coughed—"many wrong things, but our son…"

Alric followed the man's gaze to the foot of the bed but saw no one.

"He was the key to my…*our* kingdom. Should have listened to you…should have—"

"Father—"

"Lemme finish." Lambert rolled his eyes up at Alric, although the pupils were all but hidden beneath the sag of his eyelids. "Don't be like me, Son. Love is…only kingdom worth living for." A flash of alarm seized his features, and he tried to rise. "Your bride. Where is your bride? You have to save her. That witch will—"

"Deirdre is safe."

"Then go to her, lad. Leave this cesspool on earth. Now!" Lambert's breath became rapid with an infectious panic. Go! We've won. That witch brought your mother to me, but she'll take Deirdre from you. Take up the sword and save your bride."

Lambert's arm was straight as an arrow now aimed at the door. He sat upright without the support of the pillows, as if he were about to chase Alric from the room.

Ricbert's still outstretched hand lay no more than a finger's curl from the jeweled hilt of the Gleannmara sword—a finger's curl and a lifetime. Alric knelt and picked it up. A bolt of energy surged up his arm. The black sea of anguish that tossed in his brain calmed, and Abina's warning bobbed to the surface again, echoing as though she stood right at his ear and repeated it.

"Don't let your taste for revenge keep you from your bride and birthright, Son."

Wonderstruck, Alric turned back to the bed in time to see Lambert snatch Ethlinda's twisted blade from his chest and smile. Alric had never seen such joy, certainly not on his father's face. His eyes all but glowed, like stars catching the light of a full moon on a cloudless night. As though lowered by angels, Lambert, still smiling, eased back on the pillows, his last breath a long, contented sigh.

It spoke volumes, not to Alric's ear, but to his heart. His father was with his beloved.

Now it was time for Alric to join his.

THIRTY-ONE

The fog blanketing Galstead proper had tinged the night with gray, where the scattered lamps and torches glowed as though looking through from another world. It swallowed sound like a thick carpet as Deirdre and her party made their way through the pitch-black tunnel down a seemingly bottomless incline in the globe of light from Abina's lamp.

As long as it took, it should have put them out at Chesreton's gate, Deirdre thought, when at long last they emerged at the bottom. At least the eerie mist wasn't as smothering as before. The air they inhaled now held the promise of light. Restless, Cairell took up the watch, while Tor eyed him from the leash Abina clutched tightly in her arthritic hand. Deirdre helped the nurse to a seat on a flat rock as the old woman called upon heaven for angels to surround and deliver Alric safely away, if it be God's will.

Deirdre could not consider the possibility that it was not. She turned away from the nurse with her own plea. *Father, You have brought us together. It can't possibly be Your will that we part now. Surely You'd not use our hearts so unconscionably. Surely...*

"You really love him."

Realizing that she'd voiced her protest, Deirdre met her brother's gaze. "With all my heart, Cairell. God has taught me...taught Alric *and* me," she amended, "so much that we might make a good match in heaven's eye. I will cherish Alric to my dying day."

Cairell scoffed. "He's a wolf in sheep's clothing."

"Nay, he's a wolf in Christ's light." She would not let her brother's words ruffle her.

"He's a pirate, a thief—"

"He's a warrior protecting his father's shores—" the old nurse spoke up—"by seizing ships bound for Scotia Minor with arms and supplies to be used against his country. And not the least different from the

Dalraidi vessels that ply the Northumbria coast with the same purpose."

Cairell was clearly taken aback. "She speaks Irish?"

"I *am* of the Dalraidi," Abina informed him, head high. "Captured along with my mistress, Princess Orlaith of the same."

"Alric's *mother*." Deirdre smiled at her brother's shock.

"My Alric was educated by the finest teachers the Irish have to offer and certainly learned better manners than you, young man…speaking before me in a language you presumed me to be ignorant of."

The corners of Cairell's mouth struggled between humor and consternation. "My apologies, milady."

With a righteous sniff, Abina returned to her prayers.

"But it still doesn't change the fact that he chose to fight with our enemies." Obviously Cairell was still unconvinced of Alric's worthiness.

"He fought with honor for what he believed in, just like you and your friends, Cairell."

"With all due respect, miladies, neither of you have seen the handiwork of Northumbrian *honor*." Cairell thumped his chest with his fist, taking his simmering rage upon himself. "I, and my less fortunate friends, have."

His firsthand account of Ecfrith's attack on Ireland's coastal monasteries was enough to blanch Gleannmara's green hills. Worse still was the plight of slaves taken. "Mostly children, Deirdre." Cairell could not stem his disgust. "I and those who survived were taken because one of the children inadvertently called me Prince Cairell to warn me of an attacker at my back. Even so, there were four of us trying to form a fighting circle, and the devils never did figure which of us was the prince."

"What was the name of this brigand who took you?" All Deirdre had was the letter from a Frisian trader, who'd demanded the church deliver the ransom.

Cairell shrugged. "'Twas a group. They spoke so fast, I couldn't understand most of their babble."

"Your sister speaks our language flawlessly," Abina boasted to the prince. At Cairell's skeptical glance, Deirdre nodded.

A frown furrowed his brow. "You never studied it."

"It was a miraculous gift from God."

"How can you be certain?"

"Scanlan told me…and so many souls have been saved, even the king—"

Tor barked, giving them all a start. Jumping to his feet, Cairell looked into the mist.

Heavenly Father, let it be my Alric coming to me. Her Alric. The memory of his possessive ardor and sweet embrace in its aftermath would remain with her forever.

Cairell knelt to press his ear to the ground, then stood. He cut Tor a contemptuous glance. "Tell me why we brought that drooling creature with us again? 'Tis likely it was his slobber he heard smacking the ground."

"Tor is Alric's—" Deirdre broke off, recalling how the dog had come to her defense against Alric in the chapel. *"Our* dog." The beast had grown on her affections.

"Ah." Accepting his sister's explanation as an impugning explanation, Cairell settled against a large stone, staring off in the direction Tor had indicated. "I should have taken Scanlan," he said to no one in particular.

"Alric will bring him." The blade of alarm that had wedged in her chest the moment she was awakened to the sound of Alric and an unseen attacker struggling twisted with guilt. "If the poor soul's not among the dead." Scanlan had made some serious enemies. She'd been praying selfishly for Alric, forgetting Scanlan. *Please, God, let him live. He's done far more for You than I.*

"I left three good men behind as it is." The pain in her brother's voice was as thick as the fog. He shook his head. "They wanted to cover for my escape, but I refused…until I heard what had happened to you."

"What happened to *you?"* Deirdre leaned next to her brother on the stone.

In bits and snatches, between stopping to listen, Cairell told Deirdre the incredible story. The four captives were kept hidden, as though their captors did not want their comrades to know about them. Imprisoned in the hold of the Saxon ship and fed worm-eaten bread and sour wine for a week, they were at last smuggled by night to a prison in an old stone tower near the eastern sea from which the invaders had first come.

"It was a ruin; its stench was faded so that we could smell the salt air and hear the gulls."

Deirdre shivered at the thought of being confined in the hold for more than a week. Her stomach still turned with the memory of her fear and the fetid air in the hold.

"Then someone arrived with the news that you and my ransom had been captured by Alric of Galstead, and that one of Ecfrith's thanes was asking questions about me. The next thing we know, we overhear the guards talking about putting us on the next Frisian vessel bound for France. Thanks to ill-fitted shackles, I slipped overboard the first night out and swam to shore off the Essex coast. Surely God provided my way here, for I found an army forming to march on Northumbria. With my Latin, I passed as a traveling bard—"

Tor erupted suddenly in a barking frenzy, this time pulling at the leash so hard that Abina lost her grip.

"Tor!" Deirdre called out to him.

The dog disappeared into the fog, in the direction of a distant thunder.

"Alric?" She glanced at Cairell expectantly, but his shrug told her he had no more idea than she.

He hurried to Abina's side to help her to her feet. "We'll take no chances," he answered shortly. "Into the tunnel."

Having explored this hillside inside and out as a child, Alric knew exactly where he was, but Tor's throaty roar was a welcome sound to his ear. He reined in Dustan and gave the dog a chance to find him. The rain clouds and mist delayed the light of dawn, and hence the attack being mustered southeast of the walls. Even more of a blessing, the guards who'd been frightened away at the gate were remiss in regrouping and summoning help against the *demons* who'd materialized in the fog. As a result, the neatly executed escape with Wimmer and the handful of men who were in the barn had turned into a motley exodus of villagers with their women and children, as word spread of what had happened. Alric could no more abandon them than his wife's kin.

It was a miracle Scanlan lived, much less that he was able to tell them what had happened. Badly beaten and partially scalped in the manner Ecfrith's men had done to so many of the Celtic clergy, the young man was a mass of cuts and bruises swelling by the moment. Just which of the priest's bones had been broken was impossible to tell. Scanlan told Alric he owed his life to Juist. Ethlinda ordered her henchmen to subdue Scanlan while she scalped the crown of his head, and then left him to Juist and her men to finish him off. Evidently reluctant to take the life of a priest, no matter what God he served, the senior witan stopped the soldiers just before Scanlan lost consciousness for the first time.

"We must focus on the unseen," the priest mumbled, seizing Alric's arm. "What we see is temporary." He drifted in and out of his senses as the villagers placed him in a cart, while Alric and what other men they could muster stood by, weapons ready for any Mercian attempt to stop them.

"There's the mutt," Wimmer pointed out as Tor bounded out of the mist, tail wagging.

Moments later, Alric found the entrance to the cave and hailed the remainder of his party. Cairell emerged first, sword ready, but Deirdre rushed past him, her face awash with relief.

"Alric!"

Her voice truly was music to his ears.

"Were you followed?" Cairell asked as Alric slid off Dustan and caught his bride in his arms.

This was real. *This* was all that mattered, he told himself. He kissed her with a fierce thanksgiving. She was safe. Ricbert and Ethlinda would never have the chance to harm her. It would be all the queen could do to explain this black night and the murder of some of his most loyal thanes to the bretwalda.

"For the love of God, man, what manner of a parade is this?"

Cairell's exclamation took a moment to penetrate Alric's reunion with his wife. Reluctantly, Alric drew away and looked to where Cairell stood gaping at the group of men and women who had materialized in the fog. "Would you leave them to face the butchers you witnessed in the hall?" If he had to, he'd fight Gleannmara's prince then and there, but he'd not leave his people.

"Like Moses," Abina marveled, fit to burst with pride. "Orlaith and I dreamed, Son, but never to this extent."

The last thing Alric felt like was a Moses. There was no promised land for this ragged lot—at least none guaranteed this side of death. That was the only unseen he could focus on at the moment. He shoved the matter from his mind, for he wasn't certain his renewed faith was strong enough to accept that God had abandoned His children so shortly after their acceptance of Him.

"What of Scanlan?" Deirdre looked at him, lips trembling.

Alric nodded his head toward the wagon. As she turned in that direction, she took in the familiar faces that accompanied him. She swayed for a moment, causing Alric to reach for her.

"This is all?"

He understood her shock. "Most of my men were in the hall."

"And your father?" Abina queried.

"Dead."

"Oh, Alric."

He steeled himself against the tears that welled in Deirdre's eyes, lest the emotions tearing at her voice be his undoing.

"And Helewis and Gunnar?" Deirdre's question was hoarse.

"I couldn't find them. We looked as much as we dared. I can only pray they survived. Not everyone was killed. Mostly Lambert's most loyal. The rest were drugged—"

"But why—"

"Later, muirnait, later. Abina, you will ride in the cart with the priest. I want to be away from here before the mist clears. We'll go as far as Chesreton. From there, we'll decide what to do. As far as we know, though Gunnar's father is dead, his men still fortify it."

Given the extent of this treachery, Alric would not hazard to guess which army strove to lay siege to the seaport—Welsh or Mercian. For all he knew, they ran from the fat and into the fire.

"You want me to take my sister right back into the hands that—"

"*My* hands, Irish." Alric's barely suppressed anger and frustration flashed beneath the surface. "And as God is my witness now, I will cut them off for her safety. If you doubt me, then let's settle this now."

Standing his ground, hand on the hilt of his bloodied scramasax, Alric clenched his teeth, the steel gray of his gaze clashing with a blue as steely as that Deirdre had wielded against him time and again. But this time, his adversary was no comely female.

It is her brother, he reminded himself, which was nearly as much a handicap. Still, leadership had to be established. There could be only one in charge.

"Cairell!"

At Deirdre's cry, something kindled in her brother's appraisal, and Alric's senses were keen enough to recognize that it wasn't challenge. He let his hand drop from his weapon and turned to face the others. "We've a long journey ahead, so ready away," Alric shouted, turning to reach for Dustan's reins. Walking the horse to where Deirdre waited, he bowed. "Milady, I'd be honored if you share the rest of our wedding night with me."

Her smile was like the break of day in the dark swirl of his brain. "Whatever you wish, milord."

"*You* can ride in the wagon," Alric said, glancing over at Cairell, who stood without a mount.

Princely pride surely chaffed, the heir to Gleannmara acknowledged him with a gracious nod. "My feet thank you for your hospitality, sir. Mayhap I'll find out from the priest what manner of persuasion you used to addle my sister's wits."

Alric leaped onto Dustan's back behind his wife and laughed, some of the pressure building in his chest released at finding Deirdre and Abina safe. "The answer to that is simple, Lord Gleannmara. 'Twas Saxon courage and Celtic charm." Alric gave way with an *ooof!* at the sharp jab of Deirdre's elbow. "Oh, and love, let us not forget love."

THIRTY-TWO

A Welsh force camped outside Chesreton, but the beleaguered travelers from Galstead approached the city from the opposite side without event. The *Wulfshead* and three foreign ships haunted the mist hovering over the river as they crossed the bridge to the water gate of the town. Like the memories of the previous night, the sky was burdened with clouds that refused to let the sun shine through. Met at the city gate by Falk, the commander left in charge by the murdered Cedric, they learned that Owen of Emrys had come to demand restitution for the raid Ricbert had lead earlier across the Welsh lord's border.

"He claims Ricbert's retribution for a simple cattle raid was excessive," Falk informed them. "That Galstead owes Emrys some form of payment or the return of what was taken."

"He's made no move to attack?" Alric wondered at the fact.

"Not yet, sire, though we can hold him off if he does."

"Owen of Emrys?" Cairell hopped down from the cart and approached on legs stiff from the long, damp journey. "I know the man well. We studied together under Eamon of Derry. And it's not uncommon when a debt is owed to sit at the door of the obliged party."

"Actually, Owen is a distant cousin of ours," Deirdre informed Alric. "Gleannmara has been tied to Emrys by trade or blood since Queen Maire captured Rowan, lord of Emrys, and made him her husband."

"At least the circumstances of our union aren't unprecedented in your family." Alric's wryness was scant of humor. "I'll hear more of this, once we've seen to my company."

Falk looked at the humanity strung out behind him. "Begging your pardon, milord, but what's amiss at Galstead? This is hardly the average wedding celebration."

"This *is* Galstead...or what's left of it." Fatigue flattened any emotion in Alric's voice.

The commander stood dumbstruck, his reaction seesawing between disbelief and outrage.

"Summon your captains and have them meet me at the royal villa in an hour."

Falk nodded and moved aside. Deirdre heard him barking orders behind them as Alric lead his assembly to the home Lambert had given him as a wedding gift. Deirdre could only imagine her husband's anguish.

Not only had he lost his father, his closest friends, and a shire—if not a kingdom—but he'd been robbed of the teeth to avenge it. Much as she wanted to offer some word of comfort, nothing that came to mind seemed appropriate.

But then, Deirdre could hardly hold her head up from exhaustion. Despite their getting away before dawn, the travel had been extremely tedious, slowed even more by cloudbursts. She'd dozed against Alric's chest and taken comfort in the arm that occasionally tightened about her waist with affection or the brush of his lips against the back of her neck. More than once, she thanked God that they still had each other…and Cairell.

Surely God would prevail for them again.

Deirdre blinked, stiffening against her husband as she stared at the front of the villa ahead. A small figure appeared where a moment before there had only been fog. She knew instantly who the woman was.

"Aelfled!" Alric sounded no less surprised. "How did you—" He thought better of his question. "Never mind. We've grave need of your services. Have you any qualms about healing a Christian priest?"

A serene smile touched upon Aelfled's artfully formed mouth. "I delight in the company of knowledge and have no regard for those who would destroy it."

The dark-haired female seemingly floated over to where Scanlan lay in the wagon. She was too large for a fairy or an elf, yet seemed too small for a human adult. Deirdre shook the fanciful notion from her mind, but it took a stronger effort for the woman Alric had awakened in her to dismiss the possible threat of his former lover's presence.

Aelfled did indeed live up to her namesake—*elf beauty*—but she was no more some magical creature than anyone else, Deirdre told herself, watching Cairell practically fall over his own feet to help the healer into the cart. The eyes of all the men present were drawn like moths to her flame.

"Scanlan is in good hands." Obviously Alric mistook the green direction of her thoughts for a pious wariness. "I've never seen her mutter chants, much less conjure more than tea or a poultice from the herbs she collects and dries year round."

Before Deirdre could reply, the door to the villa opened and Doda rushed outside, beaming enough to make up for the lack of sunlight. "Milady, Lord Alric, welcome home!"

"Thank you, Doda," Deirdre managed, ashamed of herself for doubting the strength of her husband's vows. Even as a pirate, he honored his word. "It's good to be home."

Alric slid off the stallion and lifted Deirdre down. "Surely, you jest, milady."

What pain she heard in his murmured words. Deirdre framed his face with her hands, as though to assuage it with her touch, indeed her very soul. "I am with you, Alric. Wherever you are, it is my home, and I'm glad to be there."

He heard and digested her words, but the somber mask of his features gave none of his thoughts away, save that he was as drained by the long, wet journey and lack of sleep as she. Suddenly, as though pulling upon resources from the very tip of his reach, the warrior rallied and she, too, took heart.

"Doda," Alric said in a brighter tone, "see to my wife. And Belrap," he added, cutting off Deirdre's protest, "see what can be done to feed and lodge these good people. Use what you must, spare nothing, for these people have spared nothing in my support."

"Yes, milord." With a respectful dip, Doda put her arm around Deirdre. "Come, milady, you can tell me all about it whilst we dry out your wet clothes."

"I'll help with the guests," Deirdre informed her out of Alric's earshot.

"If you do, 'twill be in dry clothes, or I'll not budge."

"Pauls, have some of the boys find lodgings for those we cannot accommodate and spread the word that we will have a meeting in two hours." Alric set his shoulders. "If ever we needed to pull together as one people, 'tis now."

As the shadows of the day became shadows of the night, flaming cressets were raised in addition to the usual lanterns outside the villa and in the courtyard. Smoke from the baskets of wood and pitch atop the poles thickened the damp air. Alric's request that the people of the seaside shire come together with their displaced neighbors as one had already resulted in ample food and provisions. Vendors emptied their shelves, and homes opened their stores. The courtyard that had filled with travelers that afternoon as Scanlan was carried into one of the guest rooms emptied, family by family.

Dwarfed in some of Alric's spare clothes, while her wedding dress—now her only dress—dried by the hearth in the master bed-chamber, Deirdre left Aelfled tending Scanlan to join her husband and Cairell in the courtyard. Merchants and craftsmen stood with Falk and his men in the courtyard of the villa as Alric gave them what details that could be pieced together regarding the massacre at Galstead.

The latest news had come from a servant who'd made his way to Chesreton on one of the horses Alric's men scattered before leaving. When the man regained consciousness from the drugged wine, the burgh was fully occupied by the queen's brothers and their troops. All pretense of a Welsh raid had been abandoned. The servant heard one Mercian guard bragging that a second army was on its way. All the while, bodies were being tossed onto a bonfire on the common, including those of Lambert and Ricbert. The man had not seen the queen but admitted he was more concerned with escaping than with determining Her Majesty's whereabouts.

"By now you know my father and his loyal thanes have been mur-dered. Of the traitors, Ricbert and a few careless guards are dead. The queen and her Mercian relatives are in control. Had we not been fore-warned in the middle of the night, Deirdre and I might lie upon a pile of burning corpses with our throats slit as well."

Even though the tale of what had transpired swept through the city with the speed of a flame, shock still prevailed among the listeners. "From all accounts, their plan to blame the Welsh for the bloodbath was ruined by our escape." Alric's gaze met Deirdre's. "Word will get to Ecfrith that the Mercians he'd have us pay tribute to for protection were the ones we needed protection from."

The news that the bretwalda expected tribute-paying shires of his kingdom to pay for protection over and again to known enemies raised the level of emotions riding high over the assembly. The citizens were no more amenable to it than Alric and Lambert had been.

"So do you think the bretwalda will send troops to take Galstead back?" the mayor of Chesreton inquired.

Alric shook his head. "I cannot speak for Ecfrith, but I do know his forces are concentrated to keep the Scots and the Picts at bay. Even Galstead has soldiers with him. If the bretwalda would win back Galstead, it will not be a priority."

"Then what of Chesreton?"

"Aye, what of us?" Another wail joined in with the mayor's cry.

Alric waited until the questioning died down. "Chesreton will survive as it always has, under whatever rule exists at the time. The sea and ships are your holdings. The merchants who live here are the lifeblood of its prosperity. Your tariffs and fees will continue to go to whoever rules Galstead, unless you can raise a sufficient force to take the shire back yourselves."

"Or unless *you* lead us."

At the familiar voice from the rear of the crowd, Alric paled. When the people finally gave the speaker up, a whole and hearty Gunnar marched up to his friend. Seizing the stunned leader's hand, the mate raised it above his head.

"Long live Alric, the *rightful* king of Galstead!"

At that, Alric came to life. "What in Thunor's—"

The crowd picked up the cry, cutting off Alric's oath. Amid the roar, the two friends embraced, and Deirdre's eyes stung at the joy on her husband's face.

"Thank God you are alive," Alric said, as they broke away.

Deirdre laid her hand on Gunnar's arm. "Have you seen Helewis?"

"She's well, and now safe from her demon of a husband," Gunnar replied.

The people rallied around Alric, drowning out anything he might want to say. A group of men tried to raise him on their shoulders, but he threw off their well-intentioned efforts. After herding Deirdre to the safety of Cairell's company, he leaped up on the wall of the fountain as though to battle the overwhelming tide single-handedly. The slash of his arms through the air hacked the noise to a more manageable level.

"No, and I say again, *no!*"

The place fell quiet, as though death itself had swept through their number. Every muscle in Alric's arms and chest flexed with the simmering emotions tearing at his face, quivering in his jaw, pumping fast and furious through the veins that stood out with the taut chords of his neck.

"I am a soldier of the sea," he shouted in the wake of the loud and sudden hush.

"But a soldier is a soldier," the mayor objected.

"Aye, and as such, I know when it's time to fight and when it's time to retreat."

"I never thought I'd see Alric of Galstead turn coward."

The look Alric gave the official withered the man, forcing him back among his fellow townsmen. Divided opinions broke rampant throughout the enclosure. "You are entitled to your opinion, sir," Alric acknowledged.

The noisy crowd must have felt the rumble of the wolf's low growl, for it quieted at once.

"And you, sir, are welcome to lead these good people." Alric lifted his finger in warning. "But good people must not be mistaken for good fighting men. Look about you. I do not see more than a handful of men who I would lead into battle—and none that I will lead to their deaths. You are merchants, craftsmen, sailors, and fishermen."

"Then what would *you* have us do?" the mayor demanded.

"*You* are the official leader of this shire, Edgar."

"But you are king of Galstead."

"There *is* no kingdom, man!" Though clothed in anger for the crowd, Alric's howl of desolation tore at Deirdre's heart. "And if it's my advice you seek, then hear it." He paced his words, as though each were meticulously chosen and executed. "You will do the same as your fathers before you have done. You will survive. You can pay tribute to one lord as easily as to another and, believe me," he sneered, "the Mercians are no fools. They will only cut off the hand that meets theirs with a weapon, not with coin."

"And what of us who've left our means of living behind?" one of the refugees called. "The people of Chesreton won't keep us forever. Is that the cost we have to pay for following you and accepting this Christian God?"

Alric looked as if the king stone of ancient Tara had descended upon his shoulders, heavier than he could bear. Jaw clenched, he shook his head. "These are mad times. Christians pretending to be Christians persecute their brethren. Sons betray their fathers." Alric pointed to the chamber where Scanlan had been taken. "A good man, who risked his life to bring the hope of God's Word to you, lies beaten within a breath of life…scalped with the tonsure of Rome by my *unbelieving* stepmother. I am no seer or prophet. I cannot explain it all."

"I can." Deirdre reached up and took Alric's hand. "Good and evil are always at war, and we are the victims. How we survive depends on our faith…or lack of it. We mustn't despair."

Alric helped her up onto the thick fountain wall beside him. She stood tall beside her husband.

"The Christian God has done something no other god has. He has given us a book of instructions and truths to guide us. 'For I know the thoughts that I think toward you, saith the LORD, thoughts of peace, and not of evil, to give you an expected end.'" Her Saxon was flawless. "I personally know this to be true. My brother was kidnapped during Ecfrith's raid on Ireland, and I sailed with the ransom to save him. Instead of saving him, I was captured, and my faith was sorely tested. My future looked no blacker than yours appears now, and yet I stand here, rewarded by love and the safety of my brother because the God I believe in never abandoned me…and He will not abandon me—*or you*—now."

Several in the gathering spoke, but none ventured to speak above the general murmurs to each other. Her heart in her throat, she stumbled on. "My heart aches for you. You've left your homes behind and have no idea what tomorrow will bring. There was another group of people who did the same thing, and God delivered them to a new land and new beginning. Their way was not easy, but the hardship was like a smith's fire, it purified their faith like gold and made them strong as steel."

"Where will we go? Has this God provided a place for us?"

Deirdre hesitated. "He has plans for you, plans for you to prosper, to give you hope and a future." *Father, even I who have known You all my life struggled to believe this. Help me convince them of the truth of Thy Word.*

"With what fortune my ships have earned, I will purchase the land for any who choose to follow me." Alric took her hand in his. "I give my word."

Deirdre met his gaze and was embraced by it. He knew no more than she as to the how or the why, but he was willing to take the risk...the leap of faith.

"And where will you find our land?" one of the men called out skeptically. "Buy it back from Mercians and have them steal it again?"

"I don't know," Alric admitted. "I will have to search—"

"He'll find it in Ireland."

Wondering if her ears played tricks upon her, Deirdre looked to Cairell. So did others, but instead of seeing the prince of Gleannmara, all they saw was a young man in peasant garb.

A man close to Cairell sneered. "And I'm supposin' you'll be him that sells it?" Deirdre recognized the thatcher who'd put a new roof on Scanlan's chapel.

Cairell flashed a wide grin. "Aye, sir, that I will, and be the first to welcome you to your new home."

Rumbles of disdain and disbelief echoed from all around. "The beggar's crazy as a swineherd!"

"Who in thunder does that dimwit think he is?"

Alric held up his hand, waving down the uproar. "Allow me, good fellows, to introduce my brother by law, both God's and man's, to whom I owe my life…and loyalty, Prince Cairell of Gleannmara."

Wary blue eyes met wary gray as Alric offered Cairell an arm up onto the wall beside him. But the moment their hands locked, all the apprehension in their gazes melded into one sense of purpose. Deirdre's heart soared at the unspoken truce between the two men she loved. Nothing had worked out as she'd planned, but *God's* plan had proved so much better. And so it would for the people before her. She knew it, both in her heart and her soul.

THIRTY-THREE

When the last of the villa's visitors left, only lanterns were left to carry the vigil of light until morning. Alric wearily embraced Gunnar and bid him good night. Dismissing Belrap for the evening, the prince of a disintegrating kingdom meandered into the courtyard. Each step was leaden—with fatigue, with disappointment, with confusion, and self-doubt. Questions and answers were a muddle in his mind, one hardly discernible from the other. He sat on the edge of the thick, stone basin, senses numb to the night.

The graceful nymphs of the old fountain tirelessly poured an unending stream of water into its bed. It was here, in the wee hours of the night, that he often came as a child, seeking the ready company of the stone maidens—and of God. It was here that he later hurled his prayers upward as a youth, demanding to know why his mother and he were outcasts of the court. And it was here that he cursed God when he and his mother returned from her homeland, rejected and disdained.

And now what? Was this his punishment for his rebellion, his *reward* for returning to God, as the thatcher from Galstead had accused earlier? Alric had no answer. Despite the promise Deirdre championed so convincingly, he *felt* wounded, betrayed like the new Christians who'd followed him in panic to avoid Mercian retribution. Would that he had the strength of her belief, for with it the captured became the conqueror, not just of his heart but of those who heard her.

"Alric?"

He turned to see the lady of his thoughts and heart standing in the threshold to his bedchamber. Instead of wearing the silk and fine linen she deserved, she wore one of his old shirts, her freshly washed hair spilling over it like dark gold. He didn't think he'd ever seen her more beautiful, not even in the velvet and pearls that night she'd had him tripping over his brick of a tongue. The light behind her revealed the woman beneath the shirt, but it was the memory of the Scripture with which she'd calmed the stormy crowd earlier that stirred him beyond the physical.

"For I know the thoughts that I think toward you, saith the LORD, *thoughts of peace, and not of evil, to give you an expected end."*

They had given her confidence in a worse circumstance than he was in at present. She'd lost her birthright, a loved one, and hope of regaining both. Her spirit had remained indomitable to anyone, save her God. Alric had thought that everything good in this world had died with his mother, but it survived. Like a hearth fire, its light had only been banked and lay waiting, ready to warm those who flocked to it and even be carried out to other hearths, that they, too, might warm a soul with its glow.

Now it came to him, barefoot and shivering in the damp night. Deirdre reached up, raking her fingers through the length of his hair before locking them loosely behind his neck.

"You need rest, milord."

"And you need warming." He gathered her to him as though she were the last of that light in the world.

"Perhaps together, we might accomplish both," she said, with a beguiling lift of her brow.

It tugged at the muscles in the pit of his belly with an invisible string—such an insignificant gesture to carry the powerful punch delivered to his senses. No longer numb, they took in all of the woman he lifted off the cool tiles.

Deirdre. Her eyes sparkled like gems in the lantern glow, and her startled gasp-turned-to-giggle danced with delight in his ear. Meadow flowers blossomed unseen in her damp hair, while her body curled soft against his chest. That his mouth not feel neglected, Alric bent over and sampled the smile upon her lips.

At least it was meant to be a sample. Somewhere between the speed of his pulse and cessation of his breath, an intoxicating surge of renewal blurred the passing of time. Here was what he'd been missing for so long—not gold, nor power, nor land...but love. Here was the earthly birthright his mother alluded to—not

Galstead, nor Gleannmara, but one where the heart ruled, with him as its servant.

There was nothing left for him to do, save trust and obey.

Sunlight lulled Alric gently from sleep the following day. Much as he longed to awaken his bride on the first morning of their marriage, to kiss away a sleepy pout and coax her protests at being disturbed into pleas for more of his attentions, she needed rest and he needed to be about his business. Dressing quickly before temptation got the better of his discipline, Alric brushed his mouth lightly over the childlike pucker of her lips and quit the chamber.

Would it always be like this when he left her, as though a part of him remained, unable to exist without her?

Refreshed from a good night's rest, Cairell awaited Alric in the dining salon where Doda had put out fresh breads and curd sweetened with honey and porridge. The prince of Gleannmara was more suitably dressed in some of Alric's clothing, which Belrap had scrounged up for their guest. Alric recognized the shirt as the one Orlaith had made for his eighteenth birthday. He'd worn it one summer before the shoulders became too narrow. His sentimental mother must have tucked it away with her keepsakes, for this was the first Alric had seen of it since he'd outgrown it.

After an awkward moment, Alric made the first move. "Good day, sir. I take it you slept well?" He slipped into the chair at the head of the table.

"Better than in months." Cairell didn't even bother to look up from the bread he lavished with butter.

Alric didn't expect him to reciprocate. Despite Cairell's generous offer to take the refugees of Galstead, there was much to be settled. He left his guest to his brooding silence and helped himself to a loaf of bread and broke it in half. It didn't occur to him until his mouth was full to give thanks. He'd pledged to be a Christian and knew from Orlaith's upbringing that it was expected. Shoving a wad of food to the side of his mouth, Alric lowered his head.

"Thank You, God, for this food." What was it his mother used to say? She'd made him memorize it. "May it sustain us so…so that we can glorify and serve You." A dubious snort came from across the table. "And share it with others…even the Irish. Amen."

"You sound as comfortable with prayer as I am speaking Saxon."

"It doesn't come naturally," Alric conceded. He chewed the bread and swallowed. "If God's so knowledgeable and forgiving, He'll accept it as an earnest attempt."

"So, the Saxon Moses has a temper, too."

"Frig take your tongue; I'm no Moses."

"But you have the courage to match your convictions; I'll give you that."

Alric glanced up, searching for the hidden barb. The mockery in his guest's eyes, bluer than blue like Deirdre's, had disappeared.

"You handed away a kingdom for God yesterday." Cairell sopped honey up with his bread. "Now you are the shepherd of a landless flock. How does it feel?"

If his brother-in-law taunted him, Alric would take his head off. If the man were serious, then this was a subject better chewed over a thick log, with a full night ahead to watch it burn.

"I gave nothing up. God took it…or it fell apart at the foundation. A skilled blade might clear a land of its enemy, but it cannot build a kingdom of loyal subjects," he shot back. "Why?"

Cairell thought a moment. "Like you, Moses was a prince who gave up the chance to rule a kingdom to lead a group of frightened and homeless believers to safety."

Alric had forgotten Moses was a prince, the favored over the rightful heir. Nonetheless, this notion that his purpose was a godly one was nonsense. Alric wanted no unwarranted credit, especially when it came to something that smacked of the hypocrisy he'd seen in his mother's kin. It had turned what little faith he'd kept bitter in his craw.

"I gave up no chance for anything save futile bloodshed for a lost cause. I *chose* to save your sister, what men I could, and the priest. And I would hardly call that ragtag lot who straggled along God's chosen."

"All people are God's chosen. That *ragtag lot,* as you call them, chose God because of you, according to Scanlan. And you could have left them, but as I saw it, you slowed your pace to afford them protection from pursuit."

"Turns out, there was nothing to protect them from." Alric shrugged, uncomfortable as to where this was leading. "You're starting to sound like the priest…or are you having second thoughts about inviting us to settle in *your* promised land?"

He had gold enough to buy land and, in time, raise an army to defend it. If he chose Gleannmara, it would be for Deirdre.

"No. I meant it when I offered Gleannmara as a refuge. We have had a motto since its first Christian rulers, Maire and Rowan: Home to the just, enemy to the greedy and ambitious. Because we prosper in God's grace, we've always had room for our fellow man."

"Even if he's Saxon?"

"One of my good friends, a smith by trade, is a Saxon. God-fearing, hard-working people are always welcome. I've studied with some Saxon lads, intelligent as far as Saxons go." The twinkle in Cairell's eye put a good-natured edge on the jibe.

"Humph," Alric acknowledged, taking no offense. "Sounds too good to be true."

"It's as close to heaven as I'll ever see on this green earth." Affection glowed in the young prince's eyes. "It doesn't mean we are without trial or taint. We're just human and do the best we can after the example of the King of kings. At least that was the example set by King Rowan."

Alric narrowed his gaze, struck by the sincerity of his companion. "You sound too humble to be Irish."

"And you're too stubborn to be a Moses."

That again. It was like going head-to-head with a bull—a fair-haired, blue-eyed bull no less artful with a twist of the tongue than his sister. Unable to outwit the gamecock—at least at this hour—Alric called it a draw with a bellow of laughter. Cairell sealed the truce with his own. The laughter did Alric's soul good. A fleeting *Thank You, Father* came as naturally as his next heartbeat.

Belrap entered the room with slow, hesitant steps. "Excuse me, milord, but you've some visitors."

Alric sobered. "Edgar already?" It was early for the mayor to be about.

"Yes, milord, and a group of Welshmen by their look."

Even though he refused the role of king, Alric had promised to ride out to the Welsh encampment at midmorning with the mayor and Cairell of Gleannmara to settle the issue of Ricbert's raid.

"Show them in." As Belrap left, Alric took a deep breath and sighed. "Galstead haunts me still."

The two men rose to their feet as the mayor entered the room and with a sweeping bow, presented his companion.

"Milords, allow me to present Lord Owen of—"

"S'death, my eyes deceive me, else I shall have to believe in ghosts!" Struck still in his tracks, Owen of Emrys stood agape before the prince of Gleannmara.

"I am no spirit, sir," Cairell assured him as he walked around the length of the table and embraced the startled visitor. "I am a guest in the home of my new brother-in-law, the result of a story that will keep hearth fires burning long into many a night to come."

"But...but I was told you...Deirdre?" Owen shot a bewildered look at Alric. "Deirdre is alive as well?" The man threw up his hands. "Is this morning, and am I not in the Saxon port of Chesreton?"

The mayor nodded, eyes darting from one man to the other.

"The answer is yes to both your questions, sir," Alric assured the man. It always helped to have an advantage over a possible adversary. "And I am Alric, of what was once Galstead. I am, for a while, master of this villa."

Owen hardly gave Alric a passing nod. He grabbed Cairell's arms and shook him, as if expecting him to disappear in a poof. "I am beside myself with relief and joy! We received news from your mother—"

"Our stepmother," Cairell amended.

"That you and Deirdre were both dead, seized and killed by pirates. I thought Gleannmara had seen the last of the Niall dynasty die with your father."

The mischief he'd enjoyed at his Welsh friend's expense died with the blink of Cairell's eye. "What say you, Owen? You meant because

Deirdre and I have been mistaken for dead, that Father *is* the last of our line to reign."

Owen's silence spoke louder than words.

"My father is dead? Is that what you tell me?" Cairell gripped his friend's arm. "Fergal of Gleannmara is dead?"

Owen winced under the force of Cairell's grasp. Slowly, he nodded. "My father prepares to leave for Gleannmara even now to pay his respects to Queen Dealla."

Cairell stood stone still as Owen told him that the shock of losing both Cairell and Deirdre had been too much for Fergal's weakened disposition. He simply gave up his will to live. "It was his heart, I think," Owen finished grimly.

"Whose heart?"

Bright as morning sun, Deirdre came in from the courtyard entrance. The glorious mane of hair in which Alric had lost his fingers time and again was braided in a single plait down her back. With a regal sway of skirts, she approached Alric and curtseyed as pure devilment frolicked beneath the demure dip of her golden lashes. Temptation played upon the impish quirk of her lips.

"Milord, husband?" she teased. "I heard you laughing earlier. Pray tell me you do not speak so freely of your heart's fancy to your guests as you do your bride."

Alric fought the urge to seize her up and hurry her away before the news drowned the light in her eyes. Would that he could cast some spell that would preserve the loveliness and innocence that stood unwittingly on the brink of despair.

Deirdre's smile shriveled in the silence. Slowly she turned to look at her brother and Owen.

"Cairell?" She addressed her brother, but instinct drew her gaze to their visitor as the source of the uneasiness in the room. "What news, sir?"

Alric gently took her shoulders, drawing her toward him. She yielded but would not release the Welshman from her gaze.

Cairell broke first. "It's Father, Dee," he said, his voice raw with emotion. "He's dead."

THIRTY-FOUR

I t took a week to ready the *Wulfshead* for the voyage to Dublin. Deirdre watched as provisions and such belongings as the passengers had were stored in the hold of the ship, which customarily departed high and light in the water, ready for plunder. Instead, as little freeboard as was safe showed above the waterline.

The number of refugees had grown by three. Kaspar, the young dock man Deirdre had seen the day of their arrival in Chesreton harbor, signed on as a replacement on Alric's crew. His wife and new baby girl settled with the other women and children in the cover of the forward rise of the bow. The men sat ready at the oars lining both sides of the ship.

Gunnar and Helewis, hastily wed the night before by a battered but buoyant Father Scanlan, beamed in the afterglow of their wedding night. Gunnar was to keep the villa for Alric and handle the business of his merchant vessels as full partner. Undoubtedly the word of Alric's refusal to raise troops to reclaim his father's kingdom had already reached Galstead by way of the constant flow of traffic between the two shires, for a missive arrived that morning at the mayor's home from the queen's brother, informing him that no Mercian aggression would be directed at Chesreton, provided the port continued to honor the tribute due Galstead's court.

Deirdre knew the decision remained for the city of Chesreton as to whether to accept the offer or join forces with Owen of Emrys. With a full grasp of the fragility of the current regime and unable to retrieve the hostages already sold into slavery, Owen agreed to forgive the debt owed their families in exchange for a percentage of the salt from the lowland mines of the shire for a year. He also offered the protection of his troops, if Chesreton opted to choose Emrys as overlord. The mayor and shire reeve were still at odds when Alric washed his hands of the affair and walked out in disgust.

"To think, I wanted that kingdom," Alric grumbled to Deirdre and Cairell as the dock men removed the planking from the side of the ship. "They've never been of one accord on anything."

Accustomed to unquestioned obedience and a crew that worked as a cohesive unit, he'd been at the edge of his patience with everyone, save Deirdre. With her, her growling wolf became a loyal hound, sensing her pain and trying in his limited way to let her know that he suffered for her. Even the rambunctious Tor seemed to sense her grief, keeping constantly underfoot as though to protect her from further dismay.

Meanwhile, life went on all around her as though the tragedy of her father's death meant nothing to the world at large—only to her and, to a lesser degree, her brother. But then men weren't as given to emotions as women.

"How would you choose?" Cairell asked Alric, seemingly a world away from her at the moment.

How could Alric care whether the mayor and those of British blood favored a Welsh alliance, while the shire reeve and those of Saxon, Frisian, and Angle heritage leaned toward their Mercian brethren? Their father lay dead of a heart needlessly broken. Would that good news traveled half the speed of bad.

"If I were them? The Mercians," Alric answered without hesitation. "No offense intended toward your friend, for I'm certain his word is good, but I understand the Mercians better than the Welsh."

God forgive her, but she could not possibly see how Fergal's death served anything but a vile purpose.

"Even though they are heathen?" Ordinarily, she dove into discussions with relish, but instead, she foundered in a greater sea than that which lay ahead of them. Waves of questions, anger, and hurt battered her without relent.

"They worship power and wealth. That makes them more predictable. The only reason these people left—" Alric nodded toward the passengers lining the rails between the rowers' benches—"was fear of the queen's revenge, not the Mercians as a people. I should have sought her out and killed her."

Alric's vehement declaration pulled Deirdre from her woe. No, for if he had taken time to find the queen and exact revenge, then he might have been lost as well. And without him, Deirdre would be lost as well. *"The Lord giveth and the Lord taketh away, blessed be the name of the* LORD." The priest's words from her mother's funeral service emerged from her memory, like a rope tossed to her from above. God took her father but gave her Alric…and Cairell.

Stepping up to the rail, she linked her arm in her husband's. "You did exactly as you should have. And I thank God all the more for your wisdom." She meant it. *Father, forgive me for my self-pity and narrowness of thought.*

Not to be cheated of his share of affection, Tor nosed between them as the ship drifted away from the dock with the tide.

"Wisdom?" Her husband gave a halfhearted laugh, apparently to cover the anxiety that troubled his gaze. "I'm setting out with an untried crew of craftsmen and farmers and a cargo of women and children. I'd wager Noah had less trouble provisioning the ark than I have suffered this week. At least animals don't complain."

The river current caught the vessel with a sudden jerk. Startled by the movement, Tor yelped and leaped away from the rail, landing in an awkward half squat. Uncertain just who was responsible for this malady, the dog looked around him, growling.

"At least not so you can understand them," Deirdre stipulated, laughing for the first time since she'd received the news of Fergal's death. Somehow God would fit it all into perspective for her, if not in this life, surely in the next. She had the choice of growling at the shift of the ground beneath her like the disconcerted Tor, or adapting with sea legs of trust.

Deirdre knelt to comfort the dog, cooing softly and cradling him, while Alric turned his attention to the men aloft. They, at least, were veterans of the sea—most of them. Those who were not were shaken into action by the instruction of their cohorts.

"I make my circuit in the fellowship of my saint…"

Startled at the sound of Scanlan's clear voice, Deirdre rushed back to the rail. In disbelief, she saw the priest sitting in a chair that had been carried to the shore by servants. Beside him stood Aelfled, who had not left his side except to replenish her herbs. Once Scanlan refused to leave with the others, she offered him her home until he was fully recovered. When Deirdre bade him good-bye that morning, she thought she'd seen the last of him.

"Though I should travel ocean and the hard globe of the world…"

The priest's voice crossed the water as though carried on the rush of angel wings. Nearby, Deirdre and the thatcher's wife from Galstead took up the song she'd learned from Scanlan's meetings in the common. Abina, who helped Kaspar's wife with the new baby, added her high, sweet voice to the hymn.

"No harm can e'er befall me 'neath the shelter of Thy shield…"

Another voice joined in. And another and another until all Scanlan's little flock applied to the Creator for the protection of the archangel.

"O Michael, the victorious, God's shepherd thou art."

Across the water, Deirdre sought out Scanlan's gaze. More likely it was her soul that met with his and took flight in celebration. The torch they'd carried—the obedient priest by choice and the willful princess by God's design—now burned brightly where darkness had met them and in the hearts of those who left it behind. It caught upon the edge of Deirdre's black despair and consumed it with the brightness of hope and a comforting warmth.

"Everything on high or low, every furnishing and flock, belong to the Triune of glory…"

A deep voice resonated behind her and strong arms encircled her waist. She turned, mouth agape, to hear Alric finish the song with the others.

"And to Michael the Victorious…"

"What?" A lopsided grin spread across his clean-shaven face. How handsome her husband was, especially when he smiled.

"I…I didn't know you could sing, much less that you knew a hymn."

"There's a lot about me you don't know, milady, but you've a life-time to learn."

As Alric turned her in his arms, Deirdre caught a glimpse of something beyond him in the corner of her eye that sent a shiver running up her spine. Her husband's quick but thorough kiss claimed her attention, so that when she glanced back, she saw nothing but a group of women gathered around Kaspar's wife and the new baby.

Next to Deirdre, unable to find stable footing anywhere, Tor hopped from spot to spot, his bravado given over to a distressed whimper.

"We'd best put a leash on this four-legged landlubber until he gets his sea legs." Alric chuckled, turning her loose to see to the wolfhound.

Deirdre knelt and called to the dog. Like as not, her imagination was as raw edged as her emotions. She didn't even know what she thought she saw, only that it made her feel as if a splinter of ice pierced her chest. But in the wake of her husband's warm affection, it was gone.

By the following day, Tor could not stand at all. The wolfhound sat listless at Deirdre's feet and convulsed at the smallest intake of food or water.

"What's this about, mongrel?" Alric chided gently as he held the dog's head in his hands and scratched its ears. "What kind of a mariner's dog suffers from seasickness? If you seek to humiliate me before the crew, rest assured you have."

Tor's dark eyes were dull and distant, but then the wolfhound wasn't the only one who did not take readily to the water. At least half the passengers and crew kept a close vigil at the rail, while the provisions aboard went nearly untouched.

Deirdre and a handful of women kept the deck washed and coaxed watered-down wine and bread into the sufferers. One elderly lady went down in the hold, refusing to even look at the water, despite the mate's insistence that the closed-up quarters would only worsen her condition. Abina, every bit as stooped as the ailing woman, seemed to grow stronger and lighter of foot with the need of the others.

By nightfall, Tor convulsed one last time and closed his eyes, curling his long body against Deirdre on the deck. Exhausted, she didn't realize the dog was dead until Alric turned the watch over to Wimmer and checked on Tor before turning in beside her. To keep panic from spreading, Alric and Cairell quietly lowered the wolfhound over the side of the ship and into the water, while Abina and Deirdre comforted each other.

"Do you think the food is tainted?" Deirdre asked Alric, as the latter settled down next to her.

Alric shook his head. "If that were so, we'd all be sick."

"Could Tor have eaten something he shouldn't…like a dead rat or something spoiled on the dock?" Deirdre ached for her husband. Indeed, even she had become fond of the rambunctious, oversized pup.

"Tor was like the Irish here," Alric answered wryly. "He ate anything that didn't eat him first."

Forlorn as the remark was, Deirdre had to smile at the jibe aimed at Cairell. Nothing made her brother sick. He chewed the dried meat and dipped it in the cook's peas porridge with relish, even in the midst of the heaving and retching. Alric, who never flinched at the vilest gore, had twice been to the rail in sympathy with the ill—once with Tor and once after a young lad, whose idol worship of the captain resulted in a lost bellyful at Alric's feet.

"I can't help it if you can't hold down your gullet," Cairell defended himself. "There's no sense in all of us arriving at Gleannmara half starved with a hold full of food."

"Frig's mercy, man, the mite's breakfast went down in my boots. Seeing is one thing. Wearing it is another." Alric shoved his windblown hair off his face. "I mean, *God's* mercy. He of all knows we need it, what with Galstead's taint still lingering with us."

"He's seen us through worse than this." Deirdre lay her head on Alric's chest. "I'm so sorry, muirnait."

After heaving a sigh, he brushed the top of her head with his lips. "Do you suppose this archangel Michael has need of an overgrown pup?"

"I wouldn't be surprised at all," Cairell ventured.

"What the beast lacked in obedience, he made up for in love," Abina sighed.

Through her quiet tears, Deirdre smiled.

THIRTY-FIVE

Something was wrong, horribly wrong, and it wasn't the red sky heralding the break of day behind them. Alric couldn't see it, but he felt it. It raised the hair on the back of his neck. He eased Deirdre off his shoulder and over to her brother's. Cairell stirred momentarily, but at Alric's shush, he nodded off again, a willing pillow for his sister.

Sniffing the air as he made his way over and around sleeping bodies on the deck, Alric nodded to the few men who took the night shift at the oars. Wimmer maneuvered the ship to catch the contrary wind as best he could.

"How long has it been like this?" Air this thick and still bode ill.

"Not long…since the sun opened its bloodshot eye behind us," Wimmer answered, glancing over their heads. "Still as ghost's breath."

The leather sail hung limp, as though it had given up hope of catching a breeze.

"The trouble's not up there, friend, it's beneath us," Alric said, shifting easily with the faint sway of the deck. "We're sluggish as a loaded barge."

In three strides, he reached the open hold and stared into a blackness that even the ship's lantern could not penetrate in the dawn's early light. He couldn't see the danger it harbored, but he could hear it. With an oath, he went down the ladder. The easy slosh of water around the contents gave way to a splash as his boots struck water on the next to the last rung. It was cold as a northman's blood, but Alric's blood ran colder. He raised the alarm with a bellow.

"All hands to their stations, we're taking on water!"

The deck came alive as he vaulted out of the hold, barking orders at the sleep-dazed crew and passengers. Cairell reported at once, Deirdre only moments behind him.

"What can we do?"

"Form two lines with any who are able—one to bail water and the other to lighten our load to get more freeboard," Alric explained. "Deirdre, the women will have to take up the vacant oars as best they can." Reaching past her, Alric took a lantern from its hook.

"What are you going to do?" Alarm grazed her features, but her voice and manner were as calm as the sea itself. Its serenity helped quell the roaring thunder in his chest.

"God willing, I'm going below to find that leak and plug it."

"Listen up, men," Cairell shouted. "Spare nothing that doesn't draw breath. Everything comes out of there…water…goods…"

Alric joined the four men who dropped into the hold. Stepping clear of the passage, he stooped and held up the light in the low space to examine the load. Everything was tied down, exactly as it had been when he last inspected it before setting off, except that now water rose up around it, nearly to the knee.

Where was this Michael the Victorious? Alric grimaced at the cynical slip of thought. Faith did not come easily to a man so long unaccustomed to it. Hoping God sensed his regret, for there was no time for lengthy confession, he prayed, *Please give me a sign, God, anything.*

A flurry of activity drew Alric's attention to where two rats struggled to climb atop the cargo. Another swam against a tide that carried it away from the stern.

"Aft first, men." Brandishing a knife from his boot, he began to cut away the ropes securing the stored goods in place and knocked them forward when he spied a narrow passage that had been cleared through the hold. Weapon in teeth, he twisted sideways to inch through. The water swirling past him confirmed he was on the right trail. The path had been made by someone, but whether divinely inspired or maniacally made, remained to be seen. The loose ends of rope that had secured the cargo in place kindled the unthinkable suspicion that this was no accident.

Reason prevailed. What possible motive would anyone have for this?

Alric sat the lantern on top of a stack of some crates that were hastily assembled to contain the belongings of those passengers who had no trunks or means of stowing their possessions. Easing down to his knees, he felt for the strongest flow of water. The bilge stench assailed his nostrils, not nearly as strong as it should be—yet another sign of a leak, of dilution with fresh seawater. Closing his fingers around something that blocked his way, Alric lifted it from the water, ready to sling it aside until he saw what it was.

His stomach lurched like a landlubber's as he recognized the outline of a woodworker's tool, its smooth turned handles round a shaft of iron and its protruding grooved metal bit. An auger had only one purpose, and that was boring holes. Holes to sink a ship? With no time to ponder such a dark motive, Alric began feeling between the ribs of the vessel, along the seams.

Faces of the passengers flashed across his mind as he blindly searched for the deadly leak, but they evoked pity, not suspicion. Alric threw aside a dead, bloated rat coated in the slime of the bilge and sidled deeper to the stern. Whoever had done this had to be small enough to get his shoulders in the space with room to work the—

Shavings.

On a new ship, perhaps, but the *Wulfshead's* bilge had long been free of its construction debris, washed out or rotted. Alric's pulse accelerated. He scraped to the right and left of the keel with frantic fingers when he felt a steady flow of water, a little more than a finger's worth, but deadly, nonetheless. Bumping head, elbows, and knuckles, he tore off his shirt to make a makeshift plug. It would at least stifle the flow, until he fashioned a plug of wood.

"I need a man here...*now!*" he hollered, packing the twisted plug of linen into the hole with his blade.

A half a lifetime later, a second man wedged close enough to take over holding the plug in place.

"Just bail!" Alric shouted the command over his shoulder to the others as he climbed out of the hold. Considering his green crew, the lack of chaos was a credit to Deirdre's and Cairell's organization. The younger women manned the oars to Wimmer's count, while their men kept a continuous stream of cargo and water coming from the hold to the rail. Abina and the older ladies kept the children from underfoot.

"You found a leak?" Cairell inquired from the bucket brigade.

"I found the problem. We'll be all right, no thanks to a villain among us."

Alric scanned the faces on the deck as he made straight for the forward compartment, where a few scraps of wood were kept for repairs, but instead of malice, all were blanched with alarm and set with determination to survive. With a hatchet, he made quick work of a plug, tapering the wood so that it could be driven in tight. Once wet, swelling would take care of the rest.

A glance at the sky as he headed back to the hold shattered Alric's smattering of relief. Looking to the helm, he saw Wimmer nod. The mate had seen the black cluster of clouds gathering up ahead of them as well. Winded by this new threat, Alric stopped in midstride, the hatchet in one hand, the rough-hewn plug in the other.

What next? Tossing back his head with the silent challenge, he peered beyond the square of sail, which had garnered the first stirrings of a breeze. Was his confession of sin for naught, or had he committed some unpardonable deed for which God now sought vengeance? If so, was everyone aboard his ship to suffer the consequence?

Dark visions gathered as unbidden as the squall ahead—of his father lying with Ethlinda's dagger buried in his chest, of the spectacle of slain friends and crew members he desperately needed now, of Scanlan's battered body, of Tor's plaintive look before the dog lowered his head in a sleep from which he'd not awake. Each opened a raw wound, bleeding his spirit.

Now the storm swept toward him cloaked in swirling black robes like…

Like the queen's.

For as long as Alric could remember, Ethlinda threatened him in the same manner, appearing when least expected, venting her rage, and slipping out of view to await her next chance to plague him. As a child, he'd thought she floated about on a silken swirl of darkness, like some sinister fairy.

"Something troubles you, little pretender?"

God help him, he could hear the witch's taunt even now, that sing-song drawl that scraped the spine with shards of ice.

"First your dog. Then your ship—"

Alric shook himself, nightmare becoming reality.

"And now your bride."

Ethlinda—at least the old woman resembled the queen—stood back to the rail, holding Deirdre at knifepoint.

"Dee!"

"Hold, Gleannmara!" The queen snatched Deirdre's head back even further by the braid wound around her free hand as Cairell broke from the bucket brigade. "In fact, *everyone* hold."

Seeing the blade indent the smooth, white flesh he'd worshiped in what little time he and Deirdre had spent as man and wife, Alric addressed the bucket brigade.

"Do as she asks."

"She'll kill us all if we stop."

The look Alric gave the enemy was enough to wither green oak, but when he turned back, the gaze that met Deirdre's tore at her heart. She'd seen him look at the sky, watched his brow furrow, but what drew her to him could not be seen, only felt.

She'd wanted to soothe his torture, if with nothing more than a touch, but as she made her way to him, the bent old seasick woman had slipped on the deck.

Deirdre rushed to see if she was injured, but instead of a face shriveled by time, something far more hideous appeared. Dumbfounded to behold the streaked face of Galstead's pagan queen, Deirdre became easy prey. No longer bent or crippled, Ethlinda vaulted to her feet, seizing Deirdre's long braid with one hand and brandishing a dagger with the other.

"You're mad, woman." Alric made a statement without any of the emotion Deirdre had sensed earlier.

"Oh, I'm more than mad, my *little* pretender." Ethlinda's laugh was colder than the blade at Deirdre's throat. The metal warmed with each thrum of her pulse against it. If her heart pumped much harder, she'd surely feel the sting of its edge.

"I am *livid,*" the queen declared imperiously. "Thirty years of my life I waited for the day when I could cut out that old fool's heart and hand it and his kingdom over to the son of the man he murdered. I choked on Lambert's flaunting of his whore and his fair-haired bastard, but no…the little pretenderling rises like bile to spoil my delicious revenge. I want an *eye for an eye!*"

"Then take me and let the others go." Alric knelt slowly, depositing the hatchet and the spike of wood he'd made to plug the leak.

"No, Alr—" The blade at her throat nipped her flesh in warning, freezing Alric in place as he rose.

"You have always been full of yourself, little pretender. Do you think that your eyes alone will satisfy me?" the madwoman disdained. "I want them *all.*"

The woman literally trembled with seething. No human could summon the sheer evil of her presence. No human stood a chance against it.

It held them all captive in its web—all save one. The infant in Abina's arms began to wail in protest of the elderly nurse's tight hold. Deirdre felt Ethlinda stiffen behind her, imagined those painted eyes slanting toward the child as though to skewer its tiny heart.

Her breath hissed against the nape of Deirdre's neck. "Silence the whelp."

Abina shushed the baby girl, but she would not quiet. She wailed all the louder, in all her innocence of the danger. Her mother started up from the rowing bench.

"Stay put wench, or I'll have it tossed over the side."

Panic-stricken, the young woman looked across the deck to where Kaspar stood just as helpless.

Struggling to her feet, Abina began to sing, all the while rocking the distraught infant in her arms. "Thou, Michael the Victorious…"

Ethlinda's voice exploded. "I said *silence!*"

Nonplused, Abina glanced up. "You said to quiet the child. I am only obeying your command."

The baby's mother joined in. "Conqueror of the dragon, be thou at my back…"

Deirdre dared not breathe. She could already feel the warm trickle of her own blood at the hollow of her neck, but she sang with her heart. Ethlinda groaned behind her. Or was it a growl?

Certain death was a whim away, for Deirdre at least. She would not be the queen's instrument of destruction for the others. With an urgent *Father* to Him who would receive her, Deirdre met Alric's gaze. Silently, she mouthed her love for him, watching with breaking heart as he registered what she was about to do.

The child, who defied evil with complete innocence, wailed like death's banshee above the drum of the pulse in Deirdre's ear.

Abina and the new mother, maybe even others now, sang.

"Thou, ranger of the heavens—"

Deirdre raised her eyes heavenward, ready to end the standoff one way or another, when the thickening canopy of clouds split overhead, exposing a great chasm of light. Transfixed, she watched as a bolt of fire shot downward, straight at the *Wulfshead*. It struck like a giant hammer, as if to drive the mast through the bottom of ship, throwing several to the deck. An eerie blue fire danced up and down the pole, the sail evaporating in a loud puff of flame.

Ethlinda swayed backward against the rail, as if to draw away from it. The pressure of the blade slackened, and Deirdre seized the heavenly opportunity. Grabbing Ethlinda's wrist with both hands, she wrung it with all her strength. The knife fell away in the ensuing struggle, but Deirdre never heard it strike the deck.

It was as though the deck had fallen out from under them, taking the rail with it. Beyond the pale of Ethlinda's face, a yawning mouth of seawater opened wide, large enough to swallow them all. It shouted back Alric's fear-stricken "God, *no-ooo!*" and then closed its hungry jaws over the shuddering ship.

Letting go of her adversary, Deirdre reached back in the direction of her husband's voice. Something struck her from behind. Ethlinda? It didn't matter.

It hurled her through the watery abyss toward the open arms of all that mattered in this world *and* the next.

THIRTY-SIX

With the crack of thunder, Alric's heartbeats became minutes. Memories were dealt like cards flying from the hand of a master. A blinding flash of light. Deirdre struggling with Ethlinda. The jolt of the deck beneath his feet. People screaming. The rogue wave that rose like a gaping monster beyond the rail. Deirdre pulling away, running toward him. And the jeweled bolt, hurled past the corner of Alric's eye, by Cairell of Gleannmara. Ethlinda grasping its hilt in disbelief as Deirdre reached the safety of Alric's embrace. Then the cold jaws of the sea closed over them.

"I love you," Deirdre had said. Nothing else seemed real as water closed around Alric, as every shadow and shape became a nightmare vision.

God save us or take us, but keep us together.

That was what he recalled praying. So why was it Ethlinda he saw in this shadowy mire? Who, or rather *what,* were those hideous creatures tugging at her, laughing at her obvious torment? Alric had never seen the like. How he could see in the briny bellywash of the rogue wave that had swallowed them never crossed his horror-struck mind.

The creatures' voices were haunting as the cold scream of the flat stone settling on the uprights of a departed's cromlach. Nothing he saw belonged to the living. Was he dead then?

The two dark figures, which appeared more real than the life he'd lived before this moment, dragged Ethlinda and her pitiful screams for mercy deeper into the water. He heard a clamor below him that scraped the very marrow from his bones. There were more...hordes of them, coming from the black unseen of the sea floor.

He *had* to find Deirdre. He twisted away from the vision of the queen's struggle but of his wife—nay, his *life*—he saw nothing. The water slowed the hand reaching for his scramasax. It wasn't there. One of the demons—yes, that had to be what they were—brandished the weapon in its hand. Where was Deirdre? Ignoring the slash of his own blade across his chest, Alric twisted and swam toward what appeared to be the surface of the water. She would be where the light was. Her love would guide him.

He gasped for air as his head broke the surface, but one of the demons grabbed his foot, pulling him back down. Salty death seeped into his lungs, burning, smothering. Something bit him, tearing at the flesh of his shoulder. He twisted in agony, kicking at the claws tugging him deeper into the darkness. Reaching up with his good arm, he prayed. *God, if I can just get to the light…*

A hand shot down into the water. A strong forearm locked with Alric's, pulling against the tug of the demons at his feet. His joints were afire with the strain, as though at any moment he would be pulled into pieces.

That was the *Wulfshead* floating calm above him, wasn't it? *Thank God at least the passengers were safe.* Only he and Ethlinda had been washed over, he realized. Heartened, Alric used his free leg to kick at the gnarled claws tugging at the other. The two creatures would not give up their hold, but the boot did.

Shooting out of the water as if he'd taken wing, he collapsed in the arms that drew him into the boat. At first he thought his fair-haired rescuer was Cairell of Gleannmara, but this man was bigger, a magnificent specimen of a warrior with armor fashioned of pure gold. The sun glanced off it so brightly that Alric could not see his face. Was this the archangel of the hymn? Was the beating in Alric's ear his pulse or this stranger's wings…?

"And so Moses led God's people out of bondage to the old ways to freedom in a new life, like you, muirnait."

The sea seemed to fall away around him. Nothing seemed to exist but the voice and a form he knew so well.

Alric blinked. Orlaith smiled down at him. "Mother?"

As she was given to do, she fingered a lock of his hair. "Your father and I are so proud of you, my derling princeling. At last you have accepted your birthright."

Alric shook his head. He was hallucinating…or he was in heaven.

A melancholy smile lighted upon his mother's lips. She gently tucked the golden strands behind his ear. "But you must return to your flock. They need you."

His flock? What flock?

"They need to know that God chose them when they quickened in their mother's womb. They did not choose Him. Like a loving Father, He waited for His willful children to listen."

"I'm not Moses." Would that he'd had more certainty in his declaration, but certainty eluded him in this strange place.

Orlaith chuckled. "Of course not, muirnait." She tickled his nose with the curled tip of his hair. "Now get you back to your bride. She needs you."

Deirdre. Relief flooded through him. He hadn't lost her.

Leaning over him, Orlaith placed loving hands at his temples and brushed first one eye and then the other with her lips, just as she had when she'd tucked him in as a child. "Sweet dreams until tomorrow, muirnait."

She even said the same words. He couldn't open his eyes to watch her leave. He felt something heavy laid upon his chest. Unseen hands folded his fingers around the hilt of a weapon, as if he was being prepared for burial.

Then someone's palm rested over his eyes. It was a larger hand than his mother's, and stronger, though just as gentle. *Be thou the eye and champion of Gleannmara.*

What manner of madness was this? The charge was made, yet Alric had *heard* nothing. It burned into his memory. The heat was a consuming one, warming him all over at once, thawing his senses, but not his body.

Like a vessel loosed from its moorings, Alric floated on a sea of light somewhere between two worlds. Which shore lay ahead and which behind, he could not discern.

It didn't matter. The consolation that Deirdre waited for him was his wind. With God as his star, Alric would find her.

Deirdre stood on the storm-ravaged beach with the other battered and weary souls, watching numbly as the remains of the *Wulfshead* washed off the pile of rocks where Cairell and Wimmer had steered it in its death throes. Twice they'd counted heads and twice reached the same miraculous conclusion—all save two were accounted for.

She wouldn't accept that Alric was dead. He was simply missing.

Her hope was built on a Rock far greater than that which had paved the way from certain death to the safe harbor of Gleannmara's shores. It would not give way like the sand crunching beneath her feet, as she carried a makeshift sling to where Wimmer set her brother's arm with a piece of wreckage. The men had made trip after trip from the crippled ship to the beach, helping the women and children ashore first, then carrying what goods they could salvage before the *Wulfshead* broke up completely. On the last, her brother slipped and fell into a crevasse, jamming his shoulder and breaking his arm.

"Soon as we get our breath, the men are going to start searching the shoreline," Cairell assured her, wincing as she helped him into the sling. "Kaspar and I are going to head for the fishing village down the coast and get help. It can't be too far, if my bearings are correct."

Deirdre nodded. She feared that if she said anything, she'd burst into tears. She gave her brother a hug and watched as he started up the beachhead.

"We should never have left Chesreton," someone complained.

"God has deserted us!" Kaspar's wife shivered, clutching her nursing baby to her bosom.

"Nonsense." Abina sniffed. "God never deserts His children. 'Twas the work of angels that righted the ship and guided us upon yon rocks."

"I ain't never been much of a believer of nothin'," Wimmer spoke up, "but they was no land afore us before that squall took us up and turned us nigh upside down. Sure, nothin' big as that loomin' on the horizon."

Deirdre looked with others at the gentle rise of the coast upland toward Wicklow. Crowned in white clouds, her homeland seemed to stretch into heaven itself and reach down through emerald hills with knobby fingers of stone into the sea. Like a mother reaching for her children, Gleannmara nestled them in her sandy bosom. Deirdre inhaled the salt air, no longer cold, no longer weary.

"God brought us home," she said to no one in particular.

"I'm thinkin' *something* friendly moved us here," Wimmer agreed. Gleannmara beckoned them; God delivered them.

"It was a miracle none of us were washed over," the thatcher chimed in. He caught himself too late. At Deirdre's disconcerted glance, he looked at his feet. "Barrin' the cap'n, I mean."

"Oh, my Alric is alive." Abina's declaration was bright, and she winked at Deirdre. "I *know* it."

"Have you seen something, milady?" one of the others asked.

Abina was *milady* now. Of the lot of them, only she and an innocent babe had had the courage to defy Ethlinda's evil spell. She'd rallied them as one with her call to the heavens.

What's more, the heavens had answered.

All eyes shifted to where the nurse climbed to her feet with the aid of Wimmer's strong arm. Her splotched dress fell around stiff legs that had walked more miles than any of them, yet she straightened without so much as a hint of the pain that usually plagued her swollen joints.

"Young man," she answered, shaking the sand off absently. "When you get to be my age, you rely less on what you can see and more on what you believe to be." She motioned the group up from the beach with drawn hands.

"Are we going to sing again?" the little boy who'd become sick over Alric's feet asked his mother.

Abina laughed the laugh of a young woman, not one whose voice had grown brittle with age. "Nay, child. We are going to *pray!* Nothing from memory, mind you," she warned, taking Deirdre's hand in hers. "I want you to form a circle of hands, that's right…all save our new mother. You and the wee one step inside."

One or two of the people grumbled beneath their breath, but no one ventured to cross the gray-haired milady.

"Now, I want each one of you to thank God for something you have right now. I'll start."

What a strange spectacle it must have been, a circle of drenched survivors, the few things they'd salvaged scattered around them.

Overhead the midday sun bathed them in a blanket of warmth, soaking up the last remnant of their nightmare's chill.

"Father, who created us and never turns a deaf ear to our pleas, I shall sing Your praises in regal robes someday at Your throne, but for now, hear me, soaked and bedraggled, but ever so grateful for the hand that delivered us from evil in our hour of need."

Abina stopped and nudged Wimmer, who cleared his throat uneasily. "Thank ya that the rudder didn't crack till we was hard upon the rock."

"Thank you for sparing my little boy…"

"…my precious daughter…"

"…my husband…"

"…my wife…"

"…my doll…"

"…my granny…"

"…my new shoes…"

Around the circle the prayer traveled, gaining conviction with each addition, be it great or small. God had spared the significant as well as the insignificant. When at last it came Deirdre's turn, she spoke without hesitation: "My Alric."

"Alric!" A voice other than her own sounded off from the ridge of rocks behind them. It was Kaspar, jumping up and down and beckoning excitedly. "Alric!" he shouted again.

"Alric?" Deirdre echoed to Abina, afraid to trust her own ears.

With a tight squeeze of her hand, the nurse replied, "Go to him, milady. He came back for you."

THIRTY-SEVEN

I thought he was dead at first," Cairell exclaimed, not for the first time that evening.

So had Alric. When his senses came back to him, he was wet, yet baked in warmth by the glare beyond his leaden eyelids. He heard the lap of the sea nearby and the squawk of the birds. The air was heavy with salt mist. Then someone began to shake him. He felt fingers pressed to his throat, probing for the blood pumping steady and strong. Cairell's voice was most prominent in the frenzy of noises around him. Then came a sound that calmed the rest. Alric's soul quickened in recognition of his other half's voice.

He cracked open his eyes and saw her sweet face.

"He's alive, Dee," Cairell reassured the woman kneeling over Alric.

Just her nearness brought his senses to full alert. But her touch, the loving clasp of her hands about his face, the featherlight run of her fingers at his temples, the breath of her lips as she warmed his cold ones with them, broke the last of the otherworldly hold upon him.

His eyes opened fully to the face of an angel—an earthly angel.

"Welcome home, my love." Joy radiated from her face, but something contrary grazed the eyes that spilled a shower of the heart upon his cheeks.

Given the strange things he'd seen and heard, he demanded to know the nature of it. "What is it?"

Deirdre's mouth quivered in an attempt to smile and speak at the same time. "Your hair...it...it's gilded with silver as bright as your eyes. Here—" she touched his temples, just as his mother had done earlier.

"It was as eerie a sight as I've ever seen," the prince of Gleannmara told his humble host now. "There he was...washed up on the beach, laid out upon a hatch cover like a corpse, my sword folded in his hands." Several noggins of ale had dulled the pain of Cairell's injured arm and loosened his tongue considerably.

The man didn't know the meaning of the word *eerie,* but Alric kept that to himself.

"How is your head?" Deirdre ran a tender finger along a gash that had taken several of Abina's stitches to close.

"Numb," Alric answered.

His wife had not left the side of the bed that had been made from two benches, a tabletop, and fresh stuffed pallet of straw by the brewy of the seaside village. Alric had to be carried by the men to the widow's small tavern on the same hatch cover that brought him ashore. He'd gotten up well enough, but staying on his feet had been a problem. Every few steps the top of his head seemed to lift off like a wisp of ash caught up in the wind, and the next thing he knew, he was on the ground.

"The last I saw of the sword, I'd nailed that witch to the rail of the ship with it. I never thought I'd see it again." Cairell swung around to address Alric. "How *did* you come by it?"

"Someone gave it to me."

"Who?" Deirdre asked.

"Didn't see him." He had an idea, but it was so far-fetched, even he could not believe it. "I just felt the sword laid over me and my fingers folded around it." It had to have been the faceless warrior or Orlaith. It certainly hadn't been Ethlinda. Gooseflesh pebbled his skin at his last recollection of the queen, screaming in anguish, begging for mercy from—

"So you *were* laid out." Cairell stared at Alric in awe.

Alric accepted the lifeline from the nightmare gratefully. "Or I dreamed it. Given the size of this gash, I've lots of room for speculation."

"I'd suggest we let Alric rest and take a healthy dose as well for ourselves." Deirdre rose on that authoritative note. "Mistress Leary, I thank you for your hospitality. I've never been better fed nor welcomed so warmly in any royal hall."

The widow of the brewer, who'd established the small hostel more for the sake of the local fishermen than for travelers, puffed full of delight at the princess's compliment. "Bless me, milady, 'tis I who am honored by the presence of herself and himself both, and they thought to be dead by the rest o' the world."

"And thank you for keeping our presence to yourself," Alric said.

The widow came to earth. "All that know Gleannmara's *aiccid* and his sister are them right here in this room, and here they'll be stayin' until tomorrow, just as you asked, milord."

The woman, her son, and her daughter-in-law stood like soldiers at attention with the mission awarded them. Alric heaved a melancholy sigh. "I would reward each of you handsomely, had not my fortune gone down with my ship." Every bit of wealth he had at hand to purchase land for his people—coin, jewels, documents—had been in the *Wulfshead*'s hold. "Until I'm able to replenish my loss, you have my heartfelt gratitude."

He didn't feel the loss for himself, which was not like the man he had once been. Deirdre—and her God—had changed all that.

"The gratitude of Princess Deirdre's own husband is ample enough for this woman," Mistress Leary assured him. "You and your Sassenach kin have brought home Gleannmara's children. I'd shame me ancestors if I didn't make ye welcome, from prince to the wee poppet there."

Cairell was set to send a messenger ahead to Gleannmara's hall, where a royal funeral service and the crowning of his newly elected cousin was to take place on the morrow, when Alric stopped him. Unable to explain the urgent need for secrecy, he asked his brother-in-law to indulge his instincts. Whether it was due to respect or the increasingly bizarre circumstances of their journey to date, the young heir apparent relented.

After the tables were broken down and put to rest against the walls, the women and children settled on the floor of the large room for the evening. The men slept in the separate kitchen with the staff—all save Cairell and Alric, the latter of whom insisted on giving up his raised bed for a pallet next to Deirdre. The infant was the last to surrender to the night, whimpering for one last feeding. Finally, only the occasional snap and crackle of the banked fire in the center of the room disturbed the chorus of slumber.

"Will you ever tell me what happened to you?" Deirdre whispered softly, stroking the wing of silver at his temple.

Alric held Deirdre in his arms as tenderly as the new mother across the room held her precious babe. Her head rested on the shoulder that had been shredded by one of the demons in his hallucination, her arm across the slash its companion had cut across Alric's abdomen. Except that there was neither broken flesh nor sign of any injury, save the one on his head.

"I promise, I will, anmchara…when I can make sense of it myself." He'd likely struck his head on the ship's rail as he was hurled into the sea. All he knew for certain was that he'd been saved against all odds by a power beyond his understanding—that of the God he'd cried out to—and that one boot had been lost between one world and the next.

The fields around Gleannmara's *rath* and the church built by King Kieran nearly a century earlier were dotted with tents and with the banners of the visiting guests. The late Fergal had already been laid to rest in the crypt beneath the church, but such was Gleannmara's prestige that the formal service had to be scheduled to allow for the dignitaries to make the journey. Bishops from Armagh, Kildare, Derry, and Glendalough were there to take part in the ceremony on behalf of the high king and to acknowledge and crown the newly elected successor to Gleannmara's throne.

Kyras O'Dubhda, champion of Gleannmara and second cousin to the lost crown prince, was a natural choice. His fighting and leadership skills and his blood tie to the royal line made him so. Still, the news that Cairell had been so readily replaced shook the young prince to the core. He'd come prepared to mourn his father, not have the throne passed by him with so little decorum.

What spun Deirdre's head was that Dealla, her father's grieving young widow, was to marry the strapping king-elect following Kyras's crowning.

Not that there would be one, Deirdre thought as the royal party made its way toward the towering whitewashed gates, where the blue and gold of Gleannmara waved boldly against the sky in welcome. To her right, Alric, much recovered after a night's rest, rode on one of the borrowed steeds from the village. Cairell rode to her left.

Neither man seemed himself. Pain from his arm gave Cairell cause to wince if he moved it the wrong way, but he was determined to ride in as a king, not as an invalid in the wagon that trailed them with men. In case Alric's instinct that the news of Cairell's survival might not be well received, the women and children remained behind. The wagon was borrowed to expedite their journey, to avoid embarrassment for all concerned.

"Stay close to me when we get inside," Alric told Deirdre as they approached the gates. Already trumpets heralded their arrival, but their identity was yet to be revealed.

Deirdre studied her husband. "Have you seen something?"

"I exercise precaution before what is surely to be a terrible upset for some."

Aside from the "I love you more than life itself" that Alric whispered in her ear at the first stir of morning, this was all he'd had to say during the journey. Each glance she stole at him found him lost in thought.

"I agree with the need for caution," Cairell said, his attention fixed ahead of them. "If I hadn't been so excited just to get home alive, I'd have thought of it myself. The prospect of power can make men do things they wouldn't ordinarily think of. Kyras undoubtedly will be disappointed and he does have a temper."

Without a close look, no one would recognize Deirdre's brother in his tattered clothing. Or her for that matter. If Helewis could see her wedding dress now. Deirdre smiled, recalling how radiant her friend had been, waving from the dock beside her new husband. *Father, You have been so good and faithful. Surely You pave the way for us now.*

"Halt, there. Only them by invitation are to enter the rath this day, by order of the queen." One of the guards gathered at the base of the tower gate strutted, adorned in his best tunic, toward them. Cairell stopped him still in his tracks with his ringing words.

"Lew LongLegs, are you telling me I need an invitation to my own home?"

The man halted, staring, mouth agape, eyes bugging as though to spring from his head.

"He's no ghost, Lew, and neither am I," Deirdre hastily assured the stricken man. Lew had guarded the main gate for as long as she could remember. Now he was a senior member of the staff, one who reported for duty only on special occasions—like the crowning of a new king.

Coming to life, the older gentleman made short the distance between them with the stride for which he'd been named. "God be praised, what I wouldn't give for your *athair* to be seein' what *I* see! I'm pure tired of mournin', milady, pure tired," he reiterated, "but how—?"

His thick, gray-white brow knitted over a beak of a nose. She'd giggled once as a child at the impressive volume of his sneeze, only to have Lew declare that his loud snout made him the perfect sentry. He needed no trumpet.

"God works in strange ways, Lew." Cairell waved his arm toward Alric. "This good Saxon prince and his men have brought us home, and just in time I hear."

Lew's pale blue gaze widened even more. With an oath of excitement, he waved at his fellow guards. "Let them through. 'Tis Cairell, and the lady Deirdre, back from the dead!"

Word spread like ripples across a pond, preceding them as they proceeded. Lew LongLegs led the bedraggled party himself. Familiar faces flocked to both sides of them, mirroring images of shock, then thawing to joy as Cairell and Deirdre rode through the buildings and stalls that had outgrown the original rath. By the time they reached the great hall, where the crowning of the new king was about to take place, the clamor of welcome had reached a roar.

A company of Kyras's personal guards burst out of the round stone tower Deirdre's grandfather had built to replace the old one of wattle and wood. Weapons brandished, they charged down the earthen ramp to the common, slowing upon seeing a single rider break from the group to meet them. Cairell sat straight and proud, one arm in a sling and the other resting on the jeweled hilt of a sword worth more than all the steeds among his followers.

"Make way for the rightful king of Gleannmara!" At Lew's glad shout and upon recognizing Cairell, the soldiers parted in ones and twos. Weapons at rest, they knelt as Cairell led his ragged procession into the hall itself. When Cairell reached the great stone hearth in the center, he circled to the left and Deirdre to the right, their eyes fixed on the dais. Two-hundred-year-old columns carved by Gleannmara's first king held up the velvet canopy over the throne. At the throne's base, a tall, brown-haired warrior in rich robes rose from his knees before the bishops, who'd come from the most prestigious sees in all Erin.

Kyras blanched at the sight of Cairell, as though he'd truly seen a ghost. Aside from the clip-clop of Deirdre's steed coming to Cairell's side, not a sound broke the breathless hush of the room. The scene might have been a painting but for the bishop of Armagh conceding to wipe the perspiration from his brow. Standing above them was Dealla, the grieving queen. Was the grief in the tear-ravaged eyes that met Deirdre's real, or was the woman a consummate actress?

"God's timing is most remarkable and never without blessing." The queen spoke with an admirable composure.

Descending in a float of dark violet robes, walking past the landing where the holy men were about to ordain Kyras as Gleannmara's new king, she came before Cairell and knelt. "Gleannmara welcomes her king and his sister home."

As though pinched into action, not unlike a recalcitrant child in chapel, Kyras hurried forth to join her. "Indeed, I echo our queen's welcome most fervently. 'Tis truly a miracle."

"It's good to be home," Cairell declared. "And yes, good champion, it is more miracle than the imagination can conjure."

Deirdre joined the collective sigh of relief when he motioned the two to their feet. She wasn't certain what she expected to happen. Alric had been so insistent that they be prepared for trouble…but then, he was accustomed to the backstabbing of Galstead. This was Gleannmara of the just, enemy to greed and ambition.

"Help me off this steed, friend," Cairell said to the man, who, but for a few moments, would have worn the royal torque the bishop of Kildare held in his hands.

Before Kyras could reach her brother, Alric was between them, a fierce apparition that had not been there a heartbeat before. "You extend your trust too freely, Irish." His voice fairly growled his emotions—warning for Cairell, derision for Kyras.

Cairell wrestled his startled horse into submission with his one hand, but Alric stood like an immovable wall, oblivious to the danger of the steed's pawing hooves. His withering gaze would not leave Gleannmara's champion.

"Alric, what *are* you doing?" Deirdre gripped her own steed's reins. Her husband had not been himself since they'd found him on the beach. Something had changed in him, more than the silvered hair at his temples. She slid off her horse.

He didn't spare so much as a glance in her direction. "Stand back, wife!"

Dealla fell away with a gasp, following the orders intended for Deirdre. "Who is this madman? What does he mean *wife?*"

"My guards will skewer you, if you do not stand down now," Kyras threatened.

True enough; Gleannmara's finest spear throwers stood ready round the dais. Only Kyras's proximity made them hesitate.

"No!" Deirdre rushed to Alric despite his warning. "Hold your weapons. My husband is not well," she explained to Dealla and Kyras.

"You *married* this man?"

"Aye," Deirdre answered her stepmother. "And he gave up everything to save Cairell and me. But we were shipwrecked, and he was struck on the head—"

"I am clearer of mind than I have ever been, milady," Alric informed her calmly. "And of eye." Still, his steady, burning gaze had not wavered from the face of Kyras O'Dubhda.

"Then you can see that you are no match for the armed men who surround you," Gleannmara's champion pointed out.

"No, I am not. But the God of truth is, and it is He who protects me. The deceiver and those he deceives cannot see His heavenly ranger."

Deirdre shot a panicked look at Cairell, who approached Alric from the other side.

"Alric," he ventured hesitantly. *"Brother..."*

It was the first time she'd heard Cairell call Alric brother. She thought she saw the cold set of her husband's features flicker with something other than the pure contempt he had for a man he'd never seen until today.

"If you do indeed consider me your brother, Cairell of Gleannmara," Alric interrupted, "then hear my story, that you may see this cur for who he really is."

THIRTY-EIGHT

Unintimidated by his doubt-ridden audience, Alric gave a short account of the merchant who'd boasted in a Dublin tavern that a king's ransom sailed on the *Mell,* bound for Scotia Minor. If what Alric suggested was true, that the merchant was indeed Kyras O'Dubhda, then black treachery was afoot.

"You lie, Saxon!" Where shock blanched Kyras O'Dubhda's face before, purple rage mottled it now.

"I have committed many sins, but lying is not among them." Alric's reply was soft, but well Deirdre knew the beast was far more dangerous when it was quiet. And when he smiled, the blood of his prey broke into shards of ice…if the prey possessed any will to live.

The conflict appeared unsolvable without violence, even death. Kyras was the type who would not afford himself the luxury of fearing death. Deirdre's blood was shot with dread as her dark-haired cousin turned to Cairell.

"You will believe this thieving, murdering pirate over me? Cairell, we fought shoulder to shoulder when the Ulstermen tried to enforce unfair tribute."

Rallying behind their champion, the clan chiefs of Gleannmara, as well as their attending allies, began to stomp on the slate floor of the keep. As the support grew louder, the Saxons rushed to stand with Alric. King's law prohibiting weapons on such occasions—and God's grace holding tempers in check—was all that kept violence at bay.

Not unaware of the irony, Deirdre protested the brand she had once laid on Alric herself. "He's no thief nor pirate."

Too late to put the lid back on the tinderbox, she was drowned out. Such a charge should have been settled in a formal hearing, but then who could possibly have foreseen this? Royal guards formed a barrier around the crown prince's party, shoulder to shoulder, weapons out. In an attempt to restore order, Cairell signaled the heralds to their trumpets.

"I remind you all of the king's law," he shouted when the blast shocked the protests into relative silence. "The first to raise a violent hand will have it cut off, is that understood?"

He paused, until the clamor of the additional soldiers that rushed into the room to reinforce their comrades abated. The quick restoration of order was a tribute to Deirdre's father's rule.

Marching up the steps of the dais to where the bishops stood, Cairell turned and faced the crowd. "First things first. Gleannmara needs a king. Is there any man among you who has cause to challenge me for the crown? If so, say ye so now."

Deirdre was not surprised when no one offered protest. The late king had already named Cairell as aiccid, his heir apparent. It had been done with unanimous support at the time. Even the sun seemed to cast its approval of the bold young man standing before his father's empty seat, streaming through the solar balcony on the second floor and catching on the jeweled scabbard of Kieran's sword and casting brilliant colors on the stone and richly tapestried walls below.

"Then, holy fathers, I ask your *speedy* blessing and authority." Though it must have pained him immensely, Cairell managed to unsheathe the sword and handed it over to the bishop from the see of Glendalough. With a solemn grimace, he knelt before the three holy men for the ceremony.

Well aware of the need for urgency, the bishop of Kildare placed the solid gold torque around Cairell's neck with a blessing so hurried that, for all her laurels in Latin, Deirdre could not make it out. Glendalough took up Kieran's sword and touched it upon the prince's shoulders, proclaiming Gleannmara's motto in a loud voice, "Home to the Just, Enemy to the Ambitious and the Greedy." Finally, Armagh took the weapon from his holy brother and presented it to Cairell.

"By commission of the holy Triune of the heavens and the high king of Ireland, I bid you, Cairell, son of Fergal, rise and take up the sacred sword dedicated by your forefather Kieran to God and Gleannmara. Long live King Cairell!"

Surely never had there been such a crowning. Bedecked in rags and gold, the new king faced his court, the great sword raised in one hand, his other still ensconced in a sling. Recalling how it had taken all the strength of both her hands to brandish the weapon, Deirdre marveled at what seemed a miracle. And if ever there was a need for one, it was now. Her brother would need God's own hand to settle this matter fairly without dividing his court.

The crowd took up the cry, "Long live King Cairell."

Instead of filling the rafters until the wee hours of the following morning as had happened at Fergal's coronation, the cheers faded abruptly at the heralds' sharp signal.

"You have honored my father this day, and now you honor me," Cairell said in a prelude to his first speech as king. Although he was not dressed in royal robes, he carried his mean attire like one born to lead. He somehow looked bigger standing on the dais—and older.

Father God, be with him now, for he is torn…we are torn by this dark twist before us.

"I ask for one more indulgence, for my duty as king calls before my obligation as host. And this immediate concern is not one I relish." He didn't have to say it. The burden tortured his brow beyond his years. "But first, I ask you to hear me, for I will not decide between a Saxon and an Irishman this day. Nor will I weigh the word of my brother-in-law against the word of cousin and champion."

Deirdre stiffened, as thrown by her brother's declaration as those around her. "I pray for the wisdom God gave Solomon in deciding which of two mothers spoke the truth. The babe laid before Gleannmara this day is truth, and I have no desire to see it slain."

Never had she heard her brother wax so poetic. He held the attention of his audience like the druidic bards of old, who took up the Light of Christ.

"You have heard Alric of Galstead's allegation against my kin. Why do I even listen to this man, you ask?" He smiled at Deirdre. "Believe me, I was no less incredulous regarding my sister's marriage. I escaped my kidnappers, crossed a hostile country, and stole into his lodge to save her, only to have Deirdre crack my head open for trying to skewer him with my blade. I asked my sister why she *married* him." Cairell's devilish charm lighted in his gaze. "I knew then that the first man to turn my sister's head was no ordinary man…even if he was a Saxon."

A titter of laughter rose among the ladies in the hall at Deirdre's expense. Sure, she was an old maid by most standards, but she didn't care if the tale softened hearts toward Alric.

"I still wanted to slit his throat." Cairell's candor roused more male response. "Until she pointed out that Alric was no more a pirate than our Dalraidi kin's captains, who prey on ships bound for Albion with supplies and arms for our enemies." He pointed to Kyras. "Your own brother commands such a ship under the commission of Scotia Minor's kings, does he not?"

"It sounds to me as though your decision is made, the way you defend him," their cousin grumbled.

The corner of Cairell's mouth tipped up. "That's why I won't make the decision. I will leave it to our revered holy fathers. I simply speak for a stranger in an antagonistic court."

A king's testimony, even a prince's, carried much weight according to law, Deirdre knew, but sentiment was another issue. Alric and his men were being as warmly received as the plague. Love had blinded her to the reality of human nature. Before she'd left Gleannmara, she would have felt the same as those muttering among themselves.

Father, there has to be a way to get these people to see Alric as the good and noble man he is. And if he is mistaken, Lord, help him to back down. You know he's not himself. Deirdre hesitated, uncertain as to what to ask for. With a tentative heart, she added, *Thy will be done.*

"I need no one to speak for me, Irish."

"Alric, wait—" Deirdre reached for her husband, but he pulled away from the restraining hand she put on his arm.

"God will speak for me."

"This man is obviously mad." Dealla's words were filled with more compassion than condemnation. "Kyras is a loyal subject. I find it an insult to him and to me to suggest that we conspired to take Gleannmara's throne." She looked at Deirdre. "I know you never understood this, but I loved your father. My bride-price was in that ransom."

Deirdre started. Her stepmother wanted Cairell brought home so much that she'd given her own property to save him? It didn't fit the opinion Deirdre held of the woman. "Then how...how could you marry so soon after Father's death?"

"I am not you, Deirdre. I was not bred and trained to power. I haven't the strength of mind, nor the will, to govern Gleannmara."

Bemused as she was at the moment, Deirdre did not trust her own instincts. From the look on his face, Cairell was no less at a loss. Like trying to separate two fighting dogs, it was a dangerous task.

"Perhaps one of Your Worships has some advice?"

The bishops deferred to their senior of Armagh.

"Have you no trial by sword in Erin?" Alric demanded before the man could speak.

Deirdre saw the burden disappear from the older priest's shoulders as he considered Alric's challenge. No longer were the man's shoulders quite as rounded and bent. Even the furrows of his brow lightened.

"It is a viable option."

Kyras leaped at the chance. "Done! I defend my honor with my blade against this Saxon."

Yesterday, Alric was so unsteady on his feet he'd had to be carried to the tavern. Yet as Deirdre turned to object, her words died on her lips. Her husband smiled—not the pearly grin he flashed at her in flirtation or taunt, just a satisfied upturn of an otherwise set line. Try as she might, she could not fathom the trap the wolf had so obviously laid.

One of Kyras's men produced his shield and sword. The silver studs on the rich, black leather covering on both glittered as the champion accepted them.

Alric turned to Cairell. "God is my shield, but I will need that sword." He pointed to Kieran's sword. "I lost my weapon in a battle with demons, and my rescuer gave me that one."

The three holy men fell into conversation, crossing themselves at the mention of demons. With an uneasy glance at Deirdre, Cairell handed their ancestor's sacred weapon over to Alric. Around them, an uncomfortable murmur rose, not loud enough for outright defiance.

Cairell cast a glance at those gathered around them. "What Alric speaks is true. We found him unconscious, washed up on the beach on a hatch cover, and laid out as if for a warrior's burial, with the king's sword folded in his hands. It was the strangest thing I'd ever seen."

If she ever loved her brother, she loved him more now. If she ever was more frightened, she could not remember it.

Someone folded her hand in Deirdre's. She turned in surprise to see her stepmother. "I pray that you will not be left alone with the love for your Saxon that I see on your face." If Dealla said nothing more, the pain grazing her face exonerated her of any remaining suspicion that she had not felt Fergal's loss.

God forgive her, Deirdre had never really seen this side of the woman. But then, she'd never tried to see past the obvious age difference between her father and his bride.

"Have no fear, muirnait." Alric lifted her other hand and brushed her knuckles with his lips. "No one will die."

Deirdre gripped his fingers, wishing with all her heart that she could understand—and share—her husband's confidence.

THIRTY-NINE

It was easier to take the challenge outside the keep than move the guests, but most of the visitors followed Alric and the others. A circle of Gleannmara's guards marked a large arena. The royal party and the priests climbed up to a wooden parade platform over the exercise yard, where Deirdre's uncle had trained Kyras, Cairell—and even herself, when she'd give him no peace. The royal bench carved by Ryan, father of Maire, some two hundred plus years before was brought out for Cairell, along with benches for the royal ladies and the bishops.

The excitement of such a contest precipitated the inevitable wagering between noble and commoner alike. Children pressed their faces between the guards only to have them firmly but gently shoved back. Older boys and men alike crowded up on the roofs of the buildings and stalls built against the stockade. As news of the development spread to the outer keep and beyond, Cairell ordered the gates to the inner yard closed.

Deirdre's concern escalated at the sense of an almost festive atmosphere, with morbid curiosity as its companion. The crowd erupted in a roar of approval as Kyras strutted out before the raised platform and bowed before them.

"Are you certain?" Deirdre mouthed the words to the man—*her* man—who blew her a kiss over the hilt of the king's sword, for it was impossible for him to hear her over the commotion.

With a gaze that warmed her more than the afternoon sun, he nodded. Oh, to share that silent confidence! As Alric strode to the fore, she detected the faint strains of the hymn that had become such an integral part of their short time together. Her husband was...singing?

Drawn to her feet, she joined him against the drowning tide of disapproval, her hands folded in prayer. Whether they heard Alric and her with their ears or their hearts, Alric's men took up the song as well.

The familiar tune slowly struck the gathering dumb with its unfamiliar Saxon lyrics.

The bishop of Armagh smiled as he raised his hand, calling the group to order. "It is good to know that our great and omnipotent heavenly Father speaks Saxon as well as Irish. It does us well to be reminded we are *all* His children," he reminded the people gently. "God has no favorites, save the righteous."

"You've nothing to worry about, Kyras. The king's sword will not spill innocent blood," someone shouted from the mass of onlookers.

Gleannmara's champion glanced in the direction of the comment as the priest bowed his head, and Deirdre had the distinct impression her cousin was not comforted by the reminder.

It had not taken the senior bishop long to ascertain the situation. His prayer favored the love Deirdre felt toward her Saxon captor and God's willingness to forgive even blood spillers and thieves, be they pirates or soldiers of war. It lifted the ancestral pride and honor of Gleannmara represented in Kyras, but it raised God's will above all. "We look to thee for blessing, in the name of the holy Triune of Father, Son, and Spirit. Amen."

"Amen," Deirdre whispered.

She flinched with the first clash of swords but became impervious in the following succession of blows. Alric's strikes were met by Kyras's shield; the champion's blade was met by Alric's counter swing, which the Saxon followed up with an aggressive strike of his own. So lightly did he wield Kieran's sword that one might think it made of tin, not steel. While the younger man was quicker, Alric possessed a skill and grace that soon held the onlookers spellbound. Deirdre knew Alric's feral temper, but she had never seen him fight. His feet moved as if dancing to the music of the sword song. Indeed, the slashes and circles seemed to pluck chords in the air itself, a haunting sound that made the heart pound with each shrill note. Every time he dodged Kyras's raging, headlong charge, Alric smiled, which only whetted the champion's thirst for blood all the more.

Perspiration streamed down the fine physique of Alric's dark-haired opponent, streaking the film of dirt kicked up by them.

"Curse your Saxon hide, you cannot run out the day!"

"Nor can you, deceiver." Unlike Kyras's ragged gasps, Alric's breath was even. The film of his exertion made his bronzed skin glisten in the light. "Give up the truth, lad. You do not wish to see what I have seen for a forgivable mistake."

Kyras lunged at Alric with his shield, the latter knocking it away with his forearm, which was already bloodied from the studs. But when the champion's blade followed, it met the king's sword with a teeth-shattering clash. With one leg firmly planted, the muscled ridges of Alric's thigh straining against the trim fit of his trousers, he kicked with the other at the shield that had drawn the only blood that day, dislodging it from Kyras's grasp.

Face-to-face they leaned, nostrils flaring, neither giving way. Suddenly, Alric reared back his head and struck Kyras's nose hard with his skull. Deirdre gasped, the recollection of the stitches Abina had made fresh in her mind. The stalemate broke. The two adversaries staggered away from each other, one as dazed as the other. *God help him!* she prayed as Alric drove the weapon into the ground as if to pin a spinning earth into stillness. Indeed the slight wobble of his walk suggested it tried to throw him.

Without warning, still holding his bleeding nose with one hand, Kyras spun and swung his blade at the retreating Alric. This was the end. Deirdre closed her eyes, unable to watch it bite into her husband's unprotected back. A brittle crash and scrape of steel resounded, and the crowd erupted with a few shouts of gut appreciation.

Impossibly, Alric was now on the other side of the pillar of steel, which had stopped his adversary short in midswing. Unnerved, Kyras stumbled back, sword arm dragging at his side. Leaving his weapon planted in the dirt, Alric charged the younger man, plowing into him with such force that his weapon fell away. Down to ground they went, rolling over and over with the momentum of the crash.

"'E's the cap'n's now," Wimmer exclaimed, his fists drawn as if he was in the middle of the fray.

"If his head holds together," Kaspar said, echoing Deirdre's very thought.

Alric was on top, a bloodied forearm to Kyras's throat. "Give way, lad. Love'll make a man do strange things."

What an odd thing to say! Deirdre ventured a glance at Dealla, but her stepmother seemed impervious to the entire scene. One second in time away from Deirdre's watchful eye, and Alric grunted loudly. When she looked back, he was sprawled on his back, wiping his eyes furiously. Kyras vaulted to his feet and kicked Alric in the side, and then raced toward the king's sword, still standing stalwart in the sand.

"Alric, get his sword!" But Deirdre's panicked cry came against a drowning tide of cheers. The words of Kieran's dedication spilled in its midst like a balm: *"Never spill innocent blood."* Alric was innocent as a new babe, washed with the forgiveness of Christ's own sacrifice. He believed.

But he still could not see Kyras, nor the bright steel blade the champion swung at his neck. The scene that unfolded took its leisure, and as she watched, Deirdre recalled Scanlan's teaching…that lessons in faith must be etched indelibly in the mind that they might endure and be shared over and over for generations to come. Alric dropped as though he heard death's sharp breath coming at his ear, but not enough to duck it altogether. Deirdre could foresee the blood spurt from her husband's skull, imagine the top of it, along with the long golden hair she'd run adoring fingers through, coming at her like a gory dagger to her heart…

Sickness gorged her throat. She dropped to her knees.

"For I know the thoughts that I think toward you, saith the LORD, thoughts of peace, and not of evil, to give you an expected end."

An uproar deafened her to all but her claim. God promised her. He *promised* her.

"Deirdre!" Cairell's alarm sounded distant, yet she felt his hand trying to steady her. Someone else—Dealla?—was on her other side.

"Will you confess *now,* deceiver?"

It was Alric's voice that silenced the rest, for it traversed where only a soul mate's might, not through the earthly senses, but the spiritual.

Deirdre forced open her eyes. Kyras, not Alric, was lying on the ground, both hands on the blade Alric pressed to his throat. White as ash, he stared into Alric's gaze.

"For the love of God, man, *look!*" Alric shouted fiercely. His hands trembled as much as his opponent's on the bloodletting end of the weapon, as if the sword held them both with a life of its own. "Do you see *them?*"

Them? Deirdre saw nothing but two battle-weary foes, gazes locked in a pit of terror apart from the world around them.

"*Believe,* lad!" Alric half pleaded, half ordered. "Don't let them take you. Take His hand!"

Whose hand? If anyone doubted Alric's sanity now...

A sob tore from Kyras's throat as if the wolf had ripped it out with its teeth. "Jesus, *save me!*"

Alric withdrew the blade and drove it into the dirt at the foot of the platform where everyone stood—Cairell, the bishops...

A paralyzing silence engulfed them all, as though the same invisible teeth had collectively ripped out their ability to speak or move. Reaching down, Alric seized Kyras's arm and pulled the sobbing young man to his feet. They embraced, more like a father and son than victor and defeated. As the distraught champion drew away, Alric's eye met Deirdre's. No words were needed. She knew his heart. He knew hers.

Kyras moved to fall onto his knees before Cairell. "I...I'm sorry." He gave Dealla a tortured look. "I did it for you...for us."

Dealla's mouth fell open in shock. "*Us?*" She shook her head, as if she'd misunderstood.

"So you *were* in on this scheme." Cairell snapped his fingers, and two guards took Dealla by the arms.

"*No!*" The guards stilled at Kyras's agonized shout. "She knew nothing about it. Nothing!"

"*Why,* Kyras?" Tears spilled down the queen's white face. "What possessed you to do such a thing? You signed a death warrant for those innocent people." Dealla turned to Alric. "That treasure wasn't to fatten Dalraidi purses, it was to save my husband's son from being sold into slavery after *your* high king abducted him."

"I make no excuses for Ecfrith, nor do I condone what he has done in the name of God," Alric said, "but I still champion truth when I say that the bretwalda knew nothing of the prince's kidnapping. When one keeps the company of snakes, one is likely to be bitten. God's justice awaits for the bretwalda's transgressions against the Irish monasteries, perhaps to be dealt by the very serpent who sought to profit from Cairell's ransom without Ecfrith's benefit."

"Where is the ransom now?" Queen Dealla asked.

"At the bottom of the sea."

"Dealla, I have loved you since the first time I saw you." Kyras took a shaky breath. "But you were promised to the king's brother before I could prove myself...then to the king himself." He lifted his hands in despair. "How could I compete with a king?"

"You couldn't...unless you became one," Cairell observed wryly. "If I was not ransomed, I was out of the way. My sister faced either death or slavery, taking the last of Fergal's line out of the royal hierarchy. Our young, strapping champion was a natural choice to become king."

"Did you...did you do anything to harm father?" Deirdre held her breath. Fergal had thought highly of his cousin's son. She prayed he was spared the knowledge of Kyras's treachery.

Kyras shook his head. "Only by what I did to you and your brother, though I might as well have. Your loss was the dagger that stilled his heart." He turned on Alric suddenly with contempt. "Why couldn't you just *kill* me?"

Alric clamped a strong hand on the man's shoulder. "Because these godly people will forgive you. Those you saw will not."

If Alric was insane, then Kyras was as well, for it was evident that the champion knew exactly to whom the Saxon referred. For a moment, Deirdre thought the younger man might retch; such was his repugnance of the memory.

The bishop of Armagh held up his hand, seizing command of the proceedings. "Exactly what was it you did see, sons?"

Kyras shuddered, shaking his head.

"Justice on the other side," Alric provided for him. "It is unspeakable."

A tide of hush carried Alric's explanation over the crowd, echoing only the breath that bore it.

"I will seek council before I decide the nature of your sentence in this matter," Cairell told Kyras, his clear voice filling the inner rath without challenge. He nodded for the guards to take the disgraced champion into custody. "Let the rest of us retire to the hall…but *not* to celebrate my coronation." He waited for the consternate reaction of the masses to settle before continuing. "I'm sure you understand how its untimeliness robs me of any satisfaction."

Deirdre fought the grief struck fresh by the telltale quiver in her brother's voice, but he rallied as he was born to do.

"Let us instead celebrate God's triumph in our hour of darkness and deception. So, good and loyal friends, enjoy Gleannmara's hospitality." Cairell motioned to where Deirdre hopped down from the platform into her husband's arms.

She could wait no longer to touch Alric, to reinforce the eternal bond between them with the urgency of the moment.

"I bid you all show our deliverers the welcome for which we are renowned. I and my new brother and his bride will join you when we are fit to entertain those dearest to our hearts."

Everyone began to talk at once as Alric ushered Deirdre along with her brother's company back into the fine stone hall. His men climbed over each other trying to congratulate him. The nobility gave them a respectful space, many straining to hear an explanation of the miraculous sight they'd witnessed yet were loathe to believe. Alric needed no accolade. All he needed, he held under his wing.

At Deirdre's nearness, his body gave up weariness for renewal.

Alric didn't know exactly how he escaped death. At least that was what he told Cairell as they'd made their way back into the hall. Everyone was talking at once about the maneuver that deflected Kyras's blade and enabled the victim to become the victor with a lightning run of unerring kicks, blows, twists, and turns.

"Can you teach me what you did?" Cairell's eyes glowed. "Faith, I've never seen a broadsword turned away like that, much less by someone half blind with sand in his eyes."

"The blade itself announced its coming and its angle," Alric decided, replaying what he could in his mind.

"The sword song."

Alric looked surprised. "Yes, I suppose you could call it that. 'Tis a far baser note this one sings."

Cairell's face fell. "I've heard of it, but never heard it myself." He visibly wrestled with the troubling fact.

But it was more than the sword song that bade Alric move as he had. His body had suddenly thrummed with life. Like a dead piece of fat tossed on the fire, it had flashed. Or was it the sparks cast by the friction of the dirt he rubbed in his eyes? All he knew was that his limbs moved of their own accord, abandoning the sense of sight altogether. It was only when he stood over Kyras that his vision had cleared.

And as he looked down, he saw a love-stricken heart behind the treachery, devoid of greed or ambition, save love itself. He saw the dark justice that awaited it, and the sinewy, gold-banded arm reaching out of his own body for the miserable soul sinking in the dark mire beneath the sword's point. At Kyras's cry, the warrior of light left Alric altogether, and with the heavenly Spirit, so Alric's strength abandoned him.

Whether it was the archangel Michael, Christ Himself, or the Holy Spirit, Alric would not hazard to guess. Its only name to him was love—pure as the golden bracelets and bright as its light.

"Since this sword was undoubtedly gifted to you by a higher power than mine, it should be yours."

Cairell's offer penetrated the vision holding Alric spellbound. The king's sword? His? Nay, it didn't feel right.

"My appreciation knows no bounds, milord, but I was just a servant returning it to its rightful place. It belongs to Gleannmara." He handed the precious weapon he'd used as a walking stick over to the new king.

His brother-in-law refused to take it. "So do you now, Brother."

"Here, here!"

"Huzzah!"

"Alric the Just."

"Long live Alric, prince of Gleannmara!"

To Alric's amazement, it wasn't his men who started the cheers, but the clan chiefs of Gleannmara. If his knees had been wobbly before, now he felt as if he stood on water and all that kept him from sinking to the floor was belief—not in what was happening, but in the miracle of forgiveness God had wrought this day. Irish and Saxon mingled like long-lost brothers, embracing, cheering, toasting with the heady wine of God's love.

"Welcome home, Husband."

Alric looked down into the limpid pools of Deirdre's eyes, where his soul smiled back at him. Taking her in his arms, he lifted her chin with the crook of his finger. The jewels—stones and minerals—that had been his fortune lay at the bottom of the sea. Yet his heart soared like a gull streaking across the sun, singing in the safekeeping of its Creator. His voice cracked with the weight of his emotions as he repeated the very words she'd said to him when an uncertain future lay ahead.

"I am with you, beloved. Wherever you are is my home, and I'm glad to be there."

He kissed Deirdre—his wife, his life—who'd led him to an everlasting birthright, Godsent and ordained by a love that surpasses all understanding...at least on this side of heaven.

EPILOGUE

The sun climbed toward its pinnacle over the sparkling, blue-green waters. Sea birds cawed overhead, having left their cliff-side nests to fish for their breakfast—great black backs diving beside more delicate kittiwakes. To the landside of the beach, heath-land and scrub rose from the rock-strewn harbor, resplendent in the early summer bouquet of bright gorse and soft heathers, which gave life to its granite bosom. Around the round little fishing huts strung about the harbor of Skerry Town, tall, wood-framed buildings rose, birthed by the ongoing clash of iron and wood.

Filled with a hearty meal from Mistress Leary's tavern, Deirdre accompanied Alric along Water Street to where his men had embell-ished a jag of rock into a bulkhead capable of docking two seafaring ships. One such vessel was moored there now—the *Blessing,* renamed from one of the six merchant vessels the Saxon prince owned. Just returned from the Mediterranean with rich cargo coveted by merchants from all the neighboring tuaths, the crew readied the newly provi-sioned vessel for its return voyage.

The half-grown, scraggy pup trotting at Alric's heel suddenly bounded past his master, rushing to the edge of the pier and barking a friendly hello at a richly garbed young man aboard the ship.

"And good day to you as well, Wulfgar." Cairell of Gleannmara grinned from the rail of the ship at the tail-wagging wolfhound Deirdre had given Alric at Christmas. The pup was from the high king's own kennels, with bloodlines as fine as there were in all Erin.

"Wulfgar, stand fast," Alric ordered, far less amused at the pup's dis-obedience.

Deirdre's heart went out to the gangly dog. Tail tucked between his hind legs, head down, Wulfgar slunk to Alric's side and sat down. With one last shot of puppy charm, he licked the back of Alric's hand.

Laughter from the rail where the king and his company of dignitaries brought the tiny beast's tail up with renewed heart. Despite the fond smile tugging his mouth, Alric remained the strict disciplinarian.

"I did not say *come grovel,* I said *stand fast.*" He pointed behind him, maintaining eye contact in what was clearly a battle of wills.

Not too surprisingly, Wulfgar gave in first. When Deirdre did not respond to the plaintive look shot from under its furry gray brow, the pup moved behind Alric and collapsed with a whining huff into a spindly-legged sprawl.

"Abina is ruining him," Alric observed.

"He has a noble spirit. He'll grow into it," one of the bishops in the group offered graciously.

"And his name," his attendant grinned. "His back is to Prince Alric's thigh already."

All were part of the high king's commission to sail to Gaul and on to Rome in an attempt to honor Cairell's vow to his fellow captives to find them and negotiate their freedom. With highly respected members of the clergy, as well as Erin's noble families, her brother hoped to accomplish more than that. He sought to put an end to, or at least curtail, the selling of abducted Irish and Saxon children in the Mediterranean markets. The pope's latest missive to Armagh gave him hope that he had the full support of the church.

"Well, Irish," Alric called out to Cairell once the prodigal pup satisfied his order, "the *Blessing* looks ready to face its mistress sea again, but are *you?*"

It was nearly a year ago that all of them had washed up on Gleannmara's shore. Deirdre could still feel the bone-deep chill and worse, the heart-wrenching possibility that Alric had been lost to her forever. She moved closer into the crook of his arm at her waist.

"Ready and looking forward to the trip, Moses," Cairell said.

The corner of Alric's mouth tipped at the nickname that had once annoyed him. In retrospect, that's what he'd been. Not only had he provided escape for some of God's children, but he'd been instrumental in helping them rebuild their lives here on the new shore, close to the sea from which he could not bear to part.

God had had a plan for both of them, although it was some time after their arrival before Alric shared his own miracle with her—that of his mysterious rescue from the sea. It was small wonder that a premature silver now winged his temples, given the physical and spiritual warfare he'd survived and the fact that her husband had looked into the face of a heavenly savior. Deirdre understood the awe and humility her husband expressed. It made them one in a way few would ever know.

When not serving as one of Gleannmara's judges, Alric the Just devoted his time to the growth of Skerry Town and his merchant marine enterprise.

"Besides, I know I leave Gleannmara in good hands, although I had wondered if you'd make it here in time to see me off." Cairell glanced at Deirdre.

"You'll not leave till the tide does," Alric countered. "I know its pull in my veins."

"Besides," Deirdre added, "Mistress Leary's hospitality is hard to leave."

Alric added a new room onto the tavern in exchange for private lodging while their home was being built. Later, it would accommodate the increase of travelers as the port grew.

"My company had no problem departing," her brother teased, "but then we had no wives to distract us."

"'Tis a wife's duty, milord, and I'll make no excuses." The afterglow of her husband's attentions raced once more to her face, but Deirdre was unashamed. They shared God's gift to husband and wife, which surely was as glorious as it had been in Eden's innocence.

Cairell stepped away as the gangway was removed from the ship's rail and lowered, under Kaspar's supervision, by a series of ropes and pulleys to the dock. The young father, now expecting his second child, held the position of dock master. Deirdre and Alric had worked with him through the winter months, teaching him record keeping skills.

Lines tossed, the ship drifted away from the dock, riding low in the water with its load of wares, from hides and beef to salt from the marshland in the south. Men scurried aloft, unfurling the mainsail.

"Godspeed!"

"Godspeed!"

Deirdre and the man she loved more than life itself called out the blessing simultaneously.

So much had happened since Scanlan first reminded her of God's promise that his plan was to prosper, not harm. And how that promise had been fulfilled! Scanlan, now fully recovered, had returned to the Mercian-dominated Galstead. His devotion so impressed Juist, that the high priest demanded Scanlan be left unmolested to do his work as his heart led him. Deirdre's dear friend wrote of stirring conversations between himself, Juist, and, on occasion, Aelfled, who continued to keep him supplied with herbs he needed to tend his flock.

And Orna was safe, determined to live out the rest of her years on land with a young Welsh noble, who lived near the monastery where she'd been dropped off, feverish and vowing never to set foot on anything that floated again. Dutifully, she'd sent a letter to Fergal of Gleannmara stating Deirdre's predicament, but with the king already ill and Dealla devoted to his care, Kyras had easily intercepted and burned it. Now in exile for his crime of treason, the disgraced warrior served in the forces of Argyll, while the woman he loved found solace and the protection she craved with the holy sisters at Glendalough.

"Looks like a good day for a voyage," Alric observed, squinting at the sky.

No trace of the vengeful red that had nearly been their end showed its face on the eastern horizon. The sun's rays formed a golden bridge of light connecting the water to the heavens.

"The wind is with them." He pointed to the *Blessing,* his chest swelling like the sail that caught the first push of the breeze. "She'll fairly fly to Gaul."

Deirdre detected a note of melancholy in his voice. "You could have gone with them."

The restless energy he once devoted to his green mistress's whim now was spent between Gleannmara's court and its shore. But maybe that wasn't enough. As he said, the tide pulled at his blood.

Instead of answering, he steered Deirdre away from the dock to walk down the beach, as was their custom when one of his ships sailed out to sea. From the shelf of sand and rock, they watched until the departing vessel was the size of a toy in a vast pond.

A month earlier, they'd seen Gunnar and Helewis off from the same spot after their visit. They had a precious baby girl, with Helewis's golden curls and fair complexion. Alric held that the infant had her father's temperament, one that could only be assuaged by a drink—of mother's milk, in this case. "He fell straight from bosom to bottle," he teased his longtime friend.

Deirdre had carried a melancholy heart to shore that day, longing for a babe of her own, although the new school in the village kept her occupied. Still…with one cycle missed and another nearly so by her recollection, her prayers may have been answered.

She wasn't going to say anything to Alric until she was certain, but just this morning Mrs. Leary called her aside and asked her if she was expecting. Astonished, Deirdre started to share her calculation with the old female but was dismissed with a wave.

"Nonsense, milady. I know by your look. Ye've the glow of a new rose, ripe to bloom."

"All right, now you can go," Alric said to the dog, motioning toward the long expanse of beach ahead.

The pup shot off after a retreating wave, its plate-sized paws nipping at the water's edge. Deirdre giggled when another wave rolled over it, sending the half-grown hound yelping back toward dry land.

"If I didn't know any better, I'd swear that Tor had sired that halfwit," Alric remarked. Turning Deirdre in his arms, he pressed his forehead down to hers. "And I *could* have gone with the *Blessing*," he acknowledged, a twinkle lighting in his mercurial gaze. "But I couldn't leave you in your condition, even if I wanted to."

Deirdre's heart skipped. "What?" That Mrs. Leary. "Who told you?"

Alric glanced to where Wulfgar barked in hot pursuit of a copper-winged butterfly, and then returned his full attention to his wife. "I am one with the tides and the moon, muirnait, and nearly three have passed since milady's last indisposal. I wondered when you would tell me."

Deirdre felt foolish that a man kept better track of such things than she. Such was the heady effect Alric had upon her. He spun her thoughts into anticipation and intoxicated her senses with his nearness, his devilish eyes, and that irascible grin. She would offer him no excuse. "Is it too late to tell you now, milord?"

"I await your every word, sweetling." To prove it, he framed her face and met her nose to nose.

"God charges us to go forth and be fruitful," she said, moving his hands to her waist.

"And?" He circled it with his hands, his fingers all but touching.

"And I am with fruit."

The kiss she saw him moisten on his lips erupted in a loud bellow of laughter. Gathering her hands in his, he danced like an overgrown sea sprite around her, spinning and spinning until the clouds circled and Wulfgar nipped at the hem of her dress. "Her chatter will be like birdsong to your heart," he sang to the sky.

"What?" Deirdre's heart soared so high; perhaps her ears were impaired by its flight.

"Orlaith." Alric smiled at her, his eyes warm and tender. "She told me all about you and how you were the key to my birthright." He sobered, taking her into his arms as if to never let her go. "It was love, my beautiful chatter bird. Unseen—" his hoarse whispered voice sent a thrill through her—"and eternal."

As eternal as the tender-sweet homage he paid to it with his lips.

GLOSSARY

For them who'd have a smatterin' more knowledge and assistance with names and such, help yourself to a wee salmon's worth. In tryin' to curb me habit o' gettin' eighteen words to the dozen, I've kept the list as short and succinct as a Celtic heart can, with pronunciations for only them words that fool the tongue.

aiccid (ay-sid): heir apparent to kingship or clan chief.

anmchara (ahn-ca-rah): soul friend, confessor, a soul mate.

athair (a'-the): father.

brat: outer cloak or wrap; the more colors, the higher the station o' its wearer.

brehon: a judge.

bretwalda (bret-wall-dah): much like the Irish high king, *ard ri*, o' Saxon Britain.

brewy (brew'-ee): a name for a common inn and the innkeeper.

Brichriu (brik'-ree-oo): an ancient historical satirist known for stirring up trouble.

bride-price: the price paid by the groom to the bride's family for the privilege and duration o' his marriage to the lady.

churl: a freeman worth two to four hundred shillings *wergild*; owns at least one hide o' land.

cromlech: a capstone resting on two upright pillar stones, sometimes forming a passage; usually marks a grave o' someone o' importance—a hero or royalty.

curragh: a small wicker-framed boat.

Dalraidi (pl.) (dahl'-rah-dee): this was an early Ulster clan; some migrated to Scotland in the fifth century, and by the sixth century, sure they ruled it and the latter half o' that same period chose their first Christian king, Aidan.

Deirdre (deer'-drah): chatterbox; also sorrow.

derling: darling.

druid: St. Columba wrote, "My druid is Christ." Substitute *teacher* or *spiritual leader* for *druid* to catch the drift o' his meaning. The seventh-century *druid* was mostly a teacher or historian in Erin. In Britain, they were still worshipin' nature like their Germanic counterparts and the druids in *Maire,* the fifth-century book one o' this series. Ye see, the druids were not just the black-robed sacrificers reported by Julius Caesar and other foreign observers o' this secretive order, but what I'd call professionals. They were a number o' an elevated Celtic learned class—spiritual leaders, teachers, lawyers, poets, bards, historians, magicians; o'ten called magi.

There were some o' the dark kind then, mind ye, but never was any evidence o' human sacrifice found on my shores, like across the sea. And again, God used these enlightened people to pave the way for Christianity, as illustrated in the story o' Maire and Rowan's fifth-century Gleannmara.

Ecfrith (ek'-frith): the historical king o' Northumbria who raided me shores on the pretense o' religious righteousness; a scoundrel or saint, dependin' on who ye read, though his prejudice to me seemed more against the British/Irish than the Church—odd with him being half British himself.

Gleannmara (glinn-mah-rah): a fictional *tuath* or kingdom in Erin found between Wicklow and the Irish Sea; glen/valley overlooking/near the sea.

Freou-weebe: and peace weaver, a wife taken to secure a treaty o' peace by marriage.

hemmings: rawhide boots/shoes made from the skin off the hind legs o' a deer.

hide: a rectangular strip o' land equal to one-fifth o' a square mile.

maîthar (maw'-ther): mother.

muirnait: beloved.

rath: a circular fortification surrounded by earthen walls; home o' a warrior chief.

Scotland (Scotia Minor), the problem with: This became a major issue as what is today's Scotland grew. It was settled by members o' the

Dalraidi clan o' northern Erin, who owed tribute to the king o' Ulster. But it was its own province with its own king now and declared it owed allegiance to no one save the high king o' Ireland.

scramasax: a Saxon short sword.

synod: A synod was a fairlike gathering o' the provincial and *tuath* rulers and their entourages for the settlement o' political and law issues. Vendors and entertainers flocked to provide for the attendees, which attracted others whose interest was more o' a recreational nature. Games and other diversions took place when the court was not in session. These lasted for weeks due to the distances traveled to participate, so that all might put in their two cents worth prior to final decisions.

thane: a lesser king or lord, worth twelve hundred shillings *wergild*. A horse thane was the predecessor of a medieval knight.

tonsure: a style o' haircut with a section shaven; the priests' were circular with shaven center, while the druids' shaven ear to ear across top o' head to form a high brow o' intelligence. The clergy, reflectin' the druidic roots o' many o' God's servants, used both in the sixth century.

torque: a neckband often made o' gold or silver; many times took the place o' a crown for a king or queen; its degree o' elegance often indicated rank in society.

tuath (tuth): a kingdom made up o' more than one sept/clan and united under one king, to whom the clan chiefs pay tribute/homage. He in turn pays homage to the province king, who pays homage to the high king.

wergild (ver'-gild): man gold, or the worth o' a man, paid in lieu o' death punishment, much like the Irish *eric*.

Whitby, Synod of: The meeting o' druids, priests, and Oswald, King o' Northumbria, which then was the dominant rule in Britain. 'Twas here that Oswald himself decided if the future church was to follow the Celtic ways based on St. John's and Jesus' example o' ministry or on the Roman ways, which were based upon St. Peter's and St. Paul's philosophy. Ironically, the argument that won this newly saved king's favor was presented by the Roman contingent—St. Peter holds the key to heaven's gate. The aging king, bein' concerned about his eternity, decided that while both sides had merit, he was going to throw in with the man who held the keys, and so the decision was made. The prevailing church was to follow the Roman tonsure o' the bowl haircut with shaved crown over the druidic, which was long locks with a high-shaved forehead, and the Roman example o' churches and priests equivalent to palaces and kings dedicated to God's glory.

There was much to be said for both sides, which is why both concepts are prevalent throughout the world today. We have denominations that prefer to put their efforts and all moneys collected toward the needy and unsaved rather than in big cathedrals and rich garments and lifestyles, thinkin' that the collection o' souls is the kingdom Christ will return to. There are others who prepare His kingdom to receive Him royally and put much o' the wealth o' the church into the buildings and trappings themselves—all in God's honor, mind ye—and still seek to help the needy and save the unsaved. I'm in no position to judge one way or the other, but I am befuddled that a king made a decision that affected ages to come based on the bloomin' metaphor o' St. Peter's key to heaven.

BIBLIOGRAPHY

Barber, Henry. *British Family Names—Their Origin and Meaning, with lists of Scandinavian, Frisian, Anglo-Saxon, and Norman Names.* Baltimore: Genealogical Publishing Company, 1968.

Cahill, Thomas. *How the Irish Saved Civilization: The Untold Story of Ireland's Heroic Role from the Fall of Rome to the Rise of Medieval Europe.* New York: Doubleday, 1995. An interestin' peek at just what the world owes me children for preservin' light and knowledge in a darkening world.

Carmichael, Alexander. *The Sun Dances. Prayers and Blessings from the Gaelic.* London: Christian Community Press, 1960. (Reprinted Edinburgh: Floris, 1977).

Coglan, Ronan, Grehan, Ida, and Joyce, P. W. *Book of Irish First Names—First, Family & Place Names.* New York: Sterling Publishing Co., Inc. 1989. Look for the old names that described both a character and/or description, for the roots are in me history itself.

Coward, T. A. *Cheshire.* London: Methuen & Co. Ltd., 1932. A record o' cyclin' rambles, rich with historical and geographical detail of this western coastal shire.

Crossley-Holland, Kevin. *Green Blades Rising.* New York: Seabury Press, 1975. Wonderful look at the early Saxons and their way of life— war, daily living, and faith development.

Crossley-Holland, Kevin. *The Anglo-Saxon World.* Suffolk: Boydell Press, 1982. All encompassin' look at life and history in the Anglo-Saxon world, from ancient to the conquest.

Cusack, Mary Frances. *An Illustrated History of Ireland from 400 to 1800.* London: Bracken Books, 1995. 'Tis hard to pick a favorite out o' so many fine books, but this has to be among the best, written with an academic approach, but with true bardic flair. Like as not, me author will have to get a new copy, for this one's worn as an old swine's tooth.

Dunlevy, Mairead. *Dress in Ireland: A History.* Cork: Collins Press, 1989. A keeper o' the Art and Industrial Division in The National Museum of Ireland; the author packs these pages full o' information on fashion and textiles to boot, from me early days through the turn o' the twentieth century.

Fairholt, F. W. *Costume in England, Vol. II*. Detroit: Singing Tree Press, 1968. Excellent reference of costume and textile from early England to the eighteenth century.

Haywood, John. *Dark Age of Naval Power—A Reassessment of Frankish and Anglo-Saxon Seafaring Activity*. London and New York: Routledge, 1991. Eye-openin' look at ships, both for Germanic trade, war, and piracy, on the North Sea from 12 B.C. to the ninth century.

Hodgkin, R. H. *A History of the Anglo-Saxons, Vol. I*. Oxford: Clarendon Press, 1932. From early times to the eighth century, a mite tedious scholarly narrative, but informative, nonetheless.

Hughes, Thomas. *Vale Royal of England, or the County Palatine of Chester*. Manchester: E. J. Morton, 1976. A detailed census and zoning type account of Chester, the shire and the city, in old English.

Laing, Lloyd and Jennifer. *Celtic Britain and Ireland: The Myth of the Dark Ages*. New York: Barnes and Noble Books/St. Martin's Press, 1997. Ye'll never confuse *non-Roman* with *uncivilized* again.

MacManus, Seumas. *The Story of the Irish Race*. Greenwich, Conn.: The Devin Adair Co., 1971. Ach, what soul with Celtic blood flowin' through their veins couldn't fall in love with this rendition of me children's story? 'Twill tickle the funny bone, move yer heart, and light yer fancy.

Mac Niocaill, Gearóid. *Ireland Before the Vikings*. Dublin: Gill and Macmillan, 1972. We all need this kind of friend to keep us humble. 'Tis an 'in yer face' account of how things were in olden times, but I got the impression that, despite himself, this learned fella had to say some wonderful things about me and me children—all of what was true, o'course. No lore philosophizin' for this one, but full of spell-bindin' facts, some flatterin' and some, left to me, best forgotten—lessin' ye're writin' some academic paper or what not.

Mann, John. *Murder, Magic, and Medicine*. New York: Oxford University Press, 1992. Read as to how some of the medicine of the past—that what didn't kill folks, that is—is being used again by our modern medicine. Magic? Use that modern-day brain o' yours and decide for yourself. Not only will ye be entertained but enlightened as well.

Nairn, Richard and Miriam Crowley. *Wild Wicklow—Nature in the Garden of Ireland*. Dublin: Town House and Country House, 1998. This is the book for the armchair traveler who'd see the beauty and charm of me County Wicklow as it is today, with some hint of what it used to be in Gleannmara's day.

Ó Corráin, Donnchadh and Fidelma Maguire. *Irish Names*. Dublin: Lilliput Press, 1990. Now one can never have too many books on me children's names, for sure their use and meanins' are as varied as the shades o' green in Erin.

Ó Cróinín, Dáibhí. *Early Medieval Ireland (400-1200)*. New York: Longman Group Ltd., 1995. The man takes ye there and surrounds ye with all manner of information on what it was like to live in them times. 'Tis a veritable wealth of information and fascination.

Palgrave, Sir Francis. *History of the Anglo-Saxons*. London: Braken Books, 1989. An all-encompassin' look at Anglo-Saxon England, full o' legend and fact woven like a nonfiction tapestry o' time and place.

Quennell, M. and C. *Everyday Life in Roman and Anglo-Saxon Times*. New York: G. P. Putnam's Sons, 1957. Good portrayal o' this time period spannin' Roman occupation of Britain to the comin' o' the Normans.

Sadler, John. *Battle for Northumbria*. Northumberland: Bridge Studios, 1988. 'Twas a good history of struggle in this border kingdom from the sixth century through the eighteenth.

Saklatvala, Beram. *The Origins of the English People*. New York: Barnes and Noble, 1969. A concise history tracing the Anglo-Saxons from Germanic origins to the Norman Conquest with engaging narrative.

Scherman, Katherine. *The Flowering of Ireland: Saints, Scholars, and Kings*. New York: Barnes and Noble, 1996. Another favorite! 'Twas the most inspirational of all reads to this soul, for it's the memory o' how the Pentecostal Flame kindled in the hearts o' saints, scholars, and kings. Praise be, I've not been the same since. Come to think o' it, neither has the rest o' the world.

Smith, Charles Hamilton. *Ancient Costumes of Great Britain and Ireland from the Druids to the Tudors.* London: Bracken Books, 1989.

Whitelock, Dorothy. *The Beginnings of English Society, Vol. II (The Anglo-Saxon Period).* Great Britain: Penguin Books Ltd., 1952. A comprehensive look at Saxon England, life and culture, from its heathen times to the Norman Conquest. Another favorite reference.

Faith, I'd love to list a host of other books full of riveting fact and legend that contributed to the tellin' of Gleannmara's story, but I'm runnin' out of time and space. Since this work was started, the numbers of works on Ireland and its past have doubled and then some. Looks like the Golden Age of the Celts may not be over after all. Till we meet again, may the good Holy Spirit nourish ye, mind, body, heart, and soul.

Multnomah Publishers®
The publisher and author would love to hear your comments about this book. *Please contact us at:*
www.multnomah.net/firesofgleannmara

IN AN AGE OF DARKNESS COMES A FLAME THAT WILL CHANGE IRELAND AND HER PEOPLE FOREVER...

MAIRE: THE FIRES OF GLEANNMARA #1

Fierce warrior queen Maire struggles to understand her attraction to a bold yet humble, faith-filled mercenary she takes hostage. Can love spark between enemies?

ISBN 1-57673-625-3

RIONA: THE FIRES OF GLEANNMARA #2

Bestselling author Linda Windsor creates another intriguing tale! *Riona* pairs a handsome, arrogant knight with a strong-willed, compassionate gentlewoman of faith in sixth-century Ireland.

ISBN 1-57673-752-7

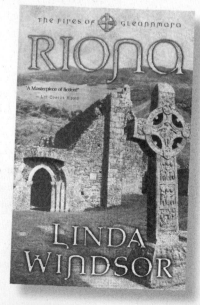